The Gift of a Falcon

The Gift of a Falcon

KENT HARRINGTON

McGraw-Hill Book Company

New York   St. Louis   San Francisco   Bogotá
Hamburg   Madrid   Mexico   Milan   Montreal   Panama
Paris   São Paulo   Tokyo   Toronto

All characters in this book are fictional and any resemblance to persons living or dead is purely coincidental.

Copyright © 1988 by Kent Harrington. All rights reserved. Printed in the United States of America. Except as permitted under the Copyright Act of 1976, no part of this publication may be reproduced or distributed in any form or by any means or stored in a data base or retrieval system without the prior written permission of the publisher.

1 2 3 4 5 6 7 8 9 DOC DOC 8 9 2 1 0 9 8

ISBN 0-07-026757-X

LIBRARY OF CONGRESS CATALOGING-IN-PUBLICATION DATA

Harrington, Kent.
    The gift of a falcon.

    I. Title.
PS3558.A6294G5 1988 813'.54 87-35256
ISBN 0-07-026757-X

BOOK DESIGN BY KATHRYN PARISE

To my wife, Toni

ACKNOWLEDGMENTS

Precious few things in this world are the creation of one person. This book is no exception. In fact, writing this story has helped me to understand just how much the help of others enables one to put words on paper. In my case, the encouragement that produced this novel began a long time ago. Now, admittedly offering too little, too late, I want to say my thanks.

To Sally and Joe Harrington, my parents, who invested four decades of love and patience. To Olga Papach, who said, "Why don't you do it?" To Mike Singer, who pushed me over the brink. To Sue Katz, my agent, who has cornered the market on enthusiasm, understanding, and faith. To Elisabeth Jakab, a superb editor and friend who was always there with the right question and suggestion. To Mary Meyer, who has never failed to listen, to invest herself, and to help me understand. To Jerry Shapiro, and Jeff and Ina Garten, who gave the gift of friendship. And most of all to Toni, who did so much to let me disappear all those nights and weekends, and was always there when I came back.

I am unable to mention several people by name who aided me with ideas and suggestions. To them and to the many others who asked the question, "How's it going?" and then actually listened to my answer—my thanks. I hope you enjoy what you read.

Given the number of spots on the globe this story covers, as well as some of its technical curiosities, there are bound to be right turns that should have been lefts, as well as an occasional dysfunctional detail. For these and any other, more egregious errors for which my literary license cannot exempt me, I am, of course, solely responsible.

CONTENTS

PART THREE: Flight

PART FOUR: The Gift

PROLOGUE

Friday, March 1, 1972

Plateau de Bolovens, Laos

Pulling out of the bombing run, Frank DiGenero felt no fear at first, only an odd annoying helplessness as he spotted the corkscrew trail climb toward him. It was impossible to mistake. Seconds before, the SAM-7 had been an inert few feet of tube, fins, and explosive on the shoulder of a man 500 feet below. Now it was alive, erratically jinking and jagging like the kind of unpracticed insect that flew only once before dying, its simple infrared sensor locked on his heat, homing in to destroy him.

DiGenero jammed the twin throttles forward, feeling the afterburners kick hard as the flame rings ignited the rush of raw jet fuel, spewing fire from the F-4D's two powerful engines.

The warning from the second seat filled his headset, "Six o'clock low, six o'clock low!"

"Got it," DiGenero craned his neck, and bit down on his lip, preparing. They had only moments, no more. The altimeter, registering 800 feet, and the airspeed indicator, at 350 knots, were winding up, recording the Phantom's climb. It wasn't fast enough. He would wait until the last second and then jam the stick hard over. The backseater would tell him when to make his move. If they had the airspeed, the F-4 would break right before the missile could correct course, zigging out of harm's way.

"Closing, closing!" Behind him, the anxiety had wrung the Boston accent out of Jimmy Clancey's voice. Clancey had flown as DiGenero's weapons systems officer, the "GIB," his guy-in-back, for the better part of eighteen months in Thailand. He was close now to going home, only days from the end of his tour. Clancey's wife and red-haired 3-year-old daughter were waiting in Needham. So were eighty days of accrued leave, and a summer back in "the World" with its Irish whiskey, Red Sox games, Cape Cod beaches, and New England boiled dinners.

In the split second the jet screamed upward, DiGenero mentally rewound the images of the bombing run. He had come in too shallow and pulled out too slow. It was his fault. Come in steep and climb out fast. Don't fuck around between 200 and 1000 feet. If you did, your ass was grass. That was the rule and he'd ignored it.

Why? Maybe you bought it at the end of a tour because it was getting too easy. He'd been here before, over this roadstop and countless others like it more times than he could remember. It was one of a hundred nodes in the complex of paths, tracks, and jungle highways that flowed down Indochina's spine, north to south, binding Vietnam, Laos, and Cambodia with the tendrils of the Ho Chi Minh Trail.

Bolovens, on the edge of the plateau, east of Muong May. It was also one of his better hunting grounds. The trucks congregated, camouflaged, and parked, waiting under the trees for drivers or fuel or orders. At night, the C-130s, the gunships, would find them with FLIR, forward-looking infrared, and their 105 cannons, probing with tracers, provoking explosions, "secondaries," and marking the "hot spots" on the map. The next day, early in the morning, they were his. The NVA, the North Vietnamese regulars, manned the antiaircraft, but their guns were visual, 23 mm's without radar to keep up with an F-4 in a 400-mile-an-hour dive. They had to see you to kill you. So did the SAM-7 shooter. If you did it right, they couldn't turn their heads fast enough to follow your track. DiGenero cursed himself. He hadn't done it right, and they had.

DiGenero swiveled, trying to look past the edge of his seat. The missile, now burning bright orange-red, was approaching, closing on his rear.

"Now!" Clancey screamed. DiGenero jammed the stick hard right, feeling the G-forces compress his chest with their weight. As the F-4 turned, wing on edge, the familiar horizon disappeared, transformed into a line bisecting green from blue.

The explosion seemed distant, heavy, dull and destructive. Clancey was already on the radio, "This is Red Fox One. We've taken a hit! We've taken a hit!"

DiGenero tried to level, but the controls moved like a broken limb, once unfailingly predictable but now crippled, refusing to follow any normal sequence of stimulus and response. The F-4, vibrating and convulsing, slewed sideways like a heavy car on ice. He was losing it. The elevators were gone, maybe the whole stabilizer assembly. His attention riveted on the cockpit. He studied the useless control column, lost in his own logic, looking for a solution, like a bright child trying to solve a difficult puzzle. Then, inside, he went all hollow as the nose pitched down.

DiGenero started to speak, but the words caught in his throat. The heat surprised him. It was under his feet, searing like a stove top. Suddenly, the smoke was around him, gray and heavy, bringing the first wave of fear. He reached for the looped red and black handle.

"Clancey, get out!" He yanked. The first explosion in the ejection sequence was instantaneous. The shock of a 300-mile-an-hour blast slammed DiGenero's head back as the long, slender Plexiglas canopy disappeared, blown away. Reflex, conditioning, and a suddenly rabid will to live made him pull hard one more time. Beneath him, the rocket motor propelled the ejection seat up its rails into the slipstream and then backward, tumbling, toward the brown plain below.

Eight hundred feet away, the chute snapped DiGenero like a manic marionette. Dazed, he pawed at his vest, finding the voice switch on the small survival radio. The built-in beacon already pulsed, transmitting his location over the preset emergency frequency. The brown-green landscape rose to meet him. Trees, a patchwork of dry rice paddies, on the edge of the field a fringe of huts, and a line—a road, actually—that disappeared into the jungle.

To his left in the sky, motion caught his eye. The two shapes were together, falling in line. The cockpit canopy glistened in the sun, dropping straight in a dedicated, downward path. The body followed, arms and legs fluttering without discipline, describing a shallow arc.

"No, no," DiGenero recoiled, hearing the horror in his own voice, screaming, as the sight wrenched the words from him. The chute, long and thin, streamed behind Clancey like a banner, as if to mark his passing. Then both forms disappeared, swallowed by the deep green of the trees. DiGenero squeezed his eyes shut, trying to blot out the image but only seeing Clancey and feeling the pain.

"Red Fox One, this is Red Fox Leader. Where are you, buddy?"

The voice was an intrusion, loud and jarring. DiGenero started, staring mindlessly at the radio on his chest. Suspended with him in the silence, its small speaker made the disembodied voice unnaturally clear. It was Merritt, his wingman. DiGenero grunted, trying to fight off his shock, but there wasn't time to answer. The trees were reaching up, rising fast, preparing to envelop him. The rice paddy was fifty yards to his right. He yanked hard on the parachute shrouds, pulling the cluster of lines above his left shoulder. The chute's nylon dome flattened on one side, speeding him downward as he slideslipped.

He yanked again but the first branches reached up to grab at his legs. DiGenero tore through the leaves, hitting the ground hard on his side, the wind knocked out of him. He gasped, digging his hands into the soil. Somehow, touching the dirt imparted an almost primordial, calming sense. He was down, the end, no more falling. Safety. The earth seemed to surround him, soft and cool, emitting the smell of decomposition and growth, the universal aromas of old and new, the end and the beginning.

DiGenero filled his lungs and half-stood, fumbling with the straps to loosen his parachute harness. His knees failed and he pitched forward. He propped himself up on his arms, breathing deeply, trying to compose himself. He was together, in one piece. Through the trees, the open space created a bright backdrop, as if it were the focal point for the morning sun. He'd missed the paddy by twenty-five yards.

"Hey, Red Fox One." It was Merritt. DiGenero remembered the radio. His wingman sounded worried, "Squawk something, will you? Frank, are you down there? Where's Clancey? We only saw one chute. Speak up, Frank."

DiGenero pushed the talk button, "I'm OK, I'm OK. I don't know where I am, but we bought it south of Muong May."

Merritt's relief was palpable, "Roger, roger."

DiGenero felt himself choke, "Clancey was a streamer."

The hiss of static recorded Merritt's pause, then, "Are you in the trees or in the clear?"

"I'm on the edge of a dry paddy. There's a road..."

DiGenero heard the low rumble of the F-4 in the distance. Merritt broke in, "Yeah, yeah. Stay under cover. I know where you are. I'm heading your way. Got any company?"

DiGenero paused. At first, there were no sounds. Then, he heard them. The voices were a magnet, radiating an invisible force. He turned slowly. He could tell they were still some distance away. Soon, they would be working the underbrush like beaters flushing prey.

He bent down, gathering the nylon around him with a clumsy scoop-

ing motion. DiGenero kicked away a layer of loose leaves and soil, goug-
ing a shallow indentation with his boot to bury the chute as best he could.
Beneath the fresh green carpet, the leaves mouldered on top of the earlier nondescript residue, releasing the rotting smell of jungle decay.

He keyed the radio, "Merritt, I've got company."

"Where are they?"

DiGenero looked at the compass on his wrist, "To the north, moving
along the far edge of the paddy, near the village."

The engines of the F-4 sounded closer. The survival radio came alive.
DiGenero recognized Udorn's call sign, "Red Fox Leader, this is Black
Jack Rescue." The transmission, fainter than Merritt's, was clear, "We
have a Jolly Green airborne, but it's going to be at least forty. What shape's
he in?"

Udorn was the closest air base, but it would take forty minutes for the
giant twin-engine rescue helicopter to reach him. DiGenero felt the first
tremor of panic. Merritt anticipated the reply that was already on his lips,
"Black Jack Rescue, he's got bad guys in the vicinity. Can't you do better
than that?"

"Negative, Red Fox Leader. We're already maxed out. Our next closest Jolly Green is an hour away."

DiGenero hastily jammed down the talk button, breaking in, "Merritt, there's more coming my direction." He could see the shapes, distant but distinct, on the perimeter of the paddy field. At 400 yards, it
was too far away to tell whether they were regulars or militia, but they
were strung out in a skirmish line, walking fast, as if they knew where
they wanted to go. "Oh, Jesus," DiGenero whispered. He knew what
came next. They'd have him long before the helicopter could arrive. He
was a dead man.

He heard Merritt relay his call to Udorn. Transfixed, DiGenero at
first barely heard the new voice on the radio. It was casual, almost laconic, "Red Fox Leader, from the sounds of it, forty minutes ain't good
enough."

Merritt's words were loaded with sarcasm, "Well, that's goddamn brilliant. Who the hell is this?"

Ten miles away, Kirby Harris touched the microphone button as he
banked toward Muong May and descended, "Red Fox Leader, this is Papa
Romeo 21."

Merritt came back at once, "You a chopper?"

"Negative."

Merritt's anger was obvious, "Well, what in the fuck good are ya? I need someone who can get that guy out of there."

"Fear not, sport," Harris's chiding reply made DiGenero smile. "I was driving airplanes when you were still using crayons in your Steve Canyon comics. Besides, I'm flying a Porter. This mother lands places ain't never seen a chopper."

DiGenero furrowed his brow. A Porter. It was a STOL, a short-takeoff-and-landing aircraft. A long-nosed tail dragger with an overhead wing and fixed gear. One engine. He'd seen them on the field at Udorn, and in Bangkok, transiting on their way up-country. They weren't Air Force, but belonged to the contract carriers, Air America, Intermountain Air. The CIA charters.

"Hey, Red Fox One, you got four or five paddies down there, right?"

The Porter was calling DiGenero. He snapped out of his daze and answered, "Affirmative."

"OK," the voice responded at once, "I know this real estate like the back of my hand. There's only one field that big due south of Muong May. I'm five minutes away, maybe less. Why don't you stroll over to the paddy. Go to the south end. But do yourself a favor. Stay in the woods and outta sight. Anybody you see in the neighborhood is NVA regular. After I put her down, get your ass ready to run. You copy?"

"Roger."

"Then go, baby."

DiGenero began to walk, stumbling over a tangle of roots and vines. It was a child's nightmare, the quintessential vision of fear, alone and chased, with nowhere to run, no matter how fast you were and how far you went. In the nightmare, if you didn't wake up, you were there forever, running. Now, if the Porter didn't come, you were there forever, dead. He shoved the branches aside, ducking and weaving as he double-timed through the underbrush toward the south end of the paddy. At the edge of the trees he knelt, surveying the open space. There were four rice paddies, like patches on a quilt, each divided by two feet of earth wall. In a month, when the rain started, they would be green. Now, the dry-season sun had baked them tan and rock hard. He bit his lip, judging the longest distance. Not much, 250 feet, maybe 275, then the dike. Seventy-five yards and the lift from the cool morning air. That was all they had.

DiGenero felt his stomach knot. On the edge of the village, the line of men had stopped and turned, facing his way. They were preparing to sweep, to move out, looking for him. Suddenly a roar deafened him. He saw the F-4 streaking skyward. It was Merritt, there and gone, leaving behind two tumbling cannisters. They hit, skipped once, and exploded in slithering, brilliant orange flame before the black smoke marred the napalm's murderous beauty. From the village, a .50-caliber heavy machine gun fired fecklessly at the empty sky. DiGenero saw that the center of the line had dissolved beneath the burning wave and smoke, leaving the two ends to rise and regroup.

Two miles away, Harris also saw the black cloud and the F-4 climbing out, its sharklike shape turning hard. He pressed the talk button on his microphone, "Take a break. I'm going in." He pushed the Porter's nose lower. A mile away, the south edge of the paddy field approached. He would come in hot, Kirby thought, just over the treetops and then hit reverse prop, literally stalling the Porter in midair. With only 200 feet to roll, he would keep the engine reversed, trying to turn before the dikes stopped him and tore out the landing gear.

DiGenero looked up as the Porter materialized from nowhere. The roar of the turboprop washed over him as the plane dropped, slamming into the hard-baked paddy. The gunmetal-gray shape shot past at 60 miles an hour. Through the open side door DiGenero glimpsed the pilot, one hand on the controls and the other on the throttle, seemingly oblivious to the dead end rushing toward him. The rudder flapped hard left, rocking the Porter as its tail wheel pivoted, swiveling 180 degrees just short of the low earthen paddy wall.

DiGenero rose, tripped, rose again, and began to run. The Porter was gaining speed, taxiing back. In the distance, he could see the muzzle flashes. They were small sunbursts, tiny adornments of light against the green-black backdrop of shrubbery and trees. The Porter raced by him. It spun again, lining up to take off. DiGenero ran like a frantic child toward the demonic roar of the turbine. At the north end of the open field, the line of men began to run, pausing to kneel and fire as they moved. From the village, the .50 caliber pounded a heavy, steady drumbeat. The shells whistled overhead, shattering limbs and trunks as they crashed into the trees. DiGenero knew they were cranking the barrel down as they fired, trying to lower the sights to zero in on the Porter.

DiGenero twisted sideways, stumbling as the prop wash hit him, then threw himself into the open doorway, landing belly-down. The Porter surged as the brakes released. He looked up. Harris, blond, suntanned, in blue jeans, workshirt, and cowboy boots, seemed nonchalant, bouncing in the seat like a bus driver whose only worry was a stretch of bad road. It was as if 200 feet of takeoff roll were 10,000.

DiGenero tried to rise to his knees, but the bouncing as the Porter accelerated threw him forward. He glanced out the open side door. He could see the small eruptions of earth as the shells struck around them. Ahead, the edge of the dike loomed. Two feet of earth, no more. It was their boundary, the limit of their world, the line between flying or losing the undercarriage and careening across the paddy, the demarcation between living and dying. One hundred feet, fifty, twenty. He closed his eyes, feeling the plane's lift and tremor. Then, he was sliding backward. He opened his eyes and looked out. The Porter pointed nose-up, banking hard. He grappled hastily for the aluminum stanchion that supported the solitary canvas sling seat as the toes of his boots caught the edge of the open doorway. Over his shoulder DiGenero could see the treetops as the Porter turned, letting the paddy slip away beneath it.

Harris leveled the plane, motioning him to the second seat. DiGenero rose, steadied himself, and stepped forward. He slipped on the headset and microphone that had been tossed casually to one side. Closer up, Harris looked older. He was lean but weathered, five or six years DiGenero's senior, maybe a little more.

The pilot extended his hand, "Kirby Harris. Backseater bought it, huh?"

DiGenero stared back in wordless acknowledgment. He remembered the picture beside Clancey's bunk, the brunette, smiling, and the little redhead, with the same expression as her mother's, only in miniature. DiGenero looked away, his eyes misting.

"Sorry about that," Harris said after a moment. "Want a cigarette?"

DiGenero nodded and took a Marlboro, hoping that Harris would light it for him so that his own trembling hands could remain disguised. The pilot obligingly extended the Zippo, striking the flame. DiGenero drew deeply and sat back. They were cruising at 90 knots and 150 feet, heading northwest.

"First time you lost a plane?"

DiGenero nodded again. He didn't quite trust himself to speak out.

"Nothing like a Porter," Harris said chattily, and reached out, affectionately patting the glare shield that extended, cowl-like, above the instrument panel. "She's a glider with an engine strapped on. Fifty feet of wing, 2600 pounds bone-dry, and 600 horsepower."

DiGenero listened, grateful for the monologue as he struggled to regain his composure.

"The Pilatus Porter." Harris spoke the words with an evident pleasure. "My favorite. First built these things in Switzerland in the fifties. Used 'em to take skiers up the glaciers." Harris leaned back, relaxed, obviously cruising over familiar ground. "They'd land on the upslope, spin around, and take off downhill. With that kind of dipsy-doodle, you don't need more than a couple hundred feet either way. Same technique works out here." Harris pointed north, "Most of the strips are on top of the mountains. We build 'em so they run uphill. Even at 5000 feet, you can land overloaded in 150 yards or less, if you know what you're doin'. Flying out empty, the takeoff's just like a ski jump. Yep," Harris smiled, "this little mother is one sweet machine."

DiGenero found his voice, "You been out here long?"

"About ten years."

"Flyin' these?"

Harris shook his head, "Started flying second seat in C-119s in Vientiane back in '62. Just before Laos went neutral." He laughed, "'Bout as neutral, that is, as a VFW post on the Fourth of July." He rubbed his chin, "Then, it was 123s out of Saigon. Very comfortable. Now, Porters in this neck of the woods, goin' here and there."

"Ten years is a long time."

"What can I say?" Harris yawned, "Spoils you. Money's good, scenery's pretty, and every night is New Year's eve."

"I don't know," DiGenero rubbed his eyes, feeling the first band of tension that gripped him beginning to ease, "Nam's winding down."

Harris shrugged, "Nothing lasts forever, does it?" He paused, looking into the distance. He seemed to concentrate for the first time, "I ought to start thinking about that, I suppose. It just beats the shit out of me what I'm goin' to do next."

Harris was quiet for a moment, then glanced over at DiGenero, "I'll drop you off in Pakse. There's a shuttle every morning and afternoon. A

C-130 or 123. Forget which. You can hitch a lift back to Udorn. Where you're from, right?"

DiGenero nodded again.

Harris continued, "I'd take you home myself but I've got to motor on up to NKP for a load of hard rice."

NKP, Nakhon Phanom, a rivertown on the Mekong, squatted between jungle and water 170 miles north of Pakse. It was a logistics base, a jumping-off point, smaller now than in the heyday of the war. Some of what was left, the warehouses and communications relays, were still operating, keeping the hill tribes in business against the Pathet Lao and the Vietnamese.

Harris smiled, "This month, I'm a combination teamster and Florence Nightingale. Freight hauler and angel of mercy. Hard rice up-country and the wounded back. You're lucky none of my little Lao buddies got zapped this week. Otherwise, I'd have had a load and wouldn't have been able to give you a lift."

DiGenero took a deep breath, "I don't know how I can pay you back."

"Remember the needy at Christmastime."

"No, seriously, what can I do for you?"

Harris shook his head. He pulled the control column back. The Porter climbed nimbly, banking northwest. The river appeared and then disappeared beyond the trees. Farther on, its course would turn west, creating the Thai border. Ahead, the waterway spread out, bending several directions at once. The Mekong. Wide, brown, and slow-flowing. In the dry season, the level was down, exposing the mud slopes that bounded the channel. On the east bank, in the distance, Pakse's tumbledown collection of tin-roofed shacks, dry dirt streets, and river docks made a cluster of confused construction.

"How about a case of whatever you drink?" DiGenero persisted.

Harris pointed, "The strip's north of town. We'll be on the ground in a few minutes. Be sure to check under your seat and in the overhead compartments for your personal belongings. On behalf of Intermountain Air, we thank you for choosing to fly with us today."

"What'll it be?" DiGenero prodded. "Johnny Walker Black, Chivas?"

Harris eyed him with a hint of aggravation, "Jesus, sonny, you don't give up, do you?"

"No," DiGenero said firmly. He was groping, struggling to find some way to say the DiGeneros always knew their obligations, but the words weren't there. Neither was the sense of self-assurance that had been his only an hour ago when he'd climbed into the F-4 at Udorn. Suddenly, he felt like a kid again in his old New York neighborhood, trying to say and do the right thing to win the favor of one of the "wise guys" who hung around the candy store on the block and flipped extra 50-cent pieces to whoever ran their errands the fastest. This was Harris's corner and Di-Genero felt out of place, too earnest, and a lifetime junior to the man in charge.

Harris frowned, "What's your name?"

"DiGenero."

The Porter turned, lining up with the single runway. "DiGenero," Harris glanced at him for a moment, appraising, "you're a pushy wop."

"Well?"

Harris sighted over the aircraft's long nose for his bearing, descending. He spoke without looking at DiGenero, "You really want to pay me back, huh?"

"Yeah."

Harris shrugged, his eyes still on the runway, "You must have landed on your head. OK, let's get this into a realistic price range for the commodity under discussion. You're bidding up the value of any standard-issue Air Force pilot way too high when you open with a case of Chivas. It just so happens I'm going to be in Bangkok next Saturday night. You can buy me a drink."

"That's all?"

"Yep."

"Where?"

"Natasha's, where else?"

"Where?"

"You don't know Natasha's?" Harris clucked his tongue, "You poor sufferin' bastard. You've been hangin' out in Patpong all this time? Natasha's is for those people who know where gettin' laid is still pleasure, not business. Nicest little bar, and sweetest little whorehouse in Bangkok."

Harris reached forward, snapping the Porter's propeller into reverse as the plane touched the strip. He turned sharply, taxiing at high speed toward the weathered Quonset adorned with the faded sign, "Pakse Airport Operations." Two dark-brown Lao in T-shirts and shorts squatted by the rusting fire extinguishers that bracketed the Quonset's open door. They ignored the Porter as it pivoted on the hardstand, its tail swinging to a stop only yards short of the Quonset.

Harris throttled back, jerking his thumb toward the rear, "Your stop, sport."

DiGenero rose and turned to face the pilot, "Natasha's?"

Harris nodded. As soon as DiGenero put his feet on the macadam, the Porter began to roll. It gathered speed, lifting off in less than 300 feet. DiGenero stood in the morning sun, watching the plane until it was gone.

The taxi crossed the canal four times, passing the same fruit stand, engine repair garage, and seamstress shop with each mistaken turn before they found the right corner. The bartender at the Erawan Hotel had written the directions down after phoning twice for instructions, but it had still taken an hour, first in the six-lane snarl of cars, jitneys, motorcycles, and cabs that clogged the crosstown streets, and then lost in the sois, the alleyways that wove with the klongs, the canals, lacing the city together.

DiGenero paid the taxi, walking the last half block. A splash of light spilled from the open front bar. The scenery on either side of the street was no different from the rest of Bangkok's sprawl, a jumble of open fronts and stands, randomly placed, rickety furniture, assorted appliances, and accumulating refuse. Despite the evening hour, the heat of the day hung heavily, mixing with the pungent lemongrass and spice aromas of meals bubbling in the rear of the dimly lit stalls.

DiGenero paused on the threshold of the bar. It was still too early for darkness to cover all Natasha's extensive blemishes. The room was nondescript, with chipped walls, a tiled floor, rock posters, colored lights, a raised bandstand, and the clumps of speakers that guaranteed the music would soon be painfully loud. At the rattan horseshoe bar under the central spine of high ceiling fans, the girls eyed him languidly, offering soft smiles.

DiGenero spotted Harris. He was sitting across from another American in the last booth on the far right side under the solitary window air-conditioner, an evident place of honor. He heard his name fill the room, "DiGenero! Well, goddamn. How many of these do you want?" There were three women in the booth also. Harris had his arms around two. They were striking, with honey-toned skin, contrasting rich, black hair, and the fine features of a perpetual childhood beauty.

DiGenero walked toward them, feeling for a moment annoyingly junior to Harris once again. He smiled and extended his hand, "I'm only configured to handle one at a time."

Harris shook it, "You gotta do better than that, sport."

At the table, the other man and the third woman, older but no less attractive, rose, making room. In his fifties and heavyset, the American wore dark slacks and a white, open-necked shirt. After eighteen months, DiGenero recognized the type. Unlike the military, they looked as if they belonged. There were more than a few of them up north, ensconced on a corner of the base with their own planes and offices. The nameplate on the door was nondescript, something like, "Far East Transport and Logistics Services." All of them were the same, with leathery tans and long tenure, the civilians who worked for the Company. The permanent party.

Harris glanced up, gesturing toward DiGenero, "This is the guy who thought his ass was worth a case of Chivas." The man smiled, nodding a silent greeting as he spoke, "No sense of value in the younger generation anymore, is there, Kirby?"

Harris shook his head seriously, "None whatsoever."

The American half-turned to Harris, "You got a ride up-country for me tomorrow?"

"Yeah," Harris replied. "Where'll you be tonight if anything comes up?"

"At the apartment. Give me a call. Otherwise, I'll see you at the plane in the morning."

DiGenero started to bid him farewell, but the man and the woman were already two tables distant and walking away.

"Well, shit," Harris said, emptying his beer, "I can't keep calling you DiGenero. What's the rest of your name?"

"Frank."

"OK, Frank, tonight's your introduction to Bangkok."

DiGenero purposefully ignored the bantering condescension, "This one's on me. It isn't exactly my maiden voyage."

Curled catlike and obliging beside Harris, the two women, smiling, listened and watched. Harris draped his arms over their shoulders, cupping his hands under their breasts, his voice assuming the melody of a country evangelist on a redemptive roll, "Captain DiGenero, we've reached our first fork in the road. You can pretend to host this party if you want, but if you're smart, you'll sit at the knee of the master and learn how to enjoy life. I can't be there to pluck your ass out of a crack every time, Lord knows. But now that I've salvaged your body, the least I can do is save your soul."

DiGenero felt the smile cross his face in spite of himself, "Is that so?"

Harris held up both hands, palms out, his face assuming a look of mock contrition, "Far be it from me to tell you what you already know. But this isn't the officer's club, with all the boys from Wichita, Detroit, and Dubuque sitting around and talking about their V-8 Chevies, campers, crabgrass, and mortgages, is it?" Harris spread his arms expansively, gesturing in a semblance of benediction, "And, you won't find hamburgers, Budweisers, the BX, or those sweet, young things who think God created only the missionary position anywhere in the vicinity.

"This is my neighborhood," Harris jerked his head skyward, "up there, and down here. I've got ten years on you, sport, enough for a bachelor's, master's, and Ph.D. That makes me the expert, and based on expert opinion I can tell you that win, lose, or draw, there won't be another war like this one." Harris turned, raising his hand to waggle a signal toward the bar, and then turned back, smiling broadly, "Or another pilot quite like me."

DiGenero sat back, wondering momentarily whether to be antagonized or amused.

The waitress, as beautiful as the two women at the table, appeared with four bottles of Singha. She poured two beers, positioning them before Harris and DiGenero with elaborate care, and then leaned forward to gently touch Harris on the cheek before she withdrew.

Harris watched her walk away, exhaling an exaggerated sigh, "This is a dirty job, but somebody's got to do it." He downed the small glassful of beer and poured another, "Where you from?"

"New York," DiGenero replied.

Harris grimaced, "My condolences."

"And you?" DiGenero asked.

"Montana," Harris answered. He paused, gently stroked the long, black hair that fell over the small shoulders of the doll-like form on his right.

"New York," Harris spoke the words with a pondering tone. "Seems like it's decided, then."

"What's that?" DiGenero asked.

Harris reached across the table, clinking his glass against DiGenero's, "You're all right, Frank."

Harris drained the beer and sat back, "New York, huh?" The question had a rhetorical tone.

DiGenero nodded.

Harris spoke, "Can't say I'd ever have a reason to go to a godforsaken place like that."

"So?"

"So?" Harris smiled, "Well, that being the case, when we get together again, you're not going to have any choice but to come looking for me."

Part One

Raptor

1

Thursday, August 16, 1984

The University Building, Salt Lake City, Utah

The late-afternoon sun had just begun to paint the high canyon slopes east of Salt Lake City a deep rose when Frank DiGenero finally swiveled away from his view of the valley and turned back to the desk. DiGenero was not by nature an indecisive man, but he had spent the last hour in his seventeenth-floor office carefully reading the official FBI file before him twice from beginning to end, watching the evening fall, and uneasily considering his options. He rubbed his temples, feeling the headache and the fatigue. He was tired, bone-tired. The choices were there, in black and white, but it still wasn't easy.

DiGenero unconsciously patted his shirt pocket. He'd smoked his last cigarette two years ago but the conditioned reflex persisted. He stared for a moment at the operation's code name, "RAPTOR," stamped slightly askew in bold block letters on the folder's buff-colored cover. There was nothing unusual about the question posed by the papers clipped inside the heavy fiberboard file: to pursue or not to pursue a case. As the "SAC," the Special Agent in Charge of the FBI's undercover strike force operating against the multimillion-dollar illegal trade in birds of prey, he'd made the decision scores of times in the last two years.

He sighed, reopening the folder. It had been buried on his desk in the end-of-week paper crunch, a pile that amounted to the standard penance for his usual sin, spending time on the street, rather than in the office shuffling memos. It was a "soft file," the initial informal record on a possible subject for investigation. Like the thousands of others in the hundreds of FBI offices across the country, the first page was the most recent "221," the standard field investigation sheet. DiGenero scanned the legal-length form until his eyes reached the box highlighted in light blue in the lower left-hand corner.

The name, typed inside with room to spare, was centered just above the preprinted subtitle, "Subject of Interest":

HARRIS, KIRBY.

That was the problem. Two words. In capital letters, directory style, last name first. Kirby was not only an FBI "Subject of Interest" but Di-Genero's subject of interest, a target of RAPTOR, his own undercover investigation.

DiGenero leaned forward and pressed the button of the office inter-com, "Hey, sweetheart, could you send in Kasiewicz?"

"Ms. McLaughlin to you, DiGenero. I'll get him. He just went down the hall."

DiGenero smiled. Nancy McLaughlin was there, morning and night, whenever he wanted. After ten years with the Bureau, all of them sup-porting undercover operations, she had more special security clearances than most agents in counterintelligence and a dedication to work she knew was important that kept her in the office even after they ordered her home. DiGenero had used three inside handlers when he was deep in the Scarlese family during his last long year in New York. She was the only one who cared, the only one who would listen late at night when he had to talk, drawing off the fear and the tension, the only one who kept the thin thread from breaking. For the next two years in Atlanta, after he'd come inside, and then in Miami, undercover again, they'd been apart, but when they gave him RAPTOR, she was the first person he'd called.

Nancy was, he thought, the closest thing he had to "family." His mother had died before he was a year old. His father also was gone. Only his sister, Teresa, was left, but she was married now and had moved again, this time to Detroit, far enough away to justify their mutual inattention. There was no one else. He'd spent his life working, alone. Have to do something about that some day, DiGenero thought, then let the recol-lection drift away as his eyes returned to business. Kirby. Kirby Harris.

DiGenero closed the file. The routing sheet and the note from Ka-siewicz were clipped on the front. The date stamps and check marks re-corded the fact that the courier had delivered the file from Missoula a week ago. According to the book, normal FBI procedure, the resident agent in Missoula would have had the "action," since his man had turned up the lead. But the illegal trapping and selling of federally protected wild falcons was RAPTOR's turf and the undercover took precedence.

The document clerk had routinely assigned the file to Kasiewicz to review and recommend action.

DiGenero stood, turning to stare back out the window. The sunset was long over now and the darkness had sharpened his reflection in the pane.

The problem with the file was a coincidence, he thought, like the image before him. If he wasn't there, it wouldn't be there. The problem and the image were both accidental combinations of his presence, the place, and the time.

Coincidence. The war and college. Law school and the FBI. The mob and RAPTOR. And now, the file and Harris. Coincidence. DiGenero smiled to himself. It was the story of his life.

Frank DiGenero had no doubt that if it hadn't been for Vietnam, he would have gone the other way. In 1963, with a high school diploma in hand, he was the son of Carlo DiGenero, who in 1913 had taken the olive grove road from Alcamo to Palermo, the boat from Sicily to Ellis Island, and the ferry from the crowded landing that faced the Battery to Manhattan's lower East Side. Fifty years later, at 18, Carlo's son, Frank, knew all the right people. They were the sons of men who had come with Frank's father but taken different paths, marked for them by Sicily's own, the Black Hand. Frank had grown up with them in New York's Little Italy, and his start was guaranteed. Not in his father's small grocery, although his beginning would have been no grander, still small-time. At first the numbers, odd jobs, deliveries, maybe some muscle chores for the loan sharks in the neighborhood. But only at first, in his case. He was tough and quick. He would have worked his way up, sooner rather than later, to become a wise guy with a piece of the action and, eventually, a place in one of the families.

He would have, that is, except for Vietnam. In 1963, he was still without a rap sheet and the Army was on his back. To beat the draft, he enrolled in City College. After a semester, something happened. He was too smart not to learn, not to see that CCNY wasn't a dodge, but an escape. Four years later, he graduated. The Army was still there in 1967, offering infantry, armor, or artillery, but so was the Air Force and he signed up for flying. The next five years took him on a straight line south and west, from officer school and pilot training in Texas to Thailand, Vietnam, and the war.

When his tour was over, DiGenero came home, trying to decide what would happen next. He stayed for a few weeks in his room over the store. The old neighbors, even some of the wise guys, looked up to him, but his friends were gone—one dead, two in Lewisburg, and the other working for the Scarlese family with a coke habit that wouldn't quit. It was as if a picture album he wanted badly to keep had disappeared, leaving only the negatives, the black images of the original prints. His last link to the past broke suddenly that July, in the heat of the day, when his father didn't return from the store's cellar after saying he'd be only a minute. When DiGenero peered down the stairway, he saw the old man was on the floor as if he'd given up looking for what he sought and lay down to rest. He knew in that cold, horrible instant that his last reason for staying, like his memories, was gone.

Law school and the FBI. It was another coincidence, he supposed. All other things being equal, after Fordham on the GI bill, his application to the Justice Department for a position as a federal trial attorney would have been one of thousands in the queue. But because of everything that should have kept him from ever being where he was, on a muggy Washington afternoon in June 1974, to the five senior FBI agents in the Bureau's Organized Crime Division who read his sheaf of government forms, Frank DiGenero was heaven-sent.

The five, the members of "MG," the Division's Undercover Management Group, had been culling candidates daily from the scores of applicant folders and interview sheets that arrived from across the country to fill the files of Justice and the Bureau. Their objective was top secret, sensitive, and in the six months since the FBI had received the Presidential Action Memorandum, still unfulfilled—to find an agent who could go deep undercover for whatever time it took to build the case that would cripple the New York mob.

Ideally, for the FBI, the world's largest and most professional law enforcement organization, the task of selecting a seasoned insider schooled in undercover operations should not have posed a problem. But for almost all of the Bureau's nearly 8000 special agents, forty years of J. Edgar Hoover's iron rule had made one message crystal clear: "undercovers" were the kiss of death. There were a few mavericks, but the computer skills bank had produced only a handful of possibles and none that matched the requirements. DiGenero was the first they'd found with the background, street savvy, and built-in connections to effect a long-term penetration. He was a natural and what they needed. Anything less and the odds were overwhelming that they would fail and bury their mistake.

With the White House waiting, DiGenero learned afterward, the rest had happened fast. It took less than forty-eight hours to get the hiring approvals that normally required six months. Their man was on the plane to New York the next day. DiGenero told the few people who cared that he had a job overseas and would return sometime.

The formal training started two weeks later, although there was no Frank DiGenero in the FBI's New Agent Class 74-10. Because he was given a different name and cover story for his short time on the inside, there also was no reference to him in the Bureau's master personnel, applicant, and national identification files. In fact, when his ninety days at the FBI Academy in Quantico were through, Frank DiGenero, alias Frank Marbury, bid farewell to his classmates, absentmindedly forgot to give them his temporary forwarding address, drove off the sprawling Marine base onto Interstate 95 alone, weaved behind the heavy trucks heading north, and disappeared.

Four years later, when the top thirty-five mafiosi from the three leading New York families were arraigned at the federal courthouse in lower Manhattan, Frank DiGenero, Brooklyn lawyer and businessman, known to some as "Frank, the brain," the Scarlese family's youngest and brightest consigliere, coincidentally disappeared once again. This time, however, to the surprise of the defendants, Frank DiGenero, FBI agent, surfaced at the prosecutor's table in his place. When he did, he earned a permanent spot on the New York mob's hit list as well as the record for the longest-running and most successful undercover in the history of the FBI.

After the Scarlese trial was over, the best jobs had come looking for him. The next two were both high-profile—one on the inside in the Atlanta field office and the last, on the outside again in Miami, by himself, at the end of the string. It was anything but the classic, career-enhancing pattern, but he was moving, making it, on the way to the top. He was golden, or so he thought.

Two years ago, when the end came, DiGenero recalled, it was no one's fault. The telephone tap had picked up the word that one of the Tattaglias, a soldier for what was left of the Scarlese family, had recognized DiGenero in a club in Key Biscayne. That was it. The Bureau pulled him out overnight. He'd argued, but even with the New York families frozen out of Miami, there were still dollar signs with big numbers after his name. He was dead if the boys from the Boroughs or New Jersey ever found him.

DiGenero looked past his reflection in the glass and into the distance. Salt Lake City's rush-hour traffic was minor league by New York standards, an orderly, steady, bright stream, politely spaced, rather than butted bumper to taillight. The headlights drew a moving line across the darkness as the cars neared the edge of the valley. There, the evening processional wound upward to the "Bench," the narrow plateau that had once been the shore of the prehistoric inland sea and now created a flared skirt along the jutting Wasatch mountain front. It was the home of the choicer suburbs, with lighted picture windows, two-car garages, crushed-gravel lawns, and imported shrubs, that looked down on the city. DiGenero glanced at his watch. It was nearly 7:00 p.m. The office was quiet.

He sat down, propping his heel on the windowsill, and laced his fingers behind his head. Being blown in Miami was only part of the reason they'd pulled him. He knew that now. He'd been undercover too long. It had been time. The facade—no, it was thinner than that—the veneer hadn't cracked. He was hanging on, onstage, performing, all day, every day. But he was waking in a cold sweat, hearing sounds every night, seeing more and more faces he thought he knew, watching longer and harder when someone, even for a moment, watched him, and reaching more quickly for the .38 that was strapped to his calf when any stranger approached, man, woman, or child.

Hanging on. That's what Jennie had said when she'd left him for the third time. Hanging on, she asked, but on which side of the edge? She told him, but he'd screamed back at her that night that he was in control, even though at that moment, when he didn't even recognize his own voice and the door shut behind her, he realized she was right. He was hanging on, but like she said, it was on the wrong side of the edge, the side with nothing beneath him. One ulcer, one failed marriage, and the toll from the scotch, cigarettes, and uppers that kept him going, leading two lives at once, twenty-four hours a day. Eight years. It was time.

And, DiGenero thought, the Bureau owed him. To their credit, they paid. DiGenero smiled to himself. The last two years had been good, although when he first arrived in Salt Lake City he couldn't decide which was more unreal—working undercover against the mob in his own backyard and surviving, or being a street-wise dago from Little Italy dropped into Utah's blond, blue-eyed promised land in order to chase cowboys who sold birds.

Still, as operations went, RAPTOR was a plum, high-profile and low-risk, with the potential for big numbers in the arrest column, a political priority in Washington that made pushing paper easy, and, if it was ever compromised, "blown" prematurely, the certain promise of the aroma of Chanel No. 5 rather than horseshit in the press. The poachers and smugglers on one side, and the FBI protecting Mother Nature's endangered species on the other. Who wouldn't love it?

DiGenero stared at the file on the desk. Two good years. Yes, he thought, the Bureau owed him and they paid. But Harris and the file? Since that day in Laos on the ground, waiting by the paddy, DiGenero had lived twelve years. Harris had given him that.

He looked up at the sound of the knock. Mitch Kasiewicz opened the door, a half-unwrapped hamburger in one hand, "Sorry, I just went across the street."

DiGenero motioned him into the room, "You're going to kill yourself eating that plastic trash." He had handpicked the 28-year-old FBI special agent from the Chicago field office a year ago. In a three-piece suit, white shirt, and conservative tie, Kasiewicz looked like a typical young big-city attorney. But DiGenero knew the look was skin-deep. The Chicago native had grown up working summers on his uncle's ranch in the Wyoming Tetons. DiGenero had chosen Kasiewicz for what he knew about ranchers and mountains rather than for his specialization in criminal procedures, accounting and tax law, and civil claims at Northwestern.

Kasiewicz saw the folder centered before DiGenero, wondering which of his cases had been singled out. He liked and admired his boss. DiGenero was uncanny, always two steps ahead of the game. And he was never condescending, or the type who gave you the odds and ends to fix, the paper clips to count and the pencils to sharpen. Instead, he handed over the case and pushed you in over your head. He had made it a good year. Salt Lake City's blue laws and bring-your-own-bottle ambiance couldn't compare with the lights, ladies, and lakeshore apartment he'd left back in Chicago, but Kasiewicz was glad the obviously tired man who sat behind the mahogany desk, sleeves rolled up, had selected him for the strike force.

DiGenero shoved the file toward Kasiewicz, who had gulped the last of the hamburger and dropped into a hands-in-pockets slouch in the chair. Questions and answers were DiGenero's style, rather than reading and solitary thinking. In this case, it also was easier to let someone else's logic help him through a difficult decision, "Well, what do you think?"

Kasiewicz eyed the name on the folder's tab, swallowing the last of the beef and bun, "I've been on it about a week. The stories from Missoula, Kalispell, and Bozeman aren't all the same, but they basically fit together. His name has come up on several occasions, although never with a lot of specifics. If he's in the business, he works by himself. He's careful and he doesn't talk much. Definitely not bush-league. My guess is he's maybe the best we've run into so far." Kasiewicz paused and shrugged, "The pieces are tantalizing, but so far they don't make enough evidence to roll him up."

DiGenero nodded. That was usually true. A soft file almost always was a collection of bits and pieces, the small, odd parts that began every investigation. Sometimes it led to more and sometimes it didn't. Kasiewicz's evaluation also sounded right, not because he believed the papers would make a case, but simply because DiGenero was sure that if Harris was trapping and selling birds, he would be the best in the trade.

Kasiewicz continued, "The pair we got last year in Kalispell were the first to mention him."

"The easy busts?"

"Yeah," Kasiewicz nodded. "They tried to peddle a gyrfalcon to O'Brian when he was the undercover working the woodsy-mossy, save-the-whales-and-snail-darters types at Glacier Park for leads. The ranchers bit and the rest fell into place. O'Brian used the Missoula resident for the buy."

DiGenero remembered the details. They had borrowed one of the agents from Missoula to avoid blowing their man at the park as well as to make the local FBI resident happy.

"The street agent followed up with the interrogation that surfaced Harris's name," Kasiewicz said. "I interviewed the ranchers again two days ago. They told me they talked to Harris a couple times when he'd

landed at the local airport. They shot the shit about birds, and about
what they could trap in the Glacier area."

"What else did they know?" DiGenero asked.

"They didn't recall Harris saying much about himself, other than the
fact he had a license to raise falcons because he worked with the breeding project at the university."

"Does he?"

"Yeah. I called the ornithology department in Missoula. He's
signed on as a supplier. Sometimes he keeps injured birds for them as
well."

A license, DiGenero thought. It wasn't a crime to raise captive-bred
birds. But a breeder's license also made a wonderful cover if you were
after wild-caught.

"Anyway," Kasiewicz said, "they saw him two seasons running, in
the spring and the fall, flying his own plane in and out of Canada. The
pieces fit together a little better when I talked to the air charter people in
Bozeman. One of the charter services said that Harris was a regular customer. I double-checked. It seems Harris uses a long hauler, a Kingair,
for trips to the east coast."

"And?" DiGenero raised his eyebrows.

"I went to the druggies first," Kasiewicz said, referring to the Drug
Enforcement Agency, DEA, "just in case. They didn't have anything on
Harris in their files."

DiGenero turned his chair halfway toward the window, appearing to
study the lights that had blinked on, outlining the grid created by Salt
Lake City's streets.

Kasiewicz continued, "I also checked for matches between the tail
numbers of any Kingairs used by known mules, drug haulers, and the
planes Harris chartered. And, I scanned the composites for descriptions
without IDs held by Customs as well as DEA that might fit Harris. The
bottom line is no drug or other smuggling connections."

The young FBI agent let himself enjoy a moment of satisfaction. He
had answered the right questions without being asked, the ones that took
a scrap of information and went beyond the puzzle where it obviously
could belong to look for others, the unusual templates with the odd, seemingly unrelated angles, that might provide the correct pattern. They were
questions that depended on carefully turning the information like a pre-

cious object slowly before your eye, a few degrees at a time, the way an appraiser examines a jewel, studying each facet from its own angle and in its own light.

The Bureau didn't teach that in its science of criminology course. By the book, it took an overwhelming mass of information, thousands of pieces, each collected one by one, to create the fabric of evidence that could make a case. The method worked, he thought, until you got outside the big-city offices. Traveling in the boonies, to the one- and two-man residences, like Elko, Twin Falls, and Pocatello, Kasiewicz had learned there were too many cases, too few hours to think each through, and no one to help but yourself. Then, you and your intuition were on your own.

College, law school, and the FBI Academy notwithstanding, he wouldn't have known how to think that way a year ago. But in the last twelve months, DiGenero had taught him, asking the right questions, over and over again, to establish the pattern, and now he did.

"Then, I went to the state police," Kasiewicz continued. "They didn't have anything in their special intelligence unit, but I checked the tax records on Harris in Great Falls. He has a family place, 4000 acres, in Broadwater County. He owns the spread. It's been there for several generations."

DiGenero smiled as Kasiewicz slipped into the kind of earnest recitation that students gave to please their favorite professors, "He seems to be doing better than most in the valley. I asked the Bozeman special agent to talk with the local banker. The ranch is paid off. Nobody thought much about it."

"Have you been out there?" DiGenero asked.

"Not yet. But maybe it's time to see what's on the place."

Kasiewicz didn't know, but DiGenero already had seen what was on the place. He had stayed in touch with Harris since Vietnam, by letter mostly, given his own obvious occupational constraints. Their reunion face-to-face had finally come last year. DiGenero had visited the ranch several times since then. Harris had made a point of showing him the falcons and with each visit of teaching him something more about the birds. It was a tutorial of sorts, serious and good-humored, but with a vaguely teasing twist, as if Kirby knew why he was in Salt Lake City. Breeding license or not, DiGenero remembered wondering from the first time he saw the falcons whether he would have trouble with Harris some day.

"Well?" Kasiewicz asked.

"Leave the file with me. I'll think about it. It's late and I'm not hitting on all eight cylinders," DiGenero said, standing to stretch. "Hey," he added, "good job."

The compliment was also a dismissal. Kasiewicz rose, glancing around to nod as he closed the door, but DiGenero's back was already turned.

There were always choices, DiGenero told himself. Obviously, if he gave Kasiewicz the go-ahead, the wheels would start to turn. When they did, it would be hard to get them to stop. Or, he could shelve it, call it off. As chief of the undercover, he would need only to write a note that said it threatened to cross wires with other priorities—an informant on the inside, or another case already under way.

Or. Or what? DiGenero craned his head back, trying to stretch the tension out of the corded muscles in his neck. He could hear the muted sounds of voices outside his door as someone, maybe Kasiewicz, ended a long day, bidding farewell. The quiet returned. Or? Or, DiGenero concluded, he could take care of it himself. That, too, was a choice. If he played it right, he could ice the problem and Harris could simply walk away.

DiGenero picked up the file. It was thin and, as Kasiewicz said, there wasn't enough inside to roll Harris up. If Harris dropped it now, that would be all they would ever have. No more, no case. DiGenero slipped the folder into his briefcase. He owed Kirby as much. No, more.

He threw his coat over his shoulder and switched off the lights. Bozeman was an hour away by air. It had been almost four months since he had last made the trip. Nancy McLaughlin looked up as DiGenero walked into the reception area. His intense expression told her immediately he was in his own world. Her good-bye was purposely exaggerated to retrieve his attention, "And you have a nice day, too."

DiGenero glanced up, smiling, and waved absentmindedly. He stepped into the hallway. The heavy oak door, adorned with the brass nameplate that declared the occupants of the suite to be "Western Associates, Management Consultants," the cover for RAPTOR's office in Salt Lake City, closed solidly behind him with the snap of the hidden security lock. He reached forward to the elevator panel and touched the button on the wall, then watched the digital counter register the elevator's progress to the seventeenth floor.

Kirby Harris and the file. DiGenero leaned against the wall, his eyes fixed straight ahead, focused not on the hallway but on a sunbaked rice paddy a long time ago, and very far away.

He flipped up the top of his briefcase, automatically checking for Harris's file as the elevator doors slid open. The file was there. Lost in thought, DiGenero stepped inside and began his descent.

2

Saturday, August 18, 1984

The Harris Ranch, Broadwater County, Montana

Against the sky, the dark shape turned in a spiral, scribing an invisible circle around them. DiGenero looked straight up and sucked in his breath. In an instant, the silhouette had changed from a cross to an arrowhead that was dropping, point down, accelerating toward the earth. Three seconds later and sixty yards away, the form swooped upward, skimming the ground. DiGenero froze, tensing his arm. The red-tailed hawk flew at him fast and low, barely above the broken wheat stalks, closing in a 50-mile-an-hour sprint. Suddenly, the hawk flared her wings and tail, braking hard to settle on his heavy leather glove in a stoop-shouldered landing. The force of her momentum startled him, jamming DiGenero's outstretched arm back toward his body. He jerked his head away as the redtail, bristling at the unexpected close quarters, jabbed a warning with her beak.

Harris's laughter welled up behind him. "She wouldn't hurt an important man like you, Frank. That's assault on a federal officer." Harris was walking toward him, slipping on a long leather gauntlet just like the one protecting DiGenero's right arm.

DiGenero eyed the hawk suspiciously, "Yeah, but does she know that?"

"You let the hawk come too close when she landed," Harris yanked on the cuff of his falconer's glove, making it snug. "And, you lowered your arm as she settled down. That makes a hawk nervous. It feels like terra firma has just dropped out from under her."

Harris raised his arm and nudged at the hawk's talons. She tightened her feathers against her body and relaxed her grip on DiGenero's arm, stepping forward onto the new glove. With his free hand, Harris took a leather hood from his pocket. Tooled and tasseled, it had a ceremonial, almost medieval look, like the knight's helmet that had once been its model. Harris deftly slipped the small cap over the redtail's head and beak. Two leather ties hung from its bell-shaped bottom. He gripped one in his free hand and the other in his teeth, pulling on the rawhide. The strands made the hood snug, sealing out the light and quieting the hawk.

The scene, DiGenero thought, was vintage Hollywood. They were in the Broadwater Valley, three miles from the ranch house, almost geographically dead center on Harris's 4000 acres. The late-afternoon light played across the freshly cut field, mellowing the brown wheat stubble to gold. Strewn with the residue of harvested grain, it was the ideal place to flush grouse as they clustered before evening to feed. Three hundred yards away, the border of wild brush mixed with the dry summer grass that was lying down to die. Beyond, a few sparse firs stood like an advance guard before a thickening dark-green stand that covered the western slope of the Big Belt Mountains, a stairstep range of the Rockies.

Against this backdrop, Harris was the picture of a Montana cowboy. Dressed in faded jeans, workshirt, ten-gallon rolled-brim hat, and a rancher's scarred boots, he stood straight as well as at ease. Only his weathering kept him from looking a decade younger than his 45 years. It was perfect, DiGenero thought, except that instead of wearing a holster and a Colt .45, Harris had a hawk on his arm and a falconer's game bag around his waist. Hanging at hip level, the soft leather satchel bulged from the bodies of the two grouse that had been flown to ground by the red-tailed hawk.

They'd brought the hawk into the field two hours before to take advantage of the Saturday afternoon before DiGenero had to return to Bozeman for his 8:00 p.m. flight back to Salt Lake City. Harris spoke as he turned, motioning DiGenero to follow him toward the pickup truck parked a quarter mile away, "The redtail's not bad for short distances." He stroked the hawk's breast with his free hand as they walked, "This one does best in spurts. The grouse are quick as hell, but when they slow down to look for a place to hide, she can get to them. If they tried to run for it, they'd do better."

Following a few steps behind, DiGenero noticed the black and white pointer that had flushed the game for them. The dog was bouncing and bumping along beside Harris, pressing against him to get his attention. It stared up, glancing back and forth between Harris and the redtail, obviously worried over its master's divided affection.

DiGenero shook his head, smiling to himself. Harris was the main attraction no matter where he went, even in the middle of a zoo parade. As always, he had the easy, self-confident gait of a man obviously at home and very much in his element. DiGenero stumbled over a hard-packed furrow. He pulled off his falconer's glove and slapped it against the leg of his jeans, raising an impressive cloud of dust.

Harris's long stride had increased the distance between them. DiGenero thought about the file, going over the possibilities once again. What did Harris know about him? About the Salt Lake City operation? There obviously were pieces he could put together. Because of the publicity when the Scarlese case broke, there was no secret about his FBI undercover assignment in New York, or later, when he came inside, about his job in Atlanta. Miami was another story, although just barely. DiGenero had never said what he was doing there, but it wouldn't have taken a genius after his vague answers to Harris's occasional questions to have figured out that he'd gone undercover again.

Even so, there was no necessary reason why Harris should have connected him to RAPTOR. When he first called Harris from Salt Lake City, he described the transfer as routine, kicked upstairs to shuffle papers after a career on the street. The story was plausible and his cover took care of the details. The "backstopping" arrangement was a "double blind," letting him hang his hat in the Salt Lake City field office, where he had his name on the directory, a mail drop, and a secretary to forward his calls. Five blocks away, at Western Associates, he ran RAPTOR under an alias.

They'd also made sure the operation had stayed clean for the last two years. When their busts went down, the newspaper stories made a day's worth of headlines in the mountain states, but so far they'd handed the arrests to the locals and to the Fish and Wildlife Service, who weren't about to turn down the credit. Even the suspects who'd been stung didn't know how they'd been had.

Harris had reached the truck and was leaning into the rear bed of the pickup. The red-tailed hawk stepped from his arm onto the cadge, the padded wood perch that was bolted to the floor behind the cab. Harris slipped the hawk's jesses, the rawhide cords tied around her legs, through the metal ring on the wooden post and looped a half hitch with one practiced motion. He walked toward the rear of the truck, slapped the tailgate, and snapped his fingers. The pointer leapt into the bed with a four-legged spring and curled up, satisfied that he was still part of the family.

DiGenero caught up, tossing his glove into the cab. The answer was still the same, he thought, frowning involuntarily. There was no reason Harris should suspect. But each time he came to visit, Harris always made a point of the hawking lessons, almost but not quite teasingly, as if telling DiGenero he knew otherwise and tempting him to ask how. And if Harris knew, the lessons would be just like him, a backhanded dare, just like a kid who knew someone was watching the cookie jar but couldn't resist letting you know he would try to stick his hand in anyway.

Harris was already behind the wheel when DiGenero reached the door on the passenger side. The beer can, frosted and dripping from the cooler on the floor, protruded through the window. DiGenero took the offering and popped the top with his thumb. The rusting hinge squawked in protest as he yanked open the door and slid onto the seat's torn upholstery.

"Keep this up, DiGenero, and some day you might learn enough to fly a wild one," Harris laughed, turning the key in the ignition. "Of course, that's only if the Feds make it legal."

DiGenero tilted his head back, half-draining the twelve-ounce can to wash down the August afternoon's dryness. He could sense Harris's eyes on him, searching for a reaction. He spoke, "Big difference with the wild ones, huh?"

"No comparison. They do what comes naturally. No need to train them to kill. You only need to convince 'em that it's worth their while to hunt for you. After they're in the air, of course, any bargains are kept strictly on their terms."

Harris slid the old Ford pickup into first gear and released the clutch. He spun the wheel one-handed. DiGenero watched the long broken speedometer gyrate wildly before it settled back against its peg, inert. They drove slowly, circling toward the ranch house.

"Yep," Harris jerked his head toward the rear and the red-tailed hawk, "the 'wild-caught' aren't like that old whore back there. Raised her from a baby. She's all right, but if you let her go on a cold, dark night, she'd

ring up to 1000 feet, spot the brightest window with the warmest fire behind it, and head straight for the spot."

DiGenero took a long swallow of beer, resting his foot on top of the
cooler that was between them on the floor. It was time, he thought.

"You read the papers, Kirby?"

Harris shook his head, "Only when I got nothin' better to do." He
raised his eyebrows, grinning, "What's happened? You got your name in
the Salt Lake City society column and want me to be impressed?"

DiGenero ignored the good-natured jibe, "Nope. I thought you might
have seen the story about the arrests for falcon poaching two or three
weeks ago."

Harris paused for several seconds, furrowing his brow, "I saw it." He
drove more slowly, letting the engine's idle speed pull them along, sipping his beer, "Fish and Wildlife. United States Department of the Interior, right?"

DiGenero nodded. "Interior's not my business, but sometimes you
hear things."

Harris glanced over, "You don't say?"

"Word is they're going after the operators, not the two-bit types, but
the ones who are trapping and selling to falcon collectors in this country,
Europe, and the Middle East. I hear the trade's a big-bucks operation
that's too large to ignore. The election year heat's on from Congress and
the conservation types. The Endangered Species Act makes getting busted
a hefty ticket. The paisans in my old neighborhood would call it 'two 5
spots'—$50,000 and five years."

"How about that?" Harris smiled faintly. So, it had come. The warning. DiGenero. He meant well. He always had. Odd, too, for an Air
Force type who hadn't even been with the Company. Frank had stayed
in touch, unlike the others, the ones he'd worked with at Intermountain
Air. One or two popped up occasionally as a drunken voice on a late-
night overseas call or a first name scrawled at the bottom of a postcard
dug out of some Central American hotel-room drawer. But beyond that,
DiGenero was it, a lifeline of sorts, his last remaining connection to the
best of times. When you got below the surface, he and Frank had more
in common than the war, but that was the most important thing.

Harris shook off the momentary reminiscence. He also could score
one. He was right after all. The arrests. It was DiGenero and the FBI,
not the "fish cops," the Fish and Wildlife Service. Now there was an-

other question. Was DiGenero's warning a general proposition or did he
know something? More to the point, did he know about Von Biemann
and the deal?

Harris hit the brake, slowing the pickup to a near stop as it approached
the main irrigation canal. The mixture of ragweed, cattail reeds, and black-
eyed Susans on the banks bowed in the breeze, covering the edges of the
dark, slowly swirling water. In the distance, the low sun reflected bloodred
in the windows of the squat, one-story ranch house that Harris called
home. The truck clattered over the heavy planks that bridged the fifteen-
foot-wide channel.

"That sure is interesting," Harris paused to finish the last of his beer,
"but I gotta ask you something personal." He held the empty out the
window, flipping it backward into the rear bed of the pickup. The pointer
jerked awake in surprise, scrambling for cover as the can clattered inside.
Harris reached across the seat, resting his hand solicitously on DiGenero's
shoulder, "You wouldn't think for a minute that an ole country boy like
me with a couple of scraggly hawks would be part of any multimillion-
dollar, international ring of poachers, would you?"

DiGenero pursed his lips and then spoke the word quietly, "Kalispell."

"Huh?"

"It's a good place to refuel on the way to Canada," DiGenero's voice
was matter-of-fact. He studied Harris's expression. He had no doubt that
Harris would remember his conversation with the two ranchers, especially after their arrest in RAPTOR's undercover operation at Glacier Park.

Harris turned his gaze back to the road. The double-rutted track led
to the ranch yard a half mile away. He spoke, his voice quieter this time,
"Do you ever think about the war, Frank?"

"Sure."

"What do you think?"

"Once is enough."

"That's not what I think."

"Oh? Miss the paycheck and the faraway places?"

Harris shook his head, "No. It's not the money, although that was
good enough, and I sure-as-shit ain't carryin' a torch for any half-assed
political causes. I just ask myself a question sometimes." Harris paused,
as if considering his words carefully and then began again, talking as much
to himself as to DiGenero, "I wonder if I'll ever be that alive again."

"Alive?"

Harris nodded, "Yeah. One thousand percent alive. The way you feel when you're walking on the edge every day, with no net, and making it to the other side."

DiGenero didn't reply. He understood Harris's question, although in his case he'd never needed to ask it, at least not quite that way. His first undercover, with its round-the-clock version of life on the brink, had answered it for him.

Harris accelerated, shifting into second gear. The pickup bounced and rattled toward the ranch's cluster of weathered buildings. He glanced at DiGenero. If he knew about Von Biemann he wasn't saying, at least not yet. Harris spoke louder over the noise, his tone good-natured, "Poachers, huh?"

"Yeah."

Harris composed his features into a mock-serious expression, "I'll tell you what. You being an officer of the court as well as a bona fide upholder of the law, I'll call you if I see anything suspicious."

DiGenero knew the conversation was over, for now. He nodded, "You do that."

"And Frank," Harris grinned, reaching over this time to clap DiGenero on the shoulder, "why don't you do the same for me?"

The shiver of apprehension, rather than the cool whisper of evening air, made Erin Dupres feel suddenly cold. From the porch of the ranch house she could see the taillights of DiGenero's rented car as they receded in the distance. Even now, the foreboding was there, as it had been since yesterday when they'd met him at the airport. She'd tried hard to dismiss it. It wasn't Frank. He'd come to the ranch before and she always liked to see him. Maybe it was the timing, Kirby's pending deal with Von Biemann and DiGenero's unexpected visit. The two were coincidental. Or were they?

Erin folded her arms, watching the dying light. It was more than that, she thought. It was also the arrests. They had been on her mind, like a fine abrasive, little by little scratching the surface of her confidence that it wouldn't, no, couldn't happen to Harris. DiGenero's visit had made the scratches into cracks. Not because of what he said, but because of who he was. FBI. For Frank, it wasn't a nine-to-five job. It made her worry, for no good reason, but worry all the same.

The sound of dead weight hitting hollow metal broke the quiet. The pickup was parked by the barn fifty yards away and Harris was loading his gear. Erin's footsteps echoed on the weathered flooring as she walked to the far edge of the porch. She watched Harris pause, hefting his favorite carbine before reaching into the cab to snap the saddle gun into the rear window rack.

Erin looked at her watch. It was 6:30 p.m. Harris still had time to reach his destination, "Sixteen," the creek that flowed from the mountain lake into the high valley, before dark. She turned. Her suitcase was beside the front door. If she left now, she could arrive in Missoula before midnight. She glanced back toward the highway. DiGenero's taillights were gone. Nonetheless, for the first time in five years with Kirby Harris, Erin Dupres was afraid.

She retraced her steps, crossing the porch to lift her suitcase, and walked toward the small Honda that was parked by the peeling picket fence, the demarcation of the ill-tended front yard. Erin opened the door and maneuvered the bag onto the rear seat. It was her annual migration, the last evening of her last weekend of her summer in the valley, the season she always spent with Harris at the ranch. Somehow, ominously, it felt more final, as if the cycles were over and she was passing the point of no return this time.

Erin shut the car door, focusing on tomorrow, trying to dismiss the thought. The next day, Sunday, would give her time to resettle in her apartment. It was two blocks from campus, where she would begin the semester on Monday. Erin frowned. The first week back was always the worst, cluttered by the chores of training new research assistants, paying the bills that had accumulated over the summer to keep the falcon research project running, and going through the drudgery of reopening the ornithology lab.

She glanced at the ranch house windows. They were dark. No one was there. For a moment she could feel as well as see the emptiness. Times like this, when leaving signaled a passage into another season, reminded her that the lives of others were more conventional. Hers could have been too, she supposed, if she hadn't met Harris five years ago. Without him, she might have found someone to give her a house, a station wagon, debts, and kids in the usual ready-made package. With him, until now, it didn't seem to matter. She'd come across other men with the impulse to take risks. But in a place like Montana where most people had enough to do to simply survive, never anyone with Kirby's success.

Erin walked slowly toward the pickup. She and Harris. She had found herself and then, found Kirby. He wasn't the first. She'd grown up in British Columbia in a small railroad town on the Revelstoke River. There, at 18, she'd married. He was the best the town had to offer, but she'd learned quickly that he would never be better than he was and she could be. At 25, when she had enough money to leave, the States and Missoula were to be her halfway house into the world. But by the time she was 31, the six years it took working part-time for a degree, her love of the Montana wilds, the beauty of the falcons that drew her to the lab, and meeting Harris had convinced her to stay.

Ahead, kneeling beside the truck, Harris was checking his pack. It was his standard preparation each time he went into the mountains. Erin leaned against the pickup, removing the comb from her hair to let it cascade down her back. She reached behind her neck, absently pulling the heavy curls over one shoulder. Harris glanced up with a brief appraising and approving stare. Erin's beauty had been enriched rather than worn by time. The sharp cut of her western jeans and the over-sized man's plaid shirt did little to disguise the curves of her tall, softly sensual body.

She watched Harris carefully fold the mesh netting for the trap, her eyes radiating their own blue light against her summer tan. It was always his last step. "Are you going to take her tomorrow?" she asked.

"No," Harris snugged down the straps on the backpack. "I want to be sure of her pattern. I'll lay the trap tomorrow night and come back with her on Monday morning. There's still plenty of time."

Erin nodded. Von Biemann's special order for a peregrine was unusual. Until the 1970s, the species had almost been wiped out by the effects of DDT, a pesticide that accumulated in their bodies as they consumed their prey, destroying their ability to produce anything but thin-shelled, fatally fragile eggs. With the ban on DDT and the help of breeding projects, the falconers' most highly prized hunter, the peregrine, was coming back slowly. But they were still rare, even more so in August with the approach of their migration time. The difficulty in finding them also accounted for the unusual price tag.

"What about delivery?" Erin asked.

"Von Biemann will let me know about the arrangements when I tell him I've got the bird."

Erin paused, her silence a preamble, "Kirby, what about Frank?"

Harris didn't look up but continued to adjust the buckles and frame of the backpack, "What about him?"

"I don't know," Erin spoke slowly, controlling her voice. "He cares about you. He wouldn't have come here if he didn't. I..." She paused again, obviously debating whether to state the implicit conclusion of her syllogism aloud, "Maybe it would be better to let this one pass."

Harris's hands stopped momentarily and then resumed work, re-cinching the shoulder straps on the pack. He looked up, grinning, "Frank's always stayed in touch, hasn't he? Never thought that giving the youngster a plane ride that day in Laos would have had such a lasting effect on the lad. Like the story in *Aesop's Fables* about the guy taking a thorn out of a lion's paw. He'll be your friend for life. Downright touching."

Irritated, Erin cut in, "I'm serious, Kirby. Von Biemann's got other people who could do it. Why take the chance? If you don't want to believe that Frank cares, fine. Then, just accept that maybe he wants to do you a favor."

Harris straightened, propping the pack on the running board of the pickup. The sarcasm hardened his voice, "So, I should kiss off the $75,000 and get an early start on the winter's whittling with the boys down at the general store?"

Erin flushed, "You know what I mean."

Harris lit a cigarette. "You think Frank has my best interests at heart and has figured all this out, eh?"

She shook her head, "I don't know, but I..."

His hand reached out to brush her hair, then lingered against her cheek. His palm was cool, almost cold. "Actually, I've been wondering why it's taken him so long."

She was surprised, "What are you talking about?"

"Come on," Harris frowned impatiently. "DiGenero's spent most of the last ten years with the FBI undercover. Remember? The guy who made the big score for the Feds against the New York mafia? Now, in the middle of his career he surfaces in Salt Lake City as a garden variety federal agent. What should happen at the same time? The law starts to crack down on the falcon business. Since when do the locals in three states get their act together enough to start arresting guys who have been trapping and selling birds for years?"

Harris flicked his cigarette away, "There's someone behind it who knows what he's doing, or thinks he does, and it's not the fish cops."

"DiGenero?" Erin's inflection made the name an answer to her own question. She shook her head slowly. It was just like Harris to play it this way, she thought. Her voice was low, almost a whisper, "That's why you're giving him the lessons, isn't it? It's a game to you. Otherwise, there's nothing to it anymore. It's gotten too easy."

Harris laughed. He pulled her against him, overcoming Erin's resistance. She spoke, her cheek against his chest, "Kirby, I'm afraid. Don't go."

"Don't worry. Frank's a friend of mine, right? He wouldn't do me wrong. Besides, you know nobody can touch me in this business." Harris smiled, "Anyway, have a little heart. DiGenero's got a tough job. He needs all the help he can get."

Harris turned her toward the car, his arm around her waist. She knew he wanted to be on his way. They walked in silence until they reached the Honda. As she looked up, Erin felt his hands close on her shoulders. His grip was almost too tight, as if an act of possession rather than an embrace. She let him kiss her once, deeply, and then stepped away, slipping behind the wheel.

Harris bent low, resting his hands on the door, "You know, you're right. DiGenero has done me a favor."

Erin turned the ignition key, hiding her annoyance at the veiled sarcasm. She looked up, starting to speak, to tell Harris to take care, but she saw there was no point. He already had stepped back from the car.

Harris stood several feet away, arms folded, "Yep, I thought the season was over and, all of a sudden, Frank comes along to add a little spice to my life. Instead of a boring trip to the bank," he winked, "he's made Von Biemann's deal much more interesting."

Harris extracted his arm from the goose-down sleeping bag and looked at his watch. 7:15 a.m., Sunday. He stretched and sat up, propping himself against the rock wall that angled away from the entrance to the railway tunnel. Beside him, the single track line emerged from the darkness on a turn, climbing the grade of the valley floor alongside "Sixteen," the creek that paralleled the railway through the mountains east of the continental divide.

He'd reached the valley shortly before dark, leaving the truck on the cattleman's road and walking through the tunnel to settle down on the embankment and wait out the night. Beside him, the tracks ran north next to the cliff and the creek. Below, on his right, on the other side of the cottonwoods and brush, the water from the high lake a mile away flowed swiftly, cascading over the rough line of rapids.

He glanced up, noticing the motion where the sun touched the serrated rock ledge, "A little ahead of schedule." Harris reached for the binoculars as the peregrine sprang from the cliff. The sun wrapped the falcon in a clear new light. He stood, keeping in the deep shadow. Flying at 800 feet, the peregrine banked across the cold face of the breeze and flew parallel to the creek below. After two weeks of watching her, Harris knew where she was going. He walked away from the cliff in the direction taken by the falcon, stepping easily along the railway embankment.

When Von Biemann had called, he had counted on her, and on her return to the eyrie, the nest that was her birthplace, when he said he could deliver a peregrine. He hadn't planned on leaving her there the year before when he'd lowered himself to the ledge to trap the two eyases, the male and female fledgling falcons. After pinning the wings of the male and pulling a sock over his body to quiet him, something had stopped him from reaching for the female. He could have taken her. She faced him, nearly full grown, with her back to the cliff wall, no longer calling her threats aloud but menacing quietly, pretending to be an adult. Her hooked beak was open and defiant and her wings half spread in a clear, although hopeless solitary challenge.

Perhaps that was it, Harris thought. Standing by herself, she seemed suddenly special, stronger somehow, as if she was no longer unsure and therefore weakened by the presence of another peregrine. Alone, as she was meant to live, even barely fledged from the nest before she had ever flown and killed, the falcon had unmistakable instincts. He saw it in her eyes, he remembered. They had captured and held him. They were extraordinary, displaying no fear. He recalled pausing and then turning away. He never really understood why, other than somehow it seemed right that she should not be caught, but left to be her own master. That was then. Now she was back, giving him another chance to ponder what he had not done last year.

Harris raised his field glasses. A half mile ahead, the falcon banked again, adjusting her flight feathers to add lift to her dagger-shaped left wing. Accelerating, she spiraled down over the streambed until at fifty feet, the peregrine turned into the wind, fanning and curving her tail. The feathers angled sharply against the air, increasing her lift and slowing her descent.

On the edge of the embankment, Harris knelt, smiling as he followed her with his glasses, "On glide path, on glide slope." He rocked out of his crouch, sitting down on his haunches as the peregrine touched ground. As he expected, she repeated her ritual survey of the landing site, the flat rock that sloped into the creek and then under the water providing a walkway to her bath, then waded into the shallows. After splashing and soaking, she emerged to preen, smoothing and oiling her feathers atop the boulder on the edge of the creek. Then, the falcon flew to the dead jack pine forty yards off.

Harris glanced at his watch. The peregrine would nap until the sun and breeze dried her. He lit a cigarette, mentally reviewing his remaining chores. He would prepare the blind and the trap that evening at twilight when the falcon would already be on the cliff.

The trap. The conversation the day before with DiGenero came back to mind. The questions were still unanswered. What did Frank know? Was he aware of Von Biemann? Did the FBI have something on the deal? If they did, he thought, yesterday's warning had been his free pass, his chance to walk courtesy of Frank. Harris shook his head. For 5 or 10, maybe, but not for $75 K. It was typical DiGenero, Harris thought. His heart was in the right place. Frank didn't owe him anything, but he could never convince him of that. Harris glanced at the dead fir. The peregrine was stirring. He smiled momentarily at the irony, "Lordy, lordy, Frankie, my poor little dago, now what happens if I don't take the hint?"

The falcon was awake. Harris shivered involuntarily at the thought of another long cold night before he could take her. Unfortunately he couldn't risk a fire or try to finesse the discomfort by arriving in the morning at a place so close to the eyrie. He crushed out the cigarette butt and lifted his binoculars. Who knows? Perhaps he and the falcon had more in common than a rendezvous at the creek in the morning. Perhaps tomorrow Frank would be waiting, too.

From the distance, he saw the peregrine hunch, anticipating the thermals, the updrafts that would raise her swiftly to altitude. Harris lowered his field glasses. It was time to find better cover. He scuttled sideways down the embankment, crouching beneath a bent tangle of brush that would hide him from above. He smiled to himself. No matter how many times he watched her, she never failed to fascinate him. She was a prima donna, as perfect in repose as she was in motion.

The peregrine left the fir with a low swoop followed by a quick rise over the creek, then went downwind in a long glide, punctuated intermittently by four or five quick wing beats. When she caught the first thermal, the falcon appeared to spiral only slightly less than straight up, turning in the rising column of air like a dancer in a seamless choreography. Harris watched her diminish to a speck against the blue sky. Alone, he thought, the peregrine was as beautiful and as deadly as any living thing on two wings.

A mile from the creek, the falcon turned windward, sideslipping to gain speed. At 1500 feet, her first long run drew a random course as she instinctively measured her own sink rate against the lift from the wind. When she reached the creek, she knew it was close to perfect, a near equivalency between gravity and the counterforce created by the airflow over her wings. She banked hard left, returning to the meadows and the thermals that boosted her to the altitude lost on her downwind leg.

Harris sat back, waiting. He remembered Erin's words. She was right in a way, he thought. Von Biemann had others he could call on, others who could provide a peregrine. But there also was something perversely appropriate about this bird and the German's $75,000 offer. The price was nearly twice the going rate. As top of the line, Harris thought, like him, the falcon was worth it, and more.

He looked up. This time, the peregrine was flying her hunting pattern, crossing, returning, and then recrossing the meadow in a weave. Harris was about to lower his glasses when suddenly, she made her first stoop. From 900 feet, the dive startled but missed the jay. It jerked sideways, plunging toward the protection of the scrub brush below. He knew the peregrine could have pursued, but had purposefully dropped on the prey with half-folded wings, keeping her velocity low. It was a warm-up. When it was over, the falcon wheeled and flew deliberately to regain height and position.

Twenty minutes later, Harris would have missed her kill as well if he hadn't kept his glasses trained. The falcon had just turned downwind over the clump of willows and aspens that formed the margin between the meadow and the creek when the three doves flushed from the water's edge. She took less than a second to isolate the low-flying bird farthest from the protection of the trees. At 800 feet, the peregrine pirouetted out of a banking downwind turn, rolling into level flight for a split second before crooking her right wing inward and extending her left for maximum lift. The maneuver flipped her sharply, head down, into a sixty-degree dive. For an instant, to control her speed as she corrected course, the falcon adjusted her wings above her body to less than their characteristic killing configuration, an uplifted, high swept-back V.

The dove reached its maximum speed just as the peregrine accelerated 400 feet above it. Approaching ninety miles an hour, the falcon's powerful legs thrust forward and locked, extending the two long, lethal rear spurs on her claws straight downward. Harris saw the explosion of gray-brown feathers as the peregrine slammed into the prey, driving her claws deep into its back, penetrating the chest cavity, and then releasing. The falcon pulled up sharply, a hook-like trajectory carrying her above the falling bird.

The peregrine made two long passes, checking security along the tree line before she landed. Finally, she moved to the dove, grasping the back with her left claw and stabbing her hooked beak between the vertebrae of the neck, with a single twist snapping the bones. Then, the peregrine flipped the dove's carcass over and began to pluck the feathers and tear the flesh from its breast.

Harris retraced his steps along the bottom of the railway embankment, staying low, hidden from the falcon. At the railroad tunnel, he collected his pack and carbine and then turned north. He would skirt the meadow, avoiding any chance that she could spot him but lengthening his walk to the cabin on the lake into two miles instead of one. Harris double-timed down the opposite slope of the railway embankment and then began to step out in a long stride, cradling the carbine comfortably in the crook of his arm. He would still have plenty of time to eat, rest, and collect the bait before he had to return for his, and the falcon's, last night at Sixteen.

3

Sunday, August 19, 1984

"Sixteen," Gallatin County, Montana

The splashing woke Harris only seconds before the cougar's snarl curled the edge of the night. He held his breath for several seconds, gauging the direction of the sound. The cat was following the elk that were coming down to the creek. Harris rolled into a shooter's prone position, feeling the gravel move to accommodate his elbows. The one-man blind was six feet inside the small thicket that edged the rocky spit where Sixteen's seasonal rise and fall had nurtured and then drowned the bushes and trees. He reached for the carbine, shouldering the stock. Beside him, the dove, disturbed by his motion, burbled and shifted in the small cage.

Harris listened, trying to discern what was just below the threshold of his hearing, but there were no sounds. The elk were downstream and the cat was padding noiselessly nearby. The creek brought the game, making the streambed a killing ground, and he was in the middle of it, but if he wanted the falcon he didn't have a choice. Harris felt his heart pound. He'd positioned himself for the night as best he could. Sixteen's curve surrounded him with water on three sides. The cliff wall was just behind the blind. The brush gave him some protection against surprises from above.

He smelled his own sweat mixing with the light aroma of gun oil as his hands warmed the rifle's lever action and his body heat filled the sleeping bag. He knew just what the thirty-year-old carbine could stop, and what it couldn't. If the cougar sensed him, depending on the balance between hunger and fear, it would stalk closer. In that case, he had a chance. Up close, he could handle the short-barreled saddle gun, if necessary, jamming it into the cat's body to fire. Harris swallowed hard. Cougars weren't the only thing that prowled at night. If a big brown or black bear stumbled across him, a .30-30 wouldn't do a hell of a lot of good.

He visualized the scene wrapped in blackness before him. The wood and net trap was ten yards away. It was a simple, spring-loaded, clamshell design. He'd staked one of the frame's two 6-foot-diameter wood bows to the ground. The netting was attached, piled unobtrusively on itself and covered with a dusting of gravel and sand. Harris reached absentmind-edly to touch the nylon filament line tied to the branch above his head. Tomorrow, one tug would release the trap's upper bow, which was hinged and clamped against the spring tension to the other bow. It would arc forward with the net to slam into the ground, closing the inescapable hemisphere.

The quiet had returned. His watch glowed softly, showing that twenty minutes had passed since the distant splashing and the cat's scream. Harris snapped the rifle's safety on and off from habit, listening. Nothing. His pulse slowed. He exhaled a long breath, slipping his finger off the trig-ger, yawned, and put his head down. In the darkness, Kirby Harris smiled self-confidently. Then, within seconds, he fell soundly asleep.

The sun woke him, shining brightly even through the tangle of brush and the tarpaulin. Harris looked at his watch: 6:45. He stretched, retrieved the thermos buried at his feet inside the sleeping bag, and poured a cup of still warm coffee. "Probably an hour before she'll show," he said, half aloud. "An hour," Harris repeated the word offhandedly.

The thought struck him. He'd made a career of hours. When he was flying, it was the measure of experience; 1000, 2000, 2500—the num-bers told you about a pilot without your having to ask for the details. He hadn't counted his hours in the mountains. Or his days, or his weeks, or even his months. But he knew the years, Harris thought. Another season and it would be his fifth anniversary. He stared at the empty cup: for the first time in a long time, remembering.

After Saigon fell, Harris thought, the first five years had had their ups and downs. Like the others on contract who got the Company's pink slips, he'd phoned the airlines from Bangkok and Hong Kong, but with more pilots than jobs and no seniority, he didn't expect much and was right. Texas was next, hauling contraband to South America, where 2000 percent tariffs on refrigerators, TVs, and stereos generated more than small change. The money was good, he recalled, for a year or two. Then, the dopers took over, driving aircraft charter rates through the ceiling. After that, it didn't pay to crank up an airplane if you weren't carrying grass or coke.

That was a choice too, he supposed, although one that he had already made. Harris grimaced. He'd seen their kind in Saigon and Bangkok and then, as before, the decision was simple. He didn't want any part of it. At any rate, in '79, after a year at home, when the new local airline called, he took a job. The odds that Montana Airways would make it were slim, but the empty seats in the back didn't matter. He still had enough cash to make ends meet and the cockpit put him somewhere between the ranch and the war. The mountains, the winter snow, and the summer thunderheads made the flying a challenge. And, he thought, he always liked a challenge.

Harris smiled to himself. He'd piloted the old Convair for close to a year, feeling almost legitimate, when Von Biemann came along. It was March 1980. The flight that day had been your typical Missoula turn-around. Outside the steamy terminal windows, the spring snow had stopped. The clouds, low and gray, were reclining against the hillsides that bounded the runway. With time to kill before his scheduled take-off, he was walking slowly toward the gate, scanning the passersby with idle curiosity, when he heard someone call his name.

"Kirby Harris!"

The man, tall, blond, and good-looking, was several steps behind. The soft, expensive casualness of his jacket and slacks distinguished him immediately from the denim-clad ranchers, rumpled college students, and double-knit small-town travelers who ebbed around him.

Harris stopped in the middle of the small concourse, "Well, I'll be goddamned..."

Klaus Von Biemann smiled broadly, "I was certain we'd meet again."

"What in the hell are you doing in Missoula?" Harris extended his hand.

"Business," Von Biemann laughed, "but if I'd known you were here, it would have been pleasure, of course." Despite half a decade, Von Biemann was unchanged, fit, tan, and urbane. "Six years," he gripped Harris's arm, "it's been too long."

They'd met at Pattaya, in a small bar that overlooked the resort beach on the Gulf of Siam, a few months before Saigon fell. German tourists already had replaced GIs two-for-one in Thailand after the Americans officially pulled out of Vietnam. Harris had arrived from up-country that morning for a few days off. It was too early for the women, who got cheaper as the night wore on. They'd passed the time talking over the din of the bad rock band and the suggestive obscenities of the half-dressed hostess between them. For Harris, Von Biemann was a diversion from the usual worn talk of a lost war, the whores, and getting back to the world. They saw each other several nights running for drinks, dinner, and more conversation, and finally, exchanged addresses.

"Hawks," Harris said as pieces of the memory fell into place.

"No," Von Biemann laughed again, correcting him, "falcons."

Harris shook his head, disagreeing good-naturedly. As a boy, he had raised hawks on the ranch as a hobby. When Von Biemann had told him casually that first night in Pattaya that he kept falcons, they'd debated at length over the qualities and distinctions.

"When can we have a drink?" Von Biemann asked.

Harris glanced at his watch just as he heard himself paged. His flight was scheduled to leave in five minutes, "I'll be back in Missoula tomorrow."

"Tomorrow, then."

"OK," Harris replied, "meet me at Russo's around 6:00 p.m. It's a little bar near the university."

"Good," Von Biemann waved.

Even then, Harris thought, he must have sensed something about the chance encounter with Von Biemann. Otherwise, why would he have chosen Russo's? It would have taken a special effort to be noticed there. The clientele—university students, the itinerant, young academics, the occasional, consciously tweedy, older professor, and the long-haired remnants of the local counterculture—was assorted, changing, and always the same. Their indifference to strangers was unusual for Montana, and combined with Russo's murkiness and oversized booths offered privacy to anyone who wanted to talk.

Harris spied Von Biemann at a far corner table when his eyes adjusted to the dark. It was a credible reunion, although Harris had seen too many players and hustlers, good and bad, not to notice the small things. It was clear Von Biemann was guiding the conversation casually but purposefully, filling in its natural spaces with talk about himself and his travels. He was in imports and exports in Munich, he said, in art, jewelry, and other things. The details were less intriguing than his style, which left a discreet but distinct impression of success.

It had occurred to Harris then that perhaps their meeting was anything but accidental. He remembered relaxing, finally, with mild amusement, and waiting to find out. After an hour, Von Biemann raised the subject, "You know, I believe that some of my business these days would interest you."

"How's that?"

Von Biemann smiled, "Falcons. A few friends of mine in the States have helped me find birds from time to time. It's really rather simple. I pinch myself occasionally to make certain I'm not dreaming when I see how much it pays. I have a market in the Middle East that is far bigger than I can supply. My customers are Saudis. They can have whatever they want—the finest estates, yachts, racing cars, private jets, prize-winning thoroughbreds, the most beautiful women—and they can afford to throw them away, whenever they like." Von Biemann shook his head in mock bewilderment, "And, they do. Money means nothing to them. But it's not that way with the birds. Like falconers everywhere, they treasure them more than anything they possess.

"It's interesting," the German continued. "The sport represents a past money can't buy, no matter how much they have. The Arabs say it's in the blood of the bedouin. Who knows?" Von Biemann shrugged. "It's a throwback to the simpler times in the desert they idealize and only the older generation actually remembers."

Harris nodded noncommittally. Von Biemann settled back in the booth and sipped his beer, lowering his voice to a near whisper, "The business is full of contradictions. The risks are low and the payback is high. The relationships with the Arabs are extraordinarily difficult to develop, but once you have them they are yours for life. The best falcons—the two-year-olds—are hard to find and trap. If you damage them, break their flight feathers, or, God forbid, injure a wing, they're worthless. But the perfect specimens bring a fortune, sight unseen.

"And, only the wild ones command the premium. 'Captive-bred' aren't the same, no matter how skillfully they're trained. The 'wild-caught' are the only ones that have the true killing instinct. I suppose, if I wanted to say something self-serving, I could tell you that my role in this little trade only ensures these exquisite creatures achieve their ultimate justification for being. But, of course," Von Biemann smiled, "I wouldn't say that."

The proposition itself, Harris recalled, was intended to be anticlimactic. Von Biemann sounded as if he was only reaffirming an old understanding between them, "Goshawks and gyrfalcons bring no less than $25,000 each, peregrines, more. Naturally, the price does not include your expenses for getting them to the border. I cover that. We've had good luck moving the birds into Canada through Detroit and Buffalo. The border crossings are always busy and customs inspections are perfunctory. We use Toronto, which has excellent connections to Europe and the Middle East. If there are any problems, we also can make shipments from New York on one of several Middle East airlines.

"There are risks, but we have good facsimiles of the necessary papers and counterfeit leg bands to show that we deal in domestically bred birds. That's legal. As you might imagine," Von Biemann raised his eyebrows, emphasizing the point, "I take great care with our security. To be caught would cost us some money, but the embarrassment would be much more serious for our clients than the size of any fine from the Fish and Wildlife Service."

A pitcher of beer later, Harris let himself be persuaded. He would trap the falcons and when his flight schedule worked out, deliver them on Montana Airways to Von Biemann in Calgary. If that wasn't possible, he would rent a plane and fly to the transfer point.

The echo of a distant bird cry pulled Harris out of his reverie. He rolled on his side, looking up. As it crested the ridge, the morning sun was deepening the pale blue of the sky. He glanced at his watch again. 7:30. Still no sign of the falcon. He craned his neck, scanning for the peregrine, and then settled back under the blind.

He remembered the feeling when he left Russo's that night. It wasn't because of the money, although that had turned out far better than he figured. He had calculated that a month or two in the mountains and a few flights east would bring him $100,000 a year. Harris shook his head. The estimate had been a world-class low ball. After five years, the ranch and his own Porter were paid for, not to mention close to a million in the bank.

It had been something else, he thought. The real high. Finally, for the first time since the war, he was back where he belonged. He was on the edge. That was Von Biemann's real offer. It was what he wanted— no, what he needed. The edge. It was ironic in a way. Frank had done the same thing for him yesterday, without intending to. Odd, too. After all these years, it still meant more than anything else. More than the money Von Biemann could pay. More than the danger from DiGenero's law. More than what Erin wanted.

Erin. To her credit, she saw that too, Harris thought, from the very beginning. Even now, five years later, he remembered their conversation that night. They'd left Von Biemann at the airport for his flight to Seattle after celebrating their new arrangement over dinner. They were riding in silence, returning to her apartment, when she spoke, "How did he find you?"

He'd glanced at her. Erin was reclining against the front seat, head back and eyes closed, her arms loosely folded over the wrappings of her coat. "He said it was an accident. He comes through Missoula a couple times a year after seeing people in Jackson and Big Sky."

"Do you believe him?" she asked.

"No," he smiled.

"I don't either."

"Why?"

Erin shook her head, "I'm not sure. There's something about him. He seems to work hard at making what he does look easy."

She turned toward Harris and spoke slowly as if she was carefully drawing together judgments from her impressions of the evening, "If you get the birds for Von Biemann, you'll make money. I don't doubt that at all. But for him, it's not the money, no matter what he says. I don't think that really matters. He's bringing you into his world, but I think it's only one aspect of his world. Somehow, I think that everything he does is this way, a part of another whole. Only he knows how it fits together. No one else."

"So?" Harris asked.

"I think he could be dangerous."

He nodded but didn't reply.

Erin smiled enigmatically, "And that's why you'd do it anyway, isn't it? Even if he didn't promise a pot of gold at the end of the rainbow." She paused, "Even if I told you not to."

Harris reached across the seat and pulled her toward him. Despite a decade exploring the easy, pleasing compliance of the Thai, the feisty allure of the Vietnamese, and the potpourri of Lao, Chinese, and Philippino women, he had never been drawn as magnetically to anyone as he was to Erin. In the six months they'd been together, he'd only begun to scratch the surface of her past, but he already knew what he saw was far more than her beauty. She was her own, fiercely, and he was certain she was drawn to the same in him. Because of that, she knew what she could ask, and what she couldn't.

He had turned to the side of the highway and stopped, he remembered. His fingers ran teasingly over the soft shape of her breasts and then paused, circling her throat, to caress the graceful line of her neck. Harris slipped his hand lower, unbuttoning her coat.

His mouth brushed hers, "You think Von Biemann's dangerous?"

Erin's lips touched his and then retreated, "And you're going to tell me you can handle it, aren't you?"

Harris didn't answer, his fingers moving lower again, gently displacing wool and silk to find her thigh, and then pressing farther, discovering the dry heat of bare skin.

"Dangerous?" Harris smiled. There was no answer, except in her eyes and the warmth of her breath. "Well," his voice was a whisper, "so am I."

The frantic fluttering told him without looking up that the falcon had just made her first low pass over the bend in Sixteen. He had tied the dove, the live bait, to a spike sunk into the creekbed with thin rawhide jesses. It could move in a circle inside the arc circumscribed by the trap. Harris scanned the creekbed, his breath tight in his throat. He glanced at his watch. 7:50 a.m. Right on schedule. With the peregrine's first flyover, the dove had thrown itself at the restraints in a vain attempt to escape. Above, the falcon wheeled, dropping lower. The dove quieted, moving in an uncharacteristically clumsy choreography.

Harris craned his neck, readying. He had the victim's-eye view as the peregrine banked in the blue dome above him. He had trapped falcons this way before, but the lightning speed of the final plunge still surprised him. The peregrine twisted, reversing direction over the creek, preparing to dive. Then, in a flash, she dropped.

He jerked the line as the peregrine touched down a foot from the dove. The blurred sight and sound of the trap arched above. The falcon reacted instantly, arresting the motion of folding her wings, but it was too late. Harris rolled from under the blind, crashing through the brush. He had only seconds. The peregrine was beating herself against the netting in vain takeoff attempts. He had ten long strides to the trap, but if a wing caught and snapped before he reached her, the $75,000 was gone.

He dropped to the ground behind the struggling falcon, using his knees to pin her beneath the mesh. His gloved hands forced her wings to her sides. The shock of his grip stilled the peregrine momentarily, allowing him to push his body firmly but gently against her. He pressed her to the ground, freeing one hand to grab his knife. Harris slashed the netting, then tossed the blade aside. He pulled a knit tube stocking from his jacket pocket and slid it one-handed over her body. It was over, and the falcon immobilized, in less than twenty seconds.

Resting on his knees, Harris heard his own breathing, hard and loud in the morning silence. He didn't know how long he knelt next to the peregrine, watching her. She was fully matured now, no longer carrying feathers tinged with the red-brown of youth. Unmoving, her eyes riveted him, examining her captor. They were the same, magnetic. Without fear. Harris wondered if she remembered. He reached for the hood in his pocket and then paused. There was something about her, as there had been before. He was reluctant to cover her head, to put her in darkness. Finally, he slipped on the cap. There was only one more step. He fastened two new leather jesses on her legs.

Harris sat back against the large boulder. A few feet away, the dove was still. He reached over, untying the bird and lifting it in his hand. Frozen in life as much as it would have been in death, it squatted, petrified in fear. He stood. "Stay of execution," he threw the dove high in the air. The wings beat frantically as the bird veered left and right, regaining its equilibrium, and then streaked down the creekbed to disappear.

He glanced at his watch. 8:05 a.m. Harris reviewed the mental checklist he had used so many times before. He would telephone Munich later in the day. Von Biemann would be pleased that it had gone well. He looked down a final time at the falcon, resting on her back. Now, they were ready. He arranged the contents of the pack carefully, using the tarp and netting as padding around the sides to create a center hollow where the peregrine would ride. When he was finished, Harris lifted the falcon and lowered it into the nook. At the bottom of the pack, her claws found the roundness of the thick dowel he had wedged there for her, closing around the improvised perch.

Harris shouldered the pack and paused, glancing around. He'd figured right. Warning or not, there was no Frank here, waiting for him as he'd waited for the falcon. DiGenero didn't know everything. He didn't know about the peregrine deal, or about Von Biemann. There was no way he could.

He picked up his rifle and walked toward the railway embankment. To his left, the sheer rock-face of the cliff rose toward the ledge, the eyrie, the falcon's home. He paused, looking up, wondering if somehow she sensed where she was now, wondering if she knew. He slowed and then stopped, as if for the peregrine's sake. "I doubt you'll see this place again, sweetheart," Harris felt the regret, obscure but there. He pushed it out of his mind and turned toward the tracks that led into the tunnel.

He walked toward the light, pacing next to the reflection that moved along the polished surface of the rails. His footfalls echoed around him. The darkness at day, the echo, and the damp cool were new to the peregrine and Harris was sure that behind him, the falcon was turning her head, listening but not seeing, trying to understand. It was only the beginning for her, he thought, only the beginning.

4

Tuesday, August 21, 1984

Minami Azabu, Tokyo, Japan

Achmed Rafsanjani, the second secretary of the Embassy of the Islamic Republic of Iran, walked through the chancery gate into the empty side street of Tokyo's fashionable Minami Azabu section at exactly 7:50 a.m. As always, the two-tone gray armored van was parked against the embassy's high concrete wall. Rafsanjani glanced at the three riot po-

licemen from the "Kidotai," the crack paramilitary force of the Tokyo
Metropolitan Police, who had just begun their morning guard shift. In
their heavily padded blue fatigues, they stood at ease, helmet visors
flipped up, five-foot batons gripped loosely, and shields propped against
the wall.

Rafsanjani shook his head. The Japanese were a mystery, an incom-
prehensible people who had none of the oil wealth, God-given righteousness, or military strength of the Islamic Republic but nonetheless ran a
world economic empire virtually second to none. A sneer crossed his face
as his thought consoled him. After three years in Tokyo, he also knew
they would sell anything to anyone for the right price, even the tools that
Iran would someday use to bring them to heel.

At the corner he paused, looking left and right. These were the police
he could see, he thought. Now, where were the ones he couldn't? He
walked uphill. The two-lane street, wide by Tokyo's standards, was ideal
for a stroll, but halfway along the block Rafsanjani abandoned it, turning
sharply right into an alley that doubled back and descended the hill. He
stepped rapidly along the walkway, examining the houses as he passed
for anyone who might be observing him. The windows were shuttered
tight. It was still early for the well-to-do city dwellers who had only a
twenty- or thirty-minute commute to their 9:00 a.m. jobs.

Rafsanjani slowed and listened intently, hearing only the rhythm of
his own heels on the uneven paving stones. He hurried on, congratu-
lating himself. He had chosen the alley because the high garden walls
on either side of it would amplify the sound of any footsteps that might
be coming toward him or following his path. At this point, he thought,
there either was no surveillance or they had yet to pick him up. Suddenly, he pivoted into another, even smaller lane and was swallowed by
its shadows.

For anyone who could observe the Iranian's route, the zigzag course
would have seemed unusual for a diplomat out on a morning walk. But
for Achmed Rafsanjani, an undercover intelligence officer of the Islamic
Republic's Revolutionary Guard, the circuitous route was part of his standard operating procedure and necessary to enhance the security of his
current assignment.

Five minutes later and 500 yards distant, Rafsanjani emerged at the
Azabu Juban, the Azabu market, at the base of the hill. He paused, look-

ing both ways along the empty shopping street, and then strolled to the
nearby cluster of vending machines. Depositing 200 yen, he bent down,
retrieving the heated can that rolled into reach. He drank the café-au-lait
slowly, eyeing the street with suspicion. It was habit, reinforced by five
years of war with the Iraqis and, for his kind, five years of deadly en-
counters in alleyways around the world, courtesy of Baghdad. Rafsanjani
ignored the first two cabs that passed despite the inquisitive stares of the
drivers before he flagged down a third.

The automatic rear door sprang open and he slid inside, "Tokyo eki
e itte, kudasai."

"Hai," the driver's reply was sharp, almost military. There were closer
spots than Tokyo Station to catch the Yamanote-sen, the commuter line
that circled the city in a twenty-one-mile loop. But fifteen minutes from
now the main station's crowds would swallow him as soon as he stepped
from the cab. The Yamanote line's trains ran three minutes apart. He
would use several, debarking and reboarding to check for unwanted companions, before reaching his final destination.

Rafsanjani settled back, relaxing momentarily. Why the rush? He wondered if Askari, the ambassador, was overreacting again. He rolled down
the window and spat. Askari was a fool, afraid for his skin twenty-four hours
a day. And well he should be. Rafsanjani had already filed his share of
reports on him. Askari's life was a festering corruption, a western educa-
tion and a career kowtowing to foreigners who had sneered at the old Iran,
America's lackey. He was marked for recall to Tehran, sooner or later, and
he knew it, Rafsanjani thought with vindictive pleasure. Whenever the
communications clerk informed Askari that a restricted message from
Tehran needed the ambassador's personal decoding, he always turned
whiter than salt. His reaction to the urgent cable late yesterday was no
exception.

Askari had refused to show the message to him, but immediately ordered him to go the next morning to Akihabara, the ten-block section of
Shitamachi, Tokyo's old "downtown," where the electronics outlets were
packed wall-to-wall, to make some purchases. Rafsanjani smiled. It was
a mission he had performed before. Tehran depended on him, very much,
to meet the highest needs. He was important, perhaps indispensable. He'd
filled secret orders scores of times, purchasing video equipment, integrated
circuitry, and two-way radio gear, and knew where to go to do even vol-
ume business with no questions asked.

He dug in his pocket for the handwritten list. This time, what was it? Five microswitches, five radio-controlled miniature solenoids, and two radio transmitters for model aircraft, plus a supply of long-life nickel-cadmium batteries. Cheap, simple. The only difference was the Intelligence Bureau wanted it now. He had to bring the order to Tehran personally. That was unusual. Why? Rafsanjani scratched his head absently. He could only guess. Perhaps it had something to do with the rumors. They were tenuous and fourth-hand, snippets from the Intelligence Bureau's grapevine about the ultimate mission, finally, to destroy the Great Satans. Rumors. That was all. Who knows? One could only hope. If they were true, perhaps he was playing a part.

The cab looped past the parklike outer grounds of the Imperial Palace into eight lanes of traffic, skirted the Marunouchi financial district, and pointed toward Tokyo Station. The driver cut through the crosswalk, bisecting the flow of pedestrians and ignoring the baleful glare of the traffic policeman, and coasted into the snarl of cars at the station's entrance.

"Massugu e itte," Rafsanjani commanded, ordering the cab closer to the curb. They lurched to a stop. As the taxi's rear door popped open, Rafsanjani thrust 1500 yen in the cabbie's hand. In five strides, he reached the terminal. Then, he stepped into the crosscurrents of 50,000 scurrying commuters and was gone.

Miss Kimiko Iida, the Japanese secretary for the consular section, bowed low when Rafsanjani reentered the Iranian embassy's small reception room. He nodded at her, walking quickly to his office. It was precisely 2:00 p.m. As he had asked, Miss Iida had typed the diplomatic note and placed it on his desk. He would carry it with him to Tehran. It identified him as a special courier. When presented at the airport, the note would confer on his luggage the privilege of diplomatic immunity, exempting the bags from search by customs or security. Rafsanjani smiled wryly. It was indeed helpful to have such courtesies extended to the Islamic Republic, despite the fact that Tehran reviled most of the governments that honored the practice.

Rafsanjani reached for the heavy canvas bag emblazoned with Iran's green, white, and red national colors that was propped beside his desk. The electronic components from Akihabara had been wrapped in a small box as he requested. He slipped it inside the canvas satchel and snapped the bag's metal clasp shut. Then, he took the steel wire, seal, and pliers out of his desk drawer. He slid the wire through the hasp of the bag, squeezing the pliers to crimp the soft lead seal around the steel strand, officially closing the diplomatic pouch.

Then he reached for the telephone and dialed Japan Airlines. The soft feminine voice of the reservations agent, in precise English, confirmed his tourist-class seat on Wednesday's first flight, at 9:20 a.m., to Beijing. Rafsanjani recited his American Express card number, charging his tickets to his Dutch branch bank account. It amused him. With Iran's currency worthless abroad, this American company, with its computerized international billing system, was always such a help in making his missions possible, and untraceable.

After he hung up, Rafsanjani buzzed the communications room on the intercom, "Send me the clerk on duty."

The sound of quickly scuffling feet in the hallway and the prompt knock pleased him, confirming again that the Intelligence Bureau always got prompt service from the foreign ministry.

He omitted any greeting to the clerk, "I want you to send a message immediately to our embassy in Beijing."

"Yessir," the pasty-faced, balding functionary looked down at his stenographic pad, poised deferentially for dictation.

"It is for my counterpart. The classification is 'Priority/Most Secret.' The text is as follows. 'You are to meet the undersigned who will arrive on a special mission on the JAL flight from Tokyo at 12:40 p.m., Wednesday. You are to hold one seat on the Iran Air flight departing Beijing on the same day for Tehran.' That is all."

Rafsanjani dismissed the clerk and sighed. He didn't relish the long flights. Day after tomorrow, on Thursday at 1:00 a.m., Iran time, when he landed, they would expect him to deliver the pouch directly to the Intelligence Bureau's headquarters. Then, there would be the usual fight to find a seat on a flight back to Beijing in order to return to Tokyo.

He hesitated for a few moments before dropping the bag into the safe and shutting the drawer. The purchase of the electronic components was commonplace but his personal delivery was not. The rumors intrigued him. To be involved in a major operation, a major success, to be part of it would move him up, closer to the power, closer to the top. Perhaps he could learn something at headquarters.

Rafsanjani felt a twinge of anxiety as he spun the safe's combination lock closed. Perhaps, although questions were dangerous. There were always those who would wonder about someone's curiosity. Sometimes it made them check, encouraging them to look into other things. He stared into the reception room. Miss Iida was typing. It didn't pay to ask too many questions. He knew others who had, or had talked too much. His mouth went dry. They had been transferred to lead the faithful at the front, to face the meatgrinder of the war.

He pushed the thought out of his mind. Besides, one version of the rumor had it that the mission belonged to a special group, that it was not one of the Intelligence Bureau's operations. He shrugged. Who knew? Maybe his trip had nothing to do with it. After all, it didn't take a genius to deduce that he'd just purchased components that could make a small, remotely detonated bomb. An antipersonnel weapon perhaps. That was nothing out of the ordinary.

Rafsanjani looked at the wall clock. It was 3:00 p.m. Miss Iida had covered her typewriter and was reaching for her coat. He sighed, anticipating. He would wait until 6:00 p.m., and then meet her at the usual place, the piano bar in the high-rise warren of clubs above Roppongi Crossing. On his way back to the embassy that afternoon, he'd bought something very brief and transparently lacy at a cheap boutique near Tokyo Station. He planned to give it to her when they returned to her apartment. Rafsanjani knew there would be little companionship during his stay in Tehran and he was anxious to have her try it on later that night. And then take it off.

At 6:00 a.m., Tokyo time, Wednesday, August 22, just as Rafsanjani awoke, his head pillowed on Miss Iida's small breasts, and groaned at the thought of his impending two days of nonstop travel, 1800 miles away, in a small hotel room in Kowloon, Hong Kong, British Crown Colony, another Iranian also was stirring. There, it was 5:00 a.m., an hour earlier, and still dark. Nonetheless, Rajid Musaani began to dress at once, pulling on the nondescript cotton slacks that were part of his workman's garb. When he finished buttoning his soiled white shirt, he leaned over to snap shut the incongruously expensive leather suitcase that held his other clothes.

Musaani carried the bag to the door, turning to check for a final time that he had left nothing in the dingy room. He stepped into the hall and walked swiftly down the dimly lit rear stairway to the narrow back street. The greengrocer's pickup was parked halfway onto the sidewalk. He placed his single piece of luggage on the seat of the truck and paused momentarily, looking up and down the deserted street. Musaani slipped behind the wheel. Then, he turned the ignition key and drove slowly away.

Like Rafsanjani, Rajid Musaani was on the way to a flight, although only after making a trip through the Harbor Tunnel to Hong Kong for his one delivery of fresh vegetables four miles away. Unbeknownst to Rafsanjani, the man in the greengrocer's truck also was the cause for his purchase in Akihabara the morning before and for his travel to Tehran that day.

Fifteen minutes later, Musaani emerged from the Harbor Tunnel exit on Hong Kong Island. Traffic was still sparse as he shifted into fourth gear, changing lanes to follow the roadsigns toward Central and Midlevels. As it approached the business district, the highway climbed upward on the overpass toward Victoria Peak. Ahead and to the right, behind the Hilton Hotel, Musaani saw the American consulate. The sight jogged his memory, dislodging a random thought. What did the Americans say when they had to meet a deadline for an important project? "The clock was running?" Yes. It already was and, after his small chore was finished today, the mission would have his undivided attention. Then, Musaani smiled, the clock would be running indeed.

5

Wednesday, August 22, 1984

Hong Kong Island, Hong Kong, B.C.C.

Even the amahs ironing in their small rooms in the back of the high-rise flats across the island on Repulse Bay had heard the explosion. Rising like a wall behind Hong Kong, Victoria Peak had only channeled the noise, magnifying the reverberations. After the blast, the rumble echoed along the harbor front, hanging in the air like a distant, persistent thunder. The shock had seemed to make all activity pause momentarily. That was unusual in Hong Kong. Unusual in a city that teemed with life, twenty-four hours a day, and never stopped. Unusual, indeed.

Chief Inspector Robert McDougall stepped from the Land Rover and touched the brim of his cap, returning the patrolman's salute in one long-practiced motion. Midlevels above Central was in his district. With Hong Kong Police headquarters a matter of blocks away, he was pleased, if not a little relieved, to be the first senior officer on the scene.

McDougall was amused at the stoic expression of the little Chinese constable who greeted him stiffly in front of the rubble, a dead giveaway for his evident pride at being Johnny-on-the-spot.

"Good day, Chief Inspector. It would appear to have been a rather large explosion, sir."

McDougall suppressed a smile, nodding gravely, "It would appear so, Officer Chin." The constable's clipped English was almost flawless, but it was clear his technical mastery of the tongue didn't extend to an appreciation of the limits on understatement.

Fate had been kind to the patrolman, McDougall thought. The man had been a block away when the blast shook the neighborhood. One street closer and he probably would still be on his own personal trajectory, heading toward splashdown in the harbor.

Standing at his habitually casual parade rest, McDougall surveyed what was left of the Iraqi consulate. He was no ordnance expert, but after seventeen years with the Hong Kong Police, he knew this had been one hell of a bomb. The row house at 64 Bonham Road was simply gone. The roof tiles and the bricks from the side walls had been blown straight up. The front stonework appeared to be the main source of the mess in the street. The rest had collapsed inward, on itself. The job had been no amateur toss-and-run affair, he thought.

McDougall stepped onto the stairs that led from the street into the one-time cellar entryway, now a macabre gangway to a disaster. The air, thick with dust, had an acrid, evil smell. A few yards in front of him, the marbled whiteness of a hand, curled like a claw, protruded from the broken bricks and plaster. Everything was down there now, he thought, including the Iraqis. McDougall pointed for the benefit of the constable, who turned to beckon the leader of the fire brigade's rescue unit.

He ran through the list of possibilities. Shiites, Iranians, Kurds, Syrians: they were the obvious candidates who either had chosen sides or were on a perennial manhunt for each other. Extraordinary timing, too. McDougall sighed, depressed at the thought of his forthcoming headaches. That was the worst of it. The special branch officer had told him only four days ago, with that irritating air of confidentiality they always assumed, that the second-in-command of Iraqi intelligence would be visiting Hong Kong this week, Wednesday, today. Doubtless he was underneath this pile, buried with the others. Now there would be hell to pay.

McDougall stepped slowly to the top of the exposed stairway. A mostly Chinese crowd eyed him from behind the police barricades on the opposite sidewalk. He looked straight ahead without seeing them. It was time to get in touch with the political adviser's shop. They would take care of the diplomatic niceties. Whitehall would receive a cable. The Foreign Office would call in the Iraqis. The Iraqis would demand to know why it had been allowed to happen and what was being done. Then, the whole process would reverse itself. The cable would arrive from London and it would be his turn again, this time to provide polite ambiguities for their unanswerable questions.

The black Rover belonging to the superintendent of police nosed to the curb. McDougall straightened slightly, clasped his hands behind him, and mentally checked to ensure his expression was sufficiently attentive and respectful. Superintendent MacDermott unlimbered through the opened rear door of the long, low sedan. The superintendent was another Scot, although that was about all they had in common, he thought. MacDermott was tall and patrician, with the chiseled profile and slightly unkempt, silver hair that seemed a prerequisite to wearing Savile Row suiting well. The right schools and the proper surroundings in the colonial service had burnished away almost all his brogue.

McDougall cleared his throat, pulled in his stomach, and tugged on his uniform tunic, feeling slightly overweight and rumpled as well as hot. The only remaining curiosity about MacDermott, he thought, was how, in the Hong Kong heat, the man always had his jacket buttoned but never managed to sweat.

MacDermott arched his eyebrows, "Well?" The superintendent's expression, the chief inspector knew, was a harbinger of an extended interrogation.

"A professional piece of work, sir," McDougall began with his only concrete conclusion, before admitting he was still well short of definite answers, "but we don't quite know who managed it yet."

Some 250 miles away, at 26,000 feet, inside the Cathay Pacific Tristar that had left Hong Kong's Kai Tak International Airport at 11:30 a.m, a half hour before the Iraqi consulate had disappeared, was the only person who did know, Rajid Musaani. Now over the South China coast, the plane banked gently to the right, climbing southwest toward the international air corridor across Vietnam and Laos. Musaani looked absently at his watch. He had made the same trip four times on four different airlines in the last four months. By now, he knew the itinerary well enough to anticipate the turns.

For anyone surveying the passengers in the executive-class section that afternoon, the dark-haired, dark-eyed young man lost in thought in window seat 16J could have belonged to any one of the several nationalities of regular business commuters on the Hong Kong to Frankfurt run. Slightly taller than average, tan but not swarthy, and handsome enough to make women take a second look, Musaani might have been an Italian, a Gulf Arab, a Latin, or an American. His clothes were casual, expensive, and designer-cut, and as relaxed as his manner.

If he'd been spoken to, he would have replied in English, but in a voice that was indistinguishably accented, and no greater help than his features or dress for any idle listener who wanted to determine his origins. He could have fit in with the late-afternoon crowd at the Hilton bar in Bahrain as easily as in Milan or São Paulo. Musaani knew that. After five years and three times as many operations in Europe and the Middle East, he also knew it was his protection. It made him a survivor. But more importantly, it helped him serve as a very effective killer, and that was what he did best.

Musaani had gotten the Hong Kong assignment months ago, when their informant in Baghdad learned of the Iraqi intelligence officer's planned visit to Asia. It was a priority task. The lead time helped considerably, although Musaani had been no less meticulous than he was on the most difficult jobs. On his first trip, he had studied the consulate from the ornate Victorian ironwork bench in the small park just across the street. He saw that while business was sparse, the pattern was regular.

The Iraqis lived in the building, opening their office late and closing early. The local help, the young handyman and the stooped, old Chinese woman who cooked, arrived every day at 11:00 a.m. They used the basement stairs, opened the unlocked gate at the bottom, and walked through the short archway beneath the building to the steel cellar door, where they were let inside. The door was about halfway under the building. From the design of the building, Musaani judged that the cellar entryway led, conveniently, through the consulate's main load-bearing wall.

Musaani mulled his options for two weeks before he decided the greengrocer disguise was best. On Mondays and Wednesdays, the white Nissan pickup arrived well before the consulate was awake with its unvarying delivery: two crates of fresh cabbage, leeks, and other vegetables, deposited in the archway beside the cellar door. The Chinese deliveryman returned late on Saturday to retrieve the crates. Musaani knew an extra crate or two were not likely to be noticed, especially on Wednesday, when empties already were stacked for pickup.

The rest took time. In Munich, he supervised the packing of the air freight shipments himself. At ten-by-four-by-two inches, each one-pound brick of plastique, the American C4 explosive, was double-wrapped, to seal in the chemical odor, and concealed in the false bottoms and sides of two steamer trunks. The bills of lading, showing the contents as brass candlesticks, hammered serving trays, and rolled carpets, described a cargo that was heavy enough to satisfy any inquiry about the weight. A split shipment was added protection. If one trunk was discovered, he would still have the materials to do the job, although with less spectacular results.

Today, Musaani thought, no one noticed that the Indian-looking chap who was new on the greengrocer's route arrived an hour early. It took barely two minutes to move the crates to their place under the empties along the rear cellar wall, and then to connect the final wire from the blasting cap to the nine-volt battery, and the Seiko alarm clock set for 12:00 p.m. He had filled the boxes with rancid table scraps, matching the contents of the others that the old cook typically used as makeshift garbage pails. It was an extra touch. Neither the greengrocer nor the handyman and amah would spot the additional crates later that morning, although there was no question they would come to the attention of the Iraqis, and most of Hong Kong, at noon.

At 38,000 feet, the westbound Tristar had just leveled off over the

white-blue curve of Vietnam's coast when the petite Malay flight attendant placed another drink by Musaani's elbow. The thigh-high split in
the silken dress molded to her body momentarily drew his eye, but not
his attention.

The Hong Kong operation had kept him occupied for the last week,
Musaani thought, and he needed to look ahead. He checked off the critical questions that faced him. Von Biemann would have the answer to
the most important: whether the American had captured the falcon. The
German's relationship with Harris was a stroke of luck, as was the American's background as a flyer who could move the peregrine without leaving a trace. If Harris produced the bird, the rest would fall into place.
Musaani's thoughts shifted to Tokyo. The materials he had ordered should
also be in the lab in Tehran soon. He would need to check on it when
he arrived in Munich.

There was no point in worrying now. Musaani stretched, trying to
relax. He might as well enjoy the flight. Or could he? He frowned, acknowledging the obvious answer. No. He had precious little time.

The mission. There were more than enough details, not to mention
ironies, he thought. Harris, for one. That an American should be a key
element in his greatest operation, one that would make their revolution
—the Islamic Republic—the unrivaled power of the Middle East. America, the Great Satan, was their adversary, but the American, Harris, however unwittingly, was their ally. America might seek to destroy them, but
it was fitting that Iran should still benefit from its associations with this
nation of rugged individualists, Musaani grinned sardonically.

And his father, he thought. That he should be involved. If his father
hadn't sent him to America to "protect" him, the plan would never have
been conceived, much less executed. That was when it all began, Musaani
remembered, when he learned he had to leave Tehran at once. That,
too, was an irony. It had been the anniversary of his own beginning. His
birthday, January 17, 1977.

It was not a time of celebration. He had walked home late from the university through one of Tehran's typically cold, clear winter nights. It was
close to midnight, and he was surprised when his father entered his bedroom. Machmed Musaani was a slight man, with thinning hair and

straight, simple features. Years spent outdoors had weathered his skin, making him appear too old for the army major's pips on the collar of his wrinkled khaki uniform.

His father sat down carefully on the edge of Musaani's straight-backed student chair, and leaned forward, his elbows on his knees. It was the posture of someone from the country, accustomed to a rough wooden stool or the narrow hearth of a farmer's brick stove. In one hand he held an envelope. Musaani had felt his stomach knot, anticipating the argument, even before his father began to speak.

"This is a ticket for you on the Pan American flight to New York and San Francisco. I have your passport with a student visa for America. Tomorrow afternoon you must go," his father didn't look at him but spoke rather at the envelope.

"I'm staying," Musaani spat out the two words as a challenge. His father raised his eyes. The silence lasted several moments.

The gaze was expressionless and hard, compelling Musaani with its authority, almost against his will, to try to explain the outburst, "I want to finish the degree. There's only one year left. I'm not political. I..."

"No!" Musaani recoiled involuntarily. His father's rejoinder echoed in the small room like a sharp slap. "Not political? How can you tell me lies? You and your activities have already almost finished our family. SAVAK is watching us. I have been questioned. Your mother lives in fear. How much more do you want? You have already done enough."

Musaani felt an instant chill at the mention of the feared secret police. He struggled to regain the initiative, "But I have stopped going to meetings, I..."

His father ignored the lie, shaking his head, "If you have gone once and they know, you have never stopped. I told you that from the start. For my sake, for your mother's sake, for the sake of your sisters, I begged you not to join the student movement. You ignored me. You knew better." His father's voice was bitter, "You were smarter, yes? Smarter than a stupid major, an old man from the farm who was lucky enough to find a home in the army, and a position at the Palace. Smarter," his father snarled the word, making it an epithet of contempt, "than everyone, yes?"

It was an old argument and now, Musaani knew, a terminal one. Angered, he sought to hide his fear of the impending unknown by striking back. Musaani's lips curved into a sneer, "Smarter? I don't know, but I know what is right and what is wrong. This place, Iran, is rotten. The Palace is evil to the core. It will fall. The people will no longer kiss the Shah's feet. Soon, it will be over for the Pahlavis and for their kind."

His father shook his head, "But even sooner for you."

"I won't go. They wouldn't touch me."

His father ignored him, "You leave tomorrow." It was an order. "Your name is on their list. Parsa, Khosrow, Nadir, and Mowlavi," the older man paused, watching his son's reaction to his fellow students' names, before continuing, "They are already gone. They will never come back. Never." Musaani felt his stomach sink. Fear gripped him. The four had not appeared at the meeting tonight. He was planning to check their homes and university dormitory rooms tomorrow. "Your name is next. It cannot be removed," his father said. "They'll use the list again, perhaps in the next few days. They told me not to doubt them."

Musaani struggled, trying to stop his own trembling. His father had told him, time and again, since his first days at the university when there was only talk against the Shah, not to join.

Musaani looked up, his fear contending with defiance, "You can stop this. You know these people. You know the bosses, the butchers at the top. Ask them. They will do you favors."

His father laughed bitterly, "They've already done me favors." He held up the ticket envelope, "That's why you're alive at this moment."

"But..."

"But what?" Machmed Musaani boomed. He appeared to rear back, raising his hand as if to strike his son as his frustration overwhelmed him. Then, he wavered, realizing how far he'd let himself go, realizing there was no point in striking anyone. He slumped in the chair, the picture of a beaten and powerless human form. His voice sounded sad, empty, "Why do you think I've told you to stay away from this 'movement,' these student groups? Because I'm one of the ruling class? Do you think I love those who come in the night to take others away simply because I happen to know them? Because I must serve them to earn my bread? Do you think I look up to them because I see their wealth in the Palace? Do you think me a fool? Do they care about me? If I became a nuisance, an impediment, I would disappear as permanently as your naive student friends. I'm nothing to them. I've tried to protect you, to keep what you've done from destroying you, us, our family. I've failed. I've done all I can for you."

For a moment, Musaani felt his father's sense of hopelessness overwhelm him, but only for a moment. He needed no lessons about SAVAK, or about their brutality. No one in Iran did. "You do what they say, always, don't you?" Musaani sneered, remembering and then casting aside the thought of the man who had looked so tall and strong, years ago, standing straight in his uniform, towering above him, a small boy. That was then, he thought. This was now. He was no longer a boy and his father was no longer tall or strong. Musaani shook his head disparagingly, "Even now, with me, you follow their orders."

"Tomorrow," his father continued, almost in a whisper, "we'll go to the airport early. I have a pass for the VIP lounge and a car with the Palace license. That will avoid the emigration check. I'll drive you directly from the lounge to the plane. It will be safer."

Musaani's voice was biting, "So, they will not kill me for the moment if you take care of me. You will do their bidding. You will exile your own son. That is 'all you can do.'"

His father started to speak and then stopped, obviously hurt but also drained of energy and anger. He rose stiffly and looked directly at Musaani. His eyes had turned flat, without reflection. Musaani still remembered his expression as well as the solitary snap of the latch as his father closed the bedroom door behind him.

Musaani stirred uneasily and looked out the window. The plane was nearing Bangkok, its first stop, descending through puffy cumulus clouds that pulled their afternoon shadows across the flat Thai landscape. The Tristar turned, slipping lower into the long, shallow final approach to the airport.

In contrast to most of the students at the university in Tehran, Musaani seemed to have no reason to want the system pulled down. His grandfather had served the Pahlavis for forty years, bequeathing his father his minor functionary's role with the Shah. They were country people, the wrong class to do very well, but their house on Tehran's north side, one of the better quarters, was more than an army major could afford and they had other advantages. When his father traveled with the royal parties to Germany or Yugoslavia, he always returned with gifts—furs, appliances, cognac. Others also knew him as one of the staff at Niavaran, the Palace. Occasionally that brought cash from those outside who hoped one day he could help them, perhaps with a discreet word, an introduction, or some business gossip. And for a time, for Musaani, the Imperial Academy appeared to promise even more.

The school, on the palace grounds, was small and elite, with European and American tutors for the Pahlavis and the select few close to them. No child from Musaani's class had ever attended, but somehow, when Musaani was 9, his father managed to get him enrolled. Musaani excelled. He was hardworking, intelligent, strong, good at sports; by his last year at the Academy, he led his form. He had mastered English and German, and was learning Arabic with a speed that continued to surprise his teachers. He was just about to enter a new world, one that his father and grandfather had only served. About to. Or so he had thought.

Musaani remembered the day his father had simply said that he had no more strings to pull. Others at the Academy could go to Europe or the United States to continue their studies, but for Musaani the universities were here, no matter how good he was. That was all.

When the rage had subsided, Musaani's anger was still there, for weeks, burning deep inside. If this was to be so, why had his father ever given him the chance at all? Better he should never have gone to the Academy. Better he should never have known how good he was, how much better than those born to wealth and position. Better he should never have realized how much they had, how much he should have. Better he should have remained an ignorant shepherd boy, living his life in the hills. Better he should have had nothing than this.

The end of his hopes was his father's fault, as it had been his father's doing that he should enter the Academy. So far and no farther. Forever second-rate, second-class. No matter what Musaani did, he was still the son of a major. No matter how well he did, he would still have to ask— no, to beg—for whatever came next. No matter how far he came, he could never go far enough to have even a fraction of what others already had because of an accident of birth. No matter that the father of the ShahanShah, the "Shah of Shahs," himself came from obscurity in the army. No others would do so. No one was to follow in those footsteps. That was 1973, the year, coincidentally, that the oil money began to wash over Iran, making the gaps between rich and poor grow into chasms.

It was not a coincidence, Musaani remembered, when the fire of anger inside him finally died, that it also was the year he truly began to hate.

The knock on his door came at 8:00 p.m., Christmas Eve 1977, just a month short of his first anniversary at Berkeley. Musaani had blended easily into the polyglot collection of foreign students on the campus that year. Most Americans didn't know or care about the growing protests in Iran, but Berkeley had enough Iranians to make him cautious about who he saw and what he said. SAVAK still had its lists. He was certain he could be singled out, noticed by those who reported to Tehran.

Musaani dropped the chain and turned the knob, peering into the obscurity of the dim hall at the caller. He had heard but ignored the footfalls on the stairs in the empty rooming house, deserted for the year-end vacation. He smiled, wondering whether he'd forgotten a holiday invitation from one of the Americans in his class, and began a reflexive apology. Both smile and words froze on his lips when he saw an Iranian he didn't know, not an American he did.

Musaani's throat closed viselike around his breath as the chill of fear drained his strength. The Iranian was medium height, slim to gaunt, and pale, with the beard, nondescript dark suit jacket, and tieless white shirt that had become a uniform among the fundamentalist expatriates on the campus. Then, in the hourlong split second he knew. If this were SAVAK, he already would be dead.

"May I come in?" The Farsi was soft, without the trace of a dialect. With his chest trembling, Musaani couldn't trust his own voice. He nodded and stepped back.

The visitor paused, taking stock of the surroundings. The furniture, battered and cheap, complemented the faded yellow paint on the walls: standard rooming house decor. The room was no different from the thousands of others in Berkeley that held the permanently temporary. Musaani motioned to one of the chairs.

The man sat down slowly, hands on knees, in an old-world pose, "I bring you greetings from Tehran."

"Who are you?"

"Abdul. I have been in the engineering department here for three years. You have been my responsibility since you arrived. I was instructed not to make contact with you until we were certain. I'm with the Committee."

Musaani tried to mask his surprise. Many in Tehran had heard whispered rumors, but few had ever heard the name spoken aloud by one of its members. A thrill ran through him. The Committee, Khomeini's underground, was a shadow, a ghost, as well as the mailed fist of the revolution. It took human form only to strike and then disappeared.

"We know why you had to leave Iran, of course," Abdul continued. "But it took time to determine to our satisfaction that you were a target of SAVAK, not sent here to do its work."

Musaani's mind raced, remembering. The Committee had approached him only once, two years ago, sending a young man he had never seen before or again with a specific request. Musaani had had to describe the layout of the walled compounds belonging to several of the Pahlavis' high advisers, as well as the family quarters of three senior SAVAK officials rumored to be the most powerful at Niavaran. He had known their children from his time at the Academy. A month later, one of the secret policemen and his family had been machine-gunned to death in bed. It had been easy enough to help, he recalled, and intrinsically satisfying.

"The Committee is aware that there is no love lost between you and your old classmates at the Academy," Abdul said. "A few are here and I've watched you keep your distance, just as you have kept your distance from others sympathetic to us." Musaani's visitor straightened in the chair, "The regime is doomed. There is much to do. You have unique connections and personal talents that are important to us. And," he paused in punctuation, "the Committee has a mission for you."

Musaani started as the pilot's amplified Australian twang announced that the flight would remain on the ground in Bangkok for forty-five minutes. He stared out at the tarmac. The shimmering heat had sterilized the afternoon sun into a flat white light. Another takeoff, then a landing in Bombay. Then, the long leg to Frankfurt. Musaani made a mental note. When he reached Munich, he would again interrogate Von Biemann closely about Harris. It was important to do it for form's sake as much as for substance, Musaani reminded himself. The German was good, charming as well as cold-blooded, but overconfident about his skills and his value to them. Von Biemann followed orders well. Didn't they all? But he was too self-assured. He could lull you into accepting his image for reality. Pricking the balloon, deflating the image, was a matter of control, he thought. Musaani felt the thin strand of tension tighten again. Given the stakes of this mission, his authority had to be unquestioned.

Musaani mentally pigeonholed the work to come. The memory of the meeting with Abdul so long ago brought back the feeling, the flood of excitement that had overcome him that first night in the rooming house. He was one of the chosen, helping those who were striking against the evil, the privilege, the power that had tried to crush out even his own existence. He'd felt their purpose in his bones. He had yet to kill, not with his own hands, but he knew then, when the time came, he could. Since that day, Musaani smiled with satisfaction, he'd proven himself with a vengeance.

Back in Berkeley in 1977, he remembered, events had moved quickly. Abdul was his handler, the source of his assignments. Musaani's task had been to work his way into the confidence of the young Iranians who were too privileged, and as yet too unknowing, to consider themselves at risk. At first, Abdul only ordered him to collect what he could to identify the network of the elite—who knew whom, who worked for whom, where the connections were made, and how the power flowed. Later, as Tehran came apart, the questions he was given were more exciting. He probed and dug harder for news from the insiders near the Shah. What were they thinking and planning? In the end, there hadn't been time. The climax came fast, faster than anyone expected.

By midsummer 1978, as the riots spread and the army lashed back, he and the others at Berkeley knew it was over. Musaani's elite new acquaintances now lived in fear. Their bravado was gone. They were on the phone every day. The stories were the same from Eşfahān, Tabrīz, and Mashhad as well as from Tehran. The killings became a bloody counterpoint to the spasms of demonstrations. Their families were leaving, fleeing at first a few at a time, then by the score, and finally, by the hundreds.

Musaani was their friend, a confidant, someone who knew, understood, and, they assumed, sympathized. He remembered their words, spilling out confused and helpless, creating for him a newsreel-like image of the multitude of cracks spreading through the foundations of the doomed regime. He had run once himself, driven from Iran by their kind. Now, it was their turn. Musaani remembered his pleasure at the little bastards' fear.

The next step came that August. Abdul had become more careful, seeing him less frequently face-to-face. There were anti-Shah demonstrations in San Francisco every week and neither was sure whether the Iranians on campus were being watched. A phone call from Abdul that mentioned the weather signaled the appearance of a letter in Musaani's post office box, which set the time and place for a meeting in two days.

As prescribed, two days later, Musaani stepped from the bus after a thirty-minute ride from Berkeley at the usual stop in Abdul's working-class-to-poor neighborhood. The patchwork quilt of small, pastel houses, postage stamp yards, and low-rise apartments confused the eye, obscuring the fact that it was on the edge of Oakland's urban decay. Small groups of black and Chicano teenage boys, shirtless in the ninety-degree heat, eyed his progress from the stoops. Musaani quickened his pace as usual whenever he came here, and walked closer to the curb and the illusion of safety in the street.

He climbed the exposed back stairway to the third-story walk-up. Musaani expected tea, some small talk, and, if the mail had arrived from Tehran, questions to follow up his last reports. The door opened at once. Abdul, uncharacteristically, was smiling. Musaani greeted him with their usual embrace and then stopped short as another man, seated at the small kitchen table, rose and walked toward him. He was tall, well built, and heavily bearded, with a presence that filled the room.

"This is Abbas," Abdul said and stepped aside. There was no question from Abdul's behavior that Abbas was somewhere near the top of the Committee's hierarchy and also no doubt in Musaani's mind that inquiries were not in order.

The stranger gestured, pointing to a place rather than inviting him to the kitchen table. Musaani sat stiffly as Abbas took a chair. It seemed un-Persian, but there were no pleasantries. The voice was low and resonant, but the words were cold. They were statements of fact, unambiguous and unadorned with emotion.

"The Committee is pleased with your work. We have looked carefully at your performance and see more for you to do, much more. When the Ayatollah returns to Iran, he will guide us in delivering justice and in carrying out the revolution. We will strike our enemies, overseas as well as at home. The Americans who kept the Shah in power all these years will try to stop us. So will the Iraqis and the Saudis, who fear our revolution. But we will strike them and before we do, we will destroy the

Iranians who have collaborated, and those who will try to collaborate again. What you are doing here—your information—helps us to be ready for that day."

Abbas turned slightly, staring at Abdul who was listening as intently as Musaani. Abdul, sensing the glance was an order, nodded, dropped his eyes, and left the room. In the few seconds that Abbas had shifted his gaze, Musaani noticed for the first time the grotesquely bent fingers of the man's left hand. The souvenir from SAVAK, he thought, explained a great deal.

"After the Shah is gone, we'll throw the Americans out," Abbas continued. "We expect retaliation. We expect the Americans and their allies to try to isolate us, to cut us off from assistance, and to keep us from attacking our enemies. We cannot afford to let that happen. For that reason, we need a handful of dedicated workers who can operate independently, anywhere, anytime."

Musaani still hadn't spoken, although the meeting obviously was not intended to be a dialogue. In any case, he knew what was coming next. "They will be special, a separate, secret organization," Abbas said. "To protect their identities, they will not come home. Only the Committee and our most senior leaders will know the group. We will call it 'Jihad,' holy war. To the outside world, it will not exist. Its members will have neither faces nor names. When they strike they will only be seen as the hand of the Imam that reaches out and destroys our enemies. Until our job is done, they will live in danger, but they also will have the greatest trust and win the greatest glory for the revolution." Abbas paused, "You will be one of its men."

The kitchen faucet dripped slowly, marking units of silence. "I know nothing about weapons or bombs or other things that I assume are part of this," Musaani chose his words carefully, implying a question, not a veiled dissent.

"You will be trained," Abbas replied. "First you will go to Lebanon to learn about arms from the Palestinians in the Bekka. They will also teach you hand-to-hand combat, surveillance, and methods of escape. Later, in Germany, our friends in the Red Army Faction will instruct you in more sophisticated ways to use explosives. Your knowledge of Arabic and German will serve you as well in the future as your English does now."

Abbas paused. Musaani noticed the battered leather briefcase next to his chair for the first time. Abbas extracted a manila file folder and placed it on the table.

"But most important now, you must have a secure base of operation. When we drive the Americans from Iran, your passport will not offer that here. Even if there are no problems renewing your student visa, it is still too vulnerable to cancellation to suit our purposes."

Abbas removed two photographs from the file. A flicker of a smile, the first since the meeting began, crossed his face, "You must have permanent resident status in the United States. To get that, you will marry an American. You have two choices."

Musaani looked down at the photographs. A brunette and a blond. Both appeared to be in their twenties, but with more wear on their features than time should have allowed. The brunette seemed heavy, tired. The blond was more attractive. From her face, Musaani judged, she probably had an acceptable body.

"They are heroin addicts," Abbas explained. "We identified them three months ago when you were first selected for Jihad. We give both the drugs they need for their habit. In return, they agreed to marry someone of our choice. We maintain an arrangement with two, of course, in case the heroin, or some stupidity on their part, accidentally costs one of them her life. You can sleep with whoever you choose or not. That's up to you. But in case the authorities investigate your application, you must live with her until you get a green card, your permanent resident alien certificate. That will take two or three months after the marriage. After that, the women have agreed to disappear. We'll give them enough heroin to make certain they live up to the bargain.

"If you marry now, you can expect to begin your training in Lebanon by March or April next year, 1979. If all goes well, you will be in Germany by the end of the summer. In the meantime, we wish you to remain here and to continue to report," Abbas concluded. Musaani nodded as Abbas rose from the table. That was that.

The marriage had not been a problem. In November 1978, shortly after his green card arrived, Dawn, the blond, had gone to San Diego with a suitcase containing an impressive quantity of heroin and enough money to support her habit for an additional six months. She had been pleasant enough and undemanding. When she wasn't stoned, she could use her imagination and body in surprisingly exciting ways in bed.

By December, events had overtaken the need for Musaani's reports.

The Shah was finished, although in Tehran his would-be successors were not, at least not quite yet. The moderates, a few new faces in the military, and the old hard-liners continued to struggle, hoping for a deal with the powers in exile who commanded the tidal wave that had smashed the throne into bits. But they were wallowing, adrift amid the debris of a ship that had broken up and all but sunk months before. The army was still in the streets and killing, but it too was in disarray. Tehran belonged to the political left and the religious right. Soon, so would Iran.

Musaani looked out as the "Fasten Seat Belt" and "No Smoking" signs came on, surprised that the time since their takeoff from Bangkok had passed so quickly. Minutes later, as the Tristar rolled to a stop at the arrival gate in Bombay, he rose, pacing the aisles to limber up. Fortunately, the ground time again was brief. Fifty minutes later, the giant airliner pushed back, paused to start engines, and then taxied toward the active runway. Without a halt, the Tristar pivoted, the whine of its three jets rising to the rumble of takeoff power, and accelerated.

Airborne ten minutes later, Musaani waved the flight attendant away, refusing a second dinner. The route would take them high above the Arabian Sea, the Persian Gulf, Iraq, and Turkey. When they reached Greece, they would follow Europe's Balkan spine and then cross the Alps. Then, Frankfurt, and for Musaani, Munich, would be only a few hours away. He eased the seat back. Munich. The next to last step. There, Musaani mused, all the pieces would come together. From Tehran, America, and Arabia. There, he would put the final touches on what he had started in San Francisco, 6000 miles away and five years before.

Nineteen seventy-nine, Musaani recalled, began as a time of waiting. On campus, he saw Abdul and the remnants of his old Iranian "friends," a shrinking group now, joining them occasionally in the small Middle East night spot in San Francisco they had frequented in "better" times. Bored, Musaani had gone there alone on the cold late January night. The club, surrounded by porno shops, X-rated movie houses, strip joints, and the sampling of hot-pillow-to-fashionable hotels that filled the blocks bounded by Union Square and Market Street, was half empty.

He'd noticed the trio, the Arab and the two American women, when they'd entered. The headwaiter's fawning over the "prince," the young man's automatic condescending air, and the name, Zahel, the Arabian ruling house, clarified the nationality. Seated in the booth next to Musaani's, the women were beautiful, expensive, and expensively dressed, with soft curves evident under satin that clung to even minor details. He noticed that they ran up a $300 tab for champagne and hors d'oeuvres in less than a half hour. It was a shame, Musaani thought, that the "prince" would probably be too drunk to perform with one, much less two, later on.

Musaani was about to call it a night when in accented English, the phrase, "revolution at home," rose above the music. He settled back, noting that the women were only feigning attention. Despite the quantity of champagne he'd consumed, the prince was still intelligible. He was making a straightforward case that the monarchy in Arabia should be overthrown. His description of the Islamic socialism that would follow was muddled, but there was no question that the prince welcomed the revolution in Iran. As he listened, Musaani knew at once that the Arab was a friend the Committee would want him to have.

"You have justice in your heart and a vision of the future," Musaani's words, polite, but not elaborately so, had a slightly formal touch. Startled, the prince turned to eye him, straining through his champagne haze to judge both Musaani's accent and looks. Musaani had continued to study Arabic at Berkeley and was nearly fluent.

Musaani continued, "My name is Rajid. From Tehran. I couldn't help overhearing your thoughts. My only concern is that friends of our revolution should not let their honest support for the cause put them in jeopardy. One never knows who may be listening."

Prince Kahlil bin Zahel, the 21-year-old grandnephew of Muhammed Kahlil abu Zahel, the king of Saudi Arabia, had just begun the second term as a freshman at U.C. Berkeley, his third American university, after Colorado and Boston, in as many years. Musaani was the first person Kahlil had met who spoke Arabic since he'd come to San Francisco two days before.

"Anyone can talk politics," the prince said. Musaani smiled. Whatever the bland ambiguity of the remark, Kahlil bin Zahel's reply in his own tongue meant that "talking politics" was just what he wanted to do. Within a few minutes, Musaani was sitting at the prince's table.

They sat, talking together, until the club closed and then, Musaani remembered, vaguely disappointed when Kahlil stuffed impressive bundles of bills into the hands of the two women, services unrendered, and dismissed them, until dawn at Kahlil's suite in the tower of the St. Francis

Hotel. Musaani pursued the relationship even before the Committee replied to his report. Kahlil kept his suite, commuting by chauffeur-driven
limousine to Berkeley for a few desultory hours of introductory political
science and economics classes. The two of them met together in San
Francisco several times a week. There were dinners, women, an occasional trip to the desert ranch owned by Kahlil's family outside Las Vegas,
and always, drinks and talk. Much, much talk.

After his years among the wealthy at the Academy, Musaani easily
recognized the type. Kahlil was spoiled, aimless, and undisciplined. It
was child's play to manipulate him. The prince's romantic view of the
revolution in Iran made it all the easier. As they sat and drank, Musaani
always listened and agreed with Kahlil's increasingly muddled ramblings
on radical Islamic socialism, although his political philosophy explained
considerably less about him than his background did.

Kahlil bin Zahel was a minor prince on a distant limb of King Zahel's
family tree. The king treated the family well. Money and travel were sta-
ples for Kahlil. A position somewhere in the government, the military,
or business was his for the asking. But in the weeks that followed, Musaani
learned what Kahlil would not admit: that his wing of the family would
never have the status and power he thought was due them. Kahlil had
plenty but it wasn't enough. He wanted more. There were too many others closer to the king and too little chance that Kahlil could move up
soon enough to suit him.

So, Musaani thought, Kahlil did the natural thing for the immature
and the overprivileged. He drank, amused himself as best he could, sulked,
and complained. None of that made him much different from the other
4000 princes in the extended royal family who might want more and
couldn't have it. But his fantasies about revolution, revenge, and his day
in the sun were different—so different, Musaani knew for a fact, that
they made Kahlil very important to Tehran.

Musaani followed the Committee's instructions, feeding Kahlil's ego,
becoming his confidant, his ally, and his friend, creating the dependency
that cemented the relationship before he left for Lebanon and Germany
that spring. He saw Kahlil each time he returned to the States from an
operation, as did others from Tehran who came to meet the prince. The
new Arabia that was his ambition, they told him, was theirs as well. The
revolution and Kahlil's future were one and the same. The effort, slow
and careful, gradually drew him into their plans. Kahlil was their pre-

cious capital—to be protected until they had just the right chance to invest it for the greatest return.

Musaani glanced out at the overcast as the engines changed pitch, matching the sensation of the Tristar's steady descent. It was an appropriate coincidence, he thought, that he had discovered that chance only a month ago in Las Vegas, the city of luck in the land of opportunity.

He'd spent the last weekend of July at Kahlil's family ranch, 1000 acres of high desert overlooking the turquoise water of Lake Mead, thirty miles east of Las Vegas. The house was contemporary, all glass and marble, long, low, and opulent. The Nevada desert offered the space and raw beauty of Arabia as well as the vices of the casinos to match the enjoyments of Dubai and Bahrain minutes outside the puritan veil of the kingdom.

They were about to start back to San Francisco when Kahlil said there was something he wanted to show him. Musaani didn't expect to see the two prairie falcons and the goshawk in the small building behind the main house. The young birds, Kahlil said, were the family's first purchases in the States. For generations in Arabia, their skills at falconry had distinguished them. They presented the king with their finest bird each year when he visited to fly his falcons over their hunting ground.

Musaani recalled the hauteur in Kahlil's voice as he emphasized his family's special standing. The king's hunt with them was a tradition, always the first stop on his annual pilgrimage to talk and to listen to the followers as well as the leaders among the Arab tribes. The idea occurred to Musaani in a flash. He had nodded absently as Kahlil talked on, repeating and embellishing his usual complaints about the king. Musaani remembered that he suddenly realized Kahlil was waiting impatiently at the falcon house door. Absorbed, he had failed twice to hear the prince when he asked if Musaani was ready to go. He mumbled an apology for his distraction and followed Kahlil to the car, already assembling the pieces of the plan in his mind.

Musaani drafted and coded the proposal later that night, transmitting it to the Committee the next day. The go-ahead came back before the week was out, including the accolade from the Supreme Revolutionary Council. Musaani felt the swell of pride again as he pictured the words on paper that congratulated him, sending the blessings of the Imam. The recognition, and now the responsibility for the mission, Jihad's most important mission, were personally his, and his alone.

The Tristar was descending, turning toward Frankfurt through overcast, the top side of a cold, late summer rain. Musaani looked at his watch. The flight was on time.

Soon, they all would be in Munich, Von Biemann, Harris, and his father, Musaani thought. Musaani had seen his father for the first time since leaving Tehran only two weeks ago, when the Committee brought him to Paris. They had talked late into the night. It had not been an easy conversation, although it would have been good if it could have been. Perhaps, Musaani thought, the old man would come to understand, to realize that his son had been right about the corruption of the old regime and the righteousness of the revolution. There would be time for that. It was the first visit in seven years, after all, and the tables had been turned. This time, Musaani smiled to himself, the meeting had been on his terms. He was providing the tickets and his father didn't have the choice.

The vibration from the landing gear and flaps in the airstream prompted Musaani to peer out. They were on final approach and the German countryside was closing on the airliner. In Paris, Musaani had only briefly sketched out what his father was to do for them. Musaani wondered what he thought. There was no choice, of course. The old man knew that. Even so, his reaction had been noncommittal. He had said only that he had done his last training a long time ago.

The Tristar's landing gear hit the runway with a heavy thump, followed by the roar of the engines at reverse thrust, although Musaani barely noticed. A long time, his father had said. That would have been 1979, Musaani thought, the final year for the throne in Iran, and the final year for his father as the falconer to the Shah.

6

Wednesday, August 22, 1984

The University Building, Salt Lake City, Utah

Frank DiGenero tossed his carry-on bag on the chair, closed his office door, and paused by the desk, shuffling through the litter of yellow telephone messages. The calls had accumulated in the two days he'd spent

in Denver, sorting out with the prosecutors whether to push for indict-
ments on three cases. Most of the slips had Washington, D.C.'s 202 area
code. Headquarters, DiGenero groaned. He swept the collection into a
wad one-handed, and dropped the loosely packed paper ball with slow,
mocking ceremony into the waste basket. If it was important, he knew
they'd call back.

Fatigued, DiGenero leaned against the wall, listening to the phones
ring outside the door, and stared out the window, looking idly for some
blue sky. The sun over Salt Lake City, hotter than usual for an August
afternoon, as well as a dirty gray smog had washed out or soiled most of
the color. Kirby was still on his mind. DiGenero wondered if his message to Harris on Saturday had gotten through. It wasn't easy playing cop
with your friends. He shrugged uncomfortably. Slapping wrists wasn't his
strong suit.

He glanced at his briefcase propped beside his bag on the chair. The
file was still inside. With a little reflection, he thought, Harris couldn't
have missed the point of his visit. Erin sure as hell hadn't. Somehow, he
recalled, she had his number the minute he climbed off the plane last
week. She hadn't been antagonistic, or even outwardly suspicious. It was
just that she seemed to sense his own uneasiness, DiGenero thought. He
couldn't put his finger on it, but she'd been different, more vulnerable,
as if she realized he knew something he wished he didn't, something that
could hurt them.

Erin. Maybe he should have told her. Maybe she could have taken
his message to Kirby. The thought of her had crossed his mind more
than once last weekend. Erin had always been easy to talk to, as if they'd
known each other for a long while. Maybe, if Kirby didn't come around
and he had to put down another marker, he'd give her a call. DiGenero
pictured her, arms folded, standing on the porch as he drove away Saturday evening. What was it that Angelo, Vince Scarlese's driver, used to
say every time he saw anything halfway decent in skirts? "Jesus, Mary,
and Joseph, whatapieceawork." He smiled to himself and then shook his
head unconsciously, suddenly afflicted with an unexpected twinge of guilt.
Harris was a friend. At this point, the last thing he needed was more
complications in the relationship.

There was a buzz on the intercom.

"Yeah, sweetheart?"

"You've got a secure call from Washington, Frank," Nancy Mc-Laughlin said.

"Shit," DiGenero muttered. He pressed the button on the small speaker box, "Can't you make it go away?"

"Come on, Frank. Commo took the call. You know the Boy Scouts always tell the truth." The tone in her voice told DiGenero she'd missed him, and his banter, while he was away.

"OK, OK." The secure telephone was in the communications room at the end of the hall. "Who is it?"

"Someone named Eddie Stockman."

"Why didn't you say so?" DiGenero smiled. Stockman had been "under" with him in New York. He was ten years DiGenero's senior, and by anybody's standards, a straight arrow, with a storybook marriage, three kids, a house in one of the homogenized, earth-toned northern Virginia suburbs outside Washington, and only a few years before a long-awaited early retirement. The two of them were different, probably too different to have ever become close in a normal field office. But being "under" wasn't the same. No one who hadn't been there could know what it was like, and the few who had never forgot.

Moments later, DiGenero punched the five-digit cipher code into the Simplex door lock, letting himself into the communication facility's antechamber. The "commo center" was a prefabricated box, a room within a room. Seated on custom-installed rubber-and-phenolic floor mounts, it was protected from prying eyes and ears—electronic or otherwise—by an insulated styrofoam jacket that soundproofed its walls, a second covering of copper shielding that kept the equipment's electromagnetic impulses inside, and a large bank vault door that ensured everyone who wasn't authorized stayed out.

DiGenero looked up at the closed-circuit security camera, complementing his usual obscene gesture to its unblinking, wide-angle eye with a beatific smile. The locking rods on the vault door released, slipping silently to the open position. DiGenero always marveled at the high-tech overkill for his odd operation, but the communications box was now standard issue for the field. Besides, who could refuse the bureaucracy's state-of-the-art generosity for his very own undercover?

"Davey baby," DiGenero clapped David Jackson on the back as he stepped up onto the raised flooring.

"Afternoon, sir," the fresh-faced young technician moved aside, smiling nervously, and closed the door behind him. DiGenero, only Jackson's second boss in his four years as an FBI communicator, still took some getting used to, especially compared to the brush-cut and spit-shined special agent in Duluth who had braced him at attention nearly every day until last month when he was transferred to Salt Lake City.

DiGenero maneuvered toward the far corner of the small chamber. It was just large enough for two men. The room housed the undercover operation's high-speed telefax data link to the FBI field office seven blocks away, a small computer terminal, two central processing units and printers, and the encrypted telephone and telegraph connection to the Bureau's nationwide communications network. It was manned sixteen hours a day by Jackson and another tech.

The communicators, as always, had the keys to any undercover operation's kingdom, the encryption codes as well as the cable traffic. For that reason, they were specially chosen, squeaky clean, usually with small-town backgrounds, all-American family values, and an uneroded respect for authority. If the pair assigned to RAPTOR had been on duty in the last days of Sodom and Gomorrah, DiGenero had no doubt they would have been the only ones spending their evenings writing home to Mom.

DiGenero lifted the handset of the gray telephone, pressing the "talk" button in the handle, "Eddie, old man, is that you? How come you don't write?"

"Because I know you can't read, Frank. How the hell are you, paisan?" DiGenero heard Stockman's familiar laugh on the other end of the tinny secure voice connection.

"Fine, how's the family in the 'burbs?"

"Taking me to the poorhouse." Two of Stockman's three children were in college, making his life a constant quest for student loans, equity financing deals, and debt rollover packages that, to DiGenero, resembled credit machinations worthy of a Wall Street financier.

"What's new in the crazy-chasing business?" DiGenero asked. Six months before, Stockman had been transferred from the Organized Crime Division to the FBI's Counterterrorism Center. DiGenero remembered commiserating. No bureaucracy accepted innovations gladly, and the politics involved in the creation of the Center had made matters even worse. Both the handwaving at the White House and the caterwauling on Capitol Hill over the terrorist threat had led the director to break more than the usual amount of crockery, wresting authority and "turf" away from other FBI divisions for the Center. Predictably, an assortment of water walkers and upwardly mobile sorts had leapt for the most visible jobs. The rest, including Stockman, had been drafted to do the real work.

"Hey, it's a jungle out there," Stockman's one-liner was mirthless. "You can't keep up with it. I'm dealing with the carriage trade, the European groups, not the bona fide lunatics, the Arabs and the Iranians, thank God. I worry mostly about the Germans and French, the ones who went wrong in the sixties and decided blowing people away was the best kind of political statement. There aren't many left, although the veterans with twenty years of practice—the Baader-Meinhof, Red Brigades, and the Action Directe types—have gotten pretty good at bang and burn." Stockman paused, "Actually, that's why I called. I need a little help."

DiGenero laughed, "You got to be shittin' me. Do you know where I am? This is Salt Lake City, Utah. Out here a radical is someone who doesn't pay his 10 percent church tithe on time. They don't even know how to spell terrorist."

"I know. I'm surprised they even let a wop like you in town," Stockman said. "But listen up and let me fill you in. Finding these guys, much less stopping them, is like looking for a needle in a haystack."

"What do you mean?" DiGenero asked. "I hear you got an army on the job."

"Yeah," Stockman shot back, "but the fact there are a handful of them and thousands of us makes it tougher, not easier. We're tripping over each other. We get intelligence from all over the world—some good, some bad. You're never sure which. Occasionally, when the trail gets warm, we're lucky. But usually we're like kids who play the whispering game at a birthday party. The same story can be repeated by ten different people and come back ten different ways. Who the hell knows what's true?

"The worst part is we also can't get at these bastards ourselves unless they come to the States, into federal jurisdiction. If we don't have the goods on an actual operation, mostly we watch and wait, trying to track the ones we've ID'd when they start to move. We have our best chance if they're traveling."

DiGenero nodded an unseen assent. The terrorism problem was different. Like his own career undercover, it was a difficult world, maybe the toughest for the Bureau, exacerbating the tension that always existed between the law enforcer who wanted to roll up his quarry and the intelligence collector who wanted to stalk it for what could be learned. Success in stopping one operation virtually guaranteed failure in learning about the next. Politicians' calls for scalps on the wall and their compulsive need for headlines in the morning press only made it worse. It was, DiGenero thought, one bad-ass account.

Stockman continued, "By the way, Frank, what I'm going to tell you is compartmented information. I know I'm asking for a favor, but you didn't hear this from me, right?"

DiGenero listened to the electronic static that passed for silence between them. He knew there were rules. The most important in any operation was that you didn't cross lines. But he also knew Stockman wouldn't have called him if he didn't need help. It was too risky for someone who could lose his monthly retirement check when he was only a short, three-year sprint from the finish line.

"I didn't hear a thing, Eddie," DiGenero answered.

"He's a German," Stockman said, "name's Klaus Von Biemann. He lives in Munich. We know his connections go back to Red Brigades. Now he's expanded, works with others, the Palestinians, the Shiites in Lebanon, and the Iranians. He's been in bed with them all."

"And, he's traveling, right?" DiGenero propped his foot on the small writing desk that held the secure telephone.

"Soon," Stockman said. The sound of shuffling papers accompanied his answer. "I think he's heading toward your neck of the woods. It's pretty solid, Frank, or I wouldn't ask you to spend your time. The German Federal Police have his place wired. We get a record of his calls."

DiGenero wondered what cops ever did before telephones and telephone taps.

"We know he made arrangements to visit a travel agent in Munich a week ago," Stockman continued. "We asked for the data that was on file in Lufthansa's reservation system for that day. According to the computer, the only record under Von Biemann's name was a reservation from Munich to Paris. We also got the number of the ticket issued him for that flight. We requested the German police to check further with Lufthansa. Because the ticket identification numbers are cross-referenced, Lufthansa could call up any subsequent booking. Von Biemann must have placed a call from somewhere else—probably a pay phone on the street—the same day he bought the ticket to Paris. We just found out that he made reservations on Air France from Paris to New York. He arrives tomorrow."

"Nice job, but what about me?"

"The phone records also show a call to the States. A Montana area code. I checked the files. Von Biemann has called the number before, once last spring and once or twice last year, but we've never had the information in time to cross-check it with his travel plans and to watch him."

"No problem," DiGenero anticipated Stockman's request. "I'll call the phone company. They'll help out. There're more telephones in the average bookie joint in Bayonne than there is in the whole state of Montana. It won't be hard to track down. We can stake out the place and put a tail on Von Biemann and his friend. I can handle it without warrants or a paper trail. The resident agents in Bozeman and Missoula owe me a few. Either one would set up a surveillance if I asked. After a lifetime of busting two-bit bad-check artists and hubcap boosters, a real live terrorist would make their day."

"Frank," Stockman interrupted, "it's not quite that easy. That's why I called you."

"Oh?" DiGenero heard the frustration in Stockman's voice.

"It's the classified information. It ties my hands. To involve the field offices, I'd need clearances for their agents to have access on the case. That's a goddamn nightmare, more pieces of paper with more signatures than you can believe, and too much time. We can't wait," Stockman said, "or we'll lose him before we get all the people clued in."

"I see." It was the quintessential example of why he never wanted to work in headquarters, DiGenero thought.

"I need you—off-line—to tell me what Von Biemann's up to. You're the only one I know who can do it. Our own people from Washington are going to put a tail on him tomorrow when he lands in New York. But Von Biemann's given us the slip before. Anything you could find from your local sources would be a world more than we've got, or could get from this end, to track him."

DiGenero broke in, "What's the number?"

"406-250-1976."

DiGenero paused uneasily for a moment, caught off guard, "Let me do a quick check. I'll be in touch." He sat back and stared straight ahead for several seconds, listening to the odd buzzing from the disconnected call, before he replaced the secure telephone in its cradle, stood slowly, and walked out of the cramped commo room.

DiGenero centered the Rolodex on his desk and turned it slowly. The drum spun. Each card was part of a catalog of numbers, names, and addresses, carefully noted with small checks and stars to ensure that he remembered which cover identity to use when he called. His thumb stopped the rotation. 406-250-1976. The number, written in pencil, was inscribed in his own hand under Kirby Harris's name.

DiGenero tapped DIGENROF, his user identification, on the computer terminal's keyboard, and waited for the response. The IBM personal computer was wedged in the corner of the communications vault, next to the old teletype machine. The system didn't need software. It was on-line twenty-four hours a day, seven days a week, as RAPTOR's window into NCSID, the Bureau's National Crime and Security Information Data Bank.

The prompting question, CLASSIFIED OR UNCLASSIFIED? painted green on black across the video display screen. DiGenero punched the keyboard, marking CLASSIFIED with a bright X, and waited for the next disembodied query. PASSWORD? He struck the keys, spelling DOORKNOCKER, although this time only asterisks appeared in the highlighted space, the program's protection for his personal access to the system. DiGenero pressed "enter" and waited. Thirty seconds and an electronic beep later he was inside the world's largest criminal information library, the guts of what made any FBI investigation tick.

DiGenero typed "201" after the small blinking carrot shape. The four-line menu appeared at once. He typed Klaus Von Biemann's name. It was a standard request, asking for a display of the German's background file. He loosened his tie and sat back to wait. The query reached Washington in an instant over the line that connected RAPTOR's terminal to the Salt Lake City field office and then to the Defense Microwave System's high-speed, 56,000-kilobit coast-to-coast data network. But a "201 call" still could take as much as five minutes, depending on the computer system's workload, the thousands of other questions being handled simultaneously by the banks of IBM 3260 mainframes in the second sub-basement of the FBI's Washington headquarters, 1900 miles away.

The terminal's quick beep less than thirty seconds later surprised Di-

Genero. COMPARTMENT PASSWORD? was centered on the screen. He swore to himself and typed DOORKNOCKER again.

The terminal beeped and blinked almost at once. INCORRECT. PLEASE ENTER CORRECT PASSWORD OR LOGOFF. YOU HAVE ONE MORE TRY.

DiGenero raised his eyebrows quizzically and retyped the eleven letters. The beep and message recurred even faster this time.

YOUR COMPARTMENT PASSWORD IS INCORRECT. YOU HAVE ONE MORE TRY OR YOU MAY LOGOFF. IF THERE IS ANOTHER INCORRECT ENTRY, YOUR ACCESS TO THE ENTIRE NCSID SYSTEM WILL BE FROZEN. SYSTEM SECURITY WILL INVESTIGATE TO DETERMINE IF UNAUTHORIZED ENTRY IS BEING ATTEMPTED. PLEASE TYPE CAREFULLY.

"Goddamn it," DiGenero snorted. The communicator looked up from his paperwork, startled.

"Can I help you, sir?"

"Nope."

DiGenero frowned at the screen. The system had him. He needed another special password for terrorism information, the subcompartment in the FBI data bank that held Von Biemann's file. There was nothing he could do. He glanced at the notepad beside him. Jackson had written down Stockman's name and secure telephone number at headquarters in the event his earlier call had been preempted or cut off. DiGenero looked at his watch. It was a little after 4:00 p.m. in Salt Lake, shortly after 6:00 p.m. in Washington. Stockman should still be at his desk. He reached for the telephone and punched in the eight-digit sequence penciled on the pad. The odd atonal melodies gave way to a series of irritating rasps before the quick rings began. The familiar voice answered in a matter of seconds.

"Hey, that was fast, Frank. What happened? You find out the phone number belonged to one of your girlfriends?"

"Eddie, I think I can give you some help, but I want to look in the files for some more information on Von Biemann. What can you do for me?"

The long pause testified to Stockman's uncertainty even before his answer confirmed it, "That could get my ass in a sling."

"I'm logged on right now. How about just giving me your password? I'll take a peek and be gone."

"No way. The password and user ID have to match. Even if I gave you both, the system would know that it's getting my request from Salt Lake City when I've been logged on the same day at the same time in Washington. It knows I can't be in two places at once and wouldn't accept the request. Besides," Stockman's voice betrayed his concern, "what do you need this stuff for anyway? No Sherlock Holmes routine, huh?"

DiGenero knew Stockman was worried. Besides Eddie's natural caution, Stockman knew his penchant for cutting the corners off the Bureau's rule book. DiGenero dissembled, "There may be a tie-in to my op. I'm not sure. I need a better feel for what source to tap."

Several seconds passed before Stockman exhaled a long, deep, obviously troubled breath, "All right. I'll make the request now. Hold on."

Stockman touched his computer terminal's keyboard, calling up the electronic menu for TERRORDAT, the FBI's data base on international terrorism. It took him less than a minute to fill in the blanks, press the "send" button, and receive ACKNOWLEDGED, IN QUEUE on his screen, confirming that his request would be processed in sequence with other queries.

Stockman picked up the phone, "All set. The hard copy, the file, should be on my desk tomorrow morning. I'll wire it to you by secure telefax. But for Christ's sake, after you read the file, destroy it. We could both go to jail if they find out."

A half hour later, as Eddie Stockman stepped from one subway into another at the Rosslyn Metrorail station across the Potomac River in Virginia, changing trains for the last stop in Alexandria, his car, and home, his request for a printed copy of the top-secret file on Klaus Von Biemann appeared on a video display screen two floors below his own in the Counterterrorism Center.

Juanita Mitchell, one of the fifteen document clerks on Wednesday's four-to-midnight shift, tapped her keyboard, first checking the security files. The bright green YES before her confirmed that STOCKMAN, the requestor, was an authorized name on the TERRORDAT access list, the roster of FBI employees cleared for highly classified terrorism data. Next, she scanned the menu to ensure its entries were correct and complete. They were, except one—the priority selection box. Tired and anxious, Stockman had forgotten to check either "Immediate" or "Priority." The correction was simple: she pressed her "enter" key. STOCKMAN's request disappeared from the screen, the omission rectified instantly by the

TERRORDAT software, which automatically assigned a "Routine" designation when none other was shown. The laser printers, collators, and finally, the registry and distribution clerks with their wire basket carts would do the rest.

The FBI's "Operating Regulations for Records and Requirements" specified that routine requests for documents would be located, printed, and delivered within seventy-two to ninety-six hours. The system rarely failed. But with the weekend two days away, Eddie Stockman's inadvertent omission of a keystroke meant that the file would not reach his desk before Monday, August 27, the day after Klaus Von Biemann, who had just arrived at Kennedy International Airport in New York, planned to be back in Munich.

At precisely 9:30 p.m., two and a half hours later, as Eddie Stockman was climbing into bed, Klaus Von Biemann stepped from a cab at the Park Avenue entrance to the Waldorf Astoria, walked up the two flights of stairs to the softly lit lobby, and strolled to the front desk. Despite the long transatlantic flight, his trim, European-cut summer suit was fresh and unwrinkled. The reception clerks were surprisingly busy for the hour, but Von Biemann stood patiently, relaxed, surveying the scene. To his satisfaction, no one reciprocated his curiosity.

Von Biemann had arrived one day earlier than specified on his tickets, his usual practice to avoid surveillance. Sometimes he used an alias, and sometimes not. In this case, he had simply checked in Munich whether seats were available on the day before he was ticketed to depart. There was plenty of room. When he arrived twenty-four hours early, Lufthansa as well as Air France, as always, accommodatingly accepted his first-class tickets without rewriting them.

Von Biemann stepped to the front desk, placing the soft leather attaché case with its gold-lettered "KVB" monogram on the high counter.

"Good evening, Mr. Von Bahrmann," the desk clerk nodded cordially, recognizing a regular guest in the tower suites. "Your rooms are ready for you, sir."

Von Biemann registered as Kurt Von Bahrmann. He would use the name to reserve his flights to Denver and Bozeman on Thursday. He handed the clerk $400, prepaying in cash for his one-night stay. He would charge nothing, and change airlines and names twice on the way to Montana. The American custom of not requesting a passport or other official identification from its hotel guests was a convenience, as was the marvelous simplicity of pay-as-you-go.

The desk clerk snapped his fingers, "Front!"

Von Biemann turned, handing his attaché case to the bellman who already held his carry-on bag. The small nook of private elevators that would whisk him thirty-three floors to his suite in the towers was across the lobby. It was going well, Von Biemann thought. Well indeed. He, Harris, and the falcon would be in Munich in less than three days.

7

Thursday, August 23, 1984

The Harris Ranch, Broadwater County, Montana

"Kirby, how are you?" With a two-time-zone edge on the day, Von Biemann sounded unnaturally alert. Groggily holding the phone to his ear, Harris snapped on the reading lamp, squinting momentarily in the glare at his watch: 4:30 a.m.

"How am I? It's too goddamn early to tell," Harris rubbed the stubble on his cheek and half-stretched. Despite the indigo darkness of the early-morning hour, he had expected the call. It was Von Biemann's usual practice to phone with the final details of his itinerary just before he began the last leg of his trip.

Two thousand miles away in New York City, a rich coffee aroma filled the Waldorf Astoria suite as the German cradled the telephone with one hand and poured a second cup of the hotel's special Jamaican Blue Mountain blend from the sterling server with the other. Von Biemann rose from his chair and stepped to the window. Thirty-three stories below, Park Avenue was empty except for the taxis that jockeyed in the southbound lanes. At 6:30 a.m., eastern daylight time, the midnight- and day-shift cabbies were beginning to flock toward Grand Central Station where the early arriving upstate commuters could provide their last or first fares of the day.

Von Biemann had slept, untroubled by any jet lag from his transatlantic flight the day before. He'd risen at 5:45 a.m., called room service for his usual breakfast of croissants, fresh orange juice, and coffee, and then showered and shaved. With ten hours of travel still before him, he dressed casually and comfortably in slip-ons, tan linen slacks, and an open-necked polo shirt. Across the sitting room, beside the suite's heavy oak double doors, his bag and briefcase were precisely aligned, ready for the bellman who would carry them to the towers' 49th Street entrance and the limousine to Kennedy Airport, forty-five minutes away.

"When are you arriving in Bozeman?" Harris yawned.

"Today, at 5:30 p.m., on Western 451 from Denver." Harris grunted an acknowledgment, scrawling the flight number on a bedside notepad. He knew the German would travel a circuitous route to Montana, using several airlines and as many names.

"You've done very well," Von Biemann said, stepping back to the table. The delicate scrape of china was audible as he finished his coffee and replaced the cup on the saucer before continuing, "I'm anxious to see her."

"Yeah," Harris replied, "she's a winner."

Von Biemann had appeared to be genuinely pleased when Harris called Munich to confirm that he had the peregrine. All things considered, Harris thought, she was in excellent shape. Another day of rest and adjustment before they started east also would help.

"When do we depart?" Von Biemann asked.

"I've made the arrangements for Saturday," Harris answered, "day after tomorrow. How's that?"

"That's fine," Von Biemann paused. "There is one change in plans. I want you to accompany me, at my expense, of course. The value of our merchandise requires some extra care. With your name on the documents, I think it would be helpful for you to assist with the customs clearance formalities. It will be added insurance that things go smoothly. I'll explain it to you when I arrive."

Harris elbowed himself into a sitting position. "I really wasn't counting on...," he began, but the German cut him off. "I insist."

In the background, Harris heard the soft three-note scale of a door chime, followed by a muted greeting. Von Biemann's voice faded momentarily as he instructed the bellman before turning back to the phone,

"I've already taken care of your tickets. Besides," he continued, "it will be worth your while. The other half of your compensation will be waiting when we arrive."

Harris tried to break in, but failed again. Von Biemann's tone was a mixture of congeniality and authority, "You should plan to spend the week with me. As my guest. Now, I must be on my way. The car is waiting. Until this evening." The line went dead before he could reply.

Harris let the phone slip from the crook of his neck and snapped off the light, lacing his fingers behind his head. On the face of it, there was no reason for him to go. As always, he'd already put his name on the peregrine's forms as breeder and owner. He only needed to draw up a bill of sale to accompany the dummied registration certificate and sign the package over to Von Biemann.

The counterfeit paperwork and the bogus transaction had been part of their standard procedure ever since they'd purchased two falcons from the breeding project at the university four years before. The pair came with documents and yellow federal leg bands that legally certified they were domestically raised, not wild-caught. He'd lost track of the number of birds they'd moved with the forms and bands, but there was no question the papers had been worth their weight in gold.

Through the window, in the distance, the light edged the foothills framing the eastern sky. Harris swung his legs off the bed and sat, thinking. A trip with Von Biemann screwed up his plans. Last night, he'd phoned Erin, promising to spend a few days in Missoula the weekend after next. DiGenero's visit had obviously bothered her. She was a big girl, Harris thought, and well aware he could take care of himself, but after five years together, he knew when his classic "pat-on-the-ass and it's-gonna-be-all-right" routine worked and when it didn't. In this case, the reassurance had come up short. He didn't want to leave it that way.

Harris stood, stretching. Von Biemann's veiled ultimatum about half of his payment waiting at the other end of the line irritated him, but the mere fact of the invitation coming after Frank's visit would bother her far more. If DiGenero had her worried about the long arm of the law, the risk of a trip would only make it worse. Harris frowned momentarily. It would be better for the two of them if he didn't go with the German, he thought. Unfortunately, with half the $75,000 at stake, that wasn't in the cards. He walked slowly toward the bathroom. "What the hell," Harris mumbled, "she'll get over it." A trip to Munich or Missoula? He snorted. It sounded like the punch line in a cornball comedy routine.

He found the wall switch, snapping on the bathroom light, and paused. In the mirror, his reflection, quizzical, stared back in a partnership of silent deliberation. Erin was one thing. Von Biemann was another. It was conceivable that he wanted to take extra care, Harris thought. The peregrine deal obviously was real money. His take told him as much. These days, his cut on a sale averaged $30,000, at a rough guess, Harris thought, probably 40 percent of the German's retail price. If he was getting $75,000 this time, that meant that the falcon would cost the buyer close to $200,000. A two-year-old peregrine was the rarest and hardest to trap as well as the hands-down favorite in any falconer's stable, but that price was well over twice the best he'd ever heard of for a wild-caught bird.

Harris spun the hot-water knob, watching the steam fill the shower stall, and then stepped into the sharp pulsating spray. Still, there was something that bothered him about Von Biemann. Something else. After five years, it wasn't like the German to let on he was nervous about a deal. Something must be up, he thought. And, Harris stood motionless in the shower, his brow furrowed, it wasn't like Von Biemann to change their pattern. Not like him at all.

Harris paused on the threshold of the old shed, leaning against the door-jamb. The falcon was hooded, but her attention had riveted onto him as soon as he'd entered. They were in the original barn behind the ranch house, divided inside by a center wall. Half the space held the debris of four Montana generations; Harris had cleared the other half. Through the old bubbled-glass windowpanes, the illusion of light made the T-shaped perches, staggered at different heights, look like incomplete crosses marking the way into the dark. He watched the peregrine as she listened for sounds of movement, trying to hear what was in store. She'd taken her first food yesterday, a good sign. He would feed her again this evening, although not enough to satisfy her hunger, waiting until tomorrow to let her gorge. It would hold her until they reached Munich.

He stepped outside, pulling shut the warped door and sliding closed its rough-hewn wood bolt, and glanced at his watch. It was after 4:00

p.m., time to pick up Von Biemann in Bozeman. Harris walked toward the house, digging in his hip pocket for the car keys. DiGenero and Von Biemann, he thought. They were two wild cards. Frank catching on, and the German changing the script.

Both worried him, although that had its pluses in a way, he thought. In addition to spicing up the game, it made him less complacent, more alert. That never hurt. Frank's "warning" was the most obvious problem. The question was still what specifically did DiGenero know? About the German? Probably not, Harris thought. And Von Biemann. Why was he changing the usual plan? Because the Feds were onto him? And if they were, would the German level with him? Who knew? One thing was for sure, Von Biemann wouldn't be pleased if he knew about Di-Genero. Moderation in all things, including candor, Harris smiled to himself. For now, or at least until he had the $75,000 in the bank, he'd keep DiGenero's warning under his hat.

Minutes later, the gravel ricocheted in the fender wells of the Blazer as Harris cut the wheels hard, turning south on the pavement, and accelerated. He glanced in the rearview mirror. No one was behind him. Only the rutted road that connected the weathered gray buildings of the ranch to the state highway receded in the distance. Flashing by, the highway mile marker noted the distance to Bozeman. He had seventy minutes to cover seventy-five miles before Von Biemann arrived.

All the details were complete, Harris thought. He'd reserved the Super Kingair 300, and paid the $4000 for the round-trip flight time. At noon he'd taken care of the final wrinkle, Von Biemann's invitation, by wiring a deposit to the charter service at Dulles, outside Washington, to reserve a pilot who could ferry the plane back to Bozeman. Other than a check of the weather along the flight path, that was it. Harris pressed down on the accelerator, winding the speedometer toward 80 miles per hour. They would be in the air on Saturday, forty-eight hours from now, and in Munich by Sunday at noon.

In the distance, beyond the highway, the sun glinted on the skin of the Western Airlines Boeing 737 that had just taken off for Tacoma after depositing the German and a handful of others at Bozeman. With Von Biemann in the seat beside him, Harris pulled into the passing lane, accelerating by a station wagon with its full load of luggage, children, and tourist paraphernalia.

"This is a very important sale, Kirby, but we've got to play it close to our vest," Von Biemann said, shifting into a more comfortable position in the passenger seat.

Harris glanced sideways, wondering for an instant whether the German already knew about DiGenero, "How's that?"

"I'm breaking the rules. The customers are Saudis but they're nowhere near the level where I prefer to do business," Von Biemann answered. "I have buyers from one end of the Persian Gulf to the other. Business is business in Kuwait, Bahrain, Oman, and the Emirates. I can sell birds to anyone who has the money. But Arabia is different. There, one way or the other, all the princes are part of the same family and you have to be careful about the hierarchy."

Tired, Von Biemann rubbed his temples and sighed, "Not all of them fly falcons, of course. But the oil money has added hundreds of new buyers, some at the top of the social ladder and others at the bottom. That makes it much more complicated. It's a matter of face and status. If I sell to one of the underlings and the word gets out, his betters won't do business with me. But if the ones at the bottom find out you're not selling to the top, they drop you too."

"Then, in this case," Harris asked, "why bother?"

"Good question. As a matter of fact, if my clients were the ultimate recipients of the peregrine, I wouldn't take the risk. But," the German paused, "they're not."

Harris raised his eyebrows, his next question obvious. Von Biemann smiled smugly, "The falcon is for the king."

The whistle of genuine surprise seemed to please the German. "What's the connection?" Harris asked.

Von Biemann shifted in his seat once again, "Every year, the king makes a pilgrimage to meet with the leaders of the bedouin tribes. Tradition has it that they honor him by presenting their finest gift, no matter the cost. Because my clients have been known for generations as falconers, they always give the king a bird from their stable. The gift of a falcon. It's a reflection on their family and its reputation, and important to them. But it's also difficult because the king is a falconer who wants for nothing. He has sakers, gyrfalcons, goshawks, laggars, and lanners. He's flown them all." Von Biemann smiled broadly. "All, that is, except a North American peregrine. I'm told," he said slowly, "he wants one very much."

"And?" Harris asked.

"And what?"

"What's in it for them?"

Von Biemann shrugged, "Giving for the Arab is an investment, not something that brings an immediate return. The king would see it that way. He's one of the last of the original breed. King Zahel also is old, almost 75. His next appointments in the government and elsewhere, the kingdom's oil monopoly, for instance, are likely to be his last. For my clients, this year's visit may be their final chance to move up, from below the salt, before he's gone. Perhaps they hope the gesture will make a difference."

Von Biemann paused, "Whether or not their wishes are granted, ours will be once we provide a falcon for the king. Our future with the House of Zahel is guaranteed. The gift will be our ultimate advertisement. That's why I've arranged for you to come with me to Munich. Our system has worked quite well over the years, but this sale is too important to take any chances. Your name on the falcon's papers as breeder and owner, rather than mine as buyer, is added security against any trouble from U.S. Customs. After that, we're home free.

"Believe me, Kirby," Von Biemann smiled, "when all is said and done, this deal will go down in history."

8

Saturday, August 25, 1984

Dulles International Airport, Washington, D.C.

At 5:00 p.m., after flying over half a continent, Kirby Harris was tired and tense, and below him, Dulles International Airport was busy. He acknowledged the Washington air traffic control center's instructions, throttling back the Kingair's two 1050-horsepower turboprop engines, and de-

scending to 4000 feet in the landing pattern. They'd left Bozeman at 6:00
a.m., before dawn. After a refueling stop outside St. Louis four hours
later, their course had drawn a line south of Indianapolis and Cincinnati
before crossing the worn, washboard rows of the Alleghenies and the Ap-
palachians. At this hour, the transcontinental flights got the straight-in
approach. On the slope of the mountains, over Front Royal, the air traffic
controller had vectored the Kingair east-southeast, away from Dulles, on
a long downwind leg.

Twenty miles from the airport, at 1500 feet, Harris turned sharply
north, holding his altitude over the Monopoly board pattern of two-story
colonials and square lawns that filled the suburban spaces between the
four-lane highways and shopping center parking lots. He pushed the nose
lower into a shallow descent at five miles out. Ahead and to the left, a
garishly painted DC-9 shuttle from New York coasted toward the parallel
runway. The pilot's voice had a tired edge as he acknowledged the final
instructions from the tower.

A few moments later, the Kingair sunk earthward over the Virginia
pines covering the airport's 10,000-acre preserve. Then, they were down.
Harris turned off the runway at the first taxiway and stopped, following
the ground controller's directions to hold his position. He leaned back
and rubbed his eyes. He'd last looked at the peregrine an hour ago. Her
cage was behind them in the cabin. She'd been traveling well.

"There it is." Beside him, in the copilot's seat, Von Biemann pointed
at the Near East Air 747's stark white fuselage. The jumbo jet was parked
at the end of the long midfield ground service building. They would leave
at 10:00 p.m. Von Biemann had arranged for a planeside check-in.

Harris stiffened. In the distance, by the transit aircraft ramp, he saw
the two dark sedans pull to a stop. FAA, Customs, FBI, or none of the
above? This was Frank's last shot, Harris thought. DiGenero had called
once, on Thursday night, just to talk, although Frank had never been
much before for idle telephone conversation. It was odd, Harris thought,
as if Frank were checking on him. Before he hung up, DiGenero had
said he might be in Bozeman again this weekend on business. Harris had
put him off, explaining he didn't know whether he'd be at the ranch or
in Missoula with Erin.

He glanced at Von Biemann who sat, relaxed, watching the trucks,
buses, and cars that were scuttling in crisscross patterns among the arriving and departing airliners.

The ground controller's laconic voice filled his earphones, "Kingair November 231, cleared to cross Runway 01 Left and proceed to the transit area."

Harris keyed his microphone, "Roger, crossing 01 Left." The two cars were still there. He released the brakes, feeling the trickle of sweat on the back of his neck, and pushed the throttles forward. The whine of the twin turboprops resonated up the scale as the Kingair started to roll. They had four hours and thirty minutes. Until 10:00 p.m. Then, Harris thought, they'd be home free.

Harris opened the medical kit, removing the disposable plastic syringe, the small vial, and the cotton gauze, and placing them on the bedside table. He looked up at the sound of ice tinkling against glass. Von Biemann stood in the doorway of the bedroom, drink in hand. The trailer, one of three beside the transit ramp, was their usual way station at Dulles. At $300 a night, the miniature mobile home had the amenities of a luxury hotel suite. It wasn't cheap, but the privacy and isolation made it ideal for their purpose.

"So, it's time to put her under," Von Biemann said.

"Yeah," Harris replied. It was a little before 9:00 p.m. "It'll take me a half hour to get her ready. Then, we'll have to go." He reached into the traveling cage and lifted the falcon from the perch, holding her gently. She was still socked and hooded. He laid her on the bed and turned to the nightstand, aspirating the diazepam in the syringe.

He paused momentarily, reluctant. He never liked to put a bird under, but this one was even harder than usual to do. Harris pictured her, free, on the ledge at Sixteen. A hell of a time for a pang of conscience, he thought. The peregrine flinched as Harris pushed the needle into the long upper-thigh muscle, a finger's breadth below the point of the graceful curve of her folded wing. The falcon lay still for several moments. The anesthetic worked quickly. In less then ten seconds, her talons relaxed and her head movements stopped. Then, she was gone.

"Perfect," Von Biemann smiled.

"I hope so. The dosage should get her to Frankfurt, and if we're in luck, keep her groggy until Munich," Harris glanced at his watch. He had until 9:15 p.m., when the car would return to pick them up, to prepare her.

Harris knelt by the bed, working deliberately. After first removing the hood and sock from the falcon, he set the carry-on bag beside him, emptying its contents. Against the peregrine, lengthwise down her back and wings, he positioned four thin, flexible strips of pinewood, sanded glass-smooth. Then, holding them in place with one hand, he wrapped her body and tail in light gauze. He stopped frequently, checking. It was important to not make the gauze too tight, to let the peregrine breathe. Satisfied, he taped the light cloth securely. It would help keep her cool and, together with the stays, protect her tail and flight feathers from damage if she happened to stir or awake.

He lifted the three-foot-long, coffinlike container from the floor beside the bed. The falcon's traveling box was perforated, allowing air to circulate freely. He placed the peregrine inside, back down, adjusting the padding to suit her. Finally, he secured the top with two hasps. It was the last step.

Harris stood and lit a cigarette. Von Biemann usually shipped his birds in the pressurized cargo bay, but this time they had three first-class tickets. Kirby Harris smiled to himself. She could have the $1800 window seat next to him.

Late evening at Dulles was the hour for European departures, not arrivals. At 9:30 p.m., the cavernous, half-lit customs inspection area echoed with Harris's footfalls as he pushed open the door, marked "U.S. Government, Official Business Only," and stepped inside.

"Now what?" he muttered, pausing for a moment to light a cigarette, uncertain. Von Biemann had the falcon outside in the transit services station wagon that was parked, waiting to take them to the Near East Air flight. Customs clearance was the last step. Twenty yards to Harris's left, the single "Exit" light glowed dull red above the door labeled "No Admittance." Behind it, Harris heard laughter combined with muted sounds of conversation.

He walked toward the voices, hesitating at the door. So far, so good, he thought, no DiGenero and no FBI. But it still boiled down to a $20,000-a-year customs inspector. Harris pulled the papers from his jacket pocket. Even if Customs didn't have the word from Frank, all it would take to screw up the deal was one jerk who didn't know a falcon from a flamingo but wanted to go through the paperwork with a fine-tooth comb because he was curious, bored, or had a bad day. This was

Von Biemann's end of the business, he frowned, not his. Why the change in routine? What the hell? Harris ground the cigarette under his heel, exhaling with a flat tuneless whistle. Then he turned the knob and stepped inside.

Twenty minutes later, and a half mile away, the transit services station wagon pulled to a halt beside the alabaster Near East Air jumbo jet. Waiting at the foot of the mobile stairs, a man in a dark three-piece suit, incongruous on the hot summer night among the T-shirted mechanics and ground crew, stepped forward, bending low to peer through the windshield. The Near East Air station manager's face brightened at the sight of Von Biemann. He opened the passenger and rear doors with a deferential nod and stepped back, preparing to escort the two men on board.

Von Biemann's hand touched Harris's shoulder. "Home free," the German sounded relieved. He stepped from the car.

"Yeah," Harris looked at the mobile stairway that led steeply upward to the 747's forward, first-class entrance. Von Biemann was already halfway to the top, obviously hurrying aboard. Harris eyed the station manager. His arm was still outstretched, welcoming, but an impatient expression had diluted his smile of hospitality.

Harris lifted the falcon's long wooden box from the seat, stepped from the car, and walked slowly to the foot of the stairs. He glanced up. The German had disappeared inside. Something about Von Biemann was different, Harris thought, very different. Above the massive wing, the fuselage spotlight was fixed on the distinctive green crescent of Islam high on the 747's five-story tail. Not exactly the Stars and Stripes, he thought. Harris paused. "Yeah," he repeated the words, half aloud, to no one in particular, "home free."

At that moment, 2000 miles away in Salt Lake City, Frank DiGenero cursed, frustrated, about to hang up the phone, when Erin's voice came on the line, "Hello?"

"Erin!" Surprised, DiGenero slid his feet off the desk. "It's Frank. How are you?"

"Oh, Frank, I just walked in from the lab," she was out of breath. "I'm looking for Kirby."

"Oh," DiGenero heard the real message in her pause, "I'm sorry, he's not here."

DiGenero wasn't surprised, "Is that right? The man's got terrible judgment. On a Saturday night, I can't understand why he'd be anywhere else in the world but with you."

"That sounds like a very old line," Erin laughed.

"Seriously," DiGenero said, "I thought he might be in Missoula this weekend."

"No, we really didn't have plans. Ah," she paused again, "I think he's away from the ranch for a few days."

"OK," DiGenero pursed his lips, "I just wanted to talk with him. Look, if you hear from Kirby, tell him to give me a call, would you?"

"Sure," Erin answered, "I'll tell him."

DiGenero put down the phone. Stockman's cable, an "Immediate, Eyes Only," was in front of him. Jackson had called him at home when it had come in three hours before and he'd been telephoning ever since, first Kirby and then Erin. Standard FBI procedure for handling "Eyes Only's" required the communications technician to put all three copies on his desk. DiGenero tore off the perforated edges of the message paper, crumpled two copies, and reread the third.

SECRET

FROM FBI HQTRS
TO RAPTOR/SLCITY

PASS TO DIGENERO FROM STOCKMAN AS EYES ONLY
DELIVERY NONDUTY AS WELL AS DUTY HOURS

BEGIN TEXT

OUR SURVEILLANCE UNABLE TO LOCATE AND FOLLOW SUBJECT VON BIE-MANN, KLAUS IN NEW YORK CITY. RESERVATION CHECK WITH LUFTHANSA AND AIR FRANCE INDICATES SUBJECT'S TICKETS USED ON FLIGHT LANDING ON WEDNESDAY, 22 AUGUST, NOT, REPEAT, NOT 23 AUGUST AS ORIGINALLY SCHEDULED. SINCE SUBJECT IN COUNTRY FULL DAY AHEAD OF EXPECTED DATE, ASSUME HE IS ALREADY IN YOUR AREA. WOULD APPRECIATE ANY EFFORT AS DISCUSSED IN PHONECON TO LOCATE AND FOLLOW. PLEASE ADVISE.

NEW ITEM. FILE ON SUBJECT PREVIOUSLY PROMISED GIVEN MISTAKEN ROUTINE PRIORITY REQUEST BY RECORDS SECTION. WILL TELEFAX SOONEST.

END TEXT

Worried, DiGenero stared at the message. Erin was a lousy liar, he thought. The German's arrival in Bozeman on Thursday, when he'd last talked to Kirby, and Harris's departure sometime yesterday or today fit together, neat and tidy. FBI rules and what he was about to do now, sure as hell didn't. DiGenero reached for the phone. Maybe, just maybe, he thought, listening to the ring, if they were very lucky, he could still help Stockman and Kirby both.

Salt Lake City Airport was still dark and quiet at 5:30 a.m., Sunday morning, August 26, when Arnold Masterson and Dwight Perkins boarded Frontier West's Twin Otter, taking the last two seats. Perkins moved to the rear, while Masterson squeezed into 6C on the aisle. Behind them, the flight attendant secured the door and began her predeparture safety check.

"My, I didn't know the phone company would make you work on Sunday," the grandmotherly woman in window seat 6D smiled, looking up from her knitting.

"Yes ma'am," Masterson nodded politely, unzipping his blue, yellow, and white striped "Bell System" windbreaker and doffing his baseball cap embossed with the phone company's logo. He always wore both on a job.

"We work seven days a week," Masterson said, "especially when we get a trouble call from one of our local companies. People out in the country deserve our best service too, you know." He extracted a technical manual from his carry-on bag, opening the loose-leaf binder on his lap. "Now, I've got to do a little homework so we can get the job done right." The old woman nodded seriously, making Masterson smile.

Perkins had made their reservations the day before, just after DiGenero had called and just before Frontier West's phones shut down for the night. The flight, the airline's first departure from Salt Lake City, arrived in Bozeman at 8:00 a.m. They'd rent a car, have the job done there by 1:00 p.m. at the latest, and then drive to Missoula. If they were lucky they could finish there in time for dinner, a good night's sleep, and the first plane back to Salt Lake on Monday morning.

Masterson looked over his shoulder at Perkins who as usual was already dozing. Both had been in the field for ten years, five as a team. For the last two years, they'd been RAPTOR's "soundmen," its audio surveillance technicians. The old-timers in the business still preferred the original label: "the black bag gang."

The white head beside him bobbed as his elderly seatmate slipped into a nap. Masterson removed the court order from his inside pocket, partially unfolding the papers. DiGenero had done a good job of dummying up the wiretap authorization. Close enough for government work, he thought. It was only meant to flash if they needed. Out here, that was usually enough to impress local phone company supervisors who challenged them. Besides, he knew Sundays were a charm. On the day of rest, none of the phone company boys on duty relished the idea of calling a third- or fourth-level boss to check further.

He replaced the papers and turned to the manual on his lap, thumbing to the entries for Broadwater County and Missoula. The 580 pages in the binder represented the regional Bell System's most current electronic map and technical specifications, "tech specs," for the north central and mountain regions. RAPTOR was on distribution courtesy of DiGenero's friends at AT&T who had helped him when he was undercover in New York.

Masterson flipped back to the exchange directory under the subheading, "Broadwater Substation, Technical Schematics." The Harris number's three-digit prefix was serviced from the local exchange on Ridgeway Drive, north of Bozeman. Then, he turned to the Missoula entry. The Dupres line ran to the university switching center on Stadium Avenue.

Thank God for computers, Masterson thought. Both local phone companies had ESS, electronic switching systems, not the old-fashioned stepper frames with their spaghettilike wire and mechanical maze of lines and contacts, once the standard equipment. Years ago, he recalled, when the locals still used 1940s technology, wire jobs had been a pain in the ass. In addition to physically connecting the wiretaps to the telephone circuit, the techs had to find a "drop," a listening post, for the position keeper or the recording equipment.

With ESS, all they needed was the documentation, the electronic "maps." Then, they simply tweaked the local company's computer program. It was a two-step process. At the local office, they typed in the target number on the computer, and then added a few lines of software coding to change its service features. The reprogramming electronically earmarked the phone. After that, a call in or out automatically closed a computer circuit, instantly duplicating the signal and forwarding it to a predesignated number. At the listening post, a keeper or the recording equipment did the rest.

Masterson thought ahead. RAPTOR already had a safe house in Missoula and another in Bozeman, where they would route the calls from the new taps. Transcribing the tapes still took time and money, but DiGenero never bitched about the cost. With his experience undercover, Frank knew all about the virtues of soundmen. No muss, no fuss, Masterson smiled to himself with pride, settling back, just a few keystrokes on the computer to "reach out and touch someone."

As Frontier West's Twin Otter lifted off the runway at Salt Lake City into the early Sunday morning sky, a half a world away and nine hours ahead on central European time, sitting in the front seat of a Mercedes station wagon winding through the Bavarian mountains, Kirby Harris knew his dull headache meant he was thoroughly fatigued. He looked at his watch. It was only 2:30 p.m., local time, but neither the Mercedes' windshield wipers nor its headlights could overcome the gloom created by the low mist and patchy fog. The driver, glum and silent, concentrated on his task.

Harris looked out, bleary-eyed. According to the last sign, they were heading toward Holzkirchen, wherever and whatever that was. Since leaving the Munich airport, he figured they had traveled about twenty miles. The twists and dips in the two-lane highway, the cordons of trees on the roadside, and the hanging clouds camouflaged the ascent, but Harris could tell they were climbing steadily.

He leaned back against the headrest and closed his eyes. After Dulles, it had gone without a hitch. Customs at Frankfurt hadn't looked twice at the sleeping falcon, and they'd caught the next Lufthansa flight to Munich without delay. An hour later, Von Biemann's people were waiting. The fact they were Middle East types, not Germans, surprised him. Von Biemann didn't introduce either of the men, he recalled, speaking only a few words to them before they got under way. After twenty-eight sleepless hours, Harris felt his consciousness begin to slip. He propped himself against the door and almost immediately started to doze.

The bump jarred Harris hard. The Mercedes had turned off the highway onto a crushed-stone road. The BMW sedan, the second car that had met them at the Munich airport, was a few yards behind. In the seconds before the foliage swallowed his view, Harris could see they'd just passed under an entry arch. On either side, a long, gray stone wall threaded through the trees. Ahead, the narrow drive inclined steeply into the woods.

Von Biemann had awoken in the rear seat, "How are you, Kirby?"

"Where are we?" Harris peered around at the dense forest, trying to crane the stiffness from his neck.

"About fifty miles from Munich, really only about thirty-five miles as the crow flies, at my home. Überspitzensee. The manor house is on top of the mountain. From there, we have a marvelous view of the Inn River. We're very close to the Austrian border. Between Überspitzensee and Innsbruck, the river valley is beautiful for us and for the birds."

"How is she?" Harris thought of the falcon.

"Fine, I'm sure," Von Biemann answered. Harris glanced at the station wagon's rear cargo space. The top was off the peregrine's traveling box. She lay quiet, unmoving, on her back.

He felt the road level at the crest. A grassy clearing widened on either side, pushing back the pines. The house, a lodge more than a manor, lay before them. It was impressive nonetheless. The same natural fieldstone as in the perimeter wall had been fitted by a craftsman's hand to create the first story. The second floor was dressed, alpine-style, in dark, weathered wood and stucco. The cedar shingle roof hung over the windows, which were each divided into a diamond pattern of leaded panes.

Harris climbed from the car and stretched. The low clouds seemed to press downward with a damp chill. Through the mist, he could see several outbuildings. He imagined one was probably a caretaker's cottage, and the others a stable or barn and, of course, a falcon house. Behind the meadow, where the fog took over, the land seemed to fall away, rolling toward the river. That would be the open space where she'd train, Harris thought. The river would be a natural attraction for the peregrine, reminding her of home on Sixteen.

Harris turned. The two drivers, Arabs or whatever they were, watched him with fixed, malevolent stares.

Von Biemann sounded unnaturally cheerful, "Let me show you your room. You need some rest."

The suggestion made Harris look toward the house. A motion in one of the second-floor windows caught his eye, as if the curtains had been pushed aside momentarily and then allowed to fall back.

Von Biemann put his hand on Harris's elbow, guiding him toward the manor, attempting to keep the nonexistent conversation alive, "Come now, we'll take good care of the falcon."

"Right," Harris said, glancing back. The two drivers still watched sullenly. It made him feel uneasy and then, for a fleeting instant, threatened and angry.

Harris frowned, trying to dismiss the thought. He was tired, overreacting. That's all. A cold rain started to fall. A half pace behind, the German seemed to hurry him along. Von Biemann clapped him on the shoulder and laughed, "And, don't worry, Kirby, my friend. We're going to take good care of you, too."

Part Two

Jihad

9

Sunday, August 26, 1984

The Thomasbraukeller, Darmstadt, West Germany

Detective Sergeant Otto Kramer, Homicide Division, Frankfurt office, West German Federal Police, was finishing a door-to-door neighborhood canvass at the end of a long and frustrating day when the bartender told him that the man in his picture, along with a woman, had entered the pub around 7:00 p.m. the previous Friday night. The police veteran looked up from his small leather notebook and smiled. Bonn was on their back and after a week of combing the suburban Frankfurt districts with double shifts and extra manpower, by rights, they should have found more. Instead, they had only scraps and theory. The bartender's memory was Kramer's first hit in six 12-hour days of nonstop questioning.

They'd found the body in the charred remains of the Opel on Monday morning, August 20, on a small dirt road near Kaiserslauten. It was badly burned, but the police report prepared half a day later, based on the autopsy, detailed the head wound, cuts, and broken bones. The bureaucratic battle over the case had taken another day as his superiors "consulted." Kramer didn't care, but others above him in the criminal investigation department who worried about such things never liked to share authority over a homicide case by asking the public prosecutor's office, the responsible agency for internal security and international matters, for help.

Kramer settled down on the high stool, hooking his heels over its well-worn lower rungs, "What do you recall?"

The old man rested his belly against the working side of the highly polished oak bar and scratched his head. His accent was Schwabian and country, but his age and hands suggested Stuttgart, factories and steel. "They sat close together in the far corner booth, ordered brandies, and left after an hour."

"Friday's a busy night, I'm sure," Kramer nodded. "What makes them stand out in your mind?"

The bartender shook his head, "Oh, not so busy. This week, yes, with the end of the summer holidays, but last week..."

The detective broke in gently, interrupting the digression, "What was it that seemed different about them?"

The bartender pointed unconsciously toward the far booth, "Well, the man's hair. It was cut close, like the Americans'." Kramer nodded. Rhine-Main Air Base, next to Frankfurt International Airport, was only twenty minutes away on the Autobahn. GIs stationed there as well as passing through were common in Darmstadt's working-class neighborhood. "But," the bartender continued, "it was odd because he was obviously an Arab, a Turk or some other Middle East sort."

"What about the woman?" Kramer interjected.

"Very pretty," the bartender rubbed his chin. "German, naturally, somewhere in her late twenties, long, straight, blond hair. Maybe a university girl, maybe not."

"Clothes?" Kramer looked up from his notes.

"Leather jacket, turtleneck sweater, and blue jeans."

"Is that all?"

The old man grinned lasciviously, "Covering a beautiful ass."

"That should narrow it down," Kramer smiled briefly. "Were they regular customers?" The question interrupted the older man's phlegmy chuckle.

"No, but strangers aren't unusual. We're so close to Frankfurt and Rhine-Main..."

The detective waved his hand, acknowledging that he understood the explanation, "Is that all?"

The old man nodded. Kramer continued to write, finishing his notes. The bartender glanced down self-consciously. Kramer's handwriting was small and precise, the script of someone used to recording details in a way that later would not be lost to memory or confused.

The detective rose, slipping the notebook and pen into his breast pocket and placing a business card on the bar, "If you think of anything else, please call me."

The bartender straightened and bowed slightly. The policeman's curt nod of thanks ended the interview without leaving any clues about why

the authorities were interested. The bartender fingered the card, holding
its edges in both hands. In the few moments before Kramer reached the
door, he thought about asking but didn't. Curiosity aside, it wasn't a German custom to question the police.

The bartender's description of the man who passed the hour in his pub
the week before was more accurate than he realized. On Friday, August
17, Staff Sergeant Ali bin Sa'al, communications specialist first class, Royal
Air Force of the Kingdom of Saudi Arabia, in fact, had visited the barbershop at the Rhine-Main Noncommissioned Officer's Club for the standard military trim. Since July, Ali's small training group in the technical
school at the American air base had convened on the 6:00 a.m.-to-12:00
noon classroom shift. On Fridays, after a stroll through the base exchange
and a stop next door to reserve his usual two-door Opel at the rent-a-car
concession, he had time for a leisurely shave, haircut, and manicure before the short drive to Dieburg, and his meeting with Ingred at her flat.

That chilly Friday, Ali bin Sa'al enjoyed the warmth of the overheated
barbershop. It was his first and only German summer, and in the damp,
sunless weather he often dreamed of Jidda's welcome blanket of heat and
humidity. But even when the dreary climate brought thoughts of home,
Ali also knew he was lucky to have been chosen, along with two others,
from the fifty final candidates for the special course at the American technical school.

He had wondered at first. When they visited the American embassy
in Riyadh, he remembered the American Air Force captain who had taken
them past the Marine guard to the doorway marked "Mutual Defense
Assistance Office." The forms, swearing his secrecy about the course,
were a peculiar custom, but he'd signed, promising on paper to protect
what he learned about the "operations and maintenance of the AN/APQ
25/26 Cryptocompatible Transceiver." It seemed odd, Ali recalled, until
his first day in the windowless classroom at Rhine-Main, when the American colonel welcomed them and spoke.

He was a thin man, more schoolmasterly than military, wearing a
uniform slightly too big for him, and he began reading, head down, from
notes, "Because of the American commitment to Arabia's security and
our close bonds of friendship, the president has authorized the deploy-

ment of an operational AN/APQ 25/26, expressly for King Zahel's use. It is the only such unit, beside the president's own. It will enable the king to communicate with his high command to protect Arabia's security, and to authorize emergency military action instantly and securely."

Lieutenant Colonel Harry Martin, United States Air Force, senior technical training officer attached to the White House Communications Agency, looked up, appearing to smile, and cleared his throat. Martin loved his work, high-tech equipment, teaching about communications, and the opportunity for the secret, temporary duty assignment to train the Saudis in Germany, but he hated giving speeches, even in front of three foreign NCOs. "I would like to congratulate you. Your government has chosen you as the specialists who will maintain this very important piece of equipment," he sighed tremulously, pleased that the worst was over, folded his notes, and removed his glasses.

Martin reached beneath the podium and retrieved a leather briefcase. He placed it on the classroom table in front of the three Saudi NCOs, "This is the AN/APQ 25/26." He began to talk again, this time more casually, "It's the latest version of the president's own 'football,' the attaché case–sized communications system that is never more than a few paces from our Commander-in-Chief." The colonel rested his palm on the brief-case, "The unit is one-of-a-kind, with a unique purpose: to link the pres-ident to the military commanders who can launch missiles and planes in a retaliatory strike if the United States comes under nuclear attack."

He paused to open the case, plainly more relaxed in his teaching role. "What we have here is a specially designed IBM 2512J microcomputer combined with triple-redundant, miniaturized, high-frequency voice and signal radio circuitry. The combination gives us a state-of-the-art secure communication system." The colonel snapped on the nearby overhead projector, laying a transparent slide in place. A stick-figure schematic di-agram appeared on the small screen behind him.

He glanced back at the depiction, pleased with the effect, and tele-scoped his pocket pointer to full length. "It's really very simple." Colonel Martin stepped to the screen and tapped at the diagram, "A signal from a transmitter at a military command center here activates the AN/APQ 25/26's microcomputer. The signal directs the software program's choice of cryptographic codes. The signal is real time and constant, allowing the command center to continuously alter the encryption used by the AN/APQ 25/26's radio transmitter/receiver."

He flipped a new slide in place on the viewgraph projector, pointing this time on the screen to the comic-book figures surrounding the AN/APQ 25/26. "The result is that this system allows the operator of the AN/APQ 25/26 to send a message without any additional steps to encrypt it. Because the remote radio signal controls the automatic encryption, the operator needs only to type his message on the units keyboard in clear text. He doesn't need to code. It's done for him."

Ali watched the pointer slide across the screen. "More important, however," the colonel continued, tapping at the box labeled military command center, "the recipients here do not need to authenticate the message from the AN/APQ 25/26. They control the code. Therefore, they are not required to double-check its messages in order to determine whether the orders are legitimate, and actually from the top of the chain of command. And, because AN/APQ 25/26 sends its messages in burst transmissions, flashes of highly compressed coded data using randomly selected frequencies that the command center's signal also controls, it is impossible to intercept or to jam along the way. Gentlemen," Colonel Harry Martin telescoped his pointer closed with a sharp snap and smiled, "it is quick, secure, and most importantly, foolproof."

Ali bin Sa'al smiled back, although for a different reason. The Saudi staff sergeant was marveling at another unique, and for him, very personal feature of the AN/APQ 25/26—the fact that it was about to transform him, the fifth generation in a family of modest shopkeepers from the Jidda bazaar, into a member of the Arabian court who would travel with the king and his successors for as long as he served. Praise Allah, he thought fervently. Life was good.

Shortly after 4:30 p.m. that Friday, as Ali bin Sa'al nudged his Opel rent-a-car into the traffic leaving the air base, blond, blue-eyed Ingred Werner stepped from the tub in her small Dieberg flat and began to run her soft, heavy towel over the upturn of her breasts, down her flat, hard stomach, and along the soft curve of her inner thigh. She straightened, pirouetting to slightly more than her five-foot-seven height to examine herself in the mirror. She smiled, pleased, slipped on her robe, and lit a cigarette.

She had an hour to herself before Ali would appear. Their date was set for 5:30 p.m., as it had been every Friday for the last three weeks. The routine was all too predictable, she thought. She would strip, undress and fondle him with feigned enthusiasm, and then let him climb on her for what was always a quick and breathless act. Ingred Werner had nothing against sex. Quite the opposite. It was just that, oddly, the three other Arabs before Ali from the NCO club had all been the same. She walked to the window and peered out to examine the rain. Perhaps it was a national trait.

It had taken her almost a month to locate the right one in the right class, but when she did Ali's eagerness to impress her made up for lost time. In fact, she thought, he'd made it quite easy, telling her about the special training course their first night. The next evening, after she received the approval from Munich, they took a cab to the flat. That was two weeks ago. Now, the pattern was set.

The phone rang once. She glanced at the clock. The call was on time, precisely 5:00 p.m. Ingred lifted the handset and listened without speaking, "Darmstadt. 8:00 p.m." The click followed promptly as the line went dead.

She replaced the receiver and walked to the small armoire, the only closet in the one-room flat, checking the drawers and hanging space to make sure they were empty. Except for the clothes she was going to wear that evening, they were. She paused, examining for a final time the tabletops and counters in the cheap room for any other personal items. The waiting had been rather dull since they'd received the approval, although the evening promised to make up for the boredom. In any case, she mused as she brushed her hair, it would be their last date.

As the bartender remembered, Ingred Werner and Ali bin Sa'al walked out of the Darmstadt pub, arm in arm, precisely at 8:00 p.m. The two brandies had warmed Ali, but the glow was short-lived in the cold darkness of the rain-blackened pavement and high brick walls that absorbed the light from the few unshuttered windows and the single, distant overhead lamp. They turned at the corner where Ali had left the Opel, thirty yards distant. He glanced ahead into the gloom of the narrow alley that bordered the pub. The side street was empty except for a black Mercedes that had parked behind the rent-a-car, half on the cobblestones and half over the curb.

A few steps from the Opel, Ali felt Ingred touch his lapel.

"One kiss," her voice was mellow. He stopped, half-turning toward her as she raised her face toward his, lips parted. As Ali bent his head, her hand followed a downward path from his lapel, moving softly across

his chest to his stomach and then between his legs. It held his attention
as the doors of the Mercedes sedan behind him flew open.

The viselike grip wrenched Ali's head back just at the moment the
truncheon slammed into his right kidney. He choked on his scream. As
intended, the pain from the smashing blow shot up and down his side,
twisting him sharply to the right. With his head locked by powerful arms,
it produced a hideous contortion that drew his knees up, pulling his feet
off the ground, and half-suspending him in the air. It was a fetal position, ideal for the two men who jammed him, head first, through the
open car door.

Ali's face, now also turned to the right, slid across the seat, slamming
hard against the opposite door. The warm blood and searing pain were a
counterpoint of sensations as the window crank tore a gash in his left
cheek, cracking the bone. For a futile instant, Ali tried to move his hands
against the heavy weight of the body that pinned them behind him. Then,
in the core of his brain, the knowledge that he was helpless combined
with the agony to overcome his shock and confusion. Ali exhaled a howl,
but it was too late for any assistance to matter. In less than a second, a
chloroformed rag muffled the yell as well as his consciousness.

Long before he fully awoke, Ali felt cold, terribly cold. His left eye
was swollen shut from the deep cut and broken cheekbone, but he could
see enough with the other to make him cry. He was naked, tied with
insulated telephone wire around his wrists and ankles on a wire bedspring
that rested at a forty-five-degree angle against the wall. The room, a cellar or basement, was gray-green and damp. It was dark except for the
small, ice-white circle of light from the bare bulb suspended above him.

Ali bin Sa'al focused on the two men who sat before him at the perimeter of the light. Both were hooded like fedayeen and wore American
Army fatigue jackets. He closed his one good eye. His body trembled
uncontrollably. The rattle of his breath and his sobs were the only sounds.

"You should not have resisted," the words were Arabic but the voice
was German. One of the pair stood. He was indistinguishable from the
other except for the piercing blue behind the two eyeholes in the knit
mask.

"No, no," Ali began to deny the accusation and then stopped. He
had not resisted, but he was lucid enough to realize that an argument
had no point.

"We know who you are, what you do, and why you are studying at the American air base. We need only a little information and then we will let you go. You do not know us and we do not want you. Tell us what we must know and it will all be over soon."

"Please...," Ali begged, but the blue eyes interrupted his soft whine. "Answer the questions and it will all be over soon." Even with the school-masterlike repetition of the instructions, the voice was not unkind. It had an even, almost clinical tone.

At first, Ali answered the questions truthfully, describing the AN/APQ 25/26 and its standard radio transceiver functions in simple detail. An hour had passed by the time they began to ask about its special coded transmissions. Ali had no doubt this was what they wanted, and he had regained sufficient composure to attempt some feeble evasions of their questions. They listened to his answers for ten minutes, asking him for information slowly, methodically, and without emotion. Then, the interrogation paused. Both men stepped back into the darkness. Ali could hear their whispers, but not their words.

When the two returned to the light, the blue-eyed questioner folded his arms, and spoke. His voice was cold and low, "You are not cooperating as we asked. That is wrong and we cannot tolerate it. We don't have the time." There was something final in the words.

"Please. I'll try. I...," Ali's request hung in the air, but the German had turned away. He spoke quietly to the other man, who moved a small table next to the bed frame from its place in the darkness beyond the light of the bare bulb. Terror made Ali's body jerk spasmodically when he saw the long straight razor and the liter bottle. For a few seconds, the fear served as a kind of powerful anesthetic, numbing the first long searing cut that laid open the skin, fat, and muscle from his chest to his groin. But when the sulfuric acid started to run in rivulets through the wound, Ali began a terrible, unending scream.

It took them three hours. By the end, Ali was breathing in short, shallow pants, on the edge of consciousness, but he was still able to feel her touch. His eyes opened, focusing slowly on Ingred. She stood next to him, the softness of her palm against his cheek.

"It's all right," her voice was quiet and soothing. He could understand the words and see her smile. She moved her hand in front of his face, beckoning him with a slow, gentle motion to raise his head. She would untie him. It was over. Ali leaned forward from the bed frame. As he did, the silencer on the .32-caliber Beretta made a sound like the popping of a pellet gun releasing its compressed air. Ali didn't hear the noise or, after his ordeal, even feel the bullet as it entered his neck to explode the medulla at the base of his skull. But in the microsecond after his heart and lungs stopped and before his last darkness fell, his one good eye did see the smile on Ingred's face turn to a sneer.

At 7:15 p.m. that Sunday, as Detective Sergeant Kramer pulled onto the Autobahn and accelerated, returning to his office in Frankfurt, Rajid Musaani stood by the window, watching the rain drum down on Überspitzensee's already rich green meadow. The water was puddling now, covering the crushed-stone drive. The rain had grown steadier since midafternoon when Von Biemann had arrived with Harris and the falcon.

As the twilight deepened, the scene in the great room behind Musaani reflected in the window in increasingly fine detail. They all were close to the fire. Seated on the hearth beside Erique Von Biemann, Klaus's younger brother, her long, blond hair half-covering her shoulders, Ingred Werner stood out. Klaus was standing nearby, sipping a drink. Muhammed, one of the two Iranians who had driven Von Biemann and Harris from the airport, was in the hall, watching Harris's second-floor bedroom door. Musaani had assigned Kamal, the other, to walk perimeter security.

Musaani turned, glancing at Klaus. He looked tired. The delivery of the falcon had gone well. So, it would appear, had the operation in Frankfurt. His connection with the German radicals had paid extraordinary dividends, Musaani thought, self-satisfied. Nine months ago, the Baader-Meinhof hit team had shot the American major in Wiesbaden simply as their own political statement. On the evening before he died, however, the American had idly told Ingred about the Saudis who were scheduled for a special training course at Rhine-Main. Naturally, Musaani's German "friends" knew then that he and Tehran would be interested. Allah be praised, Musaani smiled to himself. No one had any idea at the time just how important that information would be.

He walked toward the group. In the large arched fireplace, the dry logs snapped, throwing tracerlike sparks against the screen. The fire backlit the curves outlined by the clinging black silk of Ingred's dress. She could have stepped into an advertisement for expensive clothing or fine jewelry in any exclusive magazine or, based on what Von Biemann had said about her performance in bed, into a starring role in any hard-core porno movie. It was curious, Musaani thought, that she was so homicidal. Killing, it seemed, gave her more pleasure than sex.

Musaani listened for a moment to her voice, rather than her words. The Bavarian accent made even hard German consonants sound casually sensual, "We could go down to the river."

"True," Erique Von Biemann said, nodding. His blue eyes shone, "The current usually runs between ten and fifteen kilometers an hour. It can move whatever floats to the Danube in a few days."

Despite his lack of attention to the conversation, Musaani knew the subject without even asking.

"The river's a good choice," Ingred continued. "It would be ideal if the Austrians got involved. They would need weeks in order to check identities in their own records, as well as with the Germans and the Swiss."

Musaani walked slowly toward the small, carved bar to pour another cognac. The paper-thin crystal gave a pure, high chime as the glass lightly touched the decanter. He swirled the rich amber, letting its bouquet fill the snifter.

Ingred spoke, "And, no matter who's involved, the longer it takes, the harder it is to determine the how and the why. Natural means would minimize the risks. A few days at most in the water are all one would need to feel relatively safe about the results of any examination and inquiries."

Musaani shook his head. His unaccented German was flawless, "Not necessarily so. There is a trail, however slight, that leads here. It could be considerably more distinct if time does not work in our favor—for example, if a discovery is made after only a day or two, and if the identification is quick."

"I wonder," Ingred said, taking obvious issue with his implied caution. "Accidents happen all the time. Even if a discovery is made in a day, five or ten kilometers from here, there still will be more questions than answers about where and when it occurred, not to mention who it is."

"That's true, I suppose," Musaani spoke slowly, with a purposefully dispassionate analytic detachment. "Nevertheless, we would be leaving our fate to the river. Let's say a discovery is made a few kilometers downstream. There is little access to the Inn except from the handful of private estates in this area. The police would have no trouble in determining where the accident could have occurred. And, if for some reason an identification followed, the inquiries could focus here quite easily. It's not certain, maybe not even likely, but it is possible."

"I think there are too many ifs to convince me that it would be a problem," she said. Musaani shrugged his shoulders, diplomatically ignoring her sarcasm. He walked to the raised hearth and turned, standing beside Ingred's seated figure with his back to the flames. The radiant heat curled upward behind him, carrying the sensual fragrance of her cologne.

She glanced up at Musaani, her voice betraying her irritation, "What difference does it make where we kill him? We're not amateurs. We can make sure he's not found."

"It makes a difference," Musaani said categorically. "There can be no tie between any element in our operation and the revolution. None. That is why Harris's trip was so important. The official documents recording the peregrine's export from the United States are in the American's name. If by chance someone stumbles on the falcon's role, the bird cannot be traced to us. There is no point in taking such care if we then make ourselves more vulnerable by eliminating Harris here. He has a passport with a German entry stamp, airline tickets that take him to Munich, perhaps people who will remember him at the airport getting in a car with Klaus and my men. We do not want to chance that connection."

Ingred waved her hand, dismissing the argument, "Harris was an opportunity when you needed a falcon. Now, he's a risk. Today, tomorrow, next week? It doesn't matter? I say do it now. Get rid of him."

"Really?"

"Of course," she said impatiently. She drained her brandy glass and handed it to Erique who dutifully rose to refill it.

"Hmmm," Musaani looked down at her and then at Klaus, who had followed the path taken by his eyes. "We do have a problem, don't we?" His gaze held Von Biemann's as he continued, "To be sure, we always knew we would need to eliminate our identifiable risks." Musaani paused, "This is one case in point. On that, I think we can agree." Klaus nodded

impassively. Ingred glanced up. Musaani smiled, reaching to gently brush
the curve of blond hair that lay across her shoulder, "I think this discussion has convinced me that perhaps we should take care of it sooner rather
than later."

Harris opened his eyes and looked at his watch. 6:30 a.m., Monday. He'd
dozed off-and-on yesterday afternoon, had a drink and dinner with Von
Biemann and his acquaintances late in the evening, and returned to bed.
After sleeping most of the night, he thought, his body finally felt like it
had caught up with his mind.

He rose and walked to the window, pushing open the leaded frame.
The air was cool, almost cold, and the rain was gone, leaving behind a
clear, bright morning. Wide awake, Harris rubbed the stubble of his beard.
The bathroom, his shaving kit, and the shower were down the hall. It
was time to use all three and pretend that he was a human being again,
he thought.

Harris began to turn away when the motion in the distance, along
the tree line, caught his eye. He had to look twice before he saw the man
partially hidden in the deep morning shadows. He thought hard for a
moment, trying to pierce the haze of time zones and fatigue clouding his
recollection. Was it yesterday, last night, or this morning? Then, suddenly, the memory came back.

He'd risen and wandered to the window twice when jet lag and rest-
lessness drove him to toss and turn more than sleep, once yesterday afternoon and once after midnight, when the moonlight had replaced the
rain. Harris recalled his surprise, especially last night, when he saw someone, too far away to recognize, but there all the same.

Harris stepped to one side of the window, out of the direct line of
sight. As before, this morning the man was walking the edge of the open
meadow. He hadn't been sure yesterday, in the rain and then later in the
dark, but now he could see the weapon clearly, a carbine or an automatic, cradled in the sentry's arms. Yesterday afternoon and again last
night, more awake than asleep, Harris remembered, he'd watched for a
while. The pattern hadn't varied. The figure had passed the same point
three times at twenty-minute intervals.

He stepped from the window and sat on the edge of the bed, thinking. "Perimeter security," Harris muttered. But twenty-four-hour perimeter security? In the middle of Bavaria? On a family estate? Why? And, he scratched his head, that wasn't all. The guy in the hall, one of the two drivers. He was there, watching, at 9:00 last night, when he'd gone down for dinner, and again at 3:00 a.m., when he'd gotten up to take a leak. Who was he watching? His bedroom wasn't the only one on the second floor. They were all there. And, there was a second way down, a servants' stairs, at the far end of the hall. But his door was the first, the one closest to the landing, the only one that could be seen from the foot of the stairs.

Harris shrugged. He still needed the shave, shower, and even more than that, some coffee. He rose again and began to turn toward the door when the thought struck him. The last strange piece in the puzzle. Von Biemann's "friends." He'd met them at dinner last night. His brother and the blond, Ingred, seemed to belong. But the other, the business acquaintance, the Iranian, was odd, out of place. Somehow, Harris thought, with the Arabs, Von Biemann's clientele, lined up on the side of Baghdad in the war, the Iranian didn't fit politically, especially if the German had just jumped through hoops to put together a world-beating deal with the Arabian king. He frowned as he stepped into the hall, vaguely uneasy as well as dissatisfied with his own deductions. One thing was certain. He'd feel better on his own turf. He needed to find Von Biemann, the other half of his $75,000, and a plane ride home.

Thirty minutes later, in the great room, Harris found the full carafe of fresh coffee warming beside the plate of newly baked pastries on the bar. He was finishing his second cup when the front door opened and closed. Dressed in a heavy turtleneck sweater, rough tweed pants, and hiking boots, Von Biemann entered the room.

"Kirby, I hope you slept well."

"You look like a refugee from a Bavarian travel poster," Harris said.

Von Biemann laughed. He walked to the bar and poured some coffee, "I must show you Überspitzensee today. You've given me your hospitality many times in five years. I've waited too long to pay you back. Now it's my turn."

"I really should get home. The longer I hang around, the more it cuts into my profit margin."

Von Biemann smiled, "It's on me. Besides, I want you to meet some clients of mine, outside Bonn. I've delivered several of your birds to them in the past. They're planning to begin a breeding project that will mean large orders. We have competition, but I've assured them that I can offer the best from North America, and that you'll be my supplier."

"I don't know, Klaus."

"Humor me," Von Biemann said, clapping him on the shoulder. "It's only a one-day trip. You can relax today, fly to Bonn tomorrow, spend a day, come back on Wednesday, and be home by the weekend. Is that too much to ask?"

For a moment, Harris wondered. There was no question he wanted out of here. Von Biemann's earlier case of nerves, the guards, and the Iranian convinced him of that. In itself, the Bonn visit was plausible and from the sound of it more than an offhand idea. Von Biemann wouldn't be easily dissuaded. If something was off-key, he thought, this far from home wasn't the place to argue. "OK," Harris forced a smile. "Just for you."

Slightly less than twenty-four hours later, the sound of the car door, exaggerated in the still morning air, woke Harris with a start. In the darkness, he pawed on the night table for his watch. 6:00 a.m., Tuesday, August 28. Harris sank back against the deep feather pillow. There were voices downstairs, but he still had a little more time to sleep before he needed to shower, shave, dress, and leave for the airport in Munich.

In the foyer below Harris's room, Ingred stood beside Musaani. Erique walked through the doorway. He had just left the Mercedes, engine running and headlights on, a few yards away on the gravel drive.

"You and Ingred should wait just past the turnoff, where the road divides before reaching the gate and the main highway," Musaani said.

Erique nodded.

"Kamal will be driving him in the BMW. He knows to take the turn-off to the left, and to stop when he sees you," the Iranian continued.

Erique spoke, "Tell Kamal we'll be about fifty meters from where the main drive divides. There shouldn't be any problems. After everything is taken care of, I expect we'll be back around 7:30."

Musaani glanced down at the Walther PPK in Ingred's pocket. The butt of the automatic hung half out of her leather coat. Erique followed the Iranian's eyes. He extended his hand toward Ingred, palm up, and smiled, "My turn."

She frowned petulantly, passing him the pistol. The matte black 9-mm looked smaller in his grasp. Musaani watched the couple walk away before he shut the door behind them. In a matter of seconds, the two car doors had opened and closed. The Iranian caught the sound of the shower in Harris's bathroom at the same moment the low idling rumble of the Mercedes melded with the whine of its first gear and slowly moved away.

"Kamal will take you to the airport in time for a coffee before you catch the Cologne flight, Kirby. A car will meet you in Cologne and drive to our friends' place outside Bonn," Von Biemann said.

Harris tossed his suitbag in the backseat of the BMW. It was 7:00 a.m. and his flight left Munich at 9:00. The driver was the same one who had brought them from the airport. Given the speed of that trip, he thought, there was plenty of time.

"I thought I heard a car earlier," Harris said.

"You did," Von Biemann replied. "Erique and Ingred just went into the village for the mail and some errands."

Harris nodded and climbed into the BMW's front passenger seat as the engine roared to life. Von Biemann saw his hand appear above the roof and wave. He also heard the American's voice, although the motor drowned out the words of farewell as the car accelerated down the drive.

Klaus Von Biemann was jostling the paper and kindling in the fireplace with the poker when he heard the first sharp crack. He looked casually at his watch. 7:05 a.m. He put down the poker and rummaged in the kindling box. The next two shots came in quick succession, their sounds transmitted by the cool morning air with an almost unnatural clarity. One stick was left. He broke it in his hand, jamming the two pieces under the square split logs that had just begun to catch fire. They would need another supply to keep things going, he thought.

Twenty-five minutes later, the crunch of tires on gravel broke the si-

lence. Von Biemann heard the car engine die and a door slam. He turned
at the sound of his brother's footsteps crossing the slate foyer. Erique strode
into the great room, throwing his jacket on a nearby chair. He stopped at
the bar to pour a cup of coffee.

"7:30. Right on time," Erique said.

"Well?"

"It was no trouble, a surprise, as we intended. Musaani instructed
Muhammed to take care of the belongings," Erique continued. "He'll
have it all buried shortly. And I've got the documents. Even if anyone
chooses to look, there are no signs to worry about."

Erique Von Biemann put down his coffee cup and removed a worn
leather wallet from his pocket, handing it to his brother. Klaus turned
back to the fire. He opened the wallet and removed the paper and cards
inside, placing them on the mantel.

Von Biemann paused reflectively, turning the empty wallet in his
hand, "Best be rid of this, too, I think." He tossed it into the flames. The
leather burned slowly, giving off a brown-black smoke. He threw the papers in next, one by one, and finally, the plastic driver's license. The
laminated card caught on its edge, right side up, between two logs, with
the picture facing out. Von Biemann examined it. For a moment, Ingred
Werner's face stared back, framed by her long blond hair. Then, it too
flared and was gone.

Nine hours later, Musaani was seated, legs crossed, in the wing chair,
watching the embers of the fire. The clouds had returned, graying the
late-summer afternoon into the likeness of fall. The shadows outdoors
darkened the great room.

"I could take care of this here," Klaus Von Biemann's tone was matter-
of-fact.

Musaani shook his head, "No."

Von Biemann shrugged. Musaani rose and walked to the fire. He
stirred the ashes and coals idly with the poker before he spoke. "I realize
it's an extra step, but there can be no trace, even indirectly. If Harris
failed to return from Europe, it would be a matter of concern for those
who know him, and almost certainly produce a search. However convenient the current moment, it must occur in the States. I want you to
make the necessary arrangements for the end of next month."

"Next month? Why wait?"

"We might need Harris again before we are through," Musaani replied. "The falcon is an excellent specimen, but we don't control her either. If something happens to the peregrine in training, we would need another quickly. In that event, your connection with Harris allows us to do that as well as gives us the greatest security."

Musaani replaced the poker in its wrought-iron stand, "Given Harris's occupation, I assume it's not unusual for him to be away, out of touch." Von Biemann nodded. Musaani continued, "For a man who lives alone much of the year and flies his own airplane, a disappearance in the American mountains would be unremarkable."

Von Biemann rose from the sofa and walked to the desk. He turned the page of the small leather-bound calendar. "Actually, Canada would be best," Von Biemann said. "I would suggest the last week in September. An order for gyrfalcons would require a trip then. The gyrs will have just arrived from the north. Much later and weather conditions could be too problematic to be certain Harris could fly in," Von Biemann paused, glancing up at Musaani, "or for others to look for him after he did."

"Good," Musaani walked toward the door. "I'll make arrangements for one of our people."

"You may need to consider two."

"Two?" Musaani turned, furrowing his brow quizzically. He paused, thinking out loud, "The woman? Erin? Is that her name? Does she know enough to make it be necessary?"

"I believe so, but I am also thinking of someone else. I have no reason at this point to suspect he knows anything. It is just a possibility. Someone we need to discuss. An old friend of Harris. He stops by to see him occasionally at his ranch. A man named DiGenero. Harris mentioned him a year or so ago in passing. I didn't think it was important until now."

Musaani set his jaw hard, cursing his own failure to interrogate Von Biemann fully on every facet of Harris's background. The German's congenital overconfidence made him cavalier about details. In an operation of this magnitude, you assumed everything was important. There was no room for added risks, new uncertainties, or surprises. Musaani walked back into the great room. He eyed Von Biemann coldly, "And?"

The displeasure was obvious in the Iranian's expression. The Ger-

man had worked with him for too many years not to notice. Von Biemann cleared his throat nervously, "And he also said DiGenero is with
the FBI."

10

Tuesday, August 28, 1984

The University Building, Salt Lake City, Utah

As Mitch Kasiewicz came in, DiGenero waved him to a seat without
looking up. The conference room was windowless, decorated only with a
long wooden table, a collection of seemingly purposely mismatched chairs,
a gray two-drawer safe, and a phone. Kasiewicz eyed the wall clock. 11:30
a.m. DiGenero had been here, door closed, all morning. The atmosphere
was stale, combining the odor of old cigarette smoke, empty coffee cups,
and recycled office air. Across the table, DiGenero was writing, adding
to a list on a long, yellow legal sheet. Between them, the thermofaxed
contents of a 201 file, some papers obviously scattered and discarded and
others neatly piled, reflected an effort to organize, match and compare.

Kasiewicz idly scanned the document on the stack closest to him, waiting for DiGenero to explain the summons. In the upper left-hand corner
of the Xerox copy, the picture was too dark to make out. Kasiewicz was
adept at the investigator's skill, reading desktop papers upside down, but
DiGenero's voice interrupted before he could discern more than the fact
that the form from INS—the Immigration and Naturalization Service—
was dated sometime in 1978.

"OK," DiGenero said, tossing his pencil aside and bending back to
stretch. "You're going to help me figure this out. But you know what?"
DiGenero eyed Kasiewicz with puckish paternalism. "If anybody discov-
ers what we're doing, you're a shoo-in to run the resident agent's office
in Potato City, Idaho, for the rest of your natural life."

"Can I assume that you're trying to suggest delicately that I should
keep my mouth shut?"

DiGenero grinned, spinning the legal pad around and shoving it across the table, "I don't care what anybody else says about you. For a Polack, you're a smart young man."

Kasiewicz examined the first page. It was ruled vertically into two equal columns, one labeled "KVB" and the other "RM." DiGenero had filled the left-hand column with entries in his small, square printing. They created a chronology that began in 1976. His abbreviations, listing dates, places, and airlines in North America and Europe, recorded travels to and from the States.

"KVB is Klaus Von Biemann. He's a connection in the falcon business," DiGenero explained. "This is only the travel we know about in his true name. I'm sure he's done a hell of a lot more under alias. We don't have him cold, but I'd bet my lunch money based on the paper in front of you that he's moved more birds from this part of the country than anyone in the last ten years."

Kasiewicz reread DiGenero's chronology, noting the telltale seasonal pattern of Von Biemann's coming and going. Almost all the trips were in the spring and fall, coinciding with the best trapping periods for falcons. He counted the entries on the list. Two-thirds of the visits to the States included stops in Montana or Utah.

"Hmm," Kasiewicz spoke. "Until the late 1970s, it looks like 'KVB' moved in and out of the country via Detroit and Buffalo. Both are busy, making them easy exit points for contraband. After that, the German switched to New York and Washington. Probably when airline deregulation hit. He must have found better overseas connections."

Kasiewicz looked up, "This is good stuff, but it's circumstantial. What else do we have besides the travel?"

DiGenero reached for the paper beside him. He cleared his throat before starting to read, "Personal history. Bavarian aristocrat. Distantly related to the Hohenzollerns. Two-hundred-year-old family estate," DiGenero tapped the atlas open on the table, "still maintained outside Munich, near the German-Austrian border.

"Father. German diplomat and specialist on Arab affairs who served in various Middle East posts for the foreign ministry before World War II." He paused, looking up. Kasiewicz nodded, acknowledging the Arab connection. "Father arrested and shot by the Gestapo for suspected communist ties in 1945, just before the war ended. One younger brother, Erique. Both educated at Heidelberg in the 1960s. Student activist of left-wing persuasion in the period of Rudie the Red and all that. Since the 1960s, known as well-heeled, not to mention well-to-do. Many avocations but no career.

"Membership in numerous social, philanthropic, and sporting societies including," DiGenero said, slowing his delivery for effect, "Der Deutschen Falken und Jägern Verein."

Kasiewicz cocked an eyebrow, "Der Deutschen what?"

"Falken und Jägern Verein. The German Falcon and Hunters Society." Frank DiGenero smiled, "It's the oldest and most prestigious club for falconers in Germany."

Kasiewicz made a complimentary half bow, "He's made."

"And," DiGenero straightened in his chair, "he's also something else."

"What?"

"He's a terrorist."

DiGenero held up his hand, preempting the question already on Kasiewicz's lips, "A friend of mine in counterterrorism at headquarters called last week and asked me to track Von Biemann. That's why I've got the file."

"Why you?"

"The same reason you're here," DiGenero paused. "Kirby Harris. They turned up his phone number."

Kasiewicz sat back, a glimmer of understanding crossing his face. That connection explained what had happened to Harris's file. "They've got Von Biemann wired," DiGenero continued, "at his place in Bavaria. They know his travel plans and picked up the call to Montana. The counterterrorism group is so screwed up with classifications, compartments, and special clearances that they can't even take a piss without four pounds of paperwork," DiGenero said. "I got the call to run the tail on the German off-line."

DiGenero motioned to turn the page. Kasiewicz read the second legal sheet. It too was ruled down the middle, although the entries, unlike those on page one, filled both columns.

"Who's 'RM?'" Kasiewicz glanced up at DiGenero.

"Rajid Musaani. An Iranian who came here in 1977, enrolled at Berkeley, married, got his green card," DiGenero waved vaguely at the papers spread on the table, "and, evidently has lived in the States ever since."

"What's he doing in Von Biemann's file?"

"I don't know for sure," DiGenero shook his head. "There's one piece of paper under Von Biemann's name that could explain it, an excerpt from a wiretap transcript dated a year ago," DiGenero pointed to a document beside him. "In the phone conversation, Von Biemann mentioned a Musaani, FNU—first name unknown. Since the file system at headquarters automatically cross-references most names, my guess is that Von Biemann's name was recorded in Musaani's file and vice versa. When they printed Von Biemann's records for me, the computer program spit out this stuff on the Iranian. I imagine I'm the first one who ever asked for a hard-copy printout of the German's full file."

Kasiewicz compared the two columns. The record for "RM" and "KVB" on page two began in 1981 and ran through 1984. Kasiewicz counted down the right column. Fourteen entries showed RM's departures from the States for Europe. Each coincided with periods when KVB appeared to be in Germany. He began at the top again, counting ten others that matched RM's return to the States with KVB's arrivals. Kasiewicz ran his finger down the page a third time, tallying RM's remaining trips. There were four—to London, Rome, Athens, and Cairo. All their dates matched KVB's departures to points unknown from Germany.

Kasiewicz looked up. "Anything else?"

"Not much," DiGenero pushed two stacks of paper across the table. "Mostly bait for bottom feeders."

Kasiewicz culled through the documents, reading. When he was finished he sat back and rubbed his eyes. "Musaani's immigration papers, his application for a green card, his college attendance statements that kept his earlier student visa in good standing, and a couple of reports on his contacts in San Francisco with some Arabian prince who got a one-time surveillance from the Secret Service to see if he needed personal security protection."

Kasiewicz paused, "I don't know, Frank. You've obviously got two guys who've moved in the same orbit for years. But even if one is a terrorist suspect, you can't prove much based on the fact that they may have been in Europe and the States at the same time. Besides, immigration records are flaky. Who knows how many resident alien "Musaanis" live in the States. Maybe there's a hundred of them running around the world peddling rugs. God knows how many times their entries and exits got posted in the INS computer under the wrong names."

"So, you wouldn't pursue it?"

Kasiewicz knew the tone of DiGenero's question implied a warning to look before leaping to any conclusions, "What else you got, Frank?"

DiGenero slid the papers across the table, "Try this."

Kasiewicz examined the three parchmentlike thermofax copies. They were INS Form 111s, the Annual Status Verification for Permanent Resident Aliens, for 1982, 1983, and 1984. Musaani's name and 201 file number were typed in the upper right-hand corner. Kasiewicz flipped through them, checking each. They'd been completed properly, on time, recording Musaani's location as the law required every year.

"So?"

"Where were they filed?" DiGenero asked.

Kasiewicz looked down, "Two in San Francisco and one, in January 1984, at the American Consulate General in Munich. But Frank, that's not going to do you much good. You've got a traveling Iranian, a German, and a big goddamn city in Bavaria. This guy, Musaani, is on the road and files his annual INS registration from Germany. So what?"

"Keep looking, sport."

Kasiewicz frowned for a moment before the fine print on the bottom line caught his eye. The instructions were half-obscured under the American vice consul's notary stamp. "Respondents completing Form 111 outside the United States or its possessions who will be abroad for at least 30 days must provide a local address and telephone number in the event the data recorded above requires subsequent verification." Musaani had complied, penning "Kurhotel Sonnenbauer, Prien, Bavaria," and "33-24-90-33" in the blanks provided for street, city, and phone.

"A local address and telephone. So?"

DiGenero shook his head in mock disgust, "Keep looking."

Kasiewicz read the form from top to bottom three times before it finally caught his eye. The phone number of the American consulate, "22-98-00," was stamped along with its address in the space provided for the location of the "INS Office of Record." He glanced down at Musaani's phone number and then back at the number for the consulate at the top of the form.

"Musaani's phone number has some extra digits. An area code? Gimme Von Biemann's file."

DiGenero passed the folder. Kasiewicz flipped quickly through the

loose papers until he found the copy of Von Biemann's latest visa application. It was dated six months ago: a commercial visa at the American
Consulate General in Munich. He had listed his occupation as "art
dealer." Engrossed, Kasiewicz read the final line on the short application
aloud, "visa applicant's residence and residence telephone—Überspitzensee, Bavaria 3-11, telephone, 33-24-82-12."

"Where's Prien?" Kasiewicz asked.

"Five miles from Überspitzensee," DiGenero smiled. "Funny thing
for Musaani's hotel to have an area code and local exchange prefix the
same as Von Biemann's old homestead, isn't it?"

"Yeah," Kasiewicz nodded, "it's just funny as hell."

DiGenero stood, collecting the papers and stuffing them loosely into
a manila folder. "Harris is gone, Von Biemann is nowhere to be found,
and I haven't the faintest goddamn idea what the Iranian has to do with
any of this. I want you to go to Bozeman and find out when, where, and
how Harris and the German beat feet, OK?"

Kasiewicz asked, "Today?"

"Today." DiGenero's voice stopped him before he'd even reached the
door, "And, remember..."

"Yeah?" Kasiewicz turned, his hand resting on the knob, to see Di-
Genero's perversely solicitous smile.

"Potato City ain't even nice in the spring."

DiGenero heard the telltale sound of wax paper crinkling in the background. His call had caught Stockman eating his bologna with mustard
on Wonder bread at his desk, his unchanging daily sacrament and lunch-
time locale. DiGenero looked at his watch. It was noon in Salt Lake,
2:00 p.m. in Washington. Eddie was behind his usual schedule. "Eddie,"
he said, "I've got to talk to you."

A light belch broke the silence after DiGenero finished what he had
to say. It had been obvious that Stockman wasn't pleased even before
he'd completed making his request.

"You know, Frank, this is Alice in Wonderland," Stockman spoke
slowly. "I called you last week for a favor. You tried to give me some
help, but we lost the German. He's a smart son of a bitch. What can I
say? Don't get me wrong. I appreciate what you were willing to do. But

now, you shuffle some papers, play Dick Tracy, and want me to send you a file on some Iranian who you think is a crazy." DiGenero sighed and leaned back, putting his feet on the small table next to the secure phone in the commo center.

Stockman continued, "I could get in big trouble. This Iranian is not even in my territory. If he's on anybody's list here, he belongs to the Middle East ops section. They could hang me by the balls if they found out I'd given you that kind of compartmented information on Von Biemann, but on the raghead? Jesus...'"

"Eddie," DiGenero tried to interrupt. Stockman was speaking faster, winding himself up, "Do you know what that kind of security violation could do to me? Jesus, I'm probably already a couple inches off the ground."

"Eddie, look, I think I'm on to something that overlaps with my operation here. The German is a smuggler. I'm dead certain of that. Maybe it's his way to make a buck. Maybe it's his cover. All I know is that we have a connection with an Iranian who's not in the falcon trade. That leads me to believe either he could be buying and selling birds, which makes him my property, or he could be someone you should follow. Any way you cut it, we need to get on the case."

"Tell me, who in the hell is running what operation?" Stockman interjected. "You're in Salt Lake City on some birdwatchers' undercover, right? I'm here in this goddamn puzzle palace chasing crazies, right? With all due respect, Frank, maybe you should do your thing and I should do mine. I got kids in college, a couple years before a pension, and I need the money. They don't pay this good on the North Loading Dock. That's where we're going if we begin making our own rules so that you and I can save the world."

DiGenero shook his head. He was losing it. "OK, Eddie, OK. Just tell me what you can do for me. If you can't send me Musaani's file, what help can you give me?"

DiGenero waited out the silence, demarcated finally by Stockman's audible groan. "I'll put you on the alert network."

"What the fuck is that?" DiGenero frowned.

"You'll get the TAMs, the Terrorism Alert Messages. I can dummy up some cockamamy excuse for adding your undercover to the addressee group based on Von Biemann's trip last week. The messages are warnings, heads-up telexes. We send them to the field offices and resident

agents around the country. The word goes out whenever we have information that a suspect is on the move, or a terrorist operation may be
going down."

"That's wonderful, but what good is that going to do me?"

"For one thing, it's going to get you off my back," Stockman retorted.
"Look, Von Biemann is on the watch list. For all I know, this Iranian
may be too. When they travel and we know about it, you'll get a message. It'll tell you they're moving and whether they're coming to your
neck of the woods. The alert messages also have some background information on suspects so that the local offices involved in their cases can
update the files with the latest intelligence as soon as we have it. The
cables don't have all the details that we have here—we paraphrase the
sensitive stuff to protect the sources. But they'll give you most of it. The
TAMs are produced on a twenty-four-hour-a-day, seven-day-a-week ba-
sis and sent 'Immediate.' You can bet on getting rousted out of bed more
times than you like." Stockman paused. "Frank, it may not be what you
want, but it's the best I can do."

DiGenero hung up, left the communications room, walked slowly
back to his office, and closed the door. Von Biemann's folder lay on his
desk where he'd left it, under the yellow legal pad. He lifted the phone
and dialed Harris's number, but there was no answer. There hadn't been
for four days. He replaced the receiver and sat back, thinking. At least he
had a few angles to play. The soundmen had stopped by on Monday
morning to confirm that the wires had gone in without a hitch, giving
him a way to know now what Harris wouldn't tell him. Kasiewicz also
was on the road. Mitch was thorough and smart. The exercise with Von
Biemann's file proved that. He'd learn what he could in Bozeman.

All that, DiGenero thought, was the "good news." He flipped idly
through the legal sheets that were covered in his own hand. On the other
side of the ledger, he thought, whoever the German and the Iranian were,
nothing altered the fact that Harris was involved in the bird trade and
that he'd gone ahead with his trip despite the warning last weekend. Kirby
was Kirby. He did it his way. Harris wouldn't run scared because you
jumped out from around the corner and yelled, "Boo!" Now, however,
he wasn't shaking his bag of bones just because of RAPTOR. DiGenero
sighed and picked up the phone. All of this only demonstrated one of the
eternal verities: inside every little problem, there was always a bigger problem trying to get out.

He knew the Western Airlines number and its flight schedules by heart. The recording asked him to hold for the first available agent before it switched to canned music. DiGenero didn't even hear the tinny strings, or realize that their rendition of last year's hit movie theme had ended after only the first bars.

"Western reservations. May I help you?" The commercially cheerful female voice snapped DiGenero out of his reflection. He booked a seat on the 2:00 p.m. flight to Missoula that afternoon.

He stood and stared at the door. It wasn't as simple as it had been a week ago when he'd put Harris's file in his briefcase and walked out. Maybe, he thought fleetingly, he should have let well enough alone, allowing the wheels to grind and Kirby to take his chances. Maybe, but he couldn't. If he was in a bind, Kirby wouldn't walk away. He hadn't twelve years ago and, DiGenero thought, he knew it wouldn't be any different now. Besides, RAPTOR was only part of it. Stockman's people were throwing their net. If Kirby was caught in it, he could be in even bigger trouble, fast.

DiGenero felt his stomach tighten the way it used to when he was undercover in New York. And there was Von Biemann. His crowd played for keeps. He was worried about the German, about the risks Harris didn't know he was running. He glanced at his watch and then reached for his coat. He had forty minutes to catch the plane.

Erin Dupres was almost old enough to have bid a motherly farewell to her own freshman, but even the 17-year-olds in the crowded off-campus pub eyed her appraisingly as she crossed the room to join DiGenero. He rose from the booth. She touched his cheek with her lips, smiling, and motioned him to sit. DiGenero too had been watching her. The jeans and workshirt were gone, replaced by a light, bright printed green dress, open at the neck, that showed off her tan and cascading dark hair.

"This is a pleasant surprise, Frank. To what do I owe the honor?" He had called from the Missoula airport as soon as the flight landed. She had been at the lab. Her agreement to meet him for a drink had been friendly enough, but punctuated by a momentary pause, signaling an instant of uncertainty.

"I went out for a genuine plate of pasta in Salt Lake City and made a wrong turn."

Erin laughed as DiGenero motioned for the waitress. The Festa Room was Italian in name only, with an ersatz decor of dark wood trim, colored-glass chandeliers, checkered tablecloths, and Mexican tile. He glanced down at the menu, ordering a bottle of Chianti, before putting the cheap plastic folio aside.

DiGenero had decided on a direct approach during the hour-long flight from Salt Lake. What he knew from Stockman was off-limits. Besides, he didn't need it. RAPTOR's information was enough and it was his to use.

"I know where Kirby is and what he's doing," DiGenero paused to pour the wine. He filled the rough-cut goblets halfway. Erin's hand trembled slightly as they touched the heavy glasses in a silent toast. "And I know about Von Biemann."

She didn't drink, but centered the wineglass before her on the table, her fingers resting like supports on either side of its heavy stem, her eyes on DiGenero. He explained quietly. Erin studied him as he talked, leaning forward to hear better because of the noise. When he was through, she lifted the glass, for the first time sipping the wine, and sat back.

Several moments passed before she spoke, "Let's suppose, for the sake of discussion, that you're right about Kirby. Why are you telling me?"

"You can get the message across."

"And you can't?"

"You care about him. I owe him my life." He paused, "Look, I can bury Kirby's case."

"Bury?" Erin canted her head, her hair falling to one side. DiGenero saw the light reflect in the gold crest of her earring behind her long black curls. She was more attractive now, at that moment, than he could remember in all the times he'd seen her before. He forced himself to concentrate.

"Bury. Shelve it, put it on the bottom of the stack. It can be done. It's not right, not what I'm paid for, but...," he paused.

"But what?" she asked. "Then do it."

DiGenero sighed, "He's got to help."

"Help? Help who? You?"

"No. Help himself."

Erin's eyes flashed, "Come on. How long have you known him? Ten years. No, more. You've known him twice as long as I have. You must understand who he is, what he's done all his life. They call some people survivors. The ones who can make it no matter what, but Kirby is someone who's even rarer than that. He's his own man. He makes his own rules, picks his own game, finds his own rewards. He doesn't ask anyone else for them. No pats on the head from the boss. How many like him are there? What if he's trapping falcons? If he's doing what you say, do the birds die? Are they lost forever? Tell me, Frank, who does he hurt?"

DiGenero shifted uncomfortably, "I just don't want him to get hurt."

Erin paused. She was being unfair, she knew. All this wasn't Frank's fault. It was just that the tension had wound more and more tightly since his last visit to the ranch. He wanted to help, but she'd reacted, struck back. Her voice softened, "Do you know why you mean so much to him?"

DiGenero flushed. She spoke, "Because he sees so much of himself in you." Erin smiled, "It's true for you too, isn't it? With him. That's why you've stayed in touch all these years. You can see yourself, or maybe at least some important parts of you, in him." She reached across the table, touching DiGenero's hand, "In New York, when you were undercover, you were on the outside, alone, for a long time. You did better than survive. But the point is, when you were on the outside, you knew what it was like to take chances, to be alone, to depend on yourself. It doesn't make you better than other people, but it does make you different, perhaps irreversibly so."

She sipped her wine and repositioned the goblet carefully where it had been, studying DiGenero before she continued, "I think it's hard to come back inside, isn't it? Out there, how long was that for you? Three, four years?" she asked. DiGenero shrugged. "That's where Kirby's been his whole life. It's his choice, sure. But he doesn't do it for the money. It's something else, part challenge, part risk. It's for all the reasons people who haven't been there can't grasp." She smiled again, "But you know what it's like. Kirby sees that. He sees that you understand."

Erin's hand was still resting on his. DiGenero felt her fingers slip away as he spoke, "I've never met anyone quite like him." He laughed at the recollection, "From the first, when I tried to buy the son of a bitch a drink for picking me out of that paddy, he wouldn't take a thing."

Erin shook her head, refusing more wine as DiGenero lifted the bottle. He refilled his glass and then continued, "I know the money doesn't matter. And I know if they took every penny away, it wouldn't make a difference to Kirby. But if he takes a tumble and they lock him up, if they put him inside, I don't think he'd make it. I don't think he's built to live that way," DiGenero looked down.

The silence lasted several moments. He raised his eyes and then his glass, draining the contents. "What's in it for you?" he asked.

"What do you mean?"

"The relationship. You and Kirby. Five years is a long time."

Erin laughed, "The thirty or so before that was even longer." She ran her finger down the edge of the wineglass, tracing the pattern on its stem, "I love him. He's one of a kind. He can take chances," her eyes met DiGenero's, "I like that." Erin settled back in the booth, "And he's willing to take a chance with me, to let me do what I want, to come to me when I'm at the university rather than demanding that I come to him. He's never asked more than I can give."

"And you?" DiGenero asked. "Have you ever asked more than he can give?"

"You do know how to get personal, don't you?" It was Erin's turn to shift uncomfortably. "I...," she paused, the shadow of uncertainty crossing her face as she remembered Saturday night, "I suppose I don't know yet."

"Will you talk to him?" DiGenero asked. "You don't have to tell me. But I can't help unless he drops the connection with the German. Von Biemann is high-profile. One day, somehow, some way, he'll get caught. If Kirby's in the slipstream, he's gone too. I don't want to see that happen. You don't either. To prevent it, he needs to bail out now."

Erin turned her glass slowly, watching the candle's glow refract, stirring the soft burgundy tones of the wine. "Has Kirby ever bailed out of anything, Frank?" Her voice had dropped low, just above the background hum of the restaurant. DiGenero shook his head. She smiled, acknowledging his answer.

Erin met and held his eyes as she spoke, "For some people, warnings are challenges. It's perverse, isn't it?" She laughed softly. Her hand touched DiGenero's sleeve this time, inviting him to share the irony. "Even when you see the risk and point it out, when your message is clear, when there's no question that you care," Erin paused and looked away, "sometimes, it still doesn't work. Sometimes, the game's still the thing." Erin glanced down, removing her hand almost apologetically from DiGenero's arm. He noticed a bittersweet smile. "He's like no one I've ever met," her voice trailed off.

"Talk to him," DiGenero said. It was a request, not an order. The sounds from the bar and nearby tables surrounded them as he waited for her to break the silence. Erin nodded noncommittally.

He continued, "Tell him this isn't a game. He's got to understand that."

The two sat back, studying each other as if from different vantage points. The quiet seemed to create a momentarily shared embarrassment. Erin spoke first, "Are you going back to Salt Lake tonight?"

DiGenero shook his head, "Tomorrow."

She reached for her purse and stood, "Can I drop you somewhere?"

"No." DiGenero could see that heads already had turned at several tables around them to follow her progress.

"Think about it," he smiled. She extended her hand. It was warm against his palm. "Thanks for coming, Frank." She paused, her lips parting. For a moment DiGenero thought that Erin was about to say something more but then she turned and was gone.

DiGenero waited for the security officer to lift the chain that blocked entrance to the baggage x-ray and personnel scanner. He glanced at his watch. At 6:50 a.m., on Wednesday, August 29, there were only a few passengers in the concourse of the Missoula terminal, a typical weekday for a small-town airport, he thought, with more employees than paying customers in sight. He retrieved his bag from the x-ray machine's conveyer belt and strolled toward the last gate. The conversation with Erin was still on his mind. The tapes from the wiretap hadn't produced anything yet, but in another day or two, Kirby would be gone a week. By then, DiGenero thought, he had to call.

Twenty yards behind DiGenero in the concourse, the short, squat man with the shoulder bag paused, examining the video screen that displayed the morning's arrivals and departures. The first flight to Salt Lake City was scheduled to leave Gate 3 in twenty minutes. The phone call from Munich had provided Adman Malaek a description of his target as well as instructions. Now, it was simply a matter of finding the best location for the shot.

He walked ahead, slowing his pace a few feet from the entrance to the waiting area. The man was easy to pick out among the handful of passengers, sitting alone, in the center of a row, his back to the wall. Malaek glanced quickly around. He needed to be close and yet unobtrusive. When he was ready, he would have only one or two chances.

The facing row, across from the target, was best. Malaek picked his place, hefted the heavy shoulder bag, and walked in.

At the first sound, DiGenero started, glancing up from his newspaper. The click of the camera shutter and whir of the motor drive were loud in the quiet waiting area. Seated opposite him, the photographer was staring at the camera. The single-lens reflex, pointed in DiGenero's direction, rested on his lap atop the small carry-on bag marked with a commemorative "Tour America" logo. The man, short, rotund, and foreign, fumbled with the expensive Japanese model, trying to adjust the settings. "Very complicated," the little man spoke, glancing up sheepishly, obviously confused by the camera's controls. DiGenero nodded and looked down, turning the page of his newspaper. He ignored the shutter's second and third clicks and the photographer's muttering, and resumed his reading.

Fifteen minutes later, when the flight was called, DiGenero rose and turned toward the gate. A step from the exit, he glanced back. The five remaining passengers filed by him as he stood, surveying the empty waiting area and the section of the terminal's hallway just outside the cluster of seats.

"Sir," the passenger agent beckoned him toward the door, "you're the last to board."

DiGenero nodded. He turned, and then stopped, looking over his shoulder a final time before stepping outside and dismissing the thought. It was odd. He hadn't heard any other flights called, but the fat little man with the camera was gone.

11

Wednesday, August 29, 1984

Lowenbrau Keller, 16-18 Hohenstaufenring,
Cologne, West Germany

The Hohenstaufenring's afternoon traffic had thickened to a steady stream, blocking the view of the thin man who slouched against the front fender of the parked black Mercedes 300 sedan. Gerhardt Klammer straightened to his full height, peering over the passing cars and trucks at the beer hall across the street. Just moments before, the figure had been seated in the front window of the Lowenbrau Keller. Now he was gone.

Klammer swallowed hard, remembering the voice on the telephone on Sunday night. It had been very specific. He was to meet the American at the airport, drive him to the appointment outside Bonn, and not let the man out of his sight. Until now, his stomach churned at the thought, he had not. He leaned against the Mercedes, fidgeting with the zipper on his cheap, black leather coat. The Red Army Faction had accepted him only last month. Driving the car when they executed Bleihoff, the chairman of Dortmund Steel, had been his test, but he still couldn't afford trouble. A mistake now and he was out. A mistake that was bad enough and he was dead.

In the distance, the single chime from St. Gereon's twin spires sounded the quarter hour. 4:15 p.m. The American hadn't returned. He could go inside, looking, but it was still too early. The airport was only twenty minutes away and the plane didn't leave for Munich until 6:00 p.m. Klammer smelled the sour odor of his own sweat. He lit a Gauloises, filling his lungs with its heavy, pungent smoke. He would wait ten minutes more, one cigarette; then, he would go in.

Coincidentally, in the rear of the Lowenbrau Keller, Kirby Harris also figured he had ten minutes. He had just finished changing his bank notes for coins at the bar. Unlike his nervous driver's estimate, however, his calculation was based on the height of the German silver stacked on the phone booth shelf to pay for his international call to Erin Dupres.

The connection went through at once. At 8:15 a.m., mountain daylight time, on Wednesday, he knew Erin would still be in her apartment, wrapped in her robe, seated at the kitchen table with a mug of coffee and the newspaper. He counted the four rings it took her to walk the ten steps to the bedroom and the phone.

"How are you?" Harris asked.

"Good. What time is it and where are you?"

"It's after 4:00 p.m. I'm in Cologne."

"Cologne? Weren't you going to Munich?"

"Yeah. I'm returning there tonight. Actually, I've been in Bonn, not far from here. Klaus asked me to meet some of his friends. They've already got their share of pets. The visit was just to get acquainted, although Klaus called me later at the hotel with another order. For some white ones. I agreed to provide the supply."

Erin understood the double-talk. It was a deal for gyrfalcons. "The season's getting late, isn't it?" She knew the gyrs migrated from the Arctic early, but only into the high latitudes of northern Canada and Alaska where winter came first.

"Yeah," Harris agreed, "but there's a spot in Alberta where I'm sure I can find some at the end of September. Klaus said he'd go along for old time's sake to take them out."

"When are you coming home?"

"Tomorrow. I'll be back Friday night."

"Did everything work out?"

Harris paused, "Without a hitch."

"Just you and Klaus?"

"No, a couple of others. Klaus's brother, Erique, and an Iranian friend of his, a businessman of some sort who lives in the States."

Erin spoke, "I saw Frank yesterday."

"Frank?" Harris furrowed his brow. "What were you doing in Salt Lake?"

"No, here. He came to talk about you."

"Did he, now?" Harris leaned back.

"He knows," Erin continued. "He's worried. He cares about you, Kirby. He came to me because he wants to be sure the message gets through." Harris heard Erin's deep breath. "Maybe you should listen. Maybe..."

"Hey, you're beautiful when you're nagging."

"You may think it's a kick," Erin said, irritated, "but..."

"But what?"

"He knows about Klaus."

Harris straightened, his smile fading, "How?"

"He didn't say and I didn't ask, but he knows."

He mentally replayed his conversation with DiGenero at the ranch two Saturdays before, and ran down the sequence of events from the peregrine's capture to Von Biemann's arrival, and their departure with the falcon. Nothing he could recall was out of the ordinary, but obviously somewhere, somehow, something was.

"Kirby..."

"Don't worry about it," preoccupied, Harris cut her off. The banter was gone. "We can talk when I get home. I'll see you Friday night."

"Kirby," Erin heard the sharp click, but the words were already on her lips. "Take care."

DiGenero held the cipher lock latch aside with his thumb and opened the office door.

"Morning, sir," the National Express delivery agent handed him the small air-express parcel and the thick Sunday newspaper. DiGenero had left the paper lying in the hall beside the entrance to RAPTOR's suite a few minutes before when he'd opened the office to wait for the package. He stared at the newspaper's headlines, waiting for his change from the $20 bill. Sunday, September 2, 1984. As usual, the Salt Lake City *Tribune*'s editorial judgment on world events ran true to form: football, the height of the Great Salt Lake, and the politics of the Mormon church dominated the front page.

"Have a nice day," the delivery agent handed him 80 cents.

DiGenero pocketed the handful of coins impatiently and shut the door. He tore open the heavy mailing envelope and extracted the small spool of recording tape. The Missoula drop keeper had called the night before to tell him they had something interesting. DiGenero walked quickly down the inner corridor to the soundmen's laboratory, next to commo, at the end of the hall.

He switched on the ceiling light. Bigger boys, bigger toys, he thought. The small room, no more than ten feet by twelve feet, had a $100,000-plus inventory. It was neatly arranged, with special cabinetry and bins for the rows of audio test equipment, coaxial cable, telephone gear, multimeters, miniature recorders, directional microphones, walkie-talkies, and electronic spare components and parts. The IBM personal computer in the corner, surrounded by the technical manuals, kept track of the hardware and the miscellaneous stock.

He opened the master wall panel and reset the circuit breaker, putting power on the main equipment bench. DiGenero threaded the tape on the Teac reel-to-reel recorder. He ran several feet, stopped, rewound, adjusted the filters for static, and set the sound level. Then, he pressed "play" and sat down on the tall workbench stool to listen.

Twenty minutes later, DiGenero hit the "stop" button for the third time. The Teac's drive snapped off, quieting the amplified hiss of the remaining blank tape. He rewound and unspindled the miniature reel, laying it beside the pad where he'd jotted the details of the long-distance conversation. DiGenero studied his notes for a moment. Then, he reached for his pocket diary, thumbed to the back of the dog-eared black book, and picked up the phone.

"Doesn't he know it's the first quarter of the goddamn Redskin-Cowboys game? Tell him I'll call back!" Eddie Stockman's voice was crystal clear despite the fact he was in front of the television set in the family room of his suburban Virginia home, thirty feet from the kitchen's wall phone.

DiGenero looked at his watch and grimaced. He'd forgotten the day and his former partner's seasonal addiction. It was 11:00 a.m. in Salt Lake, 1:00 p.m., Sunday, kickoff time, in Washington. It took Dolores Stockman three more tries before DiGenero heard the shuffling in the background. From 2000 miles away, he made out Stockman's muttered profanities closing on his wife and the phone.

"Frank," Stockman omitted any hello, "you're going to ruin a wonderful relationship."

DiGenero talked fast, "Eddie, listen, the German is going to be on the move again and I think we can track him this time."

"What the hell are you talking about?" Stockman was confused as well as perturbed.

"I can't go into the details on this line," DiGenero said, "but take my word for it. He's going to be on the road soon. When is still a question mark, although where isn't. His destination is Canada, northern Alberta, for certain. It will make it easier for us to follow him since there are only a few routes for getting in and out."

"For certain?" Stockman interrupted, obviously suspicious. "How do you know?"

"Don't ask." DiGenero swore under his breath, frustrated by the need to double-talk on the open line, "Look, I don't know whether your friends, the ones who provided the tip-off the last time the German left home, can do it again, but we should give them the word. If he travels this month, we don't have much time. We should put out an alert on him. That's all I need, a heads-up, and I'll be waiting."

"All you need?" Stockman shot back. "Since when are you responsible for my account? Look, I don't know what you're up to, Frank, but I can't put this on the alert network just because you think it would be a nice thing to do." Stockman snorted. "I've got a branch chief who's going to want to see a piece of paper. I've got a division chief who checks what the branch chief does. I got a Center director who's got nothing better to do than ask the division chief questions. Why do you think I called you in the first place about the German? Because it's easy to move all these goddamn feather merchants around? You want to put the German on the alert network? Wonderful. All you need to do is document it. References, sources, a piece of paper, Frank. What about it?"

DiGenero paused. "Look, Eddie, put two and two together. You know how I got this."

"That's right," Stockman's anger surprised him, "and I'm not going to go down for you on this one, Frank. Just because you think you can play cowboy with the techies and not get into trouble doesn't mean I'm along for the ride."

"Eddie," DiGenero tried to deflect the diatribe, "I've also got something that ties into the other guy we were talking about, the Iranian."

"Huh?"

DiGenero pressed ahead, "They're connected, and..."

Stockman broke in, "You give me a piece of paper. Otherwise, no deal. You're OK, Frank, but what's say you run your operation and I'll run mine."

"Eddie..." The click was final.

"Shit," DiGenero swore vehemently at the dead receiver in his hand.

David Jackson nearly jumped a foot off the floor when DiGenero stepped from the soundmen's lab into the hall. "Sorry," DiGenero apologized. "What are you doing here?"

"That's OK," Jackson picked up his car keys where they'd fallen, "I didn't expect to see anyone else here on Sunday. I've got the duty this weekend. An 'Immediate' just came in and my beeper went off. It'll only take a minute to print the message."

DiGenero nodded as Jackson stepped to the communications vault door, deftly spinning the combination lock through its four-number sequence. Moments later, he swung the heavy door open, unlocked the inner chamber, and led the way inside.

Jackson flipped on the main power switch and turned to the keyboard of the terminal. He logged the microcomputer on-line, and scanned the inventory of current traffic in the system's memory on the video display screen.

The incoming telexes were received and stored automatically during after-duty hours. He tapped the keys, entering a series of commands to direct the messages in queue to the laser printer. Immediates would automatically appear first, followed by the lower priorities.

The rustle of spooled paper on the tractor feed and the high-pitched tearing sound of the printhead began almost at once.

DiGenero stood over the laser printer, reading.

SECRET

FROM FBI HQTRS
TO RAPTOR/SLCITY

TERRORISM ALERT MESSAGE (TAM-112)
THIS INFORMATION IS CURRENT AS OF 0900 HOURS,
2 SEPTEMBER 1984.

RELIABLE INTELLIGENCE SOURCES HAVE IDENTIFIED THE FOLLOWING TERRORIST SUSPECTS WHO MAY NOW BE TRAVELING IN YOUR AREA. IF THEY ARE ASSOCIATED WITH ONGOING CASES, THE AGENT IN CHARGE SHOULD CONTACT THE COUNTERTERRORISM CENTER (SECURE 909902) TO COORDINATE OPERATIONS AGAINST THE SUSPECT. THE INFORMATION BELOW PROVIDES THEIR LAST KNOWN LOCATION, THE DATE THEY DEPARTED THAT LOCATION, AND THEIR CURRENT STATUS. IT MAY NOT BE DISSEMINATED TO STATE OR LOCAL LAW ENFORCEMENT ORGANIZATIONS WITHOUT PRIOR PERMISSION.

NAME	LAST LOCATION	DATE	STATUS
MARTINEZ, CARLOS/ BASQUE LIBFRONT	BARCELONA	30AUG84	TRAVELING/ SAN JUAN, PUERTO RICO
O'CASEY, SHAUN/ IRA/PROVISIONAL	LONDONDERRY	29AUG84	TRAVELING/ BOSTON, MA.
MUSAANI, RAJID IRAN/JIHAD	MUNICH	1SEPT84	DESTINATION UNKNOWN

"That's the only precedence traffic in the queue, sir," Jackson logged off the printer and turned toward DiGenero, who had torn off the message and was sitting, holding the computer printout in front of him. He didn't answer, but seemed to be rereading the text. Jackson shrugged and looked away, filling out the details on his Sunday call-in in the log.

"Jesus H. Christ, now what?"

Jackson glanced back, "Sir?"

DiGenero only shook his head, staring at the piece of paper, and didn't reply.

12

Monday, September 3, 1984

Heathrow Airport, London

Lieutenant Colonel Michael Flynn was scanning the bank of television monitors in Heathrow Airport's Security Command Post, watching the passengers who had just landed in the first wave of early-morning flights, when the picture from immigration booth 13 caught his eye. He leaned forward, hands clasped behind him, squinted slightly, and studied the screen intently. Bobby Forsythe, the security officer at the controls of the camera console, felt the tap on his shoulder.

Flynn pointed to the monitor, "Thirteen. Something's not quite right."

The young policeman tapped his computer keyboard, entering the code that activated the videotape recorder in order to preserve the image now on the screen. Then, he reached to his right, moving the small toggle labeled "13" in the long row of switches to magnify and sharpen the picture on the monitor. Concealed above the immigration booths, the zoom lens of the miniature camera produced a crystal clear image. Arriving passengers were obliged to face the inspector and the video camera, because of the purposefully narrow design of the passageways between the high booths. Forsythe zoomed the lens into focus first on the passport being inspected by the immigration officer and then readjusted the controls to produce a sharp image of its bearer.

Flynn reached for the microphone on the console, flipped the selector switch to booth 13, and depressed the "talk" button.

"Take some time with this one, Miss Dorsey, if you please. I'll tell you when to let him go."

Two hundred and fifty yards away, and one floor below the Security Command Post, immigration inspector Rebecca Dorsey's miniature earpiece relayed Flynn's message. On the screen, Flynn noted her slight nod of acknowledgment as she slowly turned the pages of the passport, checking its number and photograph against the entries for stolen and forged documents, as well as for wanted passport holders, in the Tunisian section of her Immigration and Security Office Watch Book.

The small easel that held the portfolio of eleven-by-thirteen-inch photographs of known and suspected terrorists stood next to Flynn. He pulled it closer to the bank of television screens. Flipping back the heavy canvas cover marked "Secret," he turned the mounted glossies quickly, glancing up after each one to let his mind's eye recapture the image on the monitor.

He swore under his breath, "Something's bloody wrong here."

Despite his obvious skills and long seasoning as a professional intelligence officer, this aspect of the game was not Lieutenant Colonel Michael Flynn's cup of tea. Having spent fifteen of his last twenty years in the Special Air Service, Her Majesty's secret commando force and the world's best antiterrorist team, he wanted nothing more than to be back in the field. But two years before, his reputation had convinced the ad hoc Cabinet Council to pick him from among 500 of the defense ministry's candidates as the officer who could turn around the sorry state of Heathrow's security force.

Flynn had not disappointed them. Those who knew only his public record credited the results to the combination of his iron discipline, quick mind, and capacity to endure an unending series of twenty-hour days. But the handful of officials in Whitehall who had access to his secret dossier recognized that Flynn's intimate knowledge of the full spectrum of Middle East terrorists was, in fact, the special key to his success.

His expertise was firsthand and unique, deriving from service as a special security adviser to the small, oil-rich Persian Gulf sheikhdoms that the British had continued to aid even after abandoning their role east of Suez. To protect his wards, Flynn had watched, stalked, and, now and again, killed. The quarry was diverse: the Palestinian and Shiite zealots, the pathological and the rootless from Beirut's underclass who were hired and then discarded, the occasional paid hit man, and when their hand showed, their sometime masters from Tripoli, Tehran, Baghdad, and Damascus. With a decade of experience, he had acquired nearly a sixth sense in assessing the faces in Heathrow's sea of humanity. He knew which to shadow and which should be approached with weapon in hand, safety catch off.

In this instance, the face and the Tunisian passport had stopped Flynn's eye. Even given the possibility of a few Europeans and some eastern Mediterranean Arabs in the ancestry, he thought, the man and the nationality simply didn't match.

"Shit," Flynn exhaled the profanity with a hiss. He had gone back and forth over the fifty-six photographs. The man on the screen wasn't there.

He glanced at the clock above the console before shifting his eyes back to the monitor to study the slender, dark-haired figure who stood casually, apparently unperturbed by the wait. Five minutes had passed. The man on the screen had not questioned the immigration officer, fidgeted, or shifted on his feet.

Flynn folded his arms, rocking back on his heels, and thought hard. "Cool bastard, eh?" he said.

At the console, Forsythe nodded. Never mind the physical discrepancy, Flynn thought, the man's extraordinary composure alone was suspicious. He reached for the microphone, "You may release him, Miss Dorsey."

Flynn turned toward the security network radios on his right. He glanced at the schematic map of the airport facilities above the dials, digital frequency displays, and signal-output meters of the matte black transmitter/receivers. The scale depiction of Heathrow outlined the floor plans of its buildings as well as the layout of the airfield, the car parks, and the surrounding grounds. On the map, small lights registered the assigned position of each uniformed and undercover security on duty, and the locations of the mobile teams that patrolled the airport's perimeter.

Flynn keyed the microphone. "Able One and Able Three."

Inside the Security Command Post, the speakers amplified two loud clicks. The two armed agents in the immigration area had pressed the transmit buttons on their concealed walkie-talkies, acknowledging the call.

"Follow the man now leaving booth 13 and report."

The sharp metallic sound from the speakers again cut the silence, wordlessly confirming the order.

In the crowded international arrival area, a long-haired custodian, the model of a school dropout who had sunk to his permanent station in life, finished sweeping a cigarette butt into his portable dustpan. Otherwise known as Able One, Miles Townsend shouldered his broom and unobtrusively glanced up. He yawned, his boredom at the monotony of janitor's chores in character and obvious to anyone who cared to see. Shuffling toward the rear of the large room, he moved slowly at first to keep himself outside his subject's peripheral vision. Then, properly positioned, he picked up his pace, paralleling the direction of the well-dressed foreigner who had just exited from immigration booth 13.

At the same moment, twenty yards away, a short, blond woman appeared to give up her wait for an incoming passenger. She looked one last time at the immigration booths, and then turned in the direction of the terminal's exit doors. More than a few male eyes followed her motion. Her soft, straight hair, California looks and body, blue jeans, red plaid hunting shirt, running shoes, and knapsack were stereotypically American collegiate, although Sergeant Alice Brackett was anything but. A veteran of three years undercover with the British Army in Londonderry's lethal netherworld, she was a seasoned security officer and had promptly identified the Middle Eastern sort in question. Angling herself into his wake, she fell in behind him, her quickened step making the Heckler & Koch machine pistol in her knapsack bump rhythmically against the curve of her hips.

Just ahead of the blond and to the left of the custodian, Rajid Musaani strode toward the automatic doors marked "Ground Transportation." He shifted his Gucci carry-on bag, his only luggage, from his left to his right arm. The motion enabled him to glance about naturally. After two minutes in the immigration booth, Musaani had known he was under surveillance. It was impossible to quickly pick out the unusual in the arrival terminal's random sampling of humanity, but he was certain they were there. He was simply unsure who and where.

He kept a steady gait. The question, he thought, was why? It couldn't

be the passport. The East German craftsmanship was too good for anyone but an expert with a laboratory to determine it was a forgery. He
tapped his suit-jacket pocket, unconsciously confirming that the counterfeit document was still in place.

Even more important, he thought, the passport was clean. He had
never used it on an action mission and never would. It had one purpose
and one purpose only: to permit him to enter and exit the United Kingdom under an alias. Like his Moroccan, Brazilian, Syrian, and Iraqi passports, it ensured that the records of the British police and intelligence
would not hold his true Iranian name, or reveal that he and Kahlil bin
Zahel, whom he would meet later that evening, had been in the country, in the same place, at the same time.

Outside Heathrow's international terminal, the earphone connected
to the walkie-talkie in the bus dispatcher's pocket crackled with Flynn's
voice, "Watch for the man exiting now with the carry-on bag just in front
of Able Three and report."

Robby McCallum, the London police officer dressed in the bus company's blue jumper, looked toward the terminal. He patted the .357-Mag-
num Sterling revolver that was stuck in his trouser waistband under the
coveralls. As he did, Musaani walked through the exit doors. Ten steps
behind him, McCallum saw the blond brush by the custodian, who had
stopped to sweep up a few scraps of trash. Able One, the janitor, could
go no further without stretching his cover too thin.

Watching the man approach, McCallum swore silently. There were
no uniforms nearby. He had expected that Flynn would send them. He
swallowed hard. Right now, only he and Able Three were on the line if
something came unstuck.

Musaani knew he had only two choices and he quickly eliminated
one. The taxicabs were out of the question. If he took a cab, the watchers would be forced to follow him in a car. That kind of dedicated effort
would be hard to shake. Even if he could lose them, the taxi would carry
a witness, the driver, to better describe him, as well as a record, the cabbie's log, for the police, or whoever was on his case, to peruse at their
leisure.

The bus service to the West London air terminal was the only option. Musaani walked straight toward the dispatcher on the platform. The
Iranian smiled and nodded. He stepped inside the open doorway of the
bus and turned down the aisle, examining the passengers as he moved to

the back. The last row was empty. Musaani lowered himself into the window seat and waited.

At this point, he thought, it was simply a matter of logical deduction. The riders already on board were unlikely to include anyone who would be a worry. Even if he had been targeted as soon as he got off the Air France flight from Paris, they would have been uncertain about his destination and means of ground travel and thus, unable easily to plant someone in advance. More likely, Musaani judged, they would wait until he chose, and then put a watcher on board. His gaze riveted on the forward platform. It was the next passenger, therefore, who deserved his attention.

The dispatcher turned his back to the bus and rubbed his cheek with his palm, bringing the small button microphone on his watchband closer to his lips. Its tiny, voice-activated microswitch closed to relay his transmission, "He's on number 336 to West Side."

"Roger," Flynn replied, watching McCallum on the monitor that covered the bus departure area, "don't follow."

Musaani looked out at the platform. Most of the passengers from the crush of morning arrivals had gone. A blond in blue jeans, obviously an American, caught his eye as she paused momentarily before walking on toward the car park. Beneath his seat, the diesel engine rumbled, kicking into life. Musaani took a deep breath. The door closed and the rush of compressed air released the brakes.

No one. He smiled. The ride to London was nonstop. Of course, that only meant they would be waiting for him at the other end. At least, Musaani thought as the bus ground into first gear and began to move, the next forty-five minutes would offer a chance to relax.

Flynn reached for the direct telephone line to the security station at the West Side terminal. It was wired to ring as soon as he lifted the instrument from the cradle.

Police Sergeant Percy Jackson, the officer in charge of security at the city airline terminal, answered the phone almost before Flynn had the receiver against his ear.

"West Side, Jackson, sir."

"Pick up the good-looking Arab bloke with the carry-on bag on his arm. He'll probably be the last one off 336. Charcoal sports jacket, gray slacks, sweater. Take care and report to me. I'm also calling the Yard."

Flynn hung up without waiting for a reply. The feeling was so strong that it didn't do his intuition justice to call it a hunch. He thought quickly, mapping out his choices.

He lifted the secure telephone and dialed Scotland Yard's Terrorist Surveillance Unit. TSU was equipped to have a team on the street in London within five minutes. Flynn listened to a recital of odd electronic sounds from the encryption circuitry as the secure call went through. The quick beeping tones finally signaled the ring at the other end. Perhaps they'd learn more when they followed him from West Side. Perhaps, he thought, although somehow he knew that it wasn't going to be that easy.

Forty-five minutes later and some two miles from the West London air terminal, bus 336 passed the Turnham Green underground station. As it did, Rajid Musaani took the penny out from under his tongue. The use of the coin was an old trick, although it was anything but a ruse. The chemical action between his saliva and the copper had made Musaani feel as sick as he looked. It was a guarantee of prompt attention. He rose from his seat, put his hand over his mouth, and stumbled forward, dragging his bag behind him. There was no question to the passengers who stared at him that he appeared unwell.

The voice of authority echoed from the front before he reached the midpoint in the bus, "Sit down, mate. The terminal's just a bit up the road."

Musaani continued, halting unsteadily, half-leaning against the driver. Behind the panoramic windshield and large wheel, the irritated, red-faced cockney in the navy-blue uniform coat glanced up. The man bending over his shoulder was deathly pale, if not a light tinge of green. Despite the heavy Arab accent, his message came through loud and clear.

"Stop, please. I'm going to throw up."

The driver's logic was transparent in the anxiety that crossed his face. If the wog did, it was obvious where the consequences would fall.

"Take it easy, mate. Hold on."

Braking hard, he angled the bus sharply to the left against the curb, blocking the traffic behind him, and reached for the polished chrome handle that released the large double door.

Musaani tripped down the stairs. The driver looked away reflexively, averting his eyes from the sickness that was to follow. But there was no retching sound. Instead of bending over, Musaani quickly pivoted right, into the street. He was gone instantly, hidden by a large lorry in the next lane, before the driver looked back at the empty sidewalk and blurted out the first in his string of profanities at Arabs in particular and foreigners in general.

Musaani strode smartly across Cromwell Road, weaving through the cars and vans that were now snarled behind the bus. In a matter of moments, he reached the opposite curb. Without hesitation, he turned west in the direction of the Turnham Green underground, away from whoever was waiting for him at the West Side terminal two miles distant.

Ten minutes later, at 11:15 a.m., Lieutenant Colonel Flynn picked up the direct line from West Side on its second buzz. He listened in silence to Sergeant Jackson's story about the unscheduled departure from the airport bus, pausing only for a moment to think before offering a curt thank you and hanging up. A man of few words, he was not inclined to gratuitous comments, and he had no questions or further instructions.

He stroked his chin, allowing himself a brief moment to enjoy the sense of self-satisfaction, before he started to pace back and forth, head down, lips pursed, and brow furrowed. It was a habit to do this when he was thinking. From the slow rhythm of his heels striking the floor, the officer at the console knew that the lieutenant colonel was deep in contemplation.

It was, Flynn thought, a not unexpected beginning. His guess had been right. He had maintained for years that the advantage always lay with the quarry at the beginning of any chase. The observation was relevant in this case as well.

Aside from the videotape, they had little to go on, making the value of flash bulletins, dragnets, stakeouts, or any other high-energy efforts close to nil. Even if they promptly papered the country with photographs, it would take forty-eight hours to cover all the ports of entry. The would-be Tunisian's single carry-on bag as well as his theatrical exit from the bus suggested that he planned to keep his stay in London shorter than that and was well aware of his risks. It also was virtually certain that he would leave the country on another passport and, of course, as someone else.

Flynn glanced up at the monitors. They showed nothing unusual. Most of the areas were half empty now, a lull that would end at noon when Heathrow's next international influx washed over Terminal Two.

Actually, he thought, the Arab, or Iranian, or whatever he was, had acquitted himself rather well. He'd correctly assessed the dangers and acted decisively to minimize them. Flynn paused before the small easel. He flipped the classified cover sheet over the photographs and slid the tripod back to its place, squaring the legs properly with the edge of the console. He stared at the red stripe and bold letters on the heavy canvas cover that declared the pictures beneath to be "Secret."

Yes, the man was good. But then, Flynn smiled, so was he.

He turned away and continued his slow circuit of the room. In any event, he thought, success at the beginning of the chase, when the advantages were all on one side, was no guarantee of survival at the end. Flynn had spent a sufficient amount of his own career as both the hunter and the hunted to know that. Success and survival were two different things. A hundred factors could produce a success, but survival, long-term survival, depended on only two factors—not making mistakes and knowing when others did. In the final analysis, it was the same whether you were running an operation, or trying to stop one.

Flynn reached for the telephone. He dialed the in-house extension for the technical-support group at Heathrow's main security building. They would collect the videotape, copy the sequence from booth 13, and produce the photographic prints. With a routine designation, the photographs and description of Mr. FNU, LNU—First Name Unknown, Last Name Unknown—as well as copies of his documents, would be on the secure telephoto wire to the sixteen North American and Western European intelligence and security agencies that cooperated in the terrorist watch network within forty-eight hours.

It took more time than Flynn liked, but in this instance, it was all right. This was just the beginning.

"Patience," Flynn spoke the word aloud.

At the console, Forsythe glanced over his shoulder, eyeing the lieutenant colonel. Flynn was looking the other way, phone in hand, unconsciously straightening the already impeccably correct alignment of his suit jacket and tie.

Patience. His lips formed the word soundlessly as he listened to the telephone's persistent ring. Flynn's eyes returned to the bank of video monitors. Patience. It was more than a virtue, he thought. It was the most important part of the game.

✷   ✷   ✷

Four hours later, at 3:15 p.m., Mr. Brandon Smythe-Stipe, assistant manager, Piccadilly branch, Grindlay's Bank, looked up from the *Financial
Times*. It annoyed him to deal with customers without appointments at this
hour of the day, but the small furrow of irritation that marked Smythe-Stipe's
brow disappeared instantly as he recognized the man who had stopped before
his desk. He rose with a deferential smile and extended his hand, "Good afternoon, Monsieur Deleuse. It's a pleasure to see you again."

To the assistant manager, Monsieur Marc Deleuse was the personi-
fication of the ideal customer. His folder in Smythe-Stipe's file drawer
for preferred clients held a healthy stack of deposit receipts and commercial letters of credit, recording the low-risk, high-profit business he brought
to the bank. An Algerian businessman who sold wines and purchased
antiques and objets d'art, Deleuse was a frequent visitor to the Piccadilly
branch.

Deleuse returned the Englishman's smile and handshake with the
slightly condescending nod of a customer who knew full well his value.
"Good day. I really have very little business to trouble you with, but I
would like to see my security deposit box. If you please." Like his finely
tailored, London-cut, dark worsted suit, crisp white shirt, and regimentally
striped tie, the Algerian's English was flawless, with only the lightest trace
of continental lilt.

"My pleasure," the banker accepted the proffered safety deposit key.

Smythe-Stipe turned, politely motioning his customer to follow. A
few steps away, inside the vault, he opened the dark, oiled oak door and
stood aside, allowing Deleuse to precede him. The two men walked briskly
down the wood-paneled corridor to the wall of deposit boxes. The assistant manager inserted his master key alongside his customer's in number
1059 and extracted the long, heavy steel box. A minute later, Smythe-
Stipe closed the door of the small, expensively appointed private room
off the inner corridor, leaving Monsieur Marc Deleuse to his papers and
possessions.

Inside, alone and secure, Rajid Musaani, alias Marc Deleuse, smiled
as he threw the bolt. The surroundings were intended for the bank's best
customers, who deserved comfort as well as privacy and security when
they attended to their affairs. The Iranian liked that. He leaned back in
the leather-padded wing chair, put his feet on the mahogany table, and
sighed, letting the level of alertness that had sustained his survival slip a
notch.

Musaani congratulated himself on his foresight. Like the four other nonexistent businessmen he had created as preferred customers at banks in Paris, Frankfurt, Rome, and New York over the last two years, "Monsieur Marc Deleuse" had been fashioned as a valued customer of Grindlay's Piccadilly branch for one reason: as an identity that would allow him to slip, without a trace, from one cover to another. The Committee's functionaries in Tehran had raised questions about the time, travel, and money involved in making these fabrications credible. To be sure, they were expensive, Musaani agreed. But they also were necessary to deal with the kind of threat he had faced at Heathrow that morning. There was no doubt in his mind, he thought, and there would be none in the minds of others when the operation was through, that his multiple identities were worth every penny.

Musaani straightened in the chair and prepared to go to work. First, he raised the cover of the safety deposit box, placing the contents to one side on the table. Then he emptied his pockets. The forged Tunisian passport and currency, traveler's checks, counterfeit driver's license, credit cards, and miscellaneous papers that described him as a dealer in handicrafts from Bizerte made a small, neat pile. He went through his pockets twice, ensuring he had found and removed everything, before slipping the passport, credit cards, and papers into the steel box.

Musaani had memorized the details of the five different identities that were documented and stored securely in bank vaults on both sides of the Atlantic. Nonetheless, he took his time, checking the materials he had just removed from the safety deposit box in order to refresh his recollection of the identity he was about to assume.

He picked up the Syrian diplomatic passport and the residence certificate from Damascus. They established him as a foreign ministry representative, traveling on official business for Tehran's ally. The $10,000 in blank traveler's checks also were in order. He counted them, signing six of the $500 denomination checks and slipping them inside the passport before placing it in the breast pocket of his coat. The few odd restaurant and cleaning receipts that confirmed his Syrian identity lay on the table. He thumbed through the papers, mentally noting the place names and addresses as part of his cover story. They would be insurance of sorts if he was stopped, searched, and questioned.

Musaani checked his watch. It was nearly 4:00 p.m. Only a cloth-

wrapped object remained on the table. He unrolled the soft chamois and
the lightly oiled rag beneath it. Under the indirect lighting, the metal
bluing of the .38-caliber, snub-nosed Smith & Wesson Police Special
had a dull sheen. Musaani snapped open the cylinder, checking the chambers, and removed one slug. The nose of the steel-jacketed, armor-piercing
bullet was lightly etched with crosshatching. The indentations insured
that the dumdum would fracture after penetrating the target. Musaani
had needed the advantage only once before. Based on that experience
with an unfortunate Iraqi, he knew that even if it missed vital parts, the
bullet would have the force to shred a limb.

He stared at the Smith & Wesson for several seconds, recalling the
morning. Then, he slipped the pistol into the pocket of his raincoat, replaced the remaining traveler's checks and locked the safety deposit box,
and pressed the silent buzzer, summoning the assistant manager. Five
minutes later, Mr. Brandon Smythe-Stipe bid Monsieur Marc Deleuse
farewell at the door and watched as Rajid Musaani disappeared into the
late-afternoon crowd heading north on Regent toward Oxford Street, Marble Arch, and his rendezvous with Kahlil bin Zahel at the Cumberland
Hotel.

Shortly before 6:15 p.m., Musaani pushed through the large brass-and-
glass revolving door that fronted on Marble Arch and Hyde Park. The
pair of clerks who glanced up from behind the high counter of the hotel
front desk perfunctorily returned his smile. He walked to the right in the
large lobby, stopping at the entrance to the cocktail lounge. The pause
was natural, given the need for a newcomer's eyes to adjust in the bar's
dim light. But Musaani stood longer than usual on the threshold, removing his Burberry raincoat and scanning the clientele, before he acknowledged the bartender's welcoming nod and made his way to the far
corner booth.

He slid onto the oxblood leather seat of the curved settee. A corner
was his preferred position in any public place, and in this case, he was all
but obscured by the shadows that deepened to darkness in the recesses of
the lounge. Tired, Musaani closed his eyes momentarily, stretched his
legs, and settled back.

The incident at Heathrow had been a surprise, and the cause of an especially long day. He had taken no chances. After leaving the airport bus, Musaani had ridden the subway to King's Cross Road. There, in a nondescript hotel, he'd changed clothes before spending the afternoon on the streets, making certain he was not under surveillance. London, he thought, was ideal for that purpose. He had strolled in Hyde Park, taken the paths in Chelsea and Westminster by the Thames, and wandered like a tourist along the old city's narrow lanes. He used the crisscrossing byways like filters, unobtrusively doubling back, sifting those around him through a series of increasingly fine-grained screens. He had repeated the process after leaving Grindlay's Bank, turning west on Oxford Street toward the Cumberland Hotel only when he was satisfied that he was alone.

Musaani leaned forward in his seat, peering into the lobby at the ornate, four-sided Victorian railway clock over the hotel's main desk. 6:30 p.m. As usual, Kahlil was late. About that, Musaani wasn't surprised. He'd come to expect his childlike irresponsibility. Had Kahlil grown up, he would have abandoned his adolescent revolutionary dreams and gone his own way long ago. That would have made it impossible for Musaani to carry out the Committee's orders—to cultivate him, to pander to his delusions and for five long years, to hold his hand, waiting for this opportunity.

Finally, Musaani thought, the time was approaching. From the very top, the Revolutionary Council and the Committee were watching him and him alone. He was the chosen one. He felt an almost mystical sense of power. He had conceived as well as created the mission. That power, his power to create, gave the revolution the power to destroy. And in the destruction, there would be creation again. They would strike, as no operation had ever struck before. Musaani felt his pulse beating harder. The world would be in awe, and at their feet.

The vodka and orange juice he'd ordered arrived at the same moment Kahlil appeared in the entryway. Musaani lifted his drink to catch his eye, and watched him approach the table. At 26, Kahlil bin Zahel still had the face of a boy, but even $2000 worth of Bond Street tailoring couldn't hide the fact that too many pleasures and too few cares had made his body as flaccid as that of a man twice his age. The flabbiness was common among wealthy Arabs, although most hid it, save for soft hands and double chins, under flowing robes and headdresses.

Kahlil slid into the corner beside Musaani, bending forward to kiss him in traditional greeting.

"A good trip, my friend?" Musaani knew the answer without asking. Kahlil's eyes sparkled like those of a child with a secret to tell.

"Very good," Kahlil said, snapping his fingers. The slightly chubby redhead waitress who had served Musaani glanced over, noticing Kahlil's arrival and his small, scraggly goatee and guessing his nationality. She arrived with a speed that suggested the old stories in the London tabloids about rich sheikhs and their four-figure tips were fresh in her mind.

"Dom Perignon," Kahlil didn't even bother to look up. Musaani waited for the champagne to arrive before he pursued his questions. Kahlil shooed the waitress away, filling the two long-stemmed glasses himself.

"Well?" Musaani sipped slowly, his eyes on him.

"Early October," Kahlil answered.

"October," Musaani repeated. "You're certain?"

"That's half," Kahlil nodded, giggling. He raised his glass in a mock toast, and drank, clearly enjoying his control of the game.

"And?" Musaani asked.

"Jabrin," Kahlil paused momentarily for effect, "the Jabrin oasis."

Musaani smiled broadly. "Very good. We're closer because of you, my friend, much closer."

They were. Less than a month before, Musaani had sent Kahlil to Riyadh at the same time he had ordered Von Biemann to approach the American for the peregrine. Both assignments were crucial to the success of the operation, and each had its own risk: in the case of the German, whether his man in Montana could deliver the falcon; and, in the case of Kahlil, whether he could learn what they needed without bungling or arousing suspicion. Now, in the same week, they had come together— the peregrine and the place and date when King Muhammed Kahlil abu Zahel would call on the family of Kahlil bin Zahel. God willing, Musaani thought, it also would be the date and the place for the new Islamic Revolutionary Republic of Arabia to arise.

"Jabrin?" Musaani raised his eyebrows. "Could it change?"

Kahlil shook his head, "No. It is our finest hunting ground, and the king's favorite. It also will be his first hunt of the year for houbara and kairowan. He will be most eager to go."

The houbara was traditional prey. At five pounds, almost twice as big as a hawk, the bird was a fast, low flyer, and a mean fighter. Once there were thousands in Arabia, but oil money had created too many falconers, who had driven them to the brink of extinction. At Jabrin, their presence, along with the kairowan, the stone curlew, a smaller but still feisty prey, made Kahlil's family hunting ground famous.

"Do you know exactly when in October?" Musaani asked.

"The first week," Kahlil replied. "We'll learn the day shortly." He sipped the champagne and continued. "The timing is ahead of the usual schedule. The first hunt of the season normally begins in November, with the onset of winter. But it still will be good. By October, the bird migrations will be under way, and the weather will be fine. The nights will be cold and the mornings will be sharp."

"Why earlier than usual?" Musaani asked suspiciously. In any operation, the unusual troubled him, however minor the detail.

"Who knows?" The nephew of Muhammed Kahlil abu Zahel shrugged, oblivious to Musaani's serious tone. He drained and refilled his champagne glass. "The king loves to fly his falcons and he loves to hunt. They are bedouin pleasures that are hard to enjoy in Riyadh. Perhaps he's looking forward to them and that explains the early start.

"Who knows?" Kahlil repeated. He paused and then chuckled. "My uncle is old. Perhaps that's why. Perhaps," he smiled, "as the years go by, and another fall approaches, the king simply wonders whether this hunting season will be his last."

The sunlight washed through the low, charcoal clouds at precisely 7:45 a.m. on Tuesday morning, September 4, adding a touch of weak blue to the gray Channel water. On the lee side of the St. Christopher's stern promenade, the brightness warmed the small knot of travelers who watched the English coast disappear below the western horizon. A few were businessmen but most were vacationers who had purposely timed their trips for early September when the throngs on their annual August holiday had returned home, emptying the European resorts.

The ocean ferry moved smoothly through the easy swells, bound for Hamburg on its first of two weekly runs. On board, the cargo of automobiles and roll-on containers nearly filled her 7000-gross-deadweight-ton capacity, contrasting with the few passengers, inside and out, who barely accounted for three rows of the ship's comfortable, upper-deck seats.

The small manifest pleased Musaani. He turned up his raincoat collar. It made things easier, he thought. He had already strolled through second-class and most of first. The cluster on the promenade was the last he wanted to survey. Satisfied, he left the small group and stepped back inside.

With the exception of the stewards and a bartender, the upper-deck lounge was virtually empty. Musaani selected a padded deck chair on the port side and reached for the Hamburger *Zeitung* on the nearby occasional table. He could feel the steady, heavy vibration of the engine radiating through the deck. Directly beneath the two passenger levels, well below the waterline, the St. *Christopher's* 21,000-horsepower Pielstick A.P.E. Crossley diesel created an almost living pulse as it turned the giant twin screws.

"It will be a smooth trip, I'm sure."

Musaani looked up and nodded. The man, heavyset and wearing a square-cut, double-breasted suit coat and open-necked white shirt, exhaled a long, labored breath as he settled himself into the neighboring chair. In his fifties, gray-haired, with a stolid burgher's look, he made the casual statement sound like an unarguable assertion, rather than a gambit to open a conversation.

"Yes, I believe so," Musaani replied in German. He glanced at the newspaper in the newcomer's lap. "Ah," he continued in German, "you have yesterday's *Neue Frankfurter Zeitung*. If you're through, may I read it?"

"Please," said Major Wilhelm Kreutzler, the deputy chief of the Special Actions Section, Intelligence Directorate, interior ministry, the German Democratic Republic. He handed over the folded newspaper and smiled. Special Actions took care of the Directorate's liaison with the Committee, and Kreutzler handled the account. It was business, not ideology, that cemented the tie, extending the ministry's reach in the Middle East in exchange for quid pro quos in Europe and sometimes elsewhere to aid Jihad. After five years, Kreutzler knew Rajid Musaani well. Their prearranged words of recognition and reply signaled that each was prepared to conduct the meeting as scheduled.

"You are well?" Musaani asked.

Kreutzler bobbed his head once affirmatively, "Thank you, yes."

Musaani nodded in acknowledgment. The East German's ritual politeness confirmed that the ship was free of watchers. Kreutzler, too, had wandered about, examining the passengers during the first thirty minutes after the *St.Christopher*'s departure from the Harwich ferry dock. So had his three-man countersurveillance team. He had waited for the all-clear sign, which had come two minutes before when Magstadt, the team chief, had ordered coffee at the bar.

Musaani opened the newspaper. The file folder had been taped neatly inside. He turned back the cover. The pictures were stapled to the page facing the report. As ordered, Malaek had air-expressed the photos from Missoula to Munich. Musaani had only examined them briefly before passing the package to the courier who took them to Kreutzler with his request. The East Germans had cropped away the background of the airport waiting area and blown up the three-by-five-inch prints to an eight-by-ten size. The American was dressed casually in a sport jacket, blue jeans, and loafers. Musaani studied his face for several moments before he shifted his eyes to the two-page report. He read it twice before closing the folder and looking up.

"You work very quickly," he said. Kreutzler nodded at the compliment. "What do you make of it?"

"As you can see," the German began, "our information is not complete, but he has obviously had an unusual career. To the best of our knowledge, none of it has involved counterintelligence or international operations." Musaani grunted. "But, I would add," Kreutzler continued, "what he has done, in its own way, has been similar. Maybe even the same. In his case, his work undercover against the mafia in America has developed skills identical to those our profession also must have. 'Tradecraft,' the Americans call it. Perhaps," Kreutzler smiled, "he's a brother under the skin."

"Is DiGenero dangerous?" Musaani asked.

Kreutzler shrugged, "My question to you is, dangerous to what? We have provided you information from our files based on a picture and a name. You have chosen not to tell us why you are interested in him. That is your business, but without knowing more, there is little I can say. I would judge the odds are very small that DiGenero's assignment in Salt Lake City, even if it is undercover, has anything to do with you. The location is wrong, his prior experience is wrong, and there is nothing here," Kreutzler tapped the file, "to suggest he has been coopted by the counterintelligence side of the FBI."

The German paused, "On the other hand, if you are asking my opinion whether a man such as DiGenero is dangerous, my answer is, of course."

"Given what you have just said," Musaani asked, "why?"

Kreutzler smiled paternally, "Very simple. Most human beings exist in an everyday world that allows them to accept what they see, to believe what they hear, and to trust the people they know. But, Herr Musaani, you, I, and this man, DiGenero, cannot. We inhabit a world where everything, including who we are, is ambiguous and open to doubt. Why? Because of what we do. We win the confidence of others only to betray them, and we expect them to do the same to us. We live more than one identity, we are paid never to take anything or anyone at face value, we learn the limits of trust, and we teach ourselves always to doubt. We do not choose to be skeptics as a matter of philosophical or moral perspective. It is required, that is all. A prerequisite in our real, flesh-and-blood world."

The East German turned toward Musaani, "Professional skepticism, perhaps with a touch of paranoia. It is second nature for us, and I would assume for DiGenero as well. Without even thinking twice, he knows in his bones that things are never what they seem. His intuition is programmed to recognize the unusual. When he does, he will try to understand it, and to be ready for the consequences, rather than following the course most people do—explaining it away and then being surprised when life takes a strange twist. Indeed, for some of us, survival depends on that skill."

Kreutzler smiled again, "If, as this file suggests, DiGenero spent years undercover with American gangsters, I would imagine he is quite accomplished at every skill that you and I would prize highly in our work. Otherwise, I do not think he would be alive today."

Musaani leaned back in the lounge chair and closed his eyes. "Suppose, Herr Kreutzler, there was a question whether DiGenero should remain in that status?"

"What status?"

"Alive."

"Hmmm," Kreutzler pursed his lips and looked away. "I have no opinion, really. It is very hard to say. Killing an American FBI agent is not a casual matter. If I was trying to make a decision, it would depend on many things, not the least of which is how much he knows and could know."

Musaani glanced at the German, "A hypothetical question only." He lifted the two typed pages from the file, closing the folder and the newspaper. "May I?" The Iranian gestured at the papers in his hand.

"By all means," Kreutzler nodded. Musaani slipped the report into the breast pocket of his jacket.

"As always," Musaani said, "I appreciate your help and advice." Kreutzler bowed his head slightly, reciprocating the thanks. Musaani looked out. Off the stern, the English coast was gone, behind them. In DiGenero's case, he reflected, Kreutzler's criteria were partially right. The actual question, however, was not what the FBI agent knew, but who. And, by the end of this month, Musaani concluded, who DiGenero knew would not be a problem.

13

Wednesday, September 12, 1984

Überspitzensee, Bavaria, West Germany

Rajid Musaani ran his index finger down the fine print on the coding key to the last entry in the last column of three letter groups, copied "AXR," the trigraph for "end of message," and put down his pen. The four sheets of stationery before him were covered in his small script. He had worked for six hours without interruption, drafting and encoding his report. Until now, he hadn't noticed the dull throbbing behind his temples. He flexed his fingers, loosening their writer's cramp, and rolled his head to limber the corded muscles in his neck.

Musaani snapped off the compact lamp. He had bent it low over the desk to dry the disappearing ink. It was tedious and frustrating work. The thin fluid usually ran and without the heat from the high-intensity bulb, and careful penmanship, the water-soluble stationery would blot and tear. He glanced down. His last words were already fading. He crumpled the cipher key, feeling the film from the oil-impregnated paper, and tossed the wadded ball into the marble ashtray. With only a touch from the flame of his butane lighter, it flashed and was gone. All that remained was to compose an innocuous letter on the stationery as a final precaution to throw off any casual scrutiny if it was intercepted or lost. He bent to the task and was finished in a few minutes.

With the courier due to arrive for the message in two hours, he sat back, mentally reviewing his report. There was, Musaani thought, nothing else to say. All the elements of the operation, not just those he directly controlled, had to be ready by late September. He had described their manpower requirements, the remaining tasks, and the narrowing choice of alternatives if something went awry. Above all, timing was crucial. With each passing day, as they were increasingly committed to the plan, any changes became more difficult, and keeping their schedule correspondingly more important.

From outside, the sound of his father's voice broke through Musaani's concentration. Just then, the ornate clock in the corner of the great room sounded 4:00 p.m. He rose, folding the stationery, and slipped the message into his shirt pocket. His footsteps echoed hollowly as he crossed the slate foyer and stepped through the door. Musaani strolled across the crushed gravel toward the meadow. As his standing orders required, Kamal was in place fifty yards away, next to the Mercedes. The station wagon was parked diagonally across the road, blocking the narrow drive where it emerged from the trees.

Musaani looked toward the river, shading his eyes, and scanned the border of deep, green pines. In the distance, Muhammed appeared in a patch of sunlight, walking slowly. Even at 300 yards, the distinctive silhouette of the Armalite AR-18 propped on his hip stood out. Musaani had personally chosen the American automatic rifle for use on the estate. It could fire 800 rounds a minute into the underbrush or hit a target with a single shot at nearly 500 yards, minimizing the chance that an intruder would escape at either close quarters or long range.

Musaani looked upward as he stepped off the stone drive. Above him, the late-afternoon sun was conceding the day to dark clouds, and the peregrine was banking hard, tightening her circle over the grassy field. The deep beat of her wings seemed effortless as she held her altitude and speed in a constant turn. He halted halfway down the gentle slope, watching. It was the second two-hour training session of the day, a routine begun earlier in the week. Two hundred feet below the falcon, Major Machmed Musaani stood at the center of the circle described by her flight, swinging the feathered lure. At the end of his light line, the bundle of rooks' wings, tied in a clump, circled him, just above head height, in a long, easy loop. The peregrine dipped and accelerated. Her wing beats drove her low and fast across the meadow. She was lengthening her downwind leg, making her flight path into an oval, as she sped to keep her pace in the turn.

Musaani walked toward his father, stopping beside him, "Is she doing well?"

His father glanced at him and then looked up again, following the peregrine with his eyes as he swung the lure, "She is extraordinary. Her learning has taken days, not weeks. It is as if she understands what is to be done before you begin to teach her."

"And she remains healthy?"

"A perfect specimen. I have seen only a few before like this, but never one so young. She is strong and intelligent, and there is something else," his father paused, catching his breath as he swung the lure faster. "She has confidence. It is as if she is eager to show you what she can do, as if what you ask of her is a challenge, not a chore."

"Good," Musaani nodded. The last several weeks had not bridged the chasm between them, but at least he and his father could talk about the bird. As Musaani watched his father, he saw there was no question that the falconer enjoyed practicing his craft.

His father spoke, "Whoever will get this falcon should know one thing."

"Yes?" Musaani asked.

"She should only hunt one season, no more. This peregrine must return to the wild. There are too few left to keep them in captivity and also have a good conscience. That is reason enough. But she is not simply another peregrine. She must breed. There must be more like her. Offspring. Even if there is only one more from her, the world would be a far poorer place without it."

"Hmmm," Musaani shifted uncomfortably. "The value of this one, just one, is very important?"

"Just one?" His father repeated the words. Musaani felt the scrutiny in the old man's quick glance. "Just one of any living thing is important," his father said, "but this one is exceptional."

Machmed Musaani paused and then spoke, "I would always free a few, the ones I could, you know, like the Arabs do." The bedouin traditionally trapped and trained falcons only for a season, releasing them and beginning again with new birds. "The Shah had his favorites, but there were so many that I don't think he noticed very often when I let one go. Once or twice," his father's eyes smiled, "I think he knew but chose to ignore it."

"If their freedom was so important to you, and the Shah of Shahs so magnanimous, why didn't you let them all go?" Musaani smiled sarcastically, provoked as always by his father's recollections about the old days.

Musaani expected a scowl. The reaction surprised him, "A good question, Rajid. I could have, I suppose."

His father thought for several moments and then spoke, "What would have happened? Perhaps two things. First, because most of the falcons had been captive so long, freedom for all, at once, would have been difficult, at least at the beginning. There would have been struggles, for dominance, territory, and food. Most would have lived, many would have suffered, and some would have died. Finally, of course, after much confusion, the falcons would have spread over the land, each found its home, and survived." His father caught his breath again as he swung the lure. "Actually," he shrugged, "if I alone, by my action, could have given the falcons their freedom, it would have been a very good thing."

"But," the old man turned, his eyes following the peregrine as he continued, "would it have happened that way? I don't think so." He smiled, "You see, even after I freed the falcons, others would still have the power to trap, train, and control them. That is the way it has always been in Iran. The real question is not freedom for the falcons." He glanced at his son, "It is freedom from the falconer. So, if I had done what you asked, what would have happened? Of course, you know the answer. There would have been a new falconer, and then, a new falcon stable to replace the old one. And then?" His father looked up at the peregrine, "For the falcons? Who can say? Perhaps more captives, and even less chance for freedom than there was before."

Musaani's anger boiled over, "You could not understand what needed to be done then, and you cannot now."

"Is that so, Rajid?" His father glanced at his watch, "Enough for today, I must bring her in."

He shortened the line, quickening the velocity of the lure and drawing the peregrine to earth. The falcon circled, faster and closer, dipping her wings as she carved her turns in the air. Suddenly, his father dropped the feathered bundle into the thick grass and raised his left arm. The falcon banked sharply. Pivoting on one wing, she leveled into her final approach.

Even now, the peregrine's speed was awesome. Twenty feet from them, the falcon pulled up. It was only a braking motion, but the effect made her appear to hang momentarily suspended in the air before she settled, wings flared and talons extended, halfway between hand and elbow, on the heavy leather cuff of the falconer's glove.

"Now, we will have our walk," his father said, stroking the peregrine's breast with his hand. Musaani watched him walk toward the river. There was no point in arguing, he thought, regaining his composure. There never had been and never would be. His objective was to extract what he needed from the old man. The results, the mission, would speak for themselves.

Musaani turned toward the manor house. Whatever foolishness he believed, his father so far had done as he'd been told. He'd brought the falcon far, very far, in a short time. His ways were the old ways, techniques used by generations of falconers to accustom a new captive to the sight, smell, touch, and voice of a human. The combination was always the same, soft words, stroking, morsels of food, and simple patience. In less than a week, the peregrine had gone from eating warily from his hand to perching on his glove, accompanying the old man on his daily walk to the river.

Her training to the lure the following week, the next test, had gone equally well. For three days, the peregrine had fed to contentment on the fresh pigeon carcass fastened to the bundle of black wings. Then, his father made the portions smaller by lifting her off the artificial prey to finish her meals on his fist. A few days ago, the lesson moved outdoors. His father let her fly tethered to a light line as he spun the lure, calling her back for her rewards from a greater and greater distance.

Finally, late in the afternoon on her fourteenth day, they took the last step, flying the peregrine free. His father had taken the usual precautions. She was "sharp set," kept hungry to increase the appeal of the lure, and weighted with two heavy brass bells attached to her jesses. It was a risk, but if the falcon failed to turn back, the bells would tire her quickly as well as reveal her location, even at a distance and in the trees.

Musaani remembered his own tension when the peregrine launched. From his father's fist, her flight was a sprinter's dash over the meadow, back hunched and wing tips brushing the grass. She had covered 100 yards before Machmed Musaani produced the lure, but in the instant the falcon saw it arc through the air, she wheeled. The return leg was a straight course, direct and precise. The peregrine landed without hesitation beside them.

At the top of the rise, Musaani looked back. The falconer and the falcon were gone. He waved at Kamal, signaling him that the training was over for the day. Muhammed would stay near his father until he returned to the falcon house from his walk with the peregrine. Then, along with Kamal, he would check the perimeter of the estate before dark.

Musaani closed the front door of the manor house and crossed the foyer to the great room, returning to the desk. He removed the folded papers from his pocket and paused. They were close, very close to their ultimate objective. Tomorrow, they would begin "entering" the falcon, the second to last stage of the peregrine's training. "Entering," he spoke the word aloud. It was an unusual, even an odd word to describe the lethal lesson of teaching the falcon to fly straight to the kill.

.Musaani hadn't expected the courier who picked up his message at 6:00 p.m. to deliver another for him from the Committee. It was longer than usual and he only finished decoding it a little after 8:00 p.m.

TO MUSAANI/EYES ONLY

NUMBER 34/12

10 SEPTEMBER 1984

CIPHER KEY A

PRAISE TO ALLAH, THE IMAM, AND BLESSINGS ON THE BROTHERHOOD OF THE REVOLUTION:

MESSAGE STATUS: THIS IS A MESSAGE TRANSMITTING OPERATIONAL ORDERS.

BEGIN TEXT:

THE HIGHEST AUTHORITY CONGRATULATES YOU ON YOUR CONTINUED SUCCESS. FUNDS FOR YOUR OPERATIONAL STRIKE AND SUPPORT TEAM WILL BE SENT WITH THE NEXT COURIER. WIRE DEPOSITS AT DEUTSCHE HANDELSBANK, VIENNA, AND BAYRISCHE KOMMERZBANK, MUNICH, ALSO WILL BE MADE NOT LATER THAN 15 SEPTEMBER IN VON BIEMANN'S ACCOUNTS.

RASHAD AND AMIN SHAKIR WILL ARRIVE ON 15 SEPTEMBER VIA IRANAIR FLIGHT 12 IN FRANKFURT AND PROCEED TO MUNICH. PLEASE MEET.

ADDITIONAL MATERIALS TO BE PROVIDED TO YOU NOT LATER THAN 25 SEPTEMBER ARE AS FOLLOWS:

(1) TWO EGYPTIAN PASSPORTS FOR RASHAD AND AMIN SHAKIR.

INSTRUCT KAHLIL BIN ZAHEL TO OBTAIN VISAS FOR THE SHAKIRS AT EITHER THE ARABIAN CONSULATE GENERAL IN MILAN OR THE ARABIAN EMBASSY IN ROME BETWEEN 27 AND 30 SEPTEMBER. OUR AGENTS IN CONSULAR AFFAIRS WILL PROCESS HIS SPECIAL ROYAL FAMILY LETTER OF INSTRUCTION AUTHORIZING THE VISAS WITHOUT ENTERING A RECORD IN CONSULAR SECTION FILES. ZAHEL SHOULD REQUEST TO SEE ANTONIO GENOVESE, CONSULAR SECTION LOCAL EMPLOYEE, MILAN, OR SADEQ HASIM, VICE CONSUL, ROME.

(2) TWO PIECES OF MODIFIED LUGGAGE WITH CONCEALMENT COMPARTMENTS FOR TRANSPORTATION OF THE ACTION DEVICE, AND OTHER OPERATIONAL EQUIPMENT.

UPON RECEIPT OF THE MODIFIED LUGGAGE, INSTRUCT ZAHEL IN PROPER PACKING OF THE CONCEALMENT COMPARTMENTS. THE COMPARTMENTS WILL BE X-RAY SHIELDED AND HERMETICALLY SEALED. GIVEN EMIGRATION/IMMIGRATION IMMUNITIES AND PRIVILEGES GRANTED TO SAUDI ROYAL FAMILY MEMBERS, ON THE FINAL MISSION THE LUGGAGE MUST BE IN THE POSSESSION OF KAHLIL BIN ZAHEL ONLY.

(3) SCHEMATIC DIAGRAM AND OPERATING INSTRUCTIONS FOR AN/APQ 25/26 CRYPTOCOMPATIBLE TRANSCEIVER.

ENSURE THAT RASHAD SHAKIR IS FULLY CAPABLE OF PERFORMING THE SEQUENCE REQUIRED TO TRANSMIT THE STAND-DOWN INSTRUCTIONS TO THE ARABIAN MILITARY FORCES. BLAST AND FLASH EFFECTS FROM THE ACTION DEVICE SHOULD KILL OR DISABLE ALL UNPREPARED SUBJECTS WITHIN A TWENTY-FOOT RADIUS OF THE PRINCIPAL TARGET, PROVIDING SHAKIR TIME TO GAIN ACCESS TO THE TRANSCEIVER AND SEND THE STAND-DOWN ORDER.

(4) ASTRA .357-MAGNUM REVOLVER WITH SAUDI NATIONAL GUARD HANDGRIP MARKINGS.

ZAHEL SHOULD PROVIDE THE WEAPON TO RASHAD SHAKIR. IF THE BLAST/

FLASH DOES NOT KILL OR DISABLE THE COMMUNICATIONS OFFICER, SHAKIR
SHOULD DO SO AT ONCE IN ORDER TO FULFILL HIS MISSION.

(5) TWO NIPPON DENKI MINITRANSCEIVERS, 2 METERS/FM, 9 VOLT DC.

ZAHEL AND RASHAD SHAKIR SHOULD ENSURE THAT EACH UNDERSTANDS
PRIMARY AND BACKUP RESPONSIBILITY FOR DETONATION OF ACTION DEVICE.

(6) TWO ACTION UNITS.

INSTRUCTIONS ON ACTION UNITS WILL BE INCLUDED. FINAL OPERA-
TIONAL TESTING IS SCHEDULED NEXT WEEK.

PENDING ACTIONS: YOU ARE TO DISPATCH MAJOR MACHMED MUSAANI
TO TEHRAN UPON COMPLETION OF HIS TRAINING DUTIES. SINCE WE WILL
KEEP HIM IN ISOLATION UNTIL THE MISSION IS COMPLETE, YOU ALSO ARE
INSTRUCTED TO SEND A LETTER VIA THE NEXT COURIER FOR DOMESTIC
POSTING, ADVISING FAMILY MEMBERS THAT HIS RETURN TO TEHRAN WILL
BE INDEFINITELY DELAYED.

THIS IS THE END OF MESSAGE.

Musaani stood up and walked to the fire. The heat was welcome.
Despite his months in Germany, he still was not accustomed to the cold
summers and early falls. He glanced again at the message. September
15. The Shakirs would arrive in three days, sooner than he had expected.
It had taken him that long at the safe house in Bonn to select their names
from among the eighty folders sent by the Committee for his review, Musaani recalled.

He had chosen carefully. The Shakirs were exceptional, brothers and
Kurds united as sworn enemies of the Iraqis. With university study in
Cairo and London, they could pass as Palestinians, Egyptians, or Jordan-
ians who moved in the same circles as wealthy Saudis. Trained by the
Revolutionary Guards at the sabotage school at Hamadān, they also had
mastered the courses in communications, small arms, and special mu-
nitions at the expert level. And, to Musaani's everlasting good fortune,
the handwritten autobiographies in their files detailed the fact that they
came from Halabja, a mountain village in Sulaimaniya Province, two
passes west of Iranian Kurdistan, where their family had a reputation for
producing the best falconers in all of Iraq.

Musaani read the message a final time, committing the details to memory before he crumpled the paper and dropped it into the coals of the
fire. Now, he had one more step to take. He frowned. His father's hom-
ily that afternoon had not been a good omen. He could wait a day or two

if he chose, but with the Shakirs' arrival, there really was no point in a
delay. He stepped to the sideboard and pressed the servant's bell. Kamal
appeared moments later.

"Ask my father to join me for tea."

Kamal bowed deferentially and disappeared up the stairs. Musaani
listened to the heavy peasant tread scuff to the end of the second-floor
hall before walking into the dining room and sitting down to wait.

The silver samovar centered on the dining table was old and ornate,
with a look that combined wear and caring. Musaani nodded when his
father entered the room, motioning him to a chair. He reached for two
glasses and drew the strong, steaming tea. They talked idly for several
minutes before Musaani began, giving news of the Shakirs and then, finally, his instructions. When he was through, his father drained his glass
and paused. His voice was never loud, but this time he also spoke slowly,
as if taking care to ensure that his statements of fact were accurate in
every detail.

"In August, I saw you in Paris for the first time in six years. You
asked me to help you. You said you needed me to train a falcon. You
said that it was important. I have done what you asked. In the past two
weeks, we have flown the peregrine. Soon, we will enter her. She is a
superb specimen and will be ready to hunt before the month is out. That
is what she is meant for."

The clock in the great room ticked slowly, the only exception to the
silence. The empty glass in Machmed Musaani's hands held his gaze.
He turned it slowly, as if examining something subtle but distinct, before
continuing, "Now, you are asking for more."

He paused to stare down the length of the table, studying his son across
the distance. When he spoke again, his voice had the sad edge of disappointment, "You are asking me to train her for things that should not be
done."

Musaani stared back. The sound of the timepiece in the adjoining
room continued to set the meter of the moment. The old man looked
away, "What you want, Rajid, will destroy her."

"It is necessary."

The anger hardened the already spare line of his father's jaw, "Necessary? Necessary for what?"

"For our objective."

"Our objective?" The question had an acid edge. "Spare me, Rajid. I am not stupid. It does not take a genius to discern the purpose of your special training. This evening, you have asked me to do three things. To teach the falcon to fly from one handler to another. To teach her to carry something, something small. One pound, maybe two? And, you said, to teach her, then, to return to her original handler."

Musaani looked up. His father's eyes had gone as flat and cold as his voice, "And then, Rajid? Then, what? No, do not give me the answer. I will give it to you. The falcon dies. Is that not correct? In this world, is that much? Even if it is a peregrine falcon? Of course not. But you tell me something, Rajid. Who else dies? Who else are you going to kill? Do you know? Do you care? Is this what you do? Is this what you have done for the last six years? In the name of the revolution? In the name of Islam? Is this why I saved you from SAVAK? Are you any better or any different from them?"

Musaani glared at his father and then looked away. The old man's chair scraped on the floor as he rose. Musaani heard the familiar footfalls begin and then stop behind him, close to the door.

"Oh yes, Rajid, I have a final question. If I do not do this for you and those whom you serve, what then?"

His father stood half in the light of the dining room, and half in the darkness of the hall. Musaani turned toward him and spoke, "You and I are from the same place, but two different worlds. There is no hope that it will ever be different. I will not try to explain to you why this must be done, why the revolution is so important, why I am so important to it at this moment. I," Musaani's eyes flashed, "I, the major's son who was better than all of those you served, but still wasn't good enough. The one who your masters sought to destroy. I have been chosen. One of a few, a very few." Musaani felt his anger overcome him, "You should take pride in that, great pride. You should. But you do not."

He paused, his eyes cold and his tone frozen, "Why should you do this? Very simple. It is something you can understand. You and I still have the same family. They are still in Iran. You will therefore do what I ask. You have no choice," he spoke the words deliberately and without emotion, "nor do I."

The old man raised his chin, his eyes appearing to look through Musaani, as if focusing on someone else who occupied his place. Finally, his father turned and slipped out of the light. His tread sounded hollow, ascending the stairs.

Musaani felt the tremor in his arms as he unclenched his fists. He waited until he heard the bedroom door close before he pushed the button on the servant's bell. Kamal appeared through the door to the pantry, obviously half asleep.

"From this evening on, I want you to stay with my father. Night and day. He is to go nowhere without my permission."

Kamal bobbed his head perfunctorily and turned back toward the kitchen.

"Now!" Musaani's order stopped Kamal short. He looked down embarrassed, avoiding Musaani's eyes, bowed low in silent assent, and walked up the stairs.

14

Friday, September 14, 1984

The Qara Su Compound, Qom, Iran

Azhger Navadeh-Taheni put down Musaani's report, removed his wire-rimmed glasses, and rubbed the small red marks on the bridge of his nose. Then the slight, balding man rose from his desk and walked to the windows. From the spacious top-floor room, Taheni commanded a full view of the central courtyard of the Qara Su compound. The long quadrangle created by the fortress-style inner walls of the four-story building reflected an architecture totally in character with the compound's former purpose as SAVAK's regional headquarters. Little had changed in the shabby building since 1979. Except for the row of six posts, spaced six feet apart, at the far end of the courtyard, the vista below remained barren, a monotone of packed earth and mortar-gray walls. Like its previous occupants, the new tenants also had chosen not to display nameplates or signs that explained their purpose to those who passed by in the street.

The sharp knock on the door from the anteroom momentarily startled Taheni. He glanced at his watch. His appointment was for 12:30

p.m. and as always, Ayatollah Reza Hosein was exactly on time. He straightened his jacket and turned to face the door.

Hosein had been no less punctual three years ago when he had visited Taheni's former office in Qara Su to declare that Taheni's work as Qom's revolutionary magistrate, and most feared hanging judge, was complete. The Revolutionary Council, Hosein had said, was entrusting him with a new, more important mission. The honor had surprised Taheni, as had the news that his responsibilities would not require him to leave the compound, but only to move up one floor.

Even now, only thirty people in Qom knew that the north wing represented the true purpose of Qara Su. Of these, sixteen served Taheni himself, working in the cubicles along the hall outside his fourth-floor suite. Together, they made up the office of the director of the executive staff of the Committee.

Taheni straightened to an approximation of attention as he spoke, "Come."

He could see his secretary bowing low in the background as the door to his anteroom swung open. Reza Hosein entered, "Good day, Taheni, you're looking well."

"And you," Taheni replied, lowering his head in his own gesture of respect.

"Please," he motioned to the armchair and waited to be seated behind his desk until Reza Hosein had taken the place.

Ayatollah Reza Hosein was nearly six feet, four inches tall. His full beard, heavy eyebrows, and unwavering ebony stare made him doubly imposing in his cleric's flowing black robes. For the handful who understood the personal connections that bound together the Islamic Republic's inner circle, Reza Hosein was a presence and a power to be feared. As the chief of security for Khomeini, Hosein had protected the Ayatollah during his long years of exile, then founded the Committee and, as its first director, served as Taheni's only predecessor. Since 1979, he also had been the unanimous choice to hold the Revolutionary Council's most sensitive and secret portfolio: as minister for Special Actions, he was the highest official directing Iran's terror network abroad.

"I've read your operational plan," Hosein said, smiling. "It's taken a long time to reach this point, Taheni, and occasionally, I must admit, I wondered if we ever would."

"Indeed, I too wondered, but..."

"But now we have," Hosein continued, completing Taheni's sentence, "and it is none too soon."

Taheni had not spoken with Hosein in three days. Musaani's latest report had arrived by courier from Munich that morning. Taheni summarized its contents as well as filled in the remaining details, "The Shakirs and the peregrine are ready. Prince Zahel arrives in Germany next week to begin his training. Our technical unit is preparing to test the action device at the front in a few days. Then, Phase Three will be complete."

Ayatollah Reza Hosein nodded. He withdrew a small notebook from his valise and opened it on his lap. Navadeh-Taheni fell silent as Hosein flipped slowly through the pages. He knew the Revolutionary Council had met that morning for its regular session, during which Hosein always presented the Committee's weekly report. Afterward, their standing midday appointment served as Hosein's occasion to pass on new guidance as well as any special instructions from the Council.

Hosein refreshed his memory of the morning's discussion before he spoke. Finally, he looked up, "You should know, Taheni, there was some debate over this."

Taheni swallowed hard. He had wide discretion in managing the Committee's operations, but with a plan of this magnitude and consequence the Council had to give its explicit approval at each major step. His memory of the only other special action to require such approval, the attempt in London the previous year to assassinate Ghavi, the last chief of SAVAK, still woke Taheni at night in a cold sweat. The London location, and the certainty that they would need to kill Ghavi's British as well as Iraqi bodyguards, had raised the risks. It had not gone well. Ghavi had escaped, the hit team had died in a hail of bullets outside the Claridge Hotel, the ambassador and half the embassy had been ordered home by the Foreign Office, and Besharati and Dierza, Taheni's two subordinates who planned the operation, had been executed.

He watched Hosein scan further down the page. The notebook seemed incongruously small in his massive hands as he thumbed back and forth, looking for the correct spot. Taheni shifted uncomfortably in his chair. When the Ghavi mission failed, he remembered, it was Hosein's signature that had been on the bottom of the one-sentence document that ordered Besharati and Dierza shot.

Hosein cleared his throat. He had found the place.

"There are some," he said, reading, "who do not believe we should divert our resources from the Iraqi front until Saddam Hussein is finished. Until, that is, we have our heel on his throat. They want to fight to the last bullet and man. As a consequence, they question the claim our operation will make on troops, planes, and ships. They worry about dividing and weakening our forces. If we do, they predict we will lose ground."

Hosein looked up, "Nasr, the commander of the Guards, made this point very strongly. He said the war is changing and that our fortunes will turn on their own. He believes that now is not the time to take the risk."

The perspiration rolling down Taheni's neck darkened the closed collar on his tieless white shirt. "And you, Reza Hosein, what do you believe?"

Hosein smiled benignly and closed his notebook. With the powerful reach of the Committee operating through Taheni's hands, Reza Hosein knew full well that a little anxiety was a useful thing. Power, like a slowly developing disease, had unfortunate effects on even the most loyal. Under the circumstances, Hosein saw Taheni much as a doctor would view a patient who regularly needed an antidote that could suppress, albeit unfortunately not cure, a chronic condition. In this case, the prescription was simple—to never allow Taheni to doubt the need for Hosein's personal protection, or the ill effects if he attempted to operate outside his direct control.

Hosein raised his eyebrows as if puzzled by the question, "I? Why, Taheni, I, of course, supported the operation." The relief on Taheni's face was obvious. Hosein continued, his purposely neutral tone a counterpoint to the seemingly reassuring words, "You know, Taheni, like many such discussions at the Council table, the question is not where we are going. That is clear enough. The Imam has told us that Saddam Hussein and the satans in Baghdad will be destroyed."

"In truth," Navadeh-Taheni replied, nodding vigorously.

"Rather," Hosein said, clasping his hands, one over the other, in the contemplative gesture of a cleric reflecting on a difficult theological point, "the question is how farsighted we can be in getting there."

Hosein motioned toward the carafe of tea on the side table. Taheni rose immediately. His hands trembled slightly as he poured the dark, steaming liquid into the small, clear glass.

"I too believe that Saddam Hussein will fall," Hosein said, "but by itself that will not bring the end."

"To the war?" Taheni asked subserviently.

"No, Taheni," Hosein answered. "To the cause of the war. And," he reached to take the proffered glass, "the Imam agrees." Taheni nodded vigorously, making clear that he saw the wisdom at once of the Ayatollah's view.

Hosein sipped the steaming tea before he spoke, "Today, Saddam Hussein is our antagonist, to be sure. But he is only a mercenary who is paid to win time, to stave off the threat of our revolution. To eliminate him is not enough. There are more where he came from and it would only be a matter of time before they found someone else to take his place. They will arm him and, sooner or later, they will send him against us. And when that fails, they will try something else, perhaps exiles, perhaps the Americans, perhaps the Europeans. By themselves, they are only a few, but they have the wealth to challenge us again and again."

Hosein leaned forward. Even seated in the chair, his bulk seemed to loom over Taheni's desk.

"Baghdad, Taheni. Baghdad is the stage where the puppet dances. But Riyadh, Riyadh is backstage, where the puppeteer stands to pull the strings. That is why the operation is so important. That is why we must strike at Riyadh. That," Reza Hosein smiled, "is why King Zahel must die."

Hosein rose slowly from the chair, handing his empty glass to Taheni, "And, that it should happen from the inside, not from without, will be our ultimate victory." Hosein smiled at the knowledge that they shared a profoundly powerful secret. "We will, of course, assist the new regime when the true revolutionary, our own Prince Kahlil, requests our aid. It would only be natural for us to provide our military forces to protect the faithful. But the beginning, the crucial beginning, must appear to all the world as their doing, not ours. Our hand cannot show."

Hosein turned toward the door, "I am satisfied with Musaani's activities and with your effort to oversee them, but I want you to keep me advised."

Taheni stepped smartly to usher Hosein out and then remembered,

"There is one detail, Reza Hosein. The falconer. Musaani's father. We needed him and we are using him, but his background gives me pause. And," Taheni said, "he will know."

"Ah, yes, Musaani's father," Hosein repeated, pausing. He had not seen Musaani face-to-face since 1979 when he told him of his selection for Jihad in the Oakland walk-up apartment, but as the Committee's first director, and now, through Taheni, he had followed Musaani's work over the years. Taheni watched silently as Hosein rubbed his chin with his left hand, reflecting. He rarely revealed his grotesquely twisted fingers except inadvertently, when he was lost in thought.

"Where is the father now?" Hosein asked.

"At Überspitzensee." Taheni explained, "We have instructed Musaani to return him to Tehran when the training of the falcon is complete. I believe he represents a loose end, Reza Hosein, one that should be tied up permanently."

Hosein stared into the middle distance for several moments, "Hold him until it is over."

"And then?" Taheni asked.

"And then what?" Hosein eyed Taheni coldly.

Flustered, Taheni looked down, "I just thought..."

"You have your answer. Make sure his keepers know to hold him until they have further orders from me."

Hosein turned, his right hand on the doorknob, and looked back. He smiled faintly, "God go with you, Taheni."

Taheni bowed his farewell, "And with you, Reza Hosein."

15

Monday, September 17, 1984

The Eslamabad Road, Kermānshāhan Province, Iran

Nahavandian watched the first four-by-four, headlights out and gears grinding in low, crest the hill. It bounced over the summit toward the jeep, heeling precariously from one angle to another. Moments later, another, identical American Army ton-and-a-half, also painted desert-tan and gray, slewed right and left as it broached on the rise, braking to avoid the first.

"Two?" Nahavandian asked quizzically. "How many did they bring?" The rear canvas canopies shook in an odd rhythm as the battered trucks picked their way down the slope, scattering the gravel and rocks in a small cascade before them.

"Who cares?" Mirza groaned and sat up, staring through the dirty windscreen of the jeep. After driving all day and half the night from Tehran, both men were coated with desert grit. They were 50 miles east of Iraq and 350 miles west of Tehran in a long, narrowing valley that twisted north toward the border. The central range of the Zagros, rocky and bare, rose 7000 feet toward the brightening sky. The burned iron-red color of the slopes appeared to bleed slowly through the dawn's gray half-light.

Nahavandian shivered. It was time to get it over with, he thought. As assistant section chief in the Technical Development Laboratory, Intelligence Bureau, Revolutionary Guards, he managed all the details when they fabricated special orders. The projects were always the most trouble as well as the ones that he personally had to test.

He looked around. The jeep was parked on a flat, gravel-covered wash, a runoff for the winter snows. Thirty yards away, a rough border of boulders marked the edge of the alluvial fan. Beyond, the land fell away again in a steep wadi. The place was typical for the province, Nahavandian thought with distaste, harsh and lifeless.

He glanced at Mirza, who had stumbled from the rear seat to relieve himself behind the jeep. A failed engineering student, he was barely adequate as a laboratory assistant. Nahavandian shook his head, considering a variety of sarcastic remarks to salve his aggravation, but the first four-by-four skidded to a halt in front of the jeep before he could choose just the right vocabulary.

Major Jahrome Hoivedya climbed from the truck, eyeing with distaste the two men who waited for him. Nothing in the ten-hour, 150-mile drive from Dezfūl had improved his disposition. Revolution or no revolution, Hoivedya thought, he was a soldier, not a jailer. He still wore the dark-blue beret of an Imperial Army parachutist with pride, albeit without the small imperial peacock pin on its unit crest.

Hoivedya spit into the dusk, folding his arms as the two civilians approached. They were not Revolutionary Guards, Army, or police, but they were in the proper place, at the proper time, and were therefore the proper recipients for his cargo.

"Out!" Hoivedya bellowed the order.

Five soldiers piled from the first truck and four more from the last. Hoivedya motioned, pointing to either side of the second ton-and-a-half. The nine men wore a motley collection of patched and faded Iranian Army desert camouflage fatigues, but they deployed with practiced efficiency, positioning themselves in a loose ring around the truck. The metal-on-metal snap of their twenty-round magazines sounded sharply as each locked a 7.62-mm cartridge in the chamber of his Heckler & Koch G-3 rifle.

Hoivedya watched, satisfied. They were his, the remnants of the only commando team that remained intact out of the 1200 men who had once composed the First Special Forces Brigade, Imperial Army of Iran. Like him, they were not trusted. But, he thought, in a war that was entering its fifth bloody year, loyalties aside, even the zealots in Tehran knew they were too valuable to destroy.

Hoivedya turned toward Nahavandian, extracting a folded paper from his tunic's breast pocket, "You'll need to sign the receipt. Where do you want them?"

"Over there," Nahavandian pointed toward the center of the gravel delta. "Go ahead and get them out. It will take me a few minutes to prepare." He scrawled his signature on the bottom of the paper and handed it back.

Hoivedya nodded at the burly noncommissioned officer who stepped to the rear of the ton-and-a-half, threw back its canvas flap, and gestured, jerking his rifle muzzle. The prisoners emerged one by one, heads down, elbows tied with telephone wire behind their backs, and stopped dutifully in the approximate center of the armed circle. The Iraqis were still in uniform, or at least parts and pieces of what passed for military dress in the overcrowded POW camp at Dezfūl. All were young, heads close-shaven, obviously conscripts, no more than early twenties, Nahavandian guessed. He counted five. It was the correct number.

Nahavandian glanced at Mirza, "Get the box and come with me." They had work to do, but his assistant had turned pale. Mirza unsteadily retraced his steps to the jeep, lifted the small wooden container from be-

hind the passenger seat, and set off, stumbling, several paces behind Nahavandian. They halted thirty yards from the jeep, where a large flat rock
stood alone in the middle of the gravel bed. "Here," Nahavandian pointed
down at the tablelike surface.

Mirza's hands trembled as he positioned the box. Nahavandian un-
snapped its metal latches and flipped open the hinged cover, momentarily admiring the contents. It was egg-shaped, weighing slightly less than
a pound, and covered with a light-brown papier mâché. At one end, a
single, short strand of thin, plastic-coated antenna wire emerged.

Nahavandian lifted out his creation, checking it carefully. Musaani
again, he thought. He was a legend. The name wasn't even identified
with this special order, but Nahavandian knew the meticulous instructions were his trademark: in this case, to fabricate a remotely activated
antipersonnel weapon, no more than a pound in weight, that could kill
within a twenty-foot radius.

A half pound of American C4 explosive and Japanese electronic components provided the basic material. The supplies on hand in the laboratory in Tehran contained most of what was needed—the C4 and the
miniature printed circuit boards from the new, credit-card-sized AM/FM
pocket radios. The priority order from Tokyo had provided the rest. He
had modified the Sony circuit boards to receive a low-frequency FM signal and wired the model aircraft builder's microswitches and flight control surface solenoids to construct a tiny, charged capacitor fuse kit. In
the palm-sized transmitter unit, a two-meter frequency setting virtually
eliminated the danger of interference. With a nine-volt nickel-cadmium
dry-cell battery, the signal could cover a mile.

Only one specification had given him a problem, he remembered.
The required MOE, the Mandatory Operational Effectiveness. One hundred percent probability of kill within a twenty-foot radius. The usual
technique—embedding the plastique with steel that would kill as shrapnel—wouldn't work. It would make the device too heavy, over the one-
pound weight limit. More explosive also wouldn't increase the killing
probability to 100 percent. Without shrapnel, the C4's lethal effect depended on concussion, but at the critical moment the target might be
protected by someone or something from the blast.

The solution had come to him late one night when he heard an airplane taking off from Mehrabad. Titanium. Alloyed with steel, it was the

primary ingredient in the skin of high-performance aircraft. Light, in pure form, the metal could withstand a 3200-degree Fahrenheit flame. Nahavandian had embedded 700 pieces of titanium alloy, each a 2-mm cube weighing .01 ounce, in the plastique. The blast would hurl them outward at 6500 feet per second. Within twenty feet, he calculated, they would provide more than enough insurance of the desired result.

Nahavandian walked back toward the cluster of soldiers and POWs. He pulled the diagram from under his jacket, catching the major's eye, "Have your men bring them this way."

Hoivedya nodded, "Do what he says."

The NCO grunted at the squad. The soldiers formed a loose cordon, herding the Iraqis. Nahavandian walked ahead, diagram in hand. The proper spacing and postures were important. He pointed out the locations for each POW and then motioned to the NCO, "Tell them this is a simple experiment with a smoke camouflage device. Tell them also that if they move, they'll be shot."

The NCO turned, repeating the warning. Nahavandian approached Hoivedya, lowering his voice, "Have your men withdraw below the edge of the wash." Nahavandian made one circuit of the group, checking, and then strolled away. He joined the soldiers and looked back just as the sun broke through the clouds. Illuminated in the first brightness of the new day, the five Iraqis, unmoving, made a still life as Nahavandian crouched. He removed the small transmitter from his field jacket pocket and pressed the button.

The explosion reverberated against the rocky slope. Nahavandian looked up. The five remained where he had placed them, although now lying down. He motioned to Mirza, who had just vomited. The laboratory assistant, retching with dry heaves, ignored him. Nahavandian shook his head, disgusted, and walked back to the wash.

A few feet from the detonation site, he paused. The small flesh wounds had the appearance of a childhood rash, peppering the skin with angry but seemingly insignificant marks. Looks were deceiving. The force of the explosion had driven the small metal shards through the bodies. The blast effects had done the rest.

Nahavandian turned toward the groan. The POW who had been farthest from the device lay facedown where he had fallen. Nahavandian poked him with his toe. The man was quiet. He poked harder and waited, watching the pool of blood seep into the gravel. He looked up at the sound of the stones crunching behind him.

"Well?" The major's eyes as well as his voice registered his disgust.

Nahavandian didn't notice, "One hundred percent. Have your men bury them, please."

Hoivedya stood, arms folded, and spat on the ground as he watched Nahavandian walk away.

Part Three

Flight

16

Friday, September 21, 1984

The University Building, Salt Lake City, Utah

DiGenero opened the door to RAPTOR's suite with a weary shove. After six fruitless hours with the prosecutors in Tucson who were nervous about taking two of his poaching cases to trial, the flight back to Salt Lake City had been crowded, bumpy, and late. Nancy McLaughlin saw the telltale signs of DiGenero's sixteen-hour day in his expression as soon as she glanced up, "My, don't you look chipper? How about if I book a first-class on Trailways for you next time?"

He grinned, "I thought you had. Any mail from Bozeman?"

"It's in the stack on your desk."

DiGenero walked quickly into his office, tossing his suit coat on the chair. The mail filled his in-box. He shuffled anxiously through the memos, letters, and notes until he found the envelope. He slipped the small blade of his pocketknife into the flap, slicing down the paper edge with one quick motion. The two single-spaced, typewritten pages were folded neatly in thirds. Delia Conner had clipped her usual small blue note on top, as always adding an "X" beneath her name.

If he had to marry Delia to keep her on the job, DiGenero thought, 200 pounds or not, he'd consider it. She was his best transcriber and could make sense of the world's worst tapes. Margie, the other part-timer he'd hired to handle what they recorded in Missoula, wasn't nearly as good, although DiGenero conceded that transcription of this sort was a talent, not an acquired skill. A wire never produced paragraphs or even necessarily sentences, but mainly words hung suspended in a mesh of unspoken understanding. Delia had the ear. She could piece together the snippets of conversation like a practiced restorer who was able immediately to see order in a pile of broken pot shards.

He opened his briefcase and extracted the file of transcripts, laying its scant contents before him on the desk. Each week, on Friday, the courier delivered one from Bozeman followed a day later by the other from Missoula. Neither Harris nor Erin was much of a talker, hence the small stack of paper that had accumulated in the month since the soundmen had installed the wires.

In a sense, nothing was something, DiGenero thought hopefully as he dropped into his chair. Harris hadn't mentioned the German, falcons, or the pending deal on the phone in the last month. Even so, he was still looking for something positive, a sign in one or the other's comments that his message to Erin had gotten through.

DiGenero flattened the heavy bond paper with the heel of his hand, scanning down Delia's standard format. The report recorded seven days' worth of calls. The first four pages were blank, only dated and noted with the entry, "Nothing." He flipped quickly to the fifth, Wednesday, two days before.

"Bingo!" DiGenero sat up straight when his eyes reached the second line in the text.

WEDNESDAY, 19 SEPTEMBER 84

INCOMING CALL, 4:35 P.M. TO 4:38 P.M.

HARRIS: HELLO?

CALLER: KIRBY? IT'S KLAUS.

HARRIS: HOW'S IT GOING?

CALLER: FINE. I DIDN'T KNOW IF YOU'D BE AT THE RANCH OR IN MISSOULA.

HARRIS: NOPE. THE UNIVERSITY'S BACK IN SESSION. ERIN'S TEACHING AND RUN-NING THE LAB. I'VE BEEN HERE MOSTLY SINCE I GOT BACK FROM MUNICH. WHEN ARE YOU ARRIVING?

CALLER: THAT'S THE REASON FOR MY CALL. THERE'S BEEN A CHANGE IN MY PLANS.

HARRIS: OH? I... (INAUDIBLE). WHAT'S THE PROBLEM?

CALLER: NOTHING SERIOUS. ANOTHER BUSINESS OBLIGATION CAME UP. I CAN'T

RESCHEDULE. (INAUDIBLE) BUT I DON'T WANT TO INCONVENIENCE YOU. AN ACQUAINTANCE OF MINE (INAUDIBLE). HE'LL BE TRAVELING IN CANADA AND HAS AGREED TO MEET YOU AND TAKE THE MERCHANDISE.

HARRIS: I DON'T KNOW, KLAUS. THIS IS A LITTLE OUT OF THE (INAUDIBLE). MAYBE WE SHOULD (INAUDIBLE)...

CALLER: DON'T WORRY. HE AND I HAVE DONE BUSINESS BEFORE. HE'S QUITE TRUSTWORTHY. I'VE ALREADY ASKED HIM TO GO WITH YOU TO GET THE GOODS. HE'LL MAKE ALL HIS OWN ARRANGEMENTS TO BRING THEM EAST.

HARRIS: WHEN?

CALLER: YOU CAN EXPECT A CALL FROM HIM ON THE 24TH. (INAUDIBLE) FROM CALGARY.

HARRIS: WHAT ABOUT THE MONEY?

CALLER: (LAUGHTER). DON'T WORRY. HE'LL HAVE YOUR PAYMENT IN FULL.

HARRIS: OK, BUT...

CALLER: HE'S LOOKING FORWARD TO GOING NORTH WITH YOU.

HARRIS: OK, BUT...

CALLER: I'LL BE IN TOUCH. CIAO.

HARRIS: YEAH...

END OF CONVERSATION

"Shit," DiGenero tossed the transcript on the desk. He was looking for a sign and this sure as hell was a sign. The wrong sign. The next deal was going down on schedule, evidence that Harris obviously didn't give a rat's ass for what he'd said. DiGenero took a deep breath, letting the immediate rush of anger subside. More important, he thought, if he had Von Biemann's call on tape, so would the German police. And, if they had it, Stockman and the Bureau would, too.

He rubbed his eyes, trying to massage away the tension headache he'd had since Tucson. It was only a matter of time, he thought, before the law of the bureaucratic jungle would apply. The net would tighten, sooner or later, and when it did, the FBI would pull in the small fry in order to justify the operation and make the arrest numbers go up, even if they didn't catch the big one.

"Goddamn it, Kirby, wise up," DiGenero put his head in his hands, frustrated. It wasn't Laos, or Cambodia, or Vietnam anymore, and Harris wasn't flying solo in his own private war, DiGenero thought. That was over, gone. It wasn't like it used to be. This time, at home in Montana or not, Kirby was on DiGenero's territory, playing *his* game, by *his* rules, he thought.

Four blocks distant, above Temple Square, the chimes of the Mormon Tabernacle began their hourly melody. The music overflowed from the oddly austere and ornate church compound into the city streets and then receded, replaced by a slow, resonant toll. Eyes closed, he counted. 8:00 p.m. DiGenero looked up. He reached for his desk calendar, tearing off the small, square page and staring at the new date. Time, he thought. There was still some of that. He put his hand on the phone. He had to try, to make the effort to get through to Harris, once more. Monday, September 24, was still two days away.

Erin Dupres closed her eyes, feeling the whisper of Harris's breath as his lips brushed between her breasts. Her hand rested lightly on his head, following rather than guiding his motion. It was the end of a long day, but at 8:00 p.m. only the beginning of their night. After three weeks apart, the waiting had made even the imagining better. In the darkness of the bedroom, she sensed the touch of fingers, harder this time, and then the richer sensation of lips exploring the soft private stretches of her skin.

Harris had started slowly, at first undressing her, slipping off his own clothes and then, lying beside her, half-caressing, half-teasing until she pulled him between her legs. Now he was teasing again, although she willingly relinquished the initiative as he traced a long, moist line across her stomach and along her inner thigh. She raised her hips, hooking one shapely leg over his back like a dancer in an exotic choreography, and pressed his head downward, hurrying progress. Finally, his tongue began to probe, responding, just as the phone rang.

"Jesus Christ, ignore the goddamn thing," Harris groaned and resumed. The ringing persisted.

Erin glanced across the rumpled sheets of her double bed at the night table, "I'd better see who it is." Harris looked up. She smiled seductively, stroking his forehead, "Don't lose your place."

Erin lifted the phone, "Hello?"

As she lay on her side, the curve of her hips fell into a narrow waist and then rose toward full, perfectly formed breasts. She had never borne children or let herself slide into an unintended decay, maintaining with diet and exercise the body of a woman ten years her junior. Harris rolled away, watching her. Erin aroused him. Always. He ran his hand gently up her inner thigh, lightly stroking the unblemished softness. No reaction. The call seemed to have totally absorbed her.

Erin covered the receiver with her hand, "It's Frank." She extended the phone, "For you." The semidarkness masked Harris's surprise. DiGenero usually didn't call him here. He took the receiver. Erin reached toward the small table, switching on the bedside lamp.

Harris propped himself on his elbow, winked, and spoke, feigning anger, "Do you flea-bitten Feds have any idea of the kind of privacy you're invading right now?"

"I need to talk to you, Kirby," DiGenero said. His voice was serious, "My apologies for the interruption, but I tried to reach you at the ranch. I figured this was my next best bet."

Erin leaned back against the pillows. DiGenero's tone made Harris sit up, leaving behind his smile, "What can I do for you?"

"Von Biemann," DiGenero let the German's name hang in the air before he continued, choosing his words carefully. He didn't want Harris to guess about the wires. "We know about the deal with him and your meeting on Monday. We're going to take Von Biemann down. I don't want you to go down with him. I can keep that from happening, but you've got to let me."

Erin watched Harris draw his lips into a cold, tight line. In the light of the single bedroom lamp, his eyes appeared a colorless steel gray rather than blue. His expression was an odd contrast to the mocking humor in his voice, "Goddamn, Frank, you smoking something? What are you talkin' about?"

"Cut the good ol' boy routine, Kirby. I want the German. I don't want you. There's more to it than you realize. The clock is running and he's going to be had."

"And?"

"We need to talk," DiGenero replied.

"When?"

"Tomorrow."

Harris stood up, his body backlit by the brightness from the hall. His muscles defined themselves, lean and hard. "OK," he said. "Tomorrow afternoon, here. How's that?"

"Fine."

Harris hung up.

"It's Von Biemann, isn't it?" Harris turned, gazing at Erin. Her voice was calm but the apprehension had widened her eyes.

"Yeah."

"What are you going to do?" Erin asked quietly.

He knelt on the bedside, pulling her toward him, and smiled, "I told Frank I'd talk to him here, tomorrow." Harris saw her relief before she wrapped her arms around him. He felt her breathing and then, the tremble in her sigh.

"What's the matter?"

"I'm glad, Kirby. I . . . ," Erin's voice trailed off. "This time, I'm worried. You've done enough with Von Biemann, I think. You don't need this deal. I wanted you to talk to Frank." She paused, "I was afraid you wouldn't."

His caress resumed, but the warmth inside her came from more than his touch. Her fingertips brushed his cheek. Harris's lips explored the outline of her throat as he spoke, "Does that make you happy?"

Her silence lasted a moment. Then, a single tear touched his shoulder followed by a whisper, "Of course."

"Then," a thin smile crossed Harris's face as he twined her hair in his hand, only half-gently drawing her head back, "what are you going to do to show me how happy you are?"

Erin's laugh filled the room as he pretended to struggle before allowing himself to be toppled onto the bed. She straddled his body, facing him, in one easy motion and reached back with both hands, searching behind her.

"What am I going to do?" She breathed harder, closing her fingers around him, and began a slow stroking motion, "That's easy. Tonight, whatever you want."

Harris's movements in the early Saturday morning darkness woke Erin with a start. At 5:20 a.m., the bedroom was still pitch-black, but somehow she could sense that he was already dressed.

"Kirby?" Erin snapped on the lamp. "Where are you going?"

Harris was buttoning his shirt. He glanced at her sideways, expressionless, before sitting on the edge of the bed to pull on his boots.

"For a little ride."

"Where?"

Harris shrugged, "Why don't you go back to sleep?" He grinned, reaching to pat her hip under the sheet. "You deserve a rest after working so hard last night."

"When are you coming back?"

His tone was mildly mocking, "You'll be the first to know."

The sinking feeling in her stomach clarified the confusion moments before she felt the first twinge of anger that he'd lied to her. Harris stood up, looking down at her. Erin sat back against the headboard, her knees drawn up. She was rarely self-conscious, but the sense of disadvantage prompted her to pull the bedsheet higher around her breasts.

"You'd already decided last night, when Frank called, that you weren't going to wait, hadn't you?"

Harris didn't answer. She continued, fashioning her own reply, "You never meant to meet him here at all."

Harris chuckled, "Now, what would make you say a thing like that?"

Erin shifted her gaze, feeling the color rise in her cheeks, as he stepped away.

"Give Frank my best," Harris smiled sardonically, looking back. "Oh yeah, and tell him I really appreciate his help."

Erin watched Harris turn again toward the door, shaking her head slowly, "You can be a son of a bitch, Kirby, a first-class son of a bitch, without even trying." Harris didn't pause to reply. The hall carpet muffled the dull, heavy tread of his boots, although Erin could hear his soft laughter clearly even after he closed the apartment door.

*   *   *

DiGenero took the beer, nodding his thanks as they stepped out of the kitchen and turned down the hall. The living room was small but comfortable. Erin's furnishings included a few antique pieces, obviously saved for and carefully chosen, but mostly things that were comfortable, soft and worn. Despite the cool evening, the window air conditioner droned low in the background, emptying the three-room apartment of the last heat from the Indian summer day.

"Sorry about barging in on Saturday night," he said.

Erin waved away the apology. DiGenero had been scheduled to land at 2:00 p.m., on the first available flight on Saturday. But the plane was late arriving in Salt Lake City and even later departing for Missoula. By the time he'd rented a car and reached Erin's it was nearly 6:00 p.m.

"I don't suppose that my timing really mattered, did it?" Erin shook her head, wordlessly answering the question about Harris's absence. When DiGenero had knocked, five minutes before, he'd realized without asking why only she had greeted him at the door.

Erin sat down on the sofa, curling her legs beneath her, "I tried to call you, to let you know Kirby wasn't here, but I didn't have your home number."

"They took your message at the office, right?" DiGenero asked, dropping into the armchair and leaning back.

She nodded. The FBI office in Salt Lake City, his cover number, would have called him at the RAPTOR suite, but he hadn't bothered to stop by to pick up his messages before leaving for the airport. DiGenero smiled apologetically, "My home phone's unlisted. It makes things a little safer if my old friends from New York ever get the notion to come looking for me."

He sipped the beer and then spoke, "Where's Kirby?"

Erin raised her eyebrows, "The ranch, I suppose."

He leaned forward, "You know I want to help him, but my options are running out. I told you a month ago that I could shelve this. Now, I'm not so sure."

"Why?"

DiGenero sat back. There was a great deal to say, but little he could. His voice was quiet, "Things change."

"Oh?" The anxiety in Erin's eyes went through him like a knife. It was as if, alone and adrift, she had watched someone who had reached to rescue her suddenly turn away.

DiGenero cursed himself, his choice of words, and what his training, now habit, had conditioned him to do. He had begun to manipulate her without even thinking, doling out a question, then a hint of a reply, a half-suggestion, but no answer. It was the stock beginning of an interrogation, tightening the screw a turn even as he tried to draw her out. In an instant, he could see it was no good, not with her.

Erin looked down at her own hands, slowly knitting and unknitting her fingers, "I suppose I don't understand."

He spoke, "In a word, Von Biemann. He's big game. Not just in my neck of the woods. I can't control what happens when others get interested in him. And they already are."

"Who?"

He shook his head.

"Then why?"

"I can't say. But take my word for it, Kirby's in the way."

Erin studied DiGenero for several moments in silence before speaking, "I wanted to help you and to help Kirby. I did. It's really one and the same, isn't it? Helping the two of you?"

He nodded, "You could say that."

"I tried. I told him what you'd said. Last night, I told him I wanted him to stay, to talk to you."

"And?"

"Well," she laughed softly, "maybe I jumped to conclusions about him. Do you think we should check the closets?"

DiGenero flashed a smile as Erin continued, "It's not easy, you know?"

"What's that?"

She paused, as if choosing her words, "Trying to help someone who seems never to need any help. It's not just that Kirby can handle things himself. He looks for risks. He's been the same ever since Vietnam, ever since I first met him. Maybe he was always that way. Or maybe, it was the end of the war, his last war, and the fact that the excitement was gone. All those years of living on the edge and then it was over." She was quiet for a moment, "Withdrawal symptoms from a fifteen-year high? Maybe that's why. I don't know. But that's the way he wants it." Erin seemed to shrug, "From his point of view, why shouldn't he? He's done better than good. He's made out every time."

She turned her head, absently brushing back her hair, "There aren't many men like that, are there? The kind that take chances and win. I always thought it was what made him so different." The brief smile touched her eyes as her voice trailed away, "It was what attracted me to him."

"You said 'was.'" DiGenero's words seemed to snap her back to the present.

"Did I?" Erin glanced down self-consciously.

"Past tense?"

The quiet lasted several seconds before she spoke, "Sometimes I think about it another way. Sometimes I think the people who look like they can stand alone, all alone I mean, are the ones that need others the most. We all help them, you know, all of us. We admire them, we envy them, we're attracted to them." A smile touched her lips, "Some of us even love them. We think they're so different that we don't ask, no, we can't ask them to be like us. Why? If we do, we're sure they'll brush us off, go away, and we don't want to lose them. We've got the best seat in the house and we're willing to pay to keep it. So, we give them everything they want. A blank check. Love, praise, quarters, and rations."

Erin looked at the arm of the couch, running her finger slowly in a long figure eight pattern on the fabric. Finally, she spoke, "Ironic, isn't it? In a way, we make them possible. We give them everything they need so they can continue to behave as if they needed nothing, no one, at all."

"And?"

Erin's eyes met DiGenero's. "And?" She thought for a moment. "And, in return, they aren't required to give us anything. We don't ask, and they don't give. I don't think it's malicious on their part. Maybe, after a while, they're simply too old to learn. Maybe, it's just not possible, even when we ask. Despite everything, despite all their 'strength,' they don't know how. They can't do for us what we do for them."

DiGenero spoke quietly, "Even if you're right, I don't want to give up. I know what will happen to Kirby if I do."

"And I don't want you to."

Erin saw the frustration in DiGenero's eyes as he spoke, "Maybe Kirby's won them all up to now, but this one's different. We're not talk-

ing about birds, or poachers, or fish cops. That's penny ante. He can
even play games with me, but the company he's keeping now doesn't
play games."

Erin rose and stepped across the space between them. She was bare-
foot, dressed in a T-shirt and cutoff blue jeans that accentuated her long
legs and slender beauty. She knelt beside DiGenero's chair and put her
hand on his arm. Her voice was soft, as if she was trying to wrap a hard
truth in kindness, "Whoever plays games or doesn't play games, Frank,
Kirby is doing what he always does. It's not you. It doesn't matter that
you're his friend, a close friend. He's going to push you to the edge. I
don't think he can help himself. He's turning your warning into a challenge."

DiGenero's eyes flashed angrily. He started to speak, but the gentle
pressure of Erin's fingers around his wrist stopped him.

She continued, "I believed you a month ago when you said that you
wanted to help Kirby. I still do. I said then that you meant a great deal
to him and that he saw something of himself in you. I think that's true.
And yet you're not Kirby. I know that. You wouldn't be here with me
tonight if you were." She spoke slowly, "Still, I had a question for you
when we met last, and I have the same one now. I want you to think
about it." She paused, "Your warning. Are you going to turn it into a
challenge, too?"

He felt Erin's fingers brush across his arm as she stood, "You don't
have to answer right now." She smiled, "After all, I do teach for a living
and I know a pop quiz sometimes isn't fair, especially in a tough course."
She glanced at the clock. "It's late. Why don't we find somewhere for
dinner." Erin motioned toward the couch, "As for tonight, that isn't so
bad. Anyway, it's better than trying to find a motel room during a home-
game football weekend in Missoula. Now, let me change and we'll find
a restaurant."

DiGenero sat, unmoving, watching her disappear into the bedroom
and close the door. Her aroma was still in the air, around him, as were
the warmth of her presence and the mellowness of her voice. His thoughts,
at once confused and clear, tumbled over themselves.

She'd told him more about Harris than he'd expected, much more.
But that was only half of it. Erin had also told him more about himself,
more that was right, than anyone else had in years. More than his ex-
wife ever realized. More than he thought was possible. More, perhaps,

than he understood without thinking for a long time about what she'd said. It was like walking down a hallway, distracted, and turning the corner to suddenly find yourself staring into a full-length mirror. When you weren't prepared to see it, your own image appeared at first like a stranger's. It always took a moment before you realized who it was.

And the question, DiGenero thought, the "pop quiz"? He knew the answer, or at least some of it. It explained part of the reason he had put in the wires, although if Erin hadn't asked he wouldn't have admitted it to himself. He wanted to help Harris, but he also didn't want to lose, not on his turf.

DiGenero heard the sound of Erin's closet door opening and closing. He pictured her, dressing, and wondered what she'd be like, how she'd act, and react, what she'd do, how she'd feel. After what Erin had said, he thought, somehow he was certain she already knew all that about him. He shifted uncomfortably in the chair. Kirby and Erin. Was it past tense? And, if it was? He drained his beer. Erin. It had been a long time since anyone had told him something about himself that mattered. More important, though, it had been even longer since he'd found someone he'd wanted to listen to.

"Frank?"

DiGenero looked up. Erin was standing in the hallway, smiling, "You know, I called your name three times. I think you were very far away."

"Far away?" He rose from the chair. "Not as far as you'd think." DiGenero extended his arm in exaggerated gallantry. Then, they walked together out the door.

Five hours later, at 1:00 a.m., mountain daylight time, as DiGenero fell asleep finally on the couch, 2000 miles away on the fourth floor of the J. Edgar Hoover Building in Washington, D.C., Parnell Whittaker, the senior watch officer on the midnight shift in the FBI's Counterterrorism Center, looked at the clock and groaned. It was 3:00 a.m., eastern daylight time. Sunday mids was always the slowest night of the week and this shift had been no exception. Whittaker reached for the oil-stained pizza box, flipping back the top to check for any leftovers, and wrinkled his nose at the collection of half-chewed crusts.

He glanced across the expanse of the custom-made curved desk and console. Before him, the video screens that immediately displayed the incoming messages from the FBI field offices, the Defense Communications Network, the State Department, and the intelligence agencies were blank. At his left hand, there were no lights flashing on the sixty-button telephone call director, testifying to the fact that the other watch centers in Washington were in a similar lethargy. Even more telling, beneath the wall clocks recording the time in London, Moscow, Tehran, New Delhi, Bangkok, and Tokyo, the printers for Associated Press, United Press International, and Reuters sat silent. All in all, it was mute evidence that Sunday was the lousiest news day in the world.

Whittaker didn't bother to turn around at the sound of Mark Adelman's steps echoing hollowly on the raised flooring that covered the maze of wires, electrical connections, and cables for their console's communications and computer leads.

"Hot off the presses," the assistant watch officer announced. Adelman dropped the first editions of the *Washington Post*, the *New York Times*, and *USA Today* for Sunday morning, September 23, on the table behind Whittaker with a heavy thud. He rummaged in the drawer, finding a scissors, and began to clip terrorism-related stories for the "Terrorism Watch Morning Summary." The director's driver wouldn't arrive until 6:00 a.m. to pick up his "Read Folder" but at least it was something to do.

The sharp double beep of the Defense Communications Network terminal caused both men to look up.

"Well, goddamn, a Sunday morning DCN 'Immediate,'" Whittaker drawled laconically. "One of our brave boys in uniform somewhere must be awake."

Whittaker was 28 years old, with a B.A. in history from Howard University, a law degree from George Washington University, a plastic card that identified him as a special agent, FBI, and a biweekly paystub reflecting the fact that he earned a gross salary of $28,750 per year. His two roommates from law school who worked for firms in glass-walled buildings overlooking K Street N.W., less than a mile away, already took home double his gross pay, with the promise of major multiples more after a few years of faithful clerk's work. But neither knew what would appear on front pages before it happened, made decisions that helped create the stories, or could help to stop a death 5000 miles away before it occurred. Nights, boredom, cold pizza, and lousy pay or not, as senior duty officer in the Counterterrorism Center, he could. It was why he was there.

Whittaker glanced at the printer. Something was up?

He rolled his chair sideways, positioning himself before one of the three keyboards at his workstation, and typed rapidly, "DCN, xfer Whttkr." The keys clicked louder than normal in the quiet room. The beep and flashing words, "INCOMING IMMEDIATE," appeared almost instantaneously before him, signaling that the message would appear on his screen, rather than first print out on the DCN laser printer across the room.

Adelman spoke, "What's goin' on? Are we at war, or what?" Whittaker scanned the message, "Nope, it's from Bonn liaison." He read further. With incoming messages, the routine filing, retransmission to others, or the dispatch of a general alert or action message were the senior duty officer's calls.

"It looks like a TAM to me. I'll take care of it," Whittaker said.

"You're one mean bastard," Adelman chuckled. Whittaker rolled his eyes. He recognized Adelman's tone. He was cranking up for one of his monologues. Adelman stood back, addressing a nonexistent audience. "I can see it now. Across the United States of America, hundreds of patriotic, hardworking, ever-vigilant defenders of law and freedom are snuggling up to their warm, cute—or as the case may be, not so cute—squeezes. But little do they know, thousands of miles away, deep in the bowels of the FBI, their masters are about to call them to a mission."

Whittaker glanced up, "Will you shut up? I can't concentrate."

The assistant watch officer feigned shock at the insult as Whittaker turned back to the computer terminal. The software allowed him to reformat and transfer the message between the Defense Communications Network and the FBI's communications system with only three commands. Adelman stepped to the console to read the message and watch.

Whittaker shifted the screen into its "compose" mode and moved the cursor, changing the defense department format into an FBI Terrorism Alert Message. Two keystrokes automatically called up and added, from the computer program's memory, the introductory boilerplate that warned against unauthorized disclosure. Whittaker flipped through his file cards, finding the secure phone number for the geographic desks responsible for the suspects in question. In the morning, the weekend-duty desk officers would receive any incoming calls. He typed in the digits, adding the correct sequential number to the TAM, and double-checked the result. When he finished, he paged through the message, proofreading, before shifting his hand toward the keyboard's "send" button.

Adelman spoke, his voice lugubriously solemn, "Now, before you act, my duty compels me to warn that when you press the 'send' button, dispatching an 'Immediate' TAM, the army of government-issue alert beepers deployed around the continental United States are going to sound. When that happens this night, they will deprive your unseen peers and superiors forever of the chance to shake their honeys ever so gently and hope for a kind answer to the question, 'Hey dear, how about just one more?'"

Whittaker smiled with exaggerated malevolence and raised his hand, conductor fashion, letting it descend with slow drama toward the keyboard. Adelman crossed himself, pyramiding his fingers in prayer, as the key was struck. In a microsecond, the message disappeared, replaced by the boldfaced words, "SENT IMMEDIATE."

Adelman spoke, "Dearly beloved, for these few final moments, may they rest, or do whatever the laws of man, God, and the regulations of the Federal Bureau of Investigation permit, in peace."

An hour and thirty minutes later, at 2:30 a.m., Erin's voice woke DiGenero, "Frank, there's a telephone call from your office. Someone named Jackson. The phone's in here."

"OK," DiGenero answered, throwing back the sheet and slipping on his pants. As he entered Erin's bedroom, she motioned to the nightstand where the phone lay waiting, and stepped out.

Jackson's "hello" sounded wide-awake in contrast to the husky resonance in DiGenero's voice, "What's happening?"

"It's an 'Immediate,' sir. One of those special messages," Jackson said. DiGenero could picture the straight-arrow communicator nervously shifting from foot to foot, trying to decide how to talk about a classified message on the telephone. He cut in, "Look, David, my boy, just paraphrase the thing for me, would you? It doesn't do a whole shitload of good to wake me up to say there's a letter in my mailbox, but not what's in it. What special message?"

"Well, sir, I, ah...a TAM."

"Talk."

"There's two people traveling soon. When I told Mr. Kasiewicz, who gave me this phone number in Missoula, he said you'd want to know."

"Who's traveling?"

"Two of, ah...them."

DiGenero grimaced in frustration, "Who?"

"Ah..., umm..., ah...," Jackson stuttered, struggling to overcome the categorical prohibitions against security violations that had been drummed into him at communications school, before he answered, "Iranians."

DiGenero was wide-awake now. "Keep it up, sport, you're on a roll."

"There are names, but it says they use aliases, and there are no descriptions. They're known hit men. They both left Europe yesterday and are ticketed for two different destinations. One, named Sabah, will arrive in Denver and the other, named Sassanir," Jackson paused, shuffling papers, "in Calgary."

DiGenero felt the chill run the length of his spine. "The one going to Calgary. When is he supposed to get there?"

"The twenty-fourth," Jackson answered. "September twenty-fourth, Monday, tomorrow."

Erin, sitting wrapped in her robe on the couch, looked up as DiGenero reentered the living room. "Anything wrong?"

His expression answered the question, "I've got to talk to Kirby. Now."

"You can call the ranch, but I don't think he'll wait for you. It would be better if you drove." Erin paused. "Just don't push him. I know you mean well, but he won't move in any direction that you want him to go unless it's his choice." She rose, "I'll let you get ready." Erin stepped away and then turned, "And, Frank?"

"Yeah?"

"Don't take this wrong, but it may never be his choice."

DiGenero dressed in three minutes. He called, "Erin?"

Erin walked into the living room as he reached for his coat. She sat on the arm of the couch. She spoke, "It's a two-lane road most of the way. Three hours or so to the Broadwater County line, if you take it easy."

DiGenero glanced at his watch, "That'll make it about 6:00 a.m. when I arrive." He smiled, "Just in time for breakfast."

"Be careful."

DiGenero nodded and then spoke, "By the way, you were right. Pop quizzes on tough subjects aren't fair. I can't say I have an answer for you yet, but I think at least I understand the question."

Erin sat for a long while, thinking, after DiGenero closed the door.

*   *   *

The squealing tires awoke Malaek at once. Fifty yards away, at the intersection, the taillights were turning the corner. The sound of the engine, revving in gear, told him the car was moving away fast. He rubbed his eyes and looked at the parking lot alongside the garden apartments. All the tenants' cars were in their usual spots, including the Dupres woman's Honda, but the sedan that had arrived at dinnertime was gone. Malaek reached for the ignition key and then paused, cursing silently to himself. Even if he could catch up, a tail was too dangerous at this hour, too easily recognized with so few cars on the street.

He snapped on the map light, directing its small beam at his notebook, and pulled closed the curtains that shielded the side windows of the nondescript Chevy van. He checked his penciled record. The visitor had arrived at 6:00 p.m. He had stood for a moment, reading something, perhaps an address, beside the stairway to the second-floor apartments. Even from across the street, Malaek had recognized him. At the airport the morning the photographs were taken, he'd been dressed in blue jeans and sport shirt. Tonight, he wore a suit and tie.

Malaek penciled in the time of the departure. He glanced up at the apartment window. The living room light was still on. It was unusual, enough reason to inform Munich. He would do so before the woman left the apartment later that morning. Then, he would follow her to the laboratory, where she always checked the birds, and be certain of her routine for the rest of the day. As soon as her light went out, he would find a telephone and place the call. Malaek scratched his head and yawned. His orders were categorical. Omit nothing. And, he thought, reclining the seat backward to a more comfortable position, when Musaani gave such orders, there was no question that he would want to know.

17

Sunday, September 23, 1984

The Harris Ranch, Broadwater County, Montana

DiGenero pulled to a stop on the shoulder of the highway and turned off the headlights. The digital dashboard clock winked, changing the time to 6:30 a.m. The image of Erin, sitting on the edge of her couch, watching as he left, flashed through his mind. He wondered for a moment whether she was asleep or awake. Asleep, he hoped. DiGenero rubbed the stubble on his chin. He felt tired, and for the first time, uneasy.

He eyed the house. In the half light of dawn, the windows seemed bright. Even from 250 yards away, he could see Harris's figure moving inside. The Blazer was parked in front by the picket fence, tailgate open, and motor running. Two wooden crates and a box, yet to be loaded, sat near the rear wheel. DiGenero pulled forward on the sloping gravel roll of the road. He turned hard right, bottoming once on the rutted dirt track. Kirby was almost ready to leave. There was no point in waiting.

In the house, Harris, startled at the sound of the gravel under the car's tires, turned and walked to the window. It was too far away, and still too dark, to make out the driver, but he knew at once it was DiGenero. He swore under his breath. Everything he needed was loaded, except for a few boxes. Five minutes more and he would have been gone. He watched as the car pulled up and Frank opened the door. Harris turned away from the window and waited for the footsteps on the porch. There was no smile on DiGenero's face as he stepped inside.

"You don't give up, do you?" Harris asked. He leaned back, arms folded, half-sitting on the edge of the dining table.

DiGenero shook his head, "I said we needed to talk. I meant it." He motioned past Harris toward the kitchen. "You got any coffee?"

"Help yourself."

DiGenero stepped by Harris. He noticed the packing was almost complete. Only a rucksack, a sleeping bag, a small toolbox, and a coil of rope remained on the table. When DiGenero returned, Harris was standing, his back against the old-fashioned, half-glass front door.

DiGenero blew a cool breath across the top of the steaming coffee mug, "This isn't about falcons."

"Make it fast, Frank, my friend, I've got to get on the road."

DiGenero took a long swallow of coffee before he spoke, "Von Biemann..."

"If you've got something on him, that's your business. The fact is, you don't have anything on me."

DiGenero leaned against the dining table, warming his hands on the mug, "How come you're so sure?"

"Because I'm too fuckin' good," Harris's laughter was loud, louder than it needed to be. DiGenero had heard that kind of laughter before. It reminded him in an instant of the others he'd known—pilots—and their bravado, not to mention the hundreds of beers and the scores of bars. The Kitten Club, The Los Angeles, Susie's, The Black Widow's Den, The '69' Grill. Saigon, Da Nang, Nha Trang, Phan Rang, Udorn, Korat, Bangkok. There was always one, at the center of the circle, the main man. Was. Now, the others, the lesser lights who looked on, were gone. So were the honeys who orbited the pack, the Singha beer, the smoky, air-conditioned smell, and the GI joints that never closed. But the laugh was the same. Unchanged. Only the time and the place were wrong.

DiGenero spoke, "I'm not the one you've got to worry about." He paused, watching Harris's expression, "Von Biemann is."

"What are you talking about?"

"He's planning to kill you."

Harris's eyes widened slightly.

DiGenero continued, "Von Biemann's history goes back to the sixties, to the radical European underground. He's in bed with the Iranians and with their terrorism network. Your life is in danger. What I don't know is why—why you're a target. Why after all these years, Von Biemann would want you dead."

Harris's laugh was more restrained this time, "I think you've been playing cops and robbers too long, Frank. You don't think Von Biemann's going to kill the goose that lays his golden egg, do you?"

DiGenero heard the irritation and the fatigue in his own voice, "Look, I didn't spend the night driving all the way here for the fresh air. I know the call you'll receive tomorrow from Calgary won't be Von Biemann. I also know it'll be an Iranian. He's a killer. You're his contract."

Harris pursed his lips, only partially masking his surprise. He turned slowly, walked to the window, and stood, looking out, arms folded, as DiGenero continued, "At first, I only wanted you to drop the deal with Von Biemann. If you had, I could have taken care of the rest. Now, I know there's more to it than the falcon business." DiGenero paused, "So do others. Now, I need you to do more. I need your help."

Harris watched the dawn brighten, illuminating the details of the new morning sky. Von Biemann, the Iranian, the Arabian king, the peregrine, and the deal itself, the gift of a falcon, he thought. Suddenly, the pieces fit together, not perfectly, but well enough for him to make out the picture in the puzzle. It made sense of Von Biemann's case of nerves over the shipment of the bird, of his friend, the Iranian, of the goons who sat at the foot of the stairway and patrolled the perimeter at Überspitzensee. And now the assassin, coming for him.

Harris exhaled a long, silent breath. The message from DiGenero also was clear enough: it was out of Frank's hands. That was always the danger when you depended on someone else, he thought. Even if they wanted to help, they couldn't deliver. Erin didn't understand that when she told him to listen to DiGenero, to do what he wanted.

His mind raced, sorting out his options. One thing was certain. The falcon trade was over. So was whatever Frank could do for him.

Harris spoke, "Let me get this straight. You came here to help me, but now I'm supposed to help you?"

"Something like that," DiGenero said.

"Hmmm," Harris turned, grinning, "why, son, don't you know that God helps those who help themselves? I do believe if I taught you that, it'd be the most help I could give you. Make you a self-reliant young man."

DiGenero's stare hardened, "Don't screw around with me, Kirby. We're not talking about juvenile delinquents or two-bit crooks. We're talking about terrorists—killers who don't care who they hurt. It's not just you and me anymore. Von Biemann and the Iranians aren't going to have you killed unless you're smack in the middle of an operation. I've done what I can for you. Now it's up to you to play ball."

"Is it, now?" Harris unfolded his arms, hooking his thumbs loosely in his belt. He grinned, his expression matching his mocking tone, "Here we are in the middle of Montana and my old flyin' buddy from the 'Eff Bee Eye' wanders in, dressed in a $500 suit, Eye-talian loafers, and a custom-made, uptown shirt, talking about German radicals and 'Eye-rainian' hit men who are coming to get me."

Harris reached out, brushing an imaginary speck of dust from DiGenero's shoulder and straightening his lapel, "Just what do you expect a poor cowboy like me to believe?"

DiGenero pushed Harris's hand away, "Don't make it hard on yourself. I don't have to do it this way. It can be a lot tougher." He stepped back, widening the distance between them and moving a pace to the left, between Harris and the door.

Harris's hands fell free, his eyes stone-cold, "Is that so?" The change was instantaneous, as if one circuit had been broken and another closed.

DiGenero started to raise his arm, but his surprise and the coffee cup in his hand slowed his reflexes. It was too little, too late. The chopping motion struck his neck, just above the collar bone, smashing against the intricate nerve bundles that connect the cervical section of spinal cord to the shoulder, arm, and chest. His right side on fire, then numb, he pitched forward, half stunned. Harris cocked his right arm, locking the heel of his hand and wrist into place as a striking edge, but the heavy oak table by the door did the rest. Its leg met DiGenero's skull above the right temple. The concussion, a solid sound, was enough to wrap him in blackness before he hit the floor.

Harris bent down at once beside the sprawled figure, "You dumb dago, what did you hit your head for?" The angry red mark above the temple was already darkening and starting to swell. He pressed the tips of his fingers against DiGenero's neck and sighed, relieved. The carotid pulse was steady and strong. "That's better," he rose and stepped to the dining table, uncoiling the three-eighths-inch nylon rope. Unsheathing his hunting knife, he cut a six-foot section. Then, he knelt, cinching a bowline knot around DiGenero's wrists and ankles, and trussing the unconscious FBI agent's hands behind his back.

With the eight hours' difference in time zones, it was exactly 4:00 p.m., Sunday, central European time, when Von Biemann put down the phone. He walked directly upstairs, stopping at the first door to the left on the second-floor landing.

Musaani answered his knock at once, "Come in."

The Iranian was sitting at the small desk by the bedroom's single dormer window.

"Another call from the States."

"Malaek again?"

"No. That was Harris. He's changing his contact phone number for tomorrow. He'll be at a motel in Kalispell rather than at the ranch. He gave me the number. We need to tell Sassanir to call there."

"Why is the location changing?"

"He didn't say."

Musaani frowned, "Find out."

"I can't. He said he was on the road, at a public telephone. It seems he's already on his way." Von Biemann paused, "I could call him when he arrives..."

"No," Musaani stood, "no calls from here to Kalispell." He thrust his hands in his pockets and stood silently for a moment. Then, he began to pace slowly back and forth across the room.

Suddenly, Musaani stopped, "What time is it in Montana?"

Von Biemann scratched his head, "Eight hours earlier than our time." He looked at his watch. "About 8:00 a.m., Sunday morning."

"And Harris is already on the road?" Von Biemann nodded. "Is the ranch near anything? A small town, a store, a gas station?" Musaani asked.

The German shook his head, "No, it's a half hour to the nearest town. That's to the south. But to go to Kalispell, Harris would travel north. In that direction, there's nothing close by..."

"So," Musaani broke in, "to reach a pay telephone, Harris probably left early, at least a half hour before he called."

Von Biemann cocked his head indifferently, "Probably."

"And how far is it from Missoula to Harris's ranch?"

"Missoula? What's Missoula got to do with it?" Von Biemann frowned, momentarily irritated by the questioning, before it dawned on him. "It's Malaek's call about the FBI agent, isn't it?"

Musaani repeated his question more sharply, "How far?"

"I'm not sure exactly. Three, maybe four hours by car. Something like that."

Musaani turned toward the window and paused, thinking. An hour before, Malaek's unusual surveillance report from Missoula about DiGenero and Harris's woman had only been a curiosity. Unusual and therefore potentially troublesome, but still only a curiosity. Now, Musaani thought, it appeared to have been the first sign of a problem. Why had DiGenero left Missoula in the middle of the night? Why had Harris changed his plans for meeting Sassanir? Was DiGenero the cause? And, if he was, what did he know?

The Iranian stood silently for several moments, staring out the window. The diamond panes were swung open. In the distance, the meadow was still a lush summer green, although the new fall colors already tinged the low growth among the bordering pines.

"Which one of our two, Sassanir or Sabah, do you think is the best?"

Von Biemann rubbed his chin, "Sassanir, I think."

The Iranian nodded, "Is he in Calgary yet?"

Von Biemann shook his head, "No. He arrives tomorrow."

"When he arrives, get him on the phone," Musaani ordered. He turned slowly, facing Von Biemann. "After Sassanir finishes with Harris in Canada, tell him to go to Salt Lake City and await my instructions. Tell him," the Iranian paused, smiling slightly, "to be ready for another job."

The throbbing made DiGenero wince each time he took a step. The dizziness was almost gone, but not the ache. He reached up, touching the egg-sized protrusion above his temple, and jerked his hand away as the pain shot through his skull. DiGenero stopped at the end of the dirt road and glanced back at the ranch. The sun was low in the west. He looked at his watch, turned up his collar, and shivered. It was close to 5:00 p.m. and the colors of the late-afternoon clouds were warmer than the air.

DiGenero gingerly rubbed the raw skin on his wrists. He didn't know when he'd come to, but it had taken him the better part of three hours, twisting and stretching the knots, to work free. Another hour went by before he could stand. Finally, when the dizziness stopped, he'd started to move. The phone was a foregone conclusion. Harris had torn the wire out of the wall. His car keys were gone. So were the spark plug wires on the rented Ford.

DiGenero looked north and south on the highway and swore to himself. On Sunday afternoon, even the truckers took a break. He shook his head and grimaced. He'd tried. Whether Harris believed him or not, now he knew. At least Harris had a chance. He reached behind him, absentmindedly patting the snub-nosed Smith & Wesson .38 Police Special nestled in the custom holster against the small of his back. Now, DiGenero thought, Kirby and he had something else in common. They were both on the hit parade—he, on the mob's list, and Harris, on the Iranians'.

He began to walk unsteadily along the shoulder. The house in the distance looked closer than the three miles he knew lay between him and the next ranch. In a way, it didn't matter. Harris was long gone. Even if he got to a phone now, the odds were slim-to-none that they could find him before the call tomorrow from Calgary.

Calgary. DiGenero stumbled, grimacing in pain. Given Harris's destination, the Iranian almost certainly planned to meet him in Canada and make the hit somewhere isolated, out of the way. Then the assassin would have a choice. Exit the same way he entered or slip into the States to take another route out. Given Harris's destination, it made sense.

Given Harris's destination... DiGenero slowed his pace and then paused. Until that moment, he hadn't thought over Jackson's call and it simply hadn't occurred to him. Jackson had said two men were arriving on Monday, the twenty-fourth. The one, in Calgary, and the other, in Denver. Denver? DiGenero stood stock-still. Why two? And, why Denver?

"Oh, no," the vision before him was alive, real, and three-dimensional. Erin, alone, opening the door. Her smile fading to uncertainty. The hand and gun rising. The incomprehension and then the inchoate understanding. The look, smell, and taste of fear. The animal's fight-or-flight instinct. The sick, sinking helplessness. The paralysis. And at the final instant, the hopeless gesture, the arms out-thrust, trying to block the bullet but failing, warding nothing away.

DiGenero's head spun. After two years of flying from one end of the Rockies to the other, he knew that on Monday, the first plane from Denver wouldn't reach Missoula before 8:00 a.m, fifteen hours from now. Without thinking, he started to jog. The pain slashed through his concentration, doubling him over. He stumbled to a halt, gasping. Then, he started again, walking, letting the pounding in his skull subside. Finally, he straightened, clenched his jaws hard, and began to run.

Exactly twenty-four hours later, in Kalispell, Montana, Harris lifted the telephone in Room 12A of the Glacierview Motel on the first ring, "Hello?"

"Mr. Harris?"

"Yeah."

"This is Sassanir. I am a friend of Klaus."

Harris listened to the heavy accent, "Yeah."

"I am in Calgary now. How shall we meet?"

"Be at the Calgary airport tomorrow at 8:00 a.m. It'll take me about an hour and a half, give or take some, to fly up from Kalispell. I'll pick you up at Ferguson's General Aviation hangar."

"Ferguson's?" The name was obviously foreign on the caller's tongue.
"Yeah."
"That is very good."
"Say again?"
"Very good."
"Yeah."

Fifty minutes later, and forty-two miles south of Kalispell, Harris braked hard, downshifting into second gear. The Blazer slowed, bouncing from the pavement onto the corduroy road. He knew the log track well. It had been filled and raised above the bog as a dead straight shot to Plessey's Pier at Flathead Lake. Harris slipped the Blazer into third and pressed down on the accelerator. The day before, just after calling Von Biemann, he'd telephoned Plessey from Butte to make the arrangements. With the fishing season over, he knew the outfitter would be there.

Harris backed to the edge of the dock, set the brake, stepped out, and opened the tailgate. As he'd been told, the Porter's right side was moored to the pilings. Plessey did his A&E work, airframe and engine, as well as hauling and hangaring the plane for him in the winter.

Harris glanced over his shoulder, admiring the long lines of the fuselage. The Porter was his. They had been $200,000 a pop in the sixties when the Company and its contract cargo haulers had bought them by the score to carry loads up-country in Vietnam, Cambodia, and Laos. Supply and demand, Harris thought, were everything. In 1976, he'd bought the Porter for $25,000 at Whidbey Island Naval Air Station, next to Puget Sound, where they'd been lined up, wing tip to wing tip, with new numbers and no owners' names, for sale as surplus or scrap. It was a '68. With floats and the 600-horsepower Pratt & Whitney PT-6 turboprop, it was as good on water as the wheeled versions had been on mountain strips in the war. Compared to the other floatplanes he knew, the Porter was supreme. Its long wings and nine-foot prop would lift you out of most anything.

Harris pulled the snubbing lines taut, cozying the gunmetal-gray floatplane against the dock's tire fenders. He moved quickly in the lowering twilight, stepping onto the pontoon to open the starboard cargo doors. As he had requested, the rear sling seat had been removed. The Sea Eagle inflatable, the small Honda air compressor, and the fifteen-horsepower

Evinrude outboard were stowed. So was the fifty-five-gallon drum and the transfer pump. Harris double-checked the lashings and thumped the fuel drum. It was topped out, full. Satisfied, he loaded the rucksack, the cardboard box with two days' worth of provisions, the throw net, and the two cages. If the gyrs were there, the trapping would be easy enough. If they weren't, there was no point in staying.

Harris opened the right cockpit door, slid into the second seat, and turned on the ignition, checking the gauges. The two main tanks and the two auxiliaries were full. The Porter guzzled fuel, but with 227 gallons, he could stretch it close to a 1000-mile range, more than enough to cover the 640 miles from Calgary to Gypsy Lake and back to Edmonton. Even with headwinds, the drum in the rear was insurance against spending the winter up north.

There was one final chore. He switched on the cabin light, reached back for his rucksack, and uncinched the pack's nylon top. The Colt .45 automatic was a standard issue, a souvenir of sorts he'd taken with him from Indochina in 1975 after they'd turned out the lights. He hefted the pistol's four pounds and pressed the magazine release on the grip. The clip slid out. Harris pushed it back into place and grasped the automatic's receiver, retracting and releasing the slide. The snap was hard and final, cocking the pistol and chambering a round. He eased down the hammer and locked the manual safety. Now, only two motions were necessary. An inconsequential downward pressure with the thumb to release the safety, and a steady six pounds of pull with the trigger finger.

Harris replaced the rucksack and shifted across the cockpit into the pilot's position. The seat adjustment was beneath his left knee. He pressed the lever, ratcheting himself higher, and leaned down, placing the pistol, grip out toward the door, in the space that had just been created beneath the seat. Harris lowered the seat halfway and experimented. There was ample room to grasp the butt and raise the automatic.

He snapped off the cabin light and sat back. A loon's call, lonesome and distant even when close, carried across the lake. Harris glanced at his watch. It was time to get back to the motel for some sleep. He felt beneath the seat. The Colt was where it belonged. Like the fifty-five-gallon drum of fuel in the back, it was simply another form of insurance to be certain that, for him at least, tomorrow's would be a round-trip, not a one-way flight.

18

Tuesday, September 25, 1984

Gypsy Lake, Alberta, Canada

Harris stood on the cabin's sagging wood porch, admiring the palette of fall colors along the shore of Gypsy Lake. Despite the month on the calendar, his breath told him the season was all but gone. The bite in the air went hand-in-hand with the red and yellow hues of the softwoods on the far bank.

It had taken something more than three hours to fly the 420 miles from Calgary into northern Alberta, traveling north at first on the fringe of the Birch Mountains. Two hours out, they'd turned due east and climbed to 5000 feet over the evergreen carpet to find the Christina. Then, he'd followed the twisting, fast-running river north again to the lake.

Garwood—a few houses, a garage, one store, a bar, a dock, and a boat ramp—was three miles to the south. Harris had approached low and slow, just over treetops, checking the wind and the water for debris before landing. Like the other old logging and mining sites on their way to demise, Garwood was easy to spot, surrounded by several concentric rings of broken engines, discarded cars, and refuse that created a targetlike marker as well as measuring its age and state of decay. The one unpaved street that organized the buildings into a straggling row forked west out of town, heading north on one line to a dead end in the Canadian firs and straight on the other for fifty miles to Fort McMurray and Route 63.

The squeal of a spring hinge caused Harris to glance over his shoulder. Thirty yards away, across the pine-straw carpet, the privy door banged hollowly as Sassanir emerged, hitching up his pants. He was a small man with a wiry build, sallow skin, and coal-black eyes. They had spoken a few words on the flight, but the conversation had been disjointed because of both his heavy accent and the noise in the cockpit. An hour before, alone in the Porter, unloading the plane, Harris had searched one of his bags. There was nothing suspicious. Sassanir had carried the other, a student-style knapsack, and kept it hung over his right shoulder during the jeep ride to the cabin. It hung there now as he walked forward.

Harris motioned toward the inflatable boat, tethered to a log that lay half submerged at the water's edge. He already had mounted the outboard, and loaded the cage, net, ropes, and climbing irons.

"Let's go. It'll take an hour to get to the eyries on the northeast shore. We'll need to be in position before the gyrs settle for the night." Harris glanced at his watch. "With the days getting shorter, that'll be sometime between 3:00 and 4:00 p.m." Sassanir nodded, altering his course to go toward the boat.

Harris patted his shoulder holster, closing the top button of his red plaid hunting shirt to conceal the nylon chest strap. Then he stepped off the porch and strode toward the boat, too.

Two hours later, the gyrfalcons were on time. Harris had moored under the steep rock outcropping a little after 3:00 p.m. The smooth, granite-gray face formed a shallow curving shoreline. The scrapes, the gyrs' nests, were seventy to eighty feet above, commanding a view and providing protection from the northwest winds. The birds were predictably territorial and easy to spot, spacing themselves every five miles or so on the rock ledges over the deep, blue-black water or in the old ravens' nests atop the dead firs that clung, knotted and gnarled, to the crevices in the stone.

"We'll have time for one," Harris motioned with his head toward the eyrie above them. He'd mapped the locations and the easiest climbs. "Tomorrow, we'll move farther north for the others."

"May I assist you?" Sassanir asked.

Harris shook his head, "No, that's all right."

The Iranian's knapsack lay against the gunwale, several feet away. Sassanir had removed it when they left the other side of the lake in order to put on the life jacket. He had barely moved since then. Obviously nervous, he was seated, knees drawn up and arms extended, hands gripping both sides of the boat.

Harris glanced at the Iranian as he collected his gear. The small rivulet of sweat followed the line of Sassanir's jaw below the sideburn. It was perfect, he thought. As long as they were on the water, the odds he would try something were next to nil.

"No problem," Harris purposely rocked the inflatable as he slipped the rucksack onto his back, enjoying the alarm that swept across Sassanir's face. He centered the pack on his back. The net, hoods, and body socks for the falcons were inside.

Harris reached for his climbing spikes, heavy leather lineman's belt, and the coil of half-inch rope, gesturing at the sparse stand of bare-trunked pines that grew ramrod-straight from the rocks. "These'll get me up to the top." Harris fastened the logger's climbing irons to his belt. "Then, I'll work my way across to the nest. The rest is a piece of cake."

Sassanir nodded uneasily, his knuckles white as Harris stepped onto the narrow ledge. The boat bobbed erratically as his weight lifted free. Harris glanced back. The Iranian's eyes were wide with fear. There was no doubt, he thought, this guy couldn't swim. Great.

The rock wall, heated by the late fall sun, felt warm to his touch. He leaned back, fitting the climbing spikes to his legs and boots, and then turned toward the nearby fir. Harris jammed the spike on his right leg into the thick trunk, cinching the half-inch rope around his waist and the pine's girth. He pushed up, setting his left spike with a hard chunking sound. Then he leaned back and began to climb.

One hundred feet up, just below the first branches that crowned the old fir, Harris stepped across two feet of open air from the tree to the ledge. The natural path traversed the cliff, angling slightly downward along the stone face to the scrape, thirty yards to his left. Harris slipped off the irons, refastening them to his belt. He wedged his hands into a crevice, lifting himself to the next higher outcropping. It was wider, descending gently toward the nest. He moved slowly. The rock wall dropped away beneath him in a convex curve toward the water. If he fell, which he wasn't about to, the Iranian's job would be done for him. There was no forgiveness in the rocks beneath the water.

Ten minutes later and five yards from the scrape, the gyrs, already alert to his sounds, saw him. The adults were near black, half again as big as a peregrine. Startled, they took off, swooping low, and then climbed. Harris watched the pair fly overhead. They circled, keeping their distance, more perplexed than threatened. He stepped toward the young one left behind. In the late-afternoon shadows, it appeared deep gray to black. The gyr moved uncertainly, backing, hunched, trying to menace. The falcon was a flyer and full grown, but still depended on the parents. As he had expected, curious or confused, it stayed in the nest.

On the edge of the scrape, Harris slowly reached over his shoulder to remove the net from his pack. He untied the light lines that bundled it, sausagelike, in throwing order, cradling the nylon in his hands and gauging the distance. Then, ready, he lofted it with an easy, sweeping motion. The small weights carried high, spreading the net and surprising the gyrfalcon. Harris stepped forward quickly, dislodging a small pebble shower. He knelt beside the struggling bird, grasping and folding her wings with a gentle but steady pressure.

In his grip, the female quieted. He untangled her and slipped the sock and hood over her body and head. Harris fit the falcon carefully into his rucksack. He straightened and turned, looking down. The light was dimming. Eighty feet below and to the left, he could see the prow of the inflatable. The Iranian was seated, facing the stern and gripping tightly the sides of the boat, exactly where he had left him. Harris laughed out loud. Then, he made his way across the ledge the way he had come.

Five hours later, Harris poked the last pine log into the embers of the potbellied stove, shutting the heavy, cast-iron fire door, and adjusting the flue damper. Hooded and caged in the far corner, the gyrfalcon was quiet. It was after 9:00 p.m. and inside the cabin, the chill was encroaching. Harris turned up the wick of the hurricane lamp, brightening the glow. Beneath the high-pitched roof that shed the heavy winter snows, the old cabin's open-beamed ceiling seemed to absorb the light as well as the heat.

The chair scraped across the floor as the Iranian stood and picked up the flashlight, "I must go once more before we sleep."

"Watch your step," Harris nodded. The cabin door banged closed as Sassanir stepped out, heading toward the privy. Harris paused momentarily, listening to his steps descending the porch stairs. He stood up, unbuttoned his red plaid jacket, took off his hunting shirt, and unfastened his shoulder holster. Then he walked to the back of the cabin.

There were six beds, three pushed against the rear wall and three along the front, under the windows. Harris knelt, examining the perspective from the center bunk. The stove blocked his field of vision. He rose and moved left to the next. It was better. Lying on his right side, the view was clear, unobstructed. The bed also was in the darkest corner. From it, when the lamp was out, he could look toward the two front windows, where the moonlight would reflect from the lake to silhouette the room.

Harris heard the shuffle in the pine straw a moment before the footfall on the porch. He snapped the Colt's safety off, slipped the automatic beneath the pillow, and stepped back toward the table. The hinges creaked as the Iranian pushed the heavy timber door open.

"Why don't you take that one?" Harris gestured toward one of the three rough-hewn wooden bunks along the front wall. "It's got a good mattress."

Sassanir smiled perfunctorily, sliding the backpack off his shoulder. He placed the canvas satchel on the floor, then sat down and unlaced his shoes. Harris turned, busying himself with another adjustment of the stove's flue until, a moment later, he heard the bedsprings groan. The Iranian had rolled over, turning his back to the room. Harris picked up the hurricane lamp, moving it to the stool beside his bed, before he lowered the wick and blew out the flame.

He pulled off his boots and threw back the covers. Then he stretched out, shifting onto his right side. Later, the lake would magnify the flat white reflection of the half moon, but even now the darkness was slowly transforming itself into a spectrum of shadows as the soft night glow filtered into the room.

Harris grasped the .45, and slipped it downward from beneath his head to a chest-high aiming angle under the covers. Across the cabin, the Iranian stirred and then lay still. If DiGenero was wrong, he thought, it would be a long, dull night. But if he wasn't, and the little raghead made a move, what the Iranian could tell him to complete the pieces of the puzzle would be well worth his wait.

It was the deliberate step, unlike the normal sound of a man shuffling half asleep, that woke Harris and gave him a split second to save his life. The explosion and muzzle flash of his .45 filled the cabin with a deafening blindness, overwhelming the sounds of his own animal scream and Sassanir's hurried shot.

Harris barrel-rolled off the bed, gripping the Colt with both hands. In the hour-long second before he could swing the automatic toward the target again, his memory of the night seemed like demonically animated images on a fast-forward reel. He cursed wordlessly, his anger butting against his fear, for allowing himself to doze and slip away.

Halfway through his roll, Harris saw the flash from the corner of his eye. It seemed to come from another time and place, lagging oddly behind the unnatural whistle and splintering sound of wood floorboards behind his ear. Harris kicked hard, trying to accelerate his ungodly slow evasion. Spinning through his field of vision, the arm of the half-crouched figure was clearer now. It was moving, trying to follow his path. Harris righted himself, half-sitting, extending his arms straight between his knees, elbows locked, hands doubled around the Colt's knurled grip. He centered the muzzle on the dark shape. The lightning and blast enveloped him.

Sassanir buckled in the middle and sat backward, folding like a paper doll. Harris rolled again, stopping behind the potbellied stove. He flipped onto his stomach to stretch out prone. The Iranian was seated, leaning far forward, five feet away. Head down, Harris extended the .45, resting the automatic solidly against his left palm and the floor, and aimed dead center at the chest.

The pinpricks of light and color imprinted on his retinas by the muzzle flashes were slow-dancing now, beginning to fade, replaced by the black-and-white still life of the cabin at 5:00 a.m. Harris scanned right and left, feeling the tremors in his arms and legs as his first rush of adrenalin drained away. He could see the dark spreading stain on Sassanir's left side. The breathing was labored. The Iranian's gun lay a few feet from his right hand, which was resting, like a mannequin limb, palm up, on the floor.

The groan was deep and guttural.

"Don't move a goddamn muscle."

"Help me, please."

Harris crawled sideways, moving back toward his bed and then forward, approaching Sassanir from the right. He reached for the Iranian's pistol. It was a 9-mm, an Eastern European, Chinese, or Soviet design. He'd seen scores before, a few next to their dead owners but most in souvenir caches from Vientiane to Saigon. Harris depressed the thumb catch, removing the magazine, and tossed the automatic and its load across the room.

The Iranian moved his head, following Harris with his eyes. He was already white, as if the shock were purifying him before it killed. Harris pressed the muzzle of the .45 against Sassanir's temple and raised the man's shirt. He was gut shot. It was a single wound. One out of two. The bleeding was steady but there was no spurting or froth, no sign that he'd hit an artery or the lung.

Harris settled beside Sassanir, sitting Indian-style, "Why?"

"Help me, please."

He twined his fingers slowly through the Iranian's hair. It was wet with a cold sweat. Harris jerked hard, "Tell me and I help. You'll live. If you don't, you die." The moan that followed ended with a choking sound as Harris yanked Sassanir's head back. "Now."

"Musaani."

Harris paused. The picture of the Iranian and Überspitzensee materialized. Harris sat for a moment, remembering. Sassanir was breathing shallowly, his eyes closed. Harris tried to gauge how long he could last.

"Why?"

The Iranian attempted unsuccessfully to wet his lips, "Please, water."

Harris tightened his fingers, canting Sassanir's vision until it met his own eyes, "Why?"

The word formed once, soundlessly, before he managed to speak, "Jihad."

"What in the hell is that?"

Harris tightened his fingers and pulled. The Iranian gagged, and opened his eyes. They were weak and watering. He nodded a silent yes. Harris relaxed his grip. A moment passed, then two. Finally, Sassanir began to talk.

Ten minutes later, Harris rose. He had listened, interrupting only to ask questions when the Iranian drifted or his English failed. Sassanir was still conscious, but breathing more deeply, like a man who had run a long way. Harris jammed the .45 in his belt, lit the hurricane lamp, and carried it to the battered table that doubled as the cabin's kitchen counter. It was piled with soiled paper plates, plastic utensils, and his climbing gear. He pushed the remains of last night's dinner to one side, reaching for a paper cup, the thermos, and water.

Ten feet away, Muhammed Sassanir opened his eyes. He leaned back against the leg of the bunk bed and begged a silent forgiveness. The weakness of the flesh had compelled him to divulge the holy secret, breaking his blood oath of five years before. But he knew as his life ebbed and his mind composed itself in a narrowing tunnel of cold and darkness that his act of betrayal also was Allah's will.

The commanders of Jihad had directed him to kill fourteen times, any one of which could have brought his end. Instead, Allah had let him live. Sassanir shifted silently, using his right arm to reach behind him.

Now, God had determined that his own words would write his fate, final and inevitable. The broken vow meant death waited for him even if he survived, leaving no escape except one. To complete the mission, erasing the sin, purifying his soul, and earning his key to heaven.

The popping sound behind Harris as the thermos shattered, splashing him with cold water, produced an instant of confusion. He spun, grasping frantically for the Colt. The Saturday night special that had been small enough to conceal in a back pocket was difficult to see in Sassanir's shaking hand. It popped a second time, emitting a small puff of smoke, but the .22 slug went high as Harris instinctively ducked to a shooter's crouch. The .45 crashed, blasting Sassanir at point-blank range. The Iranian, straining forward to aim, slammed backward. He bounced lifelessly as Harris pulled the trigger twice more, emptying the magazine.

Two hours later, shortly before 8:00 a.m., Harris shifted the fifteen-horsepower Evinrude into neutral and throttled down. The inflatable drifted toward the shore. Around him, the mist from Gypsy Lake was steaming into the frosty Alberta morning air, a sign that the water still stored the warmth of summer even on the verge of the first snow.

Harris peered upward, surveying the ledges. He was looking for one in particular that would provide his bearing. Five years of climbing had given him a bird's-eye view of the lake's best holes, where the blue water turned indigo-black and permanently cold. The jagged rock edge, mottled with bleeding iron-red, jutted outward sixty feet above. The darkest water lay directly below. The spot was farthest from the current, where the shoreline indented and the flow, even in spring melt, would barely run slow.

Harris cut the engine and edged forward in the boat. The bundle was centered amidships. He pulled away the blankets. The Iranian was curled in a fetal form. He'd used the net and half-inch rope. The nylon was a serviceable shroud. It wouldn't deteriorate, and was strong enough to hold the 100 pounds of rocks that would keep the body eighty feet down. Harris checked the lashing. The net was stitched as well as roped closed. He dropped the 9-mm and the .22 revolver overboard, watching them fall free until at twenty feet the darkness swallowed them. They were the last of the evidence. He had charred away the bloodstains on the cabin floor with gasoline and a match, and Sassanir's clothes and luggage were already buried in the bog, two miles back along the eastern shore.

Harris moved to the left side of the boat, readying himself to counterbalance the expected heel. Slipping his arms under the body, he lifted. The body of the Iranian rolled up onto the gunwale, tilting the inflatable momentarily, before turning over with a playground tumble and a quiet splash.

Harris sat back, breathing deeply as his pulse slowed. Finally, he'd put the pieces together, each and every one. He stood, moved to the transom, and yanked the lanyard. The motor kicked into life. He shifted into forward and turned the throttle, watching the prow rise and the wake ripple outward in a widening V. Behind him, the propeller churned the ice-blue water, spinning a bubbling train that rose to temporarily roil the surface. Where he had drifted, the small cove already had smoothed again to glass.

He twisted the throttle hard, feeling the twin blades dig more deeply. An hour to the cabin. Another hour to pack and get to the plane. Then, with a refueling, another five hours or so to the States. Now, very soon, he would know how much the answer to the puzzle was worth.

19

Wednesday, September 26, 1984

550 South Higgans, Missoula, Montana

One floor below Erin Dupres's apartment, Mitch Kasiewicz raked through the sparse sprinkling of aspen leaves. Despite the morning hour, sweat darkened the back of his baggy, grass-stained white coveralls. He paused to unfasten another button of the heavy work clothes, slipping a hand inside the bloused top. The five-and-a-half pounds of Ithaca twenty-gauge stakeout shotgun hanging against his side weighted the leather sling, cutting into his shoulder.

Kasiewicz nudged the pump's pistol-grip handle into a more comfortable position under his arm and swore. He'd raked together the same scanty pile for two days straight, spreading the leaves back across the lawn again at night. In a word, the job was getting old.

His earphone crackled with DiGenero's voice, "Stop screwin' around and keep working. As a yardman, you're a great lawyer."

Twenty-five yards away, in the front seat of the flatbed truck with the pine-tree logo and lettering of the "Missoula Maintenance Service," DiGenero watched Kasiewicz stretch, noticing the solitary finger that protruded from his left hand. It was meant for his benefit. DiGenero smiled. He didn't blame him. Stakeouts were the pits. He looked away, studying the morning traffic at the intersection of South Higgans and Fifth. The few cars were moving steadily. Nothing out of the ordinary. Yet.

For the last forty-eight hours, they'd covered the building. This morning, Hightower and Morton, the two "painters," were whitewashing the foundation on the north side of the garden apartment. The Missoula resident also had loaned him Sciaratta, who was spreading mulch in the flower bed to the south. DiGenero had pulled Martin from his RAPTOR cases in Colorado. He was inside with Erin.

DiGenero squirmed, trying to make himself comfortable on the seat. The waiting gave him time to worry, allowing the uncertainty to gnaw. With himself and Kasiewicz, he had six. Six. Jesus, he hoped he'd done it right. He hoped they had enough. He looked at his watch. 10:15 a.m. Maybe the assassin would show today. The Denver field office had come up empty-handed. No one named Sabah had landed at Stapleton International Airport. They'd checked the trains and car rentals as well as the hotels. No hits. It didn't matter. Sabah would come sooner or later. DiGenero wondered uneasily whether Harris was still alive and then pushed the thought out of his mind.

He shifted again, slouching against the door to watch the cars line up at the signal light. On the clipboard beside him, the legal pad was ruled in half, the two columns labeled "Northbound" and "Southbound." DiGenero recorded the time and descriptions of the traffic. A Ford camper, a black Mazda RX-7, and a blue-and-white, late-model Mustang. The light turned green. He pushed the Mossberg 500 Bullpup aside on the seat to make room for his leg, yawning and idly drumming his fingers on the matte black thermoplastic stock of the automatic twelve-gauge shotgun. Then, he stretched and leaned back to watch and wait.

Seventy-five yards distant, third in line at the intersection, Hakkim Sabah pressed down on the accelerator of the rented Mustang, pulling away. He glanced sideways, mentally matching the scene with Malaek's photographs. The Honda was parked where it belonged. On the second floor, the apartment's curtains were drawn open, a sign, according to Malaek, that she was inside.

Sabah pulled into the left lane and signaled for a turn. All was as it should be, except for the maintenance crew. They had worked there yesterday as well. He pursed his lips, pouching his heavy cheeks. Sabah was pudgy rather than fat, with an odd softness for a man who carried 200 pounds on a six-foot-two frame. He waited for the traffic in the opposite lanes to clear. The workers were an unexpected complication, but he had dealt with bystanders before. Even if they remembered him, the shock usually riveted them in place, not to mention confusing their accounts of what happened.

He turned left, accelerating, and glanced in the rearview mirror. No one had followed. Sabah reached over, patting the dull gray sport jacket draped over the seat. The square-cut form of the Stechkin 9-mm and the smaller, tubular Interdynamic silencer that he would screw into the automatic's muzzle bulged in the breast pocket. He rolled through the stop sign, cutting the wheels hard left again, and jammed down the gas pedal. His mouth was dry.

Sabah concentrated, clearing his mind. He was the hand, the instrument of Allah's will. The killing was not a mortal's act, but an extension of the divine. His fate and the fate of the one who would die had been decreed. He turned left again on South Higgans, squealing the tires. Once more, a final check. Then, it was time.

Three minutes later, at 10:20 a.m., DiGenero looked up and reached for his pencil. Soon, the flow of cars northbound, away from the university, would begin to thicken as the day students left campus after third-period classes. Southbound, it was still sparse. He noted the Toyota and the Buick and then the third car that had joined the line. The blue-and-white Mustang again.

DiGenero furrowed his brow. Odd. The Mustang was traveling in the same direction, just like five minutes ago. He flipped up the page and ran his finger past the notations in the "Southbound" column for Tuesday, the day before.

"Goddamn...," he muttered under his breath. There were two entries, at 9:45 a.m., and at 3:20 p.m., for a blue-and-white Mustang.

He reached for the walkie-talkie, palming the miniature microphone.

DiGenero rested his left hand casually against his cheek, depressing the transmit button, "Heads up. I think we're being cased. One guy in the Mustang, just cruising by now."

Across the parking lot, Hightower and Morton folded their paint-splattered drop cloth, moving at the deliberate pace of workmen who were paid by the hour as they ambled, pushing their cart to the corner of the apartment building. There, they had already painted the foundation once. They spread the plastic sheet over the shrubbery again, positioning them-selves to cover the stairway that led to the second-floor balcony. DiGenero watched Hightower lift a canvas bundle and lay it on the grass. The M-16s, loaded, safeties off, were inside.

Thirty yards distant, Kasiewicz raked his way across the lawn toward Sciaratta. In less than a minute, both would be in place near the wrought-iron stairs to the balcony's south side. Satisfied, DiGenero turned the ignition key. The truck engine rumbled to life. He shifted into reverse and backed to the center of the parking lot, stopping parallel to the curb.

DiGenero glanced at the second story, judging the distance and the line of fire. If anyone made it up the stairs, he would cover the center stretch of balcony and Erin's door. He snapped off the ignition, praying silently that Erin was where she belonged in the back bedroom, against the wall, on the floor. DiGenero tensed his leg muscles, trying to stop the trembling. The sweat trickled into his eyes, stinging, as the click in his earphone preceded Martin's voice, "She's in the bedroom. The front door's double-locked."

He keyed the microphone twice, acknowledging the message just as the blue-and-white Mustang passed through the intersection of South Higgans and Fifth Street, slowed, and signaled a left turn into the build-ing's parking lot.

DiGenero's nerves tightened his throat. He spoke, "Get ready. He's turning in." His lips moved, silently repeating the disjointed phrases of a childhood catechism, forgotten until now. Holy Mother of God, save us now, in the hour of our need. Save us now... Everything should be fine, just fine. It was all set. Oh Jesus, all set. But was it? Had he thought of everything? Everything? Holy Mother of God, save us now, in the hour of our need...

Through the truck's right rearview mirror, DiGenero saw the Mus-tang coast into the lot. It pulled into the empty parking space next to the stairs on the south side of the building. Kasiewicz and Sciaratta were together, backs turned, twenty feet distant from the car, working on the garden. DiGenero pressed the mike button, "Kasiewicz, he's behind you, getting out now. Don't move till I say."

Twenty yards from DiGenero, the man, tall and heavyset, eased from the coupe, his back to the truck. His motion was leisurely, almost slow. He closed the car door, put on his jacket, and walked toward the stairs.

DiGenero keyed his microphone, "I'm climbing out. When you hear my command, take him." He eased open the driver's door, cradling the twelve-gauge automatic tightly against his chest. Shielded by the truck body, DiGenero crouched low, stepping quickly, and stopped at the left rear tire. He bent forward, his knees working but weak, and wiped the sweat out of his eyes. The Iranian had put another ten yards between them. He was standing at the foot of the stairs. DiGenero swore. It was far, too far for an easy shot.

DiGenero saw Sabah reach inside the breast pocket of his jacket. There wasn't any more time. He needed to make it fast, at a run, if he was going to close the gap. He stepped from behind the truck and leveled the shotgun, "Don't move, FBI!" On the command, twenty feet behind Sabah, Kasiewicz and Sciaratta spun around.

Sabah turned, recognizing instantly that the man who had called out was too distant to do him immediate harm. Without a second's hesitation, the Iranian knelt on one knee, his arms sweeping upward, leveling the Stechkin with a policeman's double-handed grip. DiGenero had barely taken his first step when Sabah's automatic barked.

The speed and the accuracy of the first shot stunned him. Sciaratta fell back from his half crouch, sitting with a bump like a small child. Then, in mute testimony to the fact that the 9-mm slug had struck his chest dead center, slightly below the sternum, lacerating and instantly stopping his heart, he rolled right and lay perfectly still. Off stride, DiGenero braced the Bullpup against his hip and pulled the trigger twice. The automatic shotgun's roar and the two slugs, aimed yards wide of their target, failed to draw the Iranian's attention.

Were it not for the fraction of a second it took Sabah to aim again, the shock that impelled Kasiewicz to glance down at Sciaratta's body would have doomed him. The blast of his twenty-gauge made the pistol shot seem insignificant by comparison, but the distraction already had taken its toll. His shotgun slug went right and high, tearing a chunk of concrete from the apartment house foundation.

Reflexively lowering his profile, Kasiewicz dropped to his knees. The Stechkin seemed inches, rather than yards away, leveled, steady, and aimed at the very source of his life. Kasiewicz jammed the shotgun's pump action back, clearing the spent shell from the chamber, reloading, and cocking, but it was too late. Sabah's bullet buried in the soft deltoid muscle, missing the right shoulder bone. The FBI agent jerked with a spasm and twisted sideways, off balance, hearing his own cry as he fired.

Kasiewicz's second blast went wild and wide. DiGenero slowed, aiming the twelve-gauge from the waist, but Sabah was already a spinning blur. He dodged the Bullpup's third and fourth shots and lunged for the stairs, taking them three at a time. Halfway across the parking lot, DiGenero knew instantly he had only one choice. To his right, Kasiewicz, bleeding bright red and obviously dazed, was trying to stand and bring the Ithaca to bear. To his left, Hightower was moving up the stairs, covered by Morton, but at half the Iranian's speed. Sabah was between them, running, but neither FBI agent could hit him before he reached Erin's door.

DiGenero knelt, shouldering the shotgun and struggling to steady his aim. He flipped up the rear sight just as Sabah leapt to the top of the stairs. His fifth shot from the Bullpup lagged by almost two paces. DiGenero's world was empty now, quiet except for his own rasping breath and above him the sound of the Iranian's pounding feet. He led the figure this time and squeezed again. The slug splintered a gaping hole in the decorative wooden railing half a step in front of Sabah. The Iranian dropped and rolled, extending his arms through the balusters and taking aim.

In a fraction of a second, in horror, DiGenero understood. Stretched prone on the balcony, looking down, Sabah had removed himself as a target for anyone below. DiGenero flinched as a 9-mm steel slug tore into macadam a foot to his right. He raised the Bullpup as the second bullet whistled to his left, but there was nothing to shoot at.

The ripping sound of Hightower's M-16 broke DiGenero's fixation on his own fatal vulnerability. Above him, the Stechkin disappeared from between the balusters and barked twice, answered by another long, full automatic burst. DiGenero glanced back and forth like a curious spectator, watching for a moment what neither man above him could see. Hightower was bent over, below the top stair, jamming another clip into the M-16. On the balcony, Sabah was rising from a squat like a weightlifter, his back flattened against the apartment wall. He was preparing to time his final few steps between the bursts of fire and find his prey inside the hallway door.

As Sabah straightened, his torso filled the Bullpup's sights. DiGenero squeezed the trigger. In the microsecond before the recoil jarred his vision, he saw the Iranian peer down at him. The twelve-gauge slug hit him squarely in the soft center belly, severing muscles, arteries, intestines, and spine as it tore through his midsection, the lumbar vertebrae, and into the brick wall. The explosion of mortar and brick shards peppered Sabah's back, blowing him forward, arms flailing, against the rail. DiGenero held the shotgun level, taking aim again, but there was no point. The Iranian's body hung momentarily and then slumped into a pile, rather than a shape, unmoving, like something discarded on Erin's second-floor porch.

An hour later, inside apartment 4B, the drone of voices filled the small living room, nearly drowning out the ringing of the telephone only a few feet away. The policewoman emerged from the bedroom, gesturing. Erin nodded and rose from the easy chair where she'd been answering questions. Against the uniforms and suits, her faded blue jeans, light-gray sweater, and sandals made her seem vulnerable, like someone who had been called unexpectedly, without time to prepare, for a formal accounting. DiGenero saw her touch the back of the couch, steadying herself. Then, like a stranger in her own home, she threaded tentatively through the standing-room-only crush of Missoula police and FBI agents and disappeared into the bedroom.

DiGenero stood up, recalling her face after it was all over and Martin had unlocked the door. Erin had looked at the body and then at him, her eyes blank, without recognition. It was as if she had come upon an accident and then glanced up to see a stranger who'd happened by. In his mind, the image of what he'd intended at that instant was so clear, so unambiguous, he could see it even now. He was reaching out, taking her in his arms, holding and protecting her. But he hadn't. He couldn't. He'd wanted to, but she'd stopped him with only a look. Then she'd turned and walked inside.

He pushed through the crowd, feeling suddenly angry at himself and at everything official and intruding. As usual, there were always ten times more police than they needed on the scene after something happened. He wanted to throw them out, all of them, on their collective ass. It was ridiculous, impossible, and he knew it, but at this moment he wanted her as his, and only his, to care for. Just him. No agents. No cops. No questions or answers. None. They were all out of bounds. All but him.

The policewoman, a bleached blond with the hard eyes of assumed authority, glanced over her shoulder, challenging DiGenero as he pushed open the half-closed bedroom door. He pointed to the FBI ID card clipped to his pocket, motioning her to step past him. He closed the door quietly, sealing off the noise and light from the hall.

Lit by a single lamp, with curtains drawn, the room was isolated, nightlike, from the day. Standing beside the bed, turned away from the door, Erin had not heard him enter. She was talking in a low voice and nodding, answering with yes or no. DiGenero leaned against the wall, watching her more than listening. Then, he heard Harris's name.

"Be careful, Kirby."

He crossed the room in only three steps, grasping Erin's wrist in one hand and taking the receiver in the other. Startled, she pulled back combatively, holding tight, before she saw it was him. Then, as if the single act of resistance had drained her, she relinquished the phone.

Harris was still on the line, "Erin?"

"No," DiGenero answered.

The surprise was obvious in the silence. "Well, well. How's the head, old buddy? Sorry you tripped and bumped into that table leg."

"Where are you?"

Harris laughed, "That's a subtle question. Is that the technique they teach you at the FBI Academy? Gimme a break."

"You've got to come in, Kirby."

"Got to?"

"No one would try a hit like this halfway around the world unless there was a bigger prize at stake."

"Gotta go, Frank."

"Kirby," DiGenero's mind raced, trying to find the words that would grab and hold Harris. "They tried to kill Erin. Don't you care about her?"

"Yeah, but you came to the rescue, didn't you?"

"For Christ's sake," DiGenero's temper flared, but Harris cut him off.

"Nice try. You're OK, Frank, but if you think I'm going to walk in for a one-way ticket to the can, you're nuts."

"Kirby..."

The connection went dead.

DiGenero slammed down the phone. Erin was sitting, her head in her hands, on the corner of the bed.

"Where is he?"

"Leave him alone," she spoke without moving.

DiGenero walked closer and stopped, standing over her, "Where is he?"

Erin straightened, looking up as if she hadn't heard him.

"I've got to find him," he said.

She shook her head and then looked away, "I can't tell you. Don't ask me."

"You have to," DiGenero tried to keep his voice low and even. "It's the right thing to do."

Erin shot back, "Don't you understand? Because I can't watch him walk on the edge any longer doesn't mean I can push him off either."

DiGenero's anger boiled up, at first over his own loss for words, and then at Harris for what he'd done, the danger he'd caused. She didn't know about the Iranians. He hadn't told her. DiGenero had only told her that Harris's deal with Von Biemann had gone bad and that they had word she was in danger because the German was out for revenge. He spoke, fists clenched, "The son of a bitch almost got you killed."

Erin eyed him coldly, "Me?" Her voice was too tired to carry the full weight of her sarcasm, "Oh, I didn't know all this was about me. I'm very flattered."

DiGenero shook his head, the frustration playing across his face. He wanted Erin, more than he'd ever wanted any woman. He knew that now. A month ago, when he had choices, when he tried to help Kirby, Harris mattered to him, very much. He still did. But now, his choices were gone, blown away, and it was Kirby's fault. And now he was in love with Kirby's woman.

DiGenero groped for something to say, some way to break through to Erin. Confused, his thoughts tumbled over themselves, coming back to the same three words. They were lousy, but there was nothing else, no other way to put it. There were no choices anymore. "Where is he?"

Erin spoke slowly, without emotion, "A minute ago you asked Kirby whether he cared about me. Do you?"

"Of course I care. I..."

"Then do what I ask. Let him go. He's not going to play your game and you can't make him."

"I can't let him go."

"You can do whatever you want."

"I tried to help him. You know that. But it didn't make any difference to him."

Erin interrupted, "You knew that before you started. He'll never change. You know that," she said, then more slowly as if admitting it to herself for the first time, "I know that." She paused, "It doesn't matter. You can still help him now. Just let him go."

"It's not that easy. I thought it was, but it's not." DiGenero looked away. "When you live two lives and keep two sets of books, sometimes you think you can pull off things other people can't. You're paid to play by your own rules, so why not do it on your own time? I thought I could. I thought I could get Kirby to move out of harm's way. I didn't expect him to fall on his knees and thank me. I just thought he'd step back, do his numbers, and say to himself, 'What are the odds? This guy's doing me a favor. Maybe I'd better shelve it for a while.'" DiGenero shrugged, "It didn't work."

Erin's eyes widened slightly, as if she had recognized a resemblance for the first time and was wondering why she hadn't seen it before. She spoke, "This is a game, isn't it?" The question startled DiGenero. Her gaze seemed as hard as her voice, "A game," she repeated the word as if it explained everything. "That's all. For you, too. A competition between the two of you—any two of you. A one-on-one. And, I'm supposed to play, aren't I? Whether I like it or not? It's just like the little boys in the sandlot. We're choosing up sides. He wants me on his team, and now, you want me on yours."

"No," DiGenero answered reflexively, but Erin's continuing words rode over his denial. "You both think this is all your own and that only you make the rules." The tears were falling slowly over the high curve of her cheeks.

"I thought you were different from him. But you're not, are you?" DiGenero shook his head, disagreeing, but Erin was making a statement, not asking a question. She watched him for a moment, seeming to reflect, and then spoke, "Or maybe you are. Maybe this is what you do every day undercover. Pretending other people matter. Making them believe you, trust you, maybe even care about you. And then?" The hurt in her voice transformed itself into contempt, "Then, you use them. You talk about right and wrong. You pretend that matters, too. Right and wrong? That's just another game, isn't it? 'Right and wrong' didn't make any difference when you were going to 'help' Kirby. But now you've got to get him. Now, your private contest is over and you've got to play by different rules. This time, it's the 'official' rules for your goddamn game."

DiGenero felt a rush of pain and then rage. He reached down, his hands closing around her arms, and jerked Erin to her feet. His words tumbled out, "I don't give a shit about falcons anymore. Harris is up to his eyeballs in terrorists."

"No," Erin said, incredulous, her eyes widening suddenly. DiGenero glared as he spoke, "Von Biemann's a terrorist. The Iranians are terrorists. The man with Harris now is a terrorist. He's a killer, just like the one in a fucking heap outside your door."

"No," she repeated the word, as if frightened as well as shocked at his vehemence. Her denial was weaker, halfhearted, "It's not true. None of it. You're lying."

DiGenero held Erin fast, his intensity overwhelming her, "Something is happening, here, in Germany, in Iran, somewhere, something very important or they wouldn't want you and Harris dead. Trying to kill you, to kill him, it's only a prelude. It's only the beginning."

Erin shook her head weakly, "Oh, my God..."

DiGenero spoke, "Kirby knows. And only Kirby knows. He's part of it and I've got to find him. Before they do. And before others die."

He paused, holding her and feeling suddenly ashamed. His words had struck like blows, one after the other. Erin stood, her body swaying, staring, trying to comprehend. Two days before, Frank had said only that there'd been a falling out, that Von Biemann was dangerous, and that she, like Harris, needed protection. She never knew. She never dreamed. She never could have believed. She thought she'd understood and come to grips with the worst of it, but she was wrong, so wrong.

"Where is he?"

Erin looked away, her lips moving soundlessly forming the word. "Where?"

DiGenero felt her weakness, as if she had become heavier in his hands. He thought he heard a word before the sob that came from somewhere deep, far inside her.

"Sixteen."

"Where?"

She whispered, "A lake. Northwest of the ranch. The cabin is there." Her voice trailed away and then began again, "With food and fuel for the plane."

"It's on the map?"

She nodded.

"Is he there now?"

Erin moved her head indecisively. She'd done it. What he'd asked. That was enough. DiGenero started to ask again, but she stiffened, then pulled free.

"There, you son of a bitch," the words choked out, like something that had been lodged inside her and finally broken free. "I did what was 'right,' for you." She stepped away. DiGenero saw she was trembling. The quiet of the room filled the space between them. She stood unsteadily for several seconds and then sat down on the bed.

"Erin, I . . . ," he started, wanting to explain how it had happened, why it had happened, how he had tried, but she interrupted. Her voice was smaller, distant, as if somehow lost and no longer part of her, "But what about Kirby?" She looked up, "Now, just what am I supposed to do for him?"

DiGenero waited, watching uncertainly for a moment. He could still feel the warmth of her on the palms of his hands.

"I'm sorry," he reached toward her and then stopped. Erin looked away, the motion neither an acknowledgment nor a rejection of the apology. DiGenero turned slowly and walked to the door. The noise from the living room seemed even harsher than before. Halfway out, he paused and looked back. When he did, he saw the heavy shudder of her shoulders and knew that finally, without a sound, she had begun to cry.

*   *   *

The frown on Ralph McCarthy's face dissipated gradually, replaced by a furrowed-brow curiosity and then a stare of fixed attention as he listened to DiGenero's half of the call to Washington on the portable phone. McCarthy, the special agent in charge of the Missoula resident office, had been angry to begin with, and the sight of DiGenero emerging from the bedroom twenty minutes before had only made him angrier.

Forty-eight hours ago, DiGenero had asked him for help to man an undercover stakeout, nothing more. Now, one of his agents was dead, one of DiGenero's was in the hospital, an unnamed corpse was in cold storage in the county morgue, the chief of the Missoula Police was in orbit, and Harold Murchison, the associate deputy director of the FBI and the head of the Counterterrorism Center, had just given him a long-distance ass-chewing. At that moment, Murchison was still on the other end of the line, listening to the answers that only DiGenero could provide.

Even without hearing Murchison's questions, McCarthy could fit the pieces together from the background and description of events outlined by DiGenero's rapid-fire replies.

"He wants to talk to you," DiGenero handed McCarthy the phone. Murchison's voice was calmer now, reflecting the fact that his legendary temper was back under a modicum of control. "Give DiGenero what he wants. He's in charge of the operation until we can get a team out there. Do you understand?"

"Yessir," McCarthy said. The cellular phone's beep and buzz signaled that Murchison had hung up, eliminating the possibility of any further discussion.

DiGenero started to speak, but McCarthy raised his hand, palm out, signaling him to hold the question. He'd heard DiGenero tell Murchison what he needed to do to find Harris. McCarthy spoke, "I've got you covered. We lease a floatplane with radar tracking gear and have a pilot on twenty-four-hour standby. I grew up in Bozeman and know the local real estate. We can take two men with us." McCarthy glanced at his watch. "Our plane's thirty minutes from here on Stevensville Lake, east of Route 93. If Harris has just flown back from Alberta to Sixteen, he'll need to refuel. If he's going on the run in the backcountry, he'll also need provisions. That'll take time. There's no guarantee we'll make it before he takes off, but we can be there in two hours. That at least is the old college try."

DiGenero nodded, "Have someone check on Kasiewicz for me. Martin will handle the paperwork on the shoot."

McCarthy reached for the phone and relayed the orders to have the floatplane fueled and the pilot waiting.

DiGenero glanced out the window. The truck was parked where he'd left it what seemed a lifetime ago. He turned, staring at the bedroom door. It was closed. He thought for a moment about going back for another word, a last try at explaining. DiGenero felt suddenly alone. Erin or Harris? Was it a choice? Had he made it already? McCarthy was staring at him, waiting. Kirby was either at Sixteen or on his way. There was no time. DiGenero slipped the magazine back into the M-16 and walked to the door, motioning to McCarthy and Hightower.

Outside, on the balcony, Sabah's body was gone, although the brick and mortar debris from his twelve-gauge slugs and most of the Iranian's blood still were there. DiGenero walked fast, stepping over the dark-brown stain. He heard the off-tempo footfalls as the others did the same. At the bottom of the stairs, he bent under the red plastic tape that festooned the building, demarcating the police lines and cordoning off the scene, and turned right, crossing the parking lot. The two patrolmen on perimeter security nodded as the three FBI agents strode past.

McCarthy had pulled his car over the curb. The portable gumball light on the roof was still rotating slowly. The FBI agent climbed into the driver's seat. He twisted the ignition, sparking the V-8 instantly to life, and waited for the other two doors to slam closed. DiGenero sat beside him, and Hightower, still in his painter's coveralls, sat in the rear.

"Say, Ralph, where are we goin'?" Hightower leaned forward from the backseat. The Dodge bottomed hard as McCarthy shifted into reverse, backed over the curb, and spun the steering wheel.

DiGenero heard the words but not the question. He wasn't listening, but instead watching Erin in his mind's eye, replaying the scene an hour ago from start to finish. He remembered his anger and frustration, but he felt the hurt they had caused each other, hers as well as his. Only that came back in his gut, but it was enough to make it all real once again. What could he have said or done? How could he have made it different? He still didn't have any answers. But there was a more important question. He had to fix it with Erin, but how could he? What in the name of Christ could he do now?

McCarthy started to talk but his voice was lost in the engine noise and squeal of rubber as he jammed down the accelerator, crossed the police line of Day-Glo orange cone markers, turned right, and sped south toward the edge of Missoula, Route 93, and Stevensville Lake in high gear.

20

Wednesday, September 26, 1984

"Sixteen," Gallatin County, Montana

Harris straightened, holding the hose that snaked down to the fifty-five-gallon drum on the dock, and listened. The drone was faint, fading and returning. He gauged the distance, and then turned back to his work, emptying the last of the fuel into the receptacle on top of the Porter's high wing. He flipped the filler cap in place, locking it shut with a final solid snap, and stepped down from the strut to the pontoon, balancing for a moment as the floatplane bobbed gently, then took a single, long stride to the dock.

The hose from the transfer pump coiled easily. He slipped it onto the Porter's rear cargo deck and paused to scan the horizon. The engine noise was steadier now, although still far away. The northwester helped carry the sound. Harris had felt the storm coming when he landed. The air was still warm, but the wind gusts carried a chill, bringing the feel of the first snow and winter, approaching, days away.

He looked west. Three hundred yards distant, the shoreline doglegged left. On the rocky spit, the row of dark, heavy spruce stood like pickets beside the water before ending abruptly against the slide. The quake of 1888 had tumbled the granite across the outlet of the valley, creating the narrow lake. He had trapped the peregrine two miles below the natural dam, where the water fell back into its old habits, running fast and white in a typical mountain stream.

Harris glanced at his watch. It was after 2:00 p.m. A few feet away, inside her cage, the hooded gyrfalcon, startled by the echo of his heels on the wooden planks, threatened with a cacking call. All other things being equal, he would have kept her. He'd unloaded the young gyr when he landed a half hour ago, delaying her release for no particular reason except perhaps that after ten years, it went against the grain to let $20,000 fly away.

Harris walked rapidly down the dock. Despite the empty sky, the sound, a single engine, was beginning to fill the high valley, a sign the plane was low, following the terrain. It had to be DiGenero, he thought. When he'd called Erin from Calgary after refueling, Frank's voice on the line had been a surprise, but not as much as her news of the second assassin. Sassanir hadn't told him there were two. Erin had been matter-of-fact, too matter-of-fact. He knew from her voice she was struggling, just barely holding herself together. That worried him. He'd tried not to react, not to push her over the brink, simply giving her the instructions on what to do next.

He glanced over his shoulder. At least, DiGenero should be able to protect her from the crazies. Even if Frank was chasing his ass, the FBI was still good for something. Besides, there was nothing he could do about Erin, at least for a couple days, even if he tried. She'd have to take care of herself. She was good at that, he reassured himself. Afterward when they were together again, he'd make up for it.

Harris hurried up the short, rocky path and crested the bank. Fifty yards distant, the cabin stood out, perched on a knoll, as if fitted into a fold in the curtain of spruce bordering the river. His grandfather had built it eighty years ago for the summer grazing time, when the cattle were loose on the high range. In the fall, they used it for elk hunting.

He skipped up the three steps to the porch and walked inside, thinking fast. His pack was on the chair. He opened the flap, checking, and then crossed the room to the cupboard. The assortment of tinned imperishables, beans, peas, stews, and peaches, were randomly stacked. He picked several, stuffing them into the pack, and then retraced his steps to the door. Two miles west, over the river, the glint of sun on glass caught his eye. The plane skimmed the horizon and then dipped low, disappearing. It was following Sixteen.

All things considered, Harris thought, it could have been worse. The Porter's tanks were almost full, good for another 800 miles. To the northeast, the clouds had pushed lower, the bottom of the gray-white bank now hanging at less than 1000 feet. When he reached their cover, he was gone. He had four more hours of daylight, less some traveling east, before he would need to set down again and rest for the night.

Harris pulled the cabin door closed and latched the heavy, rusted padlock. The .30-30 was propped against the log wall. He shouldered the pack and carbine and stepped off the porch, making his way down the slope, this time through the pines. Two minutes later, on the edge of the water, ten yards from the dock, he knelt. The brushwood and tangled weeds wove into a low-growing thicket that hung over the bank. Under the trees, the shade was full and dark.

The plane flashed into view, skirting the far shoreline 300 feet up. Harris leaned farther back into the shadows. He didn't have much time for company. And, if the company was DiGenero, he didn't have any time at all.

A half mile distant, from the rear seat, DiGenero watched over Seth Tilman's shoulder as the pilot dropped the right wing of the Maule Super Rocket, turning to follow Sixteen. Beside Tilman, in the copilot's seat, McCarthy pointed and spoke, "There, over there."

Tilman nodded. He'd flown the Montana backcountry for twenty-five years, but never this particular valley. His contract as the Bureau's standby pilot was good money—an occasional aerial search, prisoner transport, or "familiarization tour" for some Washington VIP. A piece of cake and no interference with his hiring out for the hunting and fishing season.

The cabin, dock, and plane were dead ahead. McCarthy folded the aeronautical chart he had been tracking since they'd left Missoula, an hour before.

"Jesus Christ, how the hell can he get in and out of there," Tilman said to no one in particular. He gestured with one hand at the lake as he pushed the stick away from him, dropping the Maule lower, "That can't be more than 900 feet long."

McCarthy spread the topographic map on his lap. He inched his fingers from the scale to the depiction of the lake and back to the scale, "To be exact, less than a quarter mile. Maybe 300 yards on the longest side."

DiGenero glanced at Hightower beside him in the rear seat. His eyes were closed, his color a pasty white. The Maule banked steeply over the cabin, going around. DiGenero spoke, "It's the Porter. Harris could land and take off from your backyard with it."

"Well, I sure as shit can't with this thing," Tilman said, holding the Maule in a tight circle. "I could put it down, but with three of you inside there's no way I can get off and over the trees with only 900 feet of run, not unless you want to pick pine needles out of your ass for the rest of the day."

Tilman leveled and then banked again, holding a wider, more gentle turn. He throttled back the Maule's 235-horsepower Avco flat-six engine.

McCarthy twisted to face DiGenero in the rear seat, "So?"

DiGenero shook his head, "We don't have a choice." He paused, calculating time and mileage in his head. En route, they'd called the Montana Highway Patrol for help, but the police helicopter still wasn't in sight. "Harris is there," DiGenero thought out loud, "and he knows we're up here. He doesn't know if we've got anyone coming overland or by chopper. Odds are, he probably thinks we do. So, my guess is he'll take off. Soon. That means we've either got to go in and get him before he does or hang around and follow."

Tilman broke in, "The weather in the northeast is going to knock the ceiling down to nothing within minutes." The pilot pointed to the cloud bank. Ten miles away, it was darkening and rolling toward them. "That's all the time we've got to either drive it or park it."

DiGenero nodded, "Just stay on top of him for a few more minutes. If he runs on foot, 'rabbits' into the brush, we won't find him for weeks. I don't want to chase him on the ground."

Five hundred feet below the circling Maule, Harris eyed the clouds. "Come on," he muttered impatiently. The front was moving fast. The mist and fog had just touched the ridge beyond the lake. The weather was only minutes away. Then, he heard the sound. It was what he'd been waiting for. Harris smiled, "Finally." The north wind blew harder, stirring the water. A few feet away, the lake began to break against the shore. The light chop was ideal, just enough to help the Porter lift off. Harris rose, stepping over a half-decayed log, emerged from the thicket, and walked rapidly onto the dock.

"He's on his way," DiGenero rapped his knuckle hard on the window and pointed. "Go down!" Tilman banked, sideslipping into a fast forty-degree descent, and leveled. Harris reached the Porter just as the Maule buzzed low, thirty feet above his head, pulled up, and carved a tight left turn.

Inside the Maule, the radio crackled. DiGenero listened to the conversation, cursing silently. The helicopter had been late getting off from Bozeman. It was on the way, but the Montana Highway Patrol pilot was worried about the weather.

DiGenero tapped Tilman on the shoulder, "See if you can keep Harris from taking off. Maybe the chopper can make it in time."

DiGenero looked left, craning his neck. The Porter's prop turned slowly, the long underbelly outboard exhaust pipe sputtering blue smoke from the engine. Tilman banked over the far edge of the lake, dropping down to buzz the dock again. They flashed over the Porter, pulled up hard, and went around.

"What the hell? He's getting out," McCarthy pointed at Harris, who was stepping onto the dock. The Maule, level at sixty feet, was coming in again, low and straight toward the Porter. Through the windscreen, DiGenero watched Harris reach down into the box that was sitting next to the oil drum. The gyrfalcon emerged, proud and straight on his arm, perching for a moment as if in all the world it belonged only there. Then, Harris removed its hood. Before the Maule skimmed over the dock, DiGenero could see Harris's mocking grin as the bird stretched its wings and in one powerful beat, took off, making its escape.

McCarthy looked back at DiGenero, grinning, "Well, if that isn't a goddamn kick in the butt."

DiGenero smiled involuntarily. He leaned across Hightower, trying to watch Harris as Tilman banked steeply, turning left. Harris had untied the single mooring line. By the time the Maule was over the far end of the lake again, lining up for another pass, he was back in the cockpit. The Porter's rudder flapped. Then, the water kicked up in foam and spray as Harris advanced the throttle. The long, gunmetal-gray shape swung through a graceful arc, lining up into the wind.

Tilman pressed the headset more tightly against his ear, listening. They were too low to read the radio transmissions clearly. "The police chopper is three minutes away," Tilman said. He banked the Maule hard right and then hard left, turning to come in behind the Porter. On the water, Harris accelerated, beginning the takeoff run.

"Here goes," Tilman throttled back, trying to pace the Porter and position himself ahead of Harris, an aerial roadblock that could keep him from lifting off. The Porter gained speed. DiGenero watched its tail dip ahead of them. At takeoff power, the lift generated by the 600-horsepower turboprop brought Harris's fifty feet of glider wing to life.

DiGenero yelled, "Slower, slower, pace him!" Tilman shook his head, "Can't." They were too hot, moving too fast. Harris looked up as the Maule flashed above, overshooting him. Then, he pulled back hard on the stick. The Porter seemed to rise straight up.

Tilman jammed the throttle forward and dropped the Maule's nose, gaining speed. He pulled into another tight turn and climbed, angling for position and altitude, to the rear and above the Porter. The long-winged shape, smaller now against the wider expanse of the valley, was already banking right and heading northeast toward the dark clouds.

Harris's voice, loud and clear in the headset, startled Tilman. The pilot glanced down. Harris had picked the Missoula air traffic control frequency, counting on the likelihood that they had not switched channels since taking off. Tilman flipped the radio's toggle switch to the cabin speaker.

"That you, Frank?"

Tilman passed the hand microphone back to DiGenero, who keyed the "talk" button, "Put it back on the water, Kirby, you're not going anywhere."

"Whatsamatter? You want to give me a ticket?" Harris held the mike button down, transmitting his laughter.

Tilman pointed southeast, "There's the chopper." He switched on the Collins microline police transmitter/receiver, and reached for the second microphone, "MHP Hughes 500, this is the FBI, November 220. Do you have me in sight?"

The helicopter's reply was immediate, "Roger, November 220, I have you and the Porter in sight."

Tilman keyed the microphone, "Can you help me box in the Porter? I want to turn him back to the lake."

"Roger, I'll swing wide and come in on his right if you take the left, but I don't know if we can reach him before he gets to the clouds."

The sleek Hughes cantilevered forward, accelerating, and then banked hard and climbed. DiGenero calculated the odds. The play was to bracket Harris. The chopper, 50 percent faster than the Porter, would hang in front of his nose while the Maule flew above him, forcing the Porter down or back. DiGenero sat back. It would be a long shot but possible if they were up against an average pilot, he thought. With Harris, the odds were slightly better than a snowball's chance in hell.

He looked out. The Porter was a mile ahead, and the Hughes, a mile wide right, vectoring to intercept. For a moment, they were all equidistant, like points on a blank page, needing only lines to connect them in order to create the image of a perfectly balanced three-dimensional form. But only for a moment.

Harris broke the pattern, descending and accelerating.

"See you, Frank," the radioed voice was casual, but there was no laughter this time. Harris was concentrating.

DiGenero keyed the mike, "It won't work, Kirby, this one's a tracker. We've got the radar to follow you into the clouds." There was no comeback.

The police radio crackled, "November 220, he's goin' to be in the soup before we can reach him."

DiGenero glanced over Tilman's shoulder at the altimeter. They were at 6700 feet, about 1500 feet above the valley floor. Harris was 500 feet below them and descending into the first wisps of fog and rain. DiGenero could see the muscles, corded and tense, on Tilman's neck.

DiGenero tapped the pilot on the shoulder, "Tell the cops to break it off. We'll take it from here."

"Roger MHP," Tilman replied, "we've got him on radar and will follow. Sorry for the long ride but thanks for the help." The helicopter banked at once, veering away from the weather.

DiGenero looked back, but the Porter had disappeared. Tilman had turned on the radar. The Porter was there, and only there, a green spot painted brighter once a second by the rotating cursor that translated the antennae's discoveries into the picture before them. The electronic pulse that bounced and returned put Harris in the lower-right quadrant of the eight-inch screen, ahead of and below the Maule, descending at a mile and a half through 6000 feet. DiGenero glanced at the altimeter. That also put the Porter at 800 feet above the unfamiliar and uneven ground.

The Maule passed through 6000 feet. DiGenero glanced at Hightower. His eyes were closed, squeezed tight. DiGenero felt his own pulse pounding. They dropped momentarily out of the fog. Below them, the valley rose sharply, rocks, gullies, and trees intermingled, beginning to climb upward into a high plateau. The spruce, thicker now, covered the more distant slopes.

Tilman's voice sounded strained as their visibility disappeared, "The ceiling's 750 feet or so here, but it's dropping fast." DiGenero leaned between Tilman and McCarthy, squinting at the screen. Harris's pip, fuzzier now, was still descending.

"Son of a bitch," Tilman shook his head, glancing left and right nervously. "He's about 300 feet off the deck and going lower. This is a good tracking radar but we're not AWACS." He tapped the scope, "He's giving us the slip. Your friend Harris is one smart bastard, if he lives, that is. He's taking us down where the radar signal will bounce off the trees and rocks. That'll make the scope all ground clutter. The picture won't be worth a damn. It'll obscure his pip. We're going to lose him in the blooms."

DiGenero could see the sweat on the back of Tilman's neck. On the scope, the Porter was almost invisible in the formless pattern of lightpoints and the uneven green blossoms that followed behind the cursor.

DiGenero looked out at gray cotton, rain, and dirty foam. Despite the cool cockpit, his face and hands were wet, perspiring. Zero visibility. The twin altimeters showed that the Maule was at 5600 feet above sea level, but only 400 feet over the rapidly rising Montana plateau. Ahead, at 120 knots in the murk, Harris was even lower and dropping, 100 feet over the trees. DiGenero shifted his gaze to the scope. They were passing through 300 feet. The radar was almost all green, a meaningless pattern of brightness and blurs. The Porter was gone.

"Take it up," DiGenero said. Tilman jerked back the stick, climbing into a steep left turn. Next to him, DiGenero heard Hightower's deep, tremulous, and thankful sigh.

McCarthy turned around. He was almost dead white, "I've got a suggestion. Let's not do this again, even if he's fuckin' Al Capone." DiGenero smiled weakly, his own relief evident, and looked down, noticing for the first time that his hands were shaking.

"What altitude do we need to contact Bozeman?" DiGenero asked. Tilman shrugged, "6000, 6500 will give us a clear signal."

"Get on the horn and give the Porter's course to FAA as well as MHP. Ask them to relay it to the Bureau. An APB, an All Points Bulletin, is our only hope to run him to ground." DiGenero paused, thinking about Harris's northeasterly direction, "And, tell the Canadians, too."

The Maule broke through the top of the weather into the late-afternoon sun at 6500 feet.

Tilman was about to key the microphone on the police radio when Harris's voice filled the cockpit. The regular transceiver was still set on the Missoula air traffic control frequency and the cockpit speaker.

"No need to answer, Frank, just give my love to Erin," Harris paused, laughing, "and don't forget to write."

DiGenero reached for the microphone, "This isn't going to work, Kirby."

There was no answer.

DiGenero spoke again, "Talk to me."

The speaker hissed a steady static.

Tilman glanced over his shoulder, his eyes questioning whether to make the transmission on the police radio, or to let DiGenero try again.

DiGenero sat back and frowned, frustrated. The Porter was down there, behind them, a few hundred feet off the ground, maneuvering through the valleys at 120 knots. DiGenero toyed with the microphone for a moment, thinking about what to say. The speaker was silent. He looked up. To the northeast, the clouds created a level, gray coverlet, extending to the horizon. Beneath the blanket, somewhere, Harris was putting distance between them. DiGenero reached between the two front seats, handing back the mike.

"Go ahead," he nodded to Tilman, the resignation evident in his voice. There was no point. DiGenero knew that no matter what he said, there wouldn't be an answer. For now, it was over. Harris was slipping away. The Missoula frequency was dead.

21

Thursday, September 27, 1984

Dog Lake, Ontario, Canada

The clouds were low, almost touching the water, when Claude LeBlanc and Pierre Monteau looked up from the thin, sharply angled Vs cut by their trolling lines behind the flat-bottomed bass boat. Clamped on the transom, the tiny electric outboard motor pushed them steadily at a mile an hour, creating an almost traceless wake on the dead-calm surface of the lake. The two men turned in unison. Monteau saw the gunmetal-gray plane first. It dipped briefly below the overcast before disappearing again into the mist a half mile away.

"Hey, where did he come from?" LeBlanc asked, following Monteau's raised finger and gesturing himself with a flicking motion of his gloved right hand. His Quebecois accent was hard, with sharp edges.

Monteau shrugged, "Lost, maybe." The engine noise faded quickly, wrapped in the clouds, and then seemed to hold constant, like the sound of a powerful machine, neither receding nor approaching, but running steadily and keeping its distance.

LeBlanc squinted at the murk, "I think it's coming back." The dying light, the weather, and the end of September combined to neutralize the colors in what remained of the red maple leaves along the shoreline of the western Ontario lake. This time of year, due east of Lake Superior, the land was only days from the first snow. Compared to the summer, when the tourists came west from Toronto and north from the States, it was quiet, almost deserted.

Monteau furrowed his brow, "Strange, eh? I wonder..."

LeBlanc put his finger to his lips for quiet before he spoke, "Is that the 4:30 freight?"

Monteau cocked his head, listening, "Could be." He shivered in the chill, trying to make out the distant rumble. After spending two decades listening to the earsplitting whine of lumber mill saws, Monteau had less than his share of high- and low-frequency hearing. Like the others who lived in Missanabie, the logging town where the two French Canadians had moved twenty years before from their home village in eastern Quebec, both men knew the local rail schedule by heart. The town was a stop on the Canadian Pacific line for two daily passenger trains, an east and a westbound, although Monteau was certain it was too early for the evening arrival. In any case, the sound was heavy, much more than one engine hauling a six-car passenger train.

"It's the freight," LeBlanc said. Far away, the diesels were working harder, gathering a few miles per hour before pulling their chain of cars up the grade.

Monteau bobbed his head once, "It's the 4:30." Neither man had a watch. No need. The regular train from the White River junction to Sudbury was their signal to go.

"OK. Got enough for dinner, eh?" LeBlanc said.

"Home, eh?" Monteau asked, jerking his head toward Missanabie.

"For sure," LeBlanc nodded. He opened the tackle box and reached for his pole, buttoning his red plaid hunting jacket one-handed. There would be no complaints when they walked in their kitchen doors. Their wives already knew why they were late returning from the mill's eight-to-four shift. After one call to make certain they had not stopped at Madigan's Grill, the two French Canadian women would telephone one another, just to confirm what had happened, sharpen their gutting and scaling knives, and then sit down to wait.

LeBlanc cranked the spinning reel, drawing in the deep diving lure. "We'd better go." The dampness was beginning to penetrate. Missanabie was only a little over a mile away, but at this hour, even with the forty-horsepower Johnson wide open, it was a cold ride eastward around the point.

Monteau stepped to the center of the long, flat bass boat and touched the electric starter. It whirred once, energizing the big, blue-and-white outboard. LeBlanc snapped off the power switch on the small, electric trolling motor and bent over the transom, lifting and locking it in an uptilted position beside the Johnson. Suddenly, out of the muffled silence of the lowering fog and dusk, the turboprop's roar overwhelmed them.

"Goddamn," Monteau flinched, dodging the unexpected near miss. Both men ducked involuntarily as the plane skimmed past, no more than forty feet above their heads. Their abrupt motion rocked the bass boat crazily, splashing water over the gunnels.

"Shit, what, is he nuts?" LeBlanc, startled, could feel his knees beginning to shake. Despite twenty years of fishing Ontario's lakes, he couldn't swim and loathed any surprises on the water.

Monteau nodded vigorously, "That one is too low to see in this fog. He must be going down." He hit the stop button, killing the outboard and listening for the expected crash.

The noise appeared to have been swallowed up. "He's gone," Monteau said.

"I just hear the train," LeBlanc replied. The diesel horn sounded mournfully. The two long wails signaled its warning at the unmarked crossing on the outskirts of Lochalsh, the village neighboring Missanabie, at the south end of nearby Wabatongushi Lake. The sound of the train engines grew louder, following the usual pattern. The freight would accelerate briefly before it slowed again, this time retarded by the second, much longer grade approaching Dog Lake.

"Crazy," LeBlanc muttered. Monteau punched the outboard motor's start button again with his palm. He sat down on the swivel seat and shook his head. "Better we go before the fool lands on us," LeBlanc said, but his words were already drowned in the noise of the forty-horsepower Johnson as Monteau advanced the throttle, accelerated, and turned east toward the fog, safety, and home on the other side of the point.

A mile away and seventy-five feet up, Kirby Harris glanced at the altimeter and pushed forward on the stick, leveling the Porter. The bass boat had flashed below him, materializing out of the mist. Harris had cursed, climbing into the overcast for cover and prudence's sake. The aircraft, noticeably lighter to the touch with next to no fuel, had risen swiftly. Running dry had some advantages, Harris thought wryly, lessening the Porter's weight and making it even more nimble. If he wasn't about to land, the boat wouldn't matter, but at this point, he could do without witnesses.

He cut back the throttle, quieting the engine, and stared at the gauges, calculating the fuel-flow rate. There wasn't much to record in the Porter's four tanks. The two mains held mostly fumes. With the auxiliaries, he had ten minutes remaining in the air, if that. He eyed the altimeter again and then the overcast. The ceiling was higher to the west, at the far end of the lake. He eased the controls back, letting the Porter climb to touch the fuzzy bottom of the clouds, and glanced down. The low, scudding mist and rain were thickening. He switched on the wiper, clearing the windshield, and snapped the cockpit defroster fan to the high setting. Outside, the temperature was dropping and the mist, condensing on the heavy glass, was beginning to freeze.

At 150 feet, the Porter passed over the shoreline. Harris looked back at the water, scanning again for logs, rocks, sandbars, and debris. A quarter mile distant, the lowest layer of clouds had broken open, a brief, wind-driven rending with jagged shifting edges, shaped like a newspaper tear. Harris banked toward the hole in the gray gauze and climbed, watching the altimeter wind to 500 feet. The Porter's course, a short looping out-and-back, would be his final circuit over land before touching down.

The gap in the cloud bank widened, curving like a comma to the

north and west. In the distance, he could make out the full length of the
train. The freight was where he expected, three miles away. Through the
mist and the rain, the headlight of the first diesel seemed to waver. Watching, Harris could tell that the train's speed was probably forty miles an
hour and slowing as it decelerated, coping with the grade.

Satisfied, he banked left, turning back toward the lake. He had planned
to fly due east across the States. Had. DiGenero changed all that. Yesterday, after shaking the Maule and the helicopter, Harris had tuned the
Porter's second radio, the portable Barrecrafter scanner, to the FAA's
official channel. It was the common frequency for the Feds—the Border
Patrol, Customs, the military, as well as the FBI—when they needed to
cooperate. He had made it a practice to monitor their radio traffic whenever he was moving birds. The bulletin describing the Porter had been
repeated hourly. Harris was certain the Canadians, the Civil Aviation
Authority as well as the Royal Canadian Mounted Police, the RCMP,
would have the message, although he knew from experience they had
too few people to cover the country's vastness. Then and there, he'd decided that going north was his best bet.

Harris looked down. The map was still open on the seat beside him.
His eyes traced the line he had followed east across the aeronautical chart
over the last twenty-four hours. The deep ache in his back penetrated
from his shoulders to his arms, the consequence of 1200 miles of flying,
hands on, only a few hundred feet off the deck. He craned his neck,
stretching away the muscle tension, and rapped the fuel gauges with the
back of his knuckles. It was an old habit, making the needles jump and
settle back to see if they were reading true.

The fuel in the auxiliaries was almost gone. Eight hundred miles back
and twenty hours ago, when he'd stopped for the night on the small Man-
itoba lake, south of the Trans-Canada Highway, to eat and sleep, he'd
rolled the fifty-five-gallon drum out of the Porter and cranked the transfer pump to empty the contents into the wing tanks. Harris rubbed the
stubble on his chin. Since morning, he'd followed the Canadian National's single-track line as far east as Lake Nipigon, just above Lake Superior's northern hump. Then, watching the fuel gauges drop, he'd turned
south and climbed, looking for the Canadian Pacific's right-of-way. He
found it within half an hour. It was a solitary track linking one small
town to another through the miles of forest. He'd used it, heading south.

The map showed that farther along, the railroad curved southeast, taking him in the direction he needed to go.

Harris glanced at the instrument panel. Two of his four tanks' low-fuel warning lights were blinking, telling him they were almost out. Two, already empty, glowed steady red. He had only minutes now. There would be no going around.

DiGenero knew him well enough to expect that he would fly all the way and, Harris thought, Frank was right. He would, if he had the gas. But he didn't. Simple as that. He'd thought about trying to refuel, but it was no good. That had been clear to him yesterday when he was leaving Saskatchewan, the boundary of his familiar territory. With the FBI bulletin on the air, he had no intention of bellying up to the pumps at any big-city docks. There were other places, smaller floatplane stops, but not all of them carried a turboprop's fuel and he didn't know which ones did. Besides, there was no time for wrong guesses. The train was his best choice. He'd made the decision to abandon the Porter and look for a freight two hours ago. It was a gamble, a calculated risk. But if it worked, switching from the plane to the train in the middle of nowhere would make his trail disappear. Even if DiGenero found the Porter right away, Frank wouldn't have an idea in hell as to where he'd gone.

Harris glanced back at the gauges. One of the warning lights for the auxiliary tanks had stopped blinking and was glowing steady red. He tightened his grip on the controls.

Targets, time, distance, and fuel, Harris thought, just like the war. The chance of finding a train that was traveling all the way east would have been better due south, toward Sault Ste. Marie on the main line. He'd considered it, but there, more tracks came with more roads, more people, and more chances to be seen. Instead, he'd stayed his course, searching the single-track line. It almost hadn't worked, he thought. He'd found trains, but they were westbounds or short haulers, shuttling a few cars or track repair crews between the small yards and dead-end spurs along the way.

Finally, fifteen minutes ago, he'd popped up to 1000 feet. He'd been straining to see through the spats of rain when the end of the train materialized out of gloom. It was eastbound, well over 150 cars, and stretched out, engines pulling hard, on a grade. He'd paced it long enough to estimate that the incline had slowed the string of cars to fifteen miles an hour, no more than a man's steady run.

He'd taken the Porter back down through the overcast to 300 feet, where the clouds broke open, and flown ahead. Two minutes later and four miles down the track, the marker stood out. Below him, even through the thickening mist, Harris could see the right triangle and the "5/5" numbered coding beneath it, black on white, telling the engineer to prepare for another incline, this time a 5 percent grade and a five-mile uphill pull.

Harris had banked hard right, descending. The mist was thickening to fog. Suddenly there was brightness, then, open water. He banked, this time turning hard left over the lake to parallel the tracks. Above, at seventy-five feet, the clouds and fog skittered along the top of his wing. To the north, less than a mile, a point of land jutted and bent. He dipped to forty feet, following the sharp turn of the shoreline. The opening flashed by, more than he had hoped for. The curve of land and trees formed a quiet cove, 100 yards across, clear, deep, and protected from casual sight, with a natural beach and no obstructions. He remembered glancing down at the map. He was south of the rail line over something called Dog Lake.

Harris looked down. Beneath the Porter, the water seemed to stain through the low clouds and rain, creating dark, blotchy, black-on-gray patches. Behind him, two miles away, the freight was approaching. It was time. He turned, sideslipping right in a long arc toward his final approach. The overcast closed around the Porter, dimming the cockpit. Harris throttled down, watching his airspeed fall away. A passing eddy of turbulence buffeted the wings. Suddenly the whiteout surrounded him. The clouds seemed to billow downward, keeping his pace. Descending and turning, the mist thickened, coating the windshield. Then, at seventy-five feet, in an instant, it was gone, revealing the cold, premature twilight suspended between the low brow of sky and the lake.

The blue-black water rose to meet him. Harris leveled and lowered the flaps. At seventy feet, he turned left sharply, lining up. The cove was his sanctuary, covering him, a hiding place, his protection. Fringing its mouth, the tree line seemed to reach out into the water, like gates flung open on either side of a formal entrance, at the same time demarcating and narrowing the opening. He pushed the nose lower, and throttled back. Passing through sixty knots, the Porter began to lose lift, dropping as its wings approached the edge of a stall. Harris glanced right momentarily. The lights of a town, whatever it was called, glowed and then vanished, hidden behind the point.

The brilliant flash on the panel in front of him was sudden, distracting. Startled, Harris looked at his instruments. He understood instantly. Centered just below the lip of the glare shield that protruded to shade the instrument panel, the two-inch-square master caution light pulsed. Below it, the light for the second and last auxiliary gauge shone steadily, explaining the larger, more brilliant red warning: as far as the sensors in the Porter's four tanks were concerned, he had no fuel.

"Jesus Christ, come on, baby," Harris slammed the throttle forward, reversing the propeller and hitting full power. The 600-horsepower turbine screamed, responding. The gauges couldn't read the slop in the tanks. There was always a little more, always.

At twenty feet, the Porter dropped like a stone. He grimaced as the plane smacked hard. Ahead, through the windshield, the cove's scalloped edge, a collage of earth, rocks, and timber, rushed toward him. Eighty, seventy, sixty, fifty yards. He closed fast on the shoreline. Now, he needed the power to stop, not to fly. Without the propeller's braking action, he would hit, nose on, in seconds. The plane seemed to lean forward, bowing, as the prop bit the air. Curling around him, the sound reverberated against the sides of the cove, holding and hiding both the Porter and the turboprop's roar.

Forty, thirty, twenty yards. The Porter slowed. The rocks, larger, boulders now, filled the scene framed by the windshield. Harris eased back the throttle. He kicked the rudder right, turning toward the small sand beach, and reached to cut the engine. At the instant his hand touched the throttle, the turboprop coughed. Before him, the transparent spinning blur began to reveal the outlines of the prop. He pulled up on the throttle handle, snapping it past the lockout detente into the "off" position. It was a matter of habit, not need. The engine was dead. It had sucked up the last drop of fuel. The tanks were bone-dry.

Harris sat back and rubbed his eyes. The blinking red master caution light illuminated the cockpit, accompanied in the quiet by the metronomelike tick of the solenoid that activated its pulsing glow. Above the fuel gauges, the row of four small warning lights stared back, bright red. Harris turned, looking through his own reflection in the side window, and exhaled a long sigh, "I don't want it to get around, but I may just be too fucking old for this." The Porter drifted shoreward, barely moving. Then, soundlessly, the plane grounded gently on the sand.

Harris straightened and reached behind him, grasping his pack, parka, and the .30-30. He opened the cockpit door, stepping onto the float and then to the small, curving sand spit before pausing to listen. The rain, mixed with traces of fog, created a damp, heavy dusk. In the stillness, the sound of the train was distant but closing.

He strode quickly, covering the five yards of narrow, pebbled beach, and stepped into the darkness beneath the trees, making his way to the embankment. At the foot of the gravel slope, he knelt. He would climb after the freight's four engines had passed and wait until he counted seventy-five cars, the midpoint in the string, where the distance from the center of the train to the engineer in the first cab and the brakeman in the caboose would be greatest. Then, it was simply a matter of a leg up.

Harris eased back against a tree, resting. The growl was deeper, announcing the diesels' approach. For the first time, the cold made him shiver. He zipped the parka before leaning forward to sling the pack over his shoulder.

So far, so good, Harris thought, except for one question. His next destination. Like the decision to abandon the Porter and find a train, it was a calculated risk. Calculated, that is, if you were smart enough to understand what to figure. He recalled his aerial view of the freight. All the doors on the boxcars were open. They were empties, and he knew from growing up in Montana, watching the traffic on the Great Northern's line, that out west, where towns were sparse, railroads usually put together a string of empties to make a long hauler, bringing the cars to a main marshaling yard for redistribution and reloading. There were no guarantees, Harris thought. But if this freight was doing the same, he knew its destination almost certainly was well down the line, from the looks of the map, probably Sudbury, a railway junction point, 175 miles away.

Harris shifted to one knee. At least, that was what he was counting on. At an average speed of forty miles an hour, the freight would arrive five hours from now. He looked at his watch. That was just fine, too. If he was right, Sudbury would be big enough to get lost in, and five hours would still leave him time to clean up, check on his choices for travel, and pick the best way to move on.

Above him, in the shadows thrown across the single track by the trees, the long, thin cone of light from the lead engine's headlamp played on the rails. Closer now, the rumble was palpable, like a steady physical pulse. Harris stood, tensing, and prepared to climb the bank. The noise reverberated around him. Suddenly, the four diesel units loomed above, straining at full power. Hidden in the deepening twilight, he saw the engineer, leaning against his control panel, elbow sticking out the side window, staring straight ahead.

He bent low and climbed sideways, digging his heels into the loose gravel embankment. At the top, where the grade rolled to level, Harris raised his head. The train was making ten miles an hour. At both ends, the engine and caboose were lost in the mist and darkness. As the seventieth car passed, he stood and stepped forward quickly. Finding the right stride to hit a railway tie with each pace, Harris began to jog, matching his speed to the train's. Beside him, the door to the burgundy-red Canadian Pacific boxcar gaped open. Harris reached up and slid the .30-30 onto the boxcar floor. Then, he grasped the side of the door and swung on board.

Harris landed solidly on his stomach and rolled upright, sitting. The far ends of the empty car were black, almost totally obscure. Inside, the rhythm of the boxcar's trucks, the heavy steel wheels beneath him, marked the train's slow progress. Otherwise, his own breathing, loud in the hollow quiet, made the only sound. Harris stood, moving deeper into the car. The floor was covered with loose Excelsior and packing straw. He gathered a pile for a cushion and propped his pack in the corner as a headrest.

Seventy-five cars and three diesel units ahead, the lead engine crested the grade, picking up speed. The empty boxcar rocked gently. Harris sat and leaned back, adjusting the pack behind his head. This leg of the trip sure as shit wasn't first-class, but he was dry, traveling in the right direction, and moving away from the Porter without so much as turning a single leaf that could leave a trail. With luck, he would be in Sudbury by the early hours, tomorrow morning.

He shifted into a more comfortable position, peering out from the corner. The interior momentarily glowed deep red and sounded with the toll of the warning bell as the boxcar traversed Missanabie's one and only street, passing the railroad grade-crossing signal. The street was empty and dark, except for the taillights of a pickup truck, and the bright-blue "Labatt's" sign centered in the window under the neon lettering that spelled "Madigan's Grill."

Even if it took a little longer, Harris thought, he still had forty-eight hours to cover 1000 miles. If there was any trouble and he had to cut it close, Erin also already knew where to meet him. Fortunately, there had been time enough to tell her that yesterday on the phone, before DiGenero broke in. He closed his eyes, remembering the other call he'd placed yesterday before he'd telephoned Erin. He had described, bare bones, with no details, only the bottom line, what he had to sell. The reaction had been brief and to the point. They would be waiting. When he arrived, they said, he should call again. If there was trouble and someone was following, he should go to the side door. It would be open. Once he was inside, on their territory, he was safe.

The numbness and fatigue from flying three days straight began to overcome Harris. It was not an unpleasant sensation. He turned on his side and felt himself slipping away. For now, he could sleep. Tomorrow, in Sudbury, early or late, he would find a hotel, shower, and shave. Then he would be on his way.

At that moment, 300 miles away in the Rideau Gardens section of Ottawa, Abdullah Jabir Walayd turned the key in the dead-bolt lock, securing the battered front door of his second-floor efficiency apartment, descended the dimly lit narrow stair, and stepped outside. The nondescript, four-story, old stone walk-up fronted on Beckwith Court, a quiet working-class residential street, where he turned right, walking toward Marlow Crest. At the corner, he turned right again. Walayd strode quickly north toward the intersection with Clegg and beyond, framed before him by the rain-heavy overhanging limbs, the tree-lined campus of Saint Paul University.

He buttoned the collar on his poplin coat. The rain was falling harder, beating the leaves from the maples and oaks that were draped above the street. As a Palestinian with only a third-degree honors certificate from the small business college in London's West End, Walayd knew he'd done well. He was in his third year in Ottawa as the administrative assistant to the political counselor at the Embassy of Saudi Arabia. He was one of three Palestinians at the embassy, albeit one of the hundreds in the Saudi foreign ministry, staffing a government replete with money but suffering from the dearest scarcity of all—a shortage of its own kind, not enough Saudis to manage the affairs of state.

Walayd looked ahead two blocks. He could see the lighted phone booth through the mist. He was too young to remember either rain or sun in Haifa, where his family had lived for eight generations. They had walked, carrying what they could on their backs, across the Lebanese border and settled in Sidon, scarred, poorer, bitter, and in 1948, permanently dispossessed. At 16, in high school with the others who took Fatah's training, he had vowed to return, to take the land, Palestine, back. Even in London, years later, after he began his clerk's job with the Saudis, he never forgot, and in 1981, when the Iranian approached him six months before he was transferred to Ottawa, he had said yes.

He stepped across the last intersection, looking both ways. Shia or Sunni, Iranian or Arab, Walayd thought, it hadn't mattered to him then and it didn't matter now. Their revolution was his. He would provide whatever information he could to advance the cause of Islam, including the end of Israel and the final victory of his people. But most important, Walayd stopped beside the booth and scanned the surroundings, including death to the occupiers and the return of Abdullah Jabir Walayd to his homeland, to Haifa, Palestine.

The street was empty, except for the occasional car. Waiting, he reviewed the details of the call yesterday, Wednesday, in his mind. The phone had been ringing when he entered the office. It was long-distance and the accent was American, not Canadian. Walayd had transferred him to the political counselor, listening on his extension as always for whatever could be learned. The man's name and message were simple enough to remember, as was the political counselor's reply. There was interest. The American was to come to the embassy on Saturday at 6:30 p.m.

Walayd's regular contact meeting for debriefing was still five days away and there wasn't time to wait. He had used the emergency instructions, dialing the number in Munich later Wednesday night. He gave his name as Masaad and the message for Timar, the code that told them he would be waiting tonight, at 7:00 p.m., at the predesignated number.

Walayd looked at his watch as the second hand swept past the hour. The pay phone's ring was loud, out of place in the damp and darkened street. He stepped inside the booth. The procedure was strict. There was to be no greeting or wasted words. Simply his message, repeated twice, clearly, to ensure accurate transmission of detail. Walayd lifted the receiver. He spoke slowly in English and then paused, wanting to add a thought, a bit of value, a comment that relayed his hope he had discovered something worthwhile. He didn't. The line clicked and went dead. A gust, previewing the coming storm, drove a spray of rain from the trees loudly against the glass sides of the booth. Startled, Walayd glanced out. Then he hung up the phone, backed onto the sidewalk, and strode quickly away.

Twenty-four hours later, Frank DiGenero stepped into Madigan's Grill, feeling wetter and colder than he had ever been in his life. A pace behind, Senior Constable Jeffery McCallum, Western Ontario Third District supervisor, Royal Canadian Mounted Police, closed the door just in time to prevent a thirty-mile-per-hour gust of northwest wind from driving a sheet of rain inside. McCallum watched sympathetically as DiGenero peeled off his saturated raincoat before removing his own heavy yellow slicker and dripping Mounties' hat. He was cold but at least the slicker had kept him dry, something that could not be said for that poor FBI agent who had arrived four hours before in summer suit, loafers, and lightweight raincoat.

"Out on a bad one, eh, Jeff?" Randy Madigan's voice carried over the din of Friday night drinkers who had woven themselves into a knot three-deep at the bar.

"Yeah," McCallum waved, "soaked through and through. We might as well have swum across the lake to Dimple Bay as walked around, eh?" McCallum touched DiGenero's arm, motioning him to the corner table, and then turned back toward the bar, "Randy, how about a boilermaker and a coffee to warm us up?"

"Coming your way," Madigan replied, eyeing McCallum's companion. The man was obviously miserable. DiGenero had not expected that the Canadians would serve up a hurricane when the RCMP's regional headquarters in Windsor had called that morning, telling him they'd found the Porter. To his good fortune, or so it seemed until the driving rainstorm overtook them as they walked through the woods on the other side of Dog Lake, the Bureau's Learjet had been in Salt Lake City. It was at his disposal after only one call to Associate Deputy Director Murchison in Washington. DiGenero had been airborne within an hour. One of the Mounties' Twin Otters, equipped with floats, was waiting when he landed at Sault Ste. Marie. They'd arrived at Missanabie, landing in Dog Lake after bouncing all over the Canadian sky, five minutes ahead of the storm.

DiGenero shivered. He hadn't had time to change. His suit slacks were dripping from the knees down and his loafers were a soaked-through shade of dull black, rather than their original tan. The waitress put the shotglass of Canadian whiskey and the beer in front of him. He downed the smooth whiskey with one swallow and held up a finger before she had time to turn away.

"One more?" she asked, arching an eyebrow. DiGenero nodded.

"I'm sorry we had to walk through the woods the last mile, Mr. Di-Genero," McCallum said, stirring the mug of black coffee that had been put before him, "but this place isn't exactly the suburbs."

DiGenero waved away the apology, "No need to be sorry, I wanted to look the plane over. It was my call." The Porter had been bare. Harris had taken it all. No maps, notes, papers, registration, nothing. And, the tanks were empty. DiGenero sat back, "Tell me again how you found the plane so quickly."

McCallum laughed, "Bobby Lodestar, a local Indian lad, was out fishing early, simple as that. It's more than a sport. It's the way of life around here. Anyhow, it's not every day you find an airplane parked in your favorite fishing hole, especially when the spot isn't big enough for some boats to get in. If it had landed on the lake proper, of course, someone in Missanabie would have seen it right away. We don't get many floatplanes arriving here out of season, and the view down the lake looking west from town is clear. But the chap you're after was very clever. Putting it in the cove on the back side of the point was the best hiding place, eh? It's just that it also was Bobby's spot, and he was going out for a day's fishing. Otherwise, we might not have noticed it for some time."

"And you say someone saw him land?" DiGenero asked, lifting the second whiskey. The first drink was taking effect, warming him from the inside out at the same time it went to his head, making him forget for a moment that he was cold. DiGenero wished he'd eaten. Two drinks would be it. He pushed the empty shotglass away and reached for the beer, sipping the rich Molson's and listening to McCallum's reply.

The Mountie was short and beefy, with a kind face. He shook his head, "Not exactly. It seems two chaps from the mill were out yesterday, trolling for pike, when they were buzzed by someone flying low. The weather was bad, the leading edge of the front that's washing us away right now, and they were surprised anyone was in the air, much less flying that low. The plane came over them twice before disappearing in the clouds. My deputy constable questioned them this morning, after Lodestar told him about finding the Porter, when he remembered he'd seen the two coming back to the town launching ramp at dusk last evening in their boat. He took a guess that they might have seen something."

"Good guess," DiGenero said. He paused, "OK. With no gas in the airplane, it's obvious he didn't land here by choice. Of all the places Harris could have put down, I don't think Dog Lake would have been one of them. So, where would he go?" DiGenero asked.

McCallum shrugged, "You walked the countryside and what you saw getting to the Porter is really quite typical. Woods, scrub, bog. I'm sure you could tell there's really nowhere a man on foot could go easily. Perhaps he's still around. There are a number of summer cabins closed for the season and you told me he was a Montana native, used to the out-of-doors. He could do well in this neck of the woods until the winter really set in. It would also take us a while to check all the places he might hole up."

"How about hiking to town and renting a car or taking a bus?"

"Neither is possible, I'm afraid. There's no local bus service or car rental agency. As a matter of fact, we've already checked from here to the main highway, fifty miles down the road. Nothing's been reported stolen—no cars or trucks—since yesterday morning, and no hitchhikers seen either."

DiGenero frowned. "What about the train?"

"There is local passenger service," McCallum said, nodding, "but our constable looked at the ticket register in Dawson's, the general store across the street that doubles as the depot. There's no record of anyone buying a ticket, and no one boarded the morning or evening arrival with one already in hand."

"So," DiGenero concluded, "as we say in the States, this is your basic 'you can't get there from here' situation, right?"

"As we say in the Dominion of Canada, Mr. DiGenero," McCallum responded, nodding at the irony, "'you're quite right.'"

DiGenero slouched back. He felt his first semblance of warmth, and, toying with the empty shotglass, reviewed what the Mountie had told him. "When did the two fishermen who were on the lake yesterday see the plane?" he asked.

McCallum reached for an inside pocket, extracting his notebook, and thumbed through the pages, "At 4:30, they think."

"They're not sure?" DiGenero cocked his head.

"That's right, neither evidently had a watch. It seems they heard the 4:30 freight as the plane went overhead. It's a regular. That let them fix the time."

DiGenero sat bolt upright at the same moment the light came into McCallum's eyes. "The railroad tracks were only thirty or forty yards from the cove, weren't they?" DiGenero asked.

McCallum nodded, and looked toward the bar, raising his voice, "Randy, come over here, would you?" As the bartender ducked under the formica-topped counter and stepped to the table, McCallum continued, "Randy's a part-time gandy dancer, a track repair man, for the Canadian Pacific. He'll know all there is to know about local freight traffic."

DiGenero looked up at the bartender, "Can you answer a question for me? How fast is the 4:30 freight traveling, the one that comes through every day, when it passes the cove where Bobby Lodestar found the plane this morning?"

Madigan had learned of the Porter, as had everyone else. It was always the case with any news in the small town. He scratched his head, "Oh, it's a long grade there. Maybe fifteen miles an hour. Maybe ten."

"Where is it going?"

"To Sudbury, every day, five days a week. Sometimes forty cars, sometimes four times that. It's a through train," Madigan said, turning around to search out who was banging on the bar. "I've got to go set up another round. They're getting a little rowdy."

"Thanks," McCallum said as the bartender stepped away.

DiGenero had forgotten that he was wet and cold, "Where's Sudbury?"

"East," McCallum answered, "about 200 miles."

"What is it?"

"Oh, nothing too picturesque, 80,000 people or so. Nickel mining mostly, smelting, smog, and pollution. It's also a transportation hub where the Trans-Canada Highway as well as the Canadian Pacific and the Canadian National railways come together, north of Lake Huron's Georgian Bay."

"If Harris was on yesterday's 4:30 freight, when do you suppose he would have gotten to Sudbury?" DiGenero asked.

"I don't know for sure," McCallum answered, "but my guess is trains around here would do well to make forty or fifty miles an hour on average. That would put him in Sudbury this morning, sometime around midnight or 1:00 a.m."

DiGenero's face fell, "And Harris could get anywhere from there."

"Indeed, he could. By rail, car, or air." McCallum paused, and then continued, "I could call ahead. The Canadian Pacific has its own railway police who monitor the yards for security, safety, and all that. They might have spotted someone. If they did, it could give you a fix on when he arrived and a description to help in subsequent identification. There's an outside chance they might have arrested and held him, but in any case, they would record whatever they did, even if they just questioned Harris, you know."

McCallum was visibly surprised when DiGenero jumped to his feet. "Record! The wire on Erin's phone," DiGenero said, talking to himself. He sat down again, "In all the confusion, the shooting, the chase, the hassling with headquarters, Kasiewicz, my guy who was shot, your call, the trip out here, in all that, I forgot."

It was a statement of fact. Since the shooting at the stakeout the day before, DiGenero had slept all of two hours, the time he had in the Missoula airport lounge this morning and the flight time back to Salt Lake City. The rest had been close to forty hours of nonstop work, a string of meetings in Missoula to pick up the pieces of the case and put them together, the paperwork, and the scores of calls to and from Washington with questions from every layer of the criminal as well as the counterterrorism bureaucracy requiring answers and explaining. There had been no time to step back and think things through. And, with Kasiewicz in the hospital, there was no one to help who knew anything about what DiGenero had already done. No one who would have thought to check the wires.

"Shit," DiGenero cursed himself for overlooking the obvious, the tap on Erin's phone.

"I'm sorry, I don't follow you," McCallum said.

"Hey," DiGenero slapped the Mountie on the shoulder, "I've got to make a long-distance call." The FBI agent rose impatiently and then sat down again, realizing from McCallum's expression that he owed an explanation.

DiGenero spoke quickly, "Last month, when I began to wonder about Harris's connection with several terrorist suspects, I put a tap on his phone and on the phone of a friend of his, a woman, in Missoula. When Harris called her yesterday, I took the phone, but not until they'd spoken for a few moments. I don't know what he said, but it's possible, just barely possible, that he may have told her what he planned to do next. When you mentioned recording things, the light went on. Given the lead Harris has, right now, it's our only hope."

McCallum nodded, "Well, if you're in luck, you may have something. The phone's in the back. Maybe your office in Missoula will be able to pull the tape and run it for you in short order, eh?"

DiGenero rolled his eyes, "It's not that easy. The Missoula office and my headquarters don't know about the wire. What's the best way to put this?" DiGenero paused momentarily, "The paperwork's still in the mail."

"Oh," McCallum smiled slightly, "I see. Then?"

DiGenero completed the sentence, "I need to call my office in Salt Lake. It would be easier for them to help out. At least, I won't get my ass in the wringer with Washington right away. They'll call the drop keeper in Missoula who can unload the machine and play the tape back to my guy in Salt Lake over the phone." DiGenero glanced around, "Now, where did you say I could go to make a call?"

McCallum pointed to the rear. The booth, an open cubicle, was sandwiched between the doors to the men's and ladies' rooms. DiGenero angled his way through the crowd, picked up the receiver, covered his ear to close out the din from the bar, and dropped two quarters in the slot. The operator gave him Salt Lake City information and three minutes later, Arnold Masterson, RAPTOR's senior soundman, accepted DiGenero's collect call and came on the line.

"Frank, where the hell are you calling from? The Bronx Zoo at feeding time?"

"What did you say?" DiGenero could barely hear the technician. He frowned at the noise, glancing at his watch. It was 9:45 p.m. eastern day-

light time in Missanabie and 7:45 p.m. mountain daylight time in Salt
Lake. Masterson repeated himself. DiGenero shouted into the phone,
"Knock it off, Arnie. I need your help and fast." Since Masterson had
installed the wires, he was familiar with the details of who to contact in
Missoula and what to ask for. DiGenero began to talk quickly, explain-
ing what he wanted Masterson to do.

Twelve hundred miles away, Erin Dupres looked up and felt her heart
leap into her throat. The man walking toward her was tall, with a dark
suit and white shirt. She looked down quickly and then back, unable to
tear her gaze away. He seemed to be examining faces as he passed, one
by one, as if searching for someone he knew was there, somewhere, as
yet undiscovered. She glanced away, her stomach knotting. Her pulse
marked the seconds. It had been easy, too easy.

The touch, firm on her arm, startled her. "Your seatbelt. Could you
fasten it, please?" The stewardess, pausing beside her, was pointing at
Erin's lap.

"Oh, yeah, sure," she looked up, her eyes drawn ineluctably to the
dark suit before her. He had stopped, facing her, a row ahead. Then,
Erin saw the notebook. He'd balanced it on the arm of the aisle chair as
he turned and slid into the middle seat. The IBM logo was embossed on
the binder's cover, white on blue. Erin closed her eyes, feeling a combination of welcome relief and sudden weakness. He wasn't one of Frank's.
They weren't coming to get her, to bring her back.

She peered out the window at the baggage crew, loading the plane,
and thought of DiGenero again. He had been on her mind more than
she had expected after what had happened in the bedroom. His anger
had frightened her, but not the look in his eyes, his pain when she'd
lashed back. He cared and she'd hurt him. She knew that. Now, when
she remembered, it hurt her. The baggage trucks drove away. They were
ready to go. Was she? Was she doing the right thing?

Forward, beyond the passageway's gathered curtain and the bulkhead
that separated first-class, the door thudded closed. Erin felt the bump
and roll as the tow tractor pushed the Boeing 737 backward. Moments
later, the voice from the small speaker above her head began the usual
declamation, "Good evening, ladies and gentlemen, I'd like to welcome

you on Western's flight 992 to Salt Lake City with connections to Chicago and New York. Now, would you please familiarize yourself with the card in the seat pocket in front of you."

Erin's attention trailed away. Strange that the questions about Frank, about what was "right," should occur to her at this moment. She hadn't given them any thought earlier that afternoon as she watched the darkness approach from the apartment window. Now, remembering, it was a surprise how everything had fallen into place. She'd waited until she knew there would be just enough time. Before he left for Salt Lake that morning, DiGenero had called to tell her the two FBI agents would stay with her, for security, until things were safe. An hour and a half ago, Erin had told them she had to check the birds at the lab. They obligingly drove her to the university. The parking lot in front of the lab was empty. As she asked, they'd waited in the car while she went inside.

The wall phone was in the corridor, outside her office door. The call to the airline came first, and then the call for the campus cab. She'd slipped out the back, through the fire exit, keeping in the shadows of the zoology building. The student union's rear entrance was a short diagonal across the quad. She walked through the basement past the cafeteria, climbed the stairs to the first floor, and then strode quickly out the main door and down the steps. The cab had been waiting.

The click in the public address speaker and the captain's voice retrieved her attention, "We've been cleared for takeoff, ladies and gentlemen. Flight attendants, please take your seats." The airliner turned sharply as the engines wound up to their high pitch. They were looking for her now, but they wouldn't find her. In an hour, maybe less, Frank would know she was gone. In a day or two, maybe they'd discover where she was, but by then it wouldn't matter.

Erin put her head back, feeling the acceleration, and closed her eyes. Two days ago when the Iranian died; today, as she left; Sunday, when Frank arrived to tell her she was in danger; a month before, on the ranch when he came to warn Kirby. It was a web, all one piece, but seamless, with no point she could identify as beginning and still no known end.

Faces floated in front of her. Kirby, Frank, the killer on the balcony, eyes open, staring with the look of terminal surprise, and others she couldn't recall, the police and the FBI, the blur of features, expressions, hard, curious, questioning, surrounding and watching her. Erin shook her head involuntarily, trying to erase the worst of it, but the unreality came back, like a floating sensation, suspending her, conscious but adrift, above the solid ground she knew she had left somewhere a few hours, or a few weeks, or, was it a lifetime, ago.

She looked out at the line of streetlights that marked the edge of Missoula as the plane climbed, turning south, into the night. Why do it? she thought. Why go to him? Why now, when she saw a right and a wrong, a good and a bad, when she recognized them clearly, and when there was nothing compelling her, not blind love, not unquestioning trust, not ignorance? Why go through with it?

Why? Erin looked down, examining her hands. On both, a network of fine lines made similar patterns across her tanned skin. She interlaced her fingers, schoolgirl-like, in her lap. Why? She was old enough to know better. She'd spent the day picking up and examining her excuses as well as her reasons like shells on a beach, keeping some and discarding others. Put together, it wasn't hard to explain.

As in all things, there was more than one answer. The easiest had come first, two days ago, almost like a reflex, at the same time DiGenero had pulled her to her feet. She'd told him about the cabin in the hope that only part of the truth would be enough, enough to let Frank bring Kirby back from the brink. Enough but not too much. Enough without revealing the whole confidence. Enough without fingering her, if Frank succeeded, as the one who gave Kirby up. Without really believing it, she'd also convinced herself after DiGenero returned from Sixteen empty-handed that she would say more if he asked. He hadn't asked and she didn't.

The whole truth. Why didn't she tell what she knew yesterday? Erin thought. Yesterday, it was because of Kirby. After five years, she was part of him, part of what he was and part of what he'd done. She remembered going over and over the same ground, trying to put it together, to traverse all the territory, including the fact that because of him, people she had never known wanted her dead. But she always came back to where she began. He needed her, for the first time and maybe the last. He was over the edge. He'd asked for her help. After five years, that mattered, and after five years, she couldn't say no.

Erin turned to the window. To the east, 20,000 feet below, the lights of Anaconda and Butte were slipping under the wing. She brushed her hand across her cheek, wiping away the damp traces left behind by the tears that had disappeared into the folds of her sleeve. And tonight? Why not the whole truth? Tonight why leave? Why go through with it? She knew that DiGenero was right, morally, legally, personally, unequivocally right. And, he cared. She knew that too. For Kirby and for her. She'd helped Frank for all those reasons. Now she was going to Kirby.

Why? Tonight, Erin thought, she was down to basics. No tactical explanations, no evasions, no deep analyses of relationships, no moral rationales. Tonight, it was simple enough. She loved Kirby and wanted what everyone wanted. She wanted to have it both ways.

Erin reached for her purse, extracting her tickets. She opened the booklet, double-checking. With the layover in Salt Lake City, she would arrive in Chicago at 3:00 a.m., Saturday morning, local time. Her next flight, Air Canada, left O'Hare International Airport at 7:00 a.m., with an intermediate stop in Toronto to clear customs and immigration. Erin closed the ticket folder, calculating the time-zone changes. That meant she would land at her final destination at noon, Saturday, eastern daylight time.

She dug into her purse for the scrap of paper. She'd written down the name. L'Auberge du Voyageur, on Montreal Road. She would rent the car at the airport and find the motel. Then, in Ottawa, as Kirby had asked, she would wait.

Six thousand miles east of the invisible north-south track being drawn down the North American continent by Erin's Western Airlines flight on its course to Salt Lake City, it was already Saturday morning in Munich, although still two hours before the light would begin to warm the cold German dawn. In the far corner of the Hauptbanhoff, the main Munich train station, Musaani stepped from the alcove that housed the telephone kiosks, walking casually across the old tile floor toward the main entrance. The bent forms of the two cleaning women turned and straightened at the sound of his heels echoing in the empty concourse. The only passerby in the station, he was worth a glance, before they turned back to their mops and pails.

Musaani paused on the station's threshold. Before him, half of the bank of doors were open, revealing the darkened Bahnhofplatz and in the distance, beyond Lenbachplatz and the Karlstor Gate, the brilliant beams that bathed the Frauenkirche's twin spires. Lit like medieval missiles pointing upward into a moonless night, the church steeples dominated the darkness. To the left and right, Dachauer Strasse and Schillerstrasse, a wide and a narrow street respectively, led away to the north and south. Both were empty. So was the train station plaza except for the Mercedes station wagon that was waiting for Musaani, motor running.

He descended the steps, slipped into the backseat of the Mercedes, and closed the door. Musaani mused, thinking of two telephone calls as the car pulled away. Sassanir's call and the one from the Palestinian agent in the Saudi embassy in Ottawa. They transmitted two very different kinds of messages—on the one hand, the expected that didn't occur, and on the other, the unexpected that did. Sassanir was supposed to have called. He hadn't. The Palestinian was never to call unless there was something exceptional. He had.

Putting the two together, Musaani thought, led to only one conclusion. It was plain enough. Sassanir was dead, Harris knew about the operation, and the American was about to tell.

Musaani leaned back, watching Munich's dark streets pass by silently in the early hour between night and day. His own call from the telephone booth in the train station to Bazargan in New York had taken only a few minutes. Under normal circumstances, he wouldn't even have contemplated making direct contact, much less using him on such a mission, but the situation was extraordinary and he had no choice. In any case, the wheels were turning. It was still Friday evening, around 10:00 p.m., in New York. Bazargan would leave on the first flight in the morning. Musaani had already cabled the coded instructions to the Iranian embassy in Ottawa. There, his contact would have a selection of weapons, whatever Bazargan needed.

He frowned. It was not his preferred way to do business. Bazargan was too good an assassin to send without adequate preparation, and on general principles, Musaani abhorred making last-minute decisions. But there was no time and no other option. Allah had given them another chance. A single opportunity. At 6:30 p.m., on Saturday. And, Allah willing, at 6:30 p.m., on Saturday, this time Kirby Harris would die.

22

Saturday, September 29, 1984

L'Auberge du Voyageur Inn, Ottawa, Canada

DiGenero sneezed, shivered, then awkwardly wiped his nose, feeling every bit as uncoordinated as he looked. For the last several minutes an impressive series of chills had absorbed his attention, offering a change of physical pace from the feverish perspiration that had preceded them. He reached for the dashboard, pushing the thermostat and heater fan switches to high, and turned up the collar of his raincoat. The squad car was already warm, but the mere act of trying to cope with his own condition was a therapy of sorts, creating the momentary illusion that he could do something to make himself feel better.

The gust, sudden from the north, slapped the eddy of fall leaves whirling through the parking lot against the sides of the car. The wind had started as the rain had stopped, turning the air sharply colder. At 5:30 p.m., with Ottawa's sky drooping low, it was almost totally dark. The radio by DiGenero's knee crackled, emitting the universally flat, affectless tones of the police dispatcher's voice. DiGenero listened without real curiosity. The RCMP's communications network was busy with the assortment of cryptic calls that sounded like the standard litany of police chores the world over.

DiGenero rubbed the back of his hand across the windshield, wiping a clear swath through the condensation. The unmarked blue Chevrolet sedan was parked, nose to the curb, in front of the motel office's half-open front door. Inside, DiGenero could only see Chief Inspector Michael Cavanaugh's back, and the top of the innkeeper's bald crown, but it was enough to tell him the story. The man behind the dark-stained, French country-style front desk was shaking his head from side to side nonstop, something less than an encouraging sign. DiGenero sneezed again. The chills had ceased and the fever was coming back. He blew his nose and looked out. Cavanaugh seemed to be saying farewell, preparing to turn and walk back toward the car.

It had been a hell of a day, not to mention night, DiGenero thought. Masterson hadn't called Missanabie until 4:00 a.m. It had taken him until 2:00 a.m. to contact the drop keeper in Missoula and another two hours to get the tape from Erin's phone collected and played. The phone had rung again at 6:00 a.m., this time an agent he didn't know from Missoula with the message that Erin was gone.

DiGenero rubbed his eyes and tilted his head against the seat back, trying unsuccessfully to breathe through his nose. Thanks to his walk through the woods to find the Porter yesterday, he had developed a world-class head cold and flu combination. He remembered trying to figure out what to do last night. Or was it this morning?

For openers, there were only a few minor problems, like the fact his case on Harris was out in legal left field. The Bureau, he knew, wouldn't be pleased. There was no warrant for the wiretap on either Kirby or Erin, no paperwork in process to get a warrant, no evidence, at least not the kind that was legally admissible, to prepare the paperwork, and, he thought, until a few hours ago, sitting in Missanabie, Ontario, socked in by a rainstorm without Harris's file, no way to fabricate the legal documents even if he wanted to try.

Then, there was the RCMP. With Harris already two jumps ahead, he needed their help, a surveillance team, stakeout people, and a detention order, an international agreement to pick up and hold an American on Canadian soil. It was far more than the pro forma department-to-department courtesy normally provided. Asking for all that by the book required a "sign-off," an OK, by an associate deputy director, in this case Murchison, and the United States attorney, not to mention everything that came afterward, the formalities, ID information on Harris, and cables back and forth to Ottawa. There was no way for him to do it, to generate the bureaucratic hocus-pocus that would put the Bureau and the RCMP in gear, to find Harris in time. Not from legal ground zero and a party-line phone in western Ontario.

That was when he remembered Cavanaugh. It was a long shot, but he tried RCMP headquarters in Ottawa at 8:00 a.m., as soon as the switchboard opened. The operator had looked up the name. She said he was chief of domestic security and something or other and that he could call Cavanaugh in the office on Monday. He'd wheedled the home number from her and finally reached him at 10:30 a.m., just as the storm over Missanabie was lifting. Fortunately, Cavanaugh agreed to help, no questions asked.

DiGenero shivered as he watched the senior Royal Canadian Mounted Police inspector walk toward the car. Cavanaugh was built like a linebacker, or a cop. They'd worked together on an undercover operation five years before, an Appalachian-style meeting like the mob summit in upstate New York in the late fifties, only this time, in the Laurentians and smaller, more intimate, involving only three bosses, one each from New York, Montreal, and Toronto. They'd wired, videoed, and bugged the capos and their four lieutenants, in their private meeting rooms, in bed with their honeys, in the bar, in the sauna, in the pool, in their cars, you name it. It was textbook technical op all the way. The capos couldn't take a piss without making the audio meters dance. It hadn't hurt either of their careers. And, DiGenero sneezed, they'd gotten along, as they say.

The car door opened, admitting a cold gust along with the Canadian police detective. Cavanaugh was dressed in a navy-blue North Face parka, early for the season but more than appropriate for the raw weather. He examined DiGenero with the concerned look of a friend, "You look worse than when I picked you up at the airport an hour ago. I think I'd better take you home for some sleep."

DiGenero shook his head, "No. Anything from the manager?"

"You sure, Frank?" Cavanaugh asked, ignoring the question. "I don't want to ship you back to Salt Lake City in a bag. Too many forms to fill out, you know."

"I'm OK."

Cavanaugh nodded reluctantly. "She's gone," the Canadian said, "like the desk clerk told us on the phone." Cavanaugh still had a leftover tan from his late-summer vacation at the family cottage on the St. Lawrence. A second-generation English immigrant without the usual ruddy-pasty complexion of the stock, he looked atypically healthy. He'd put on weight since DiGenero had seen him last, which accentuated his heavyset frame and square-jawed features. Both were professionally useful, giving him the appearance of a man who couldn't be ignored and didn't lose arguments.

DiGenero frowned, "Did he know anything that would help at all?"

Cavanaugh put his arm over the seat back, "Not really. She checked in at 1:30 p.m. and left her key at the desk on the way out at 2:00, just five minutes before our stakeout team arrived." He looked down, scratching his chin with an out-of-character sheepishness, "I'm sorry it took that long, Frank. I tried to get the group together sooner, but it was a little tough on short notice finding five guys who would work off-line and keep their mouths shut, especially on a soccer and football afternoon."

DiGenero mustered the strength to give the Canadian's shoulder a weak slap, "Hey, we haven't lost the inning yet."

"Anyway," Cavanaugh continued, "Ms. Dupres hasn't been back since. The manager said she received one phone call. At 1:50 p.m. My guess is Harris, giving her directions."

DiGenero bobbed his head, "They could be anywhere." The cold, flu, or whatever was expanding its repertoire of symptoms, making his temples throb in four-four time.

"That's true," Cavanaugh replied, "but unless they're planning to tour the country by car, we've got the exits from town covered. The word is out at the other points of departure, the airport and rail terminals. And, the APB, the All Points Bulletin, is on the air with their description and the car's for the Ottawa city cops."

"I wonder why we haven't spotted them," DiGenero said.

"So do I," Cavanaugh put his hands on the wheel, "but there's no point in waiting here." He nodded in the direction of the van parked across the street. Cavanaugh knew that behind the long, smoked-glass side windows, two RCMP plainclothesmen stared back. "The surveillance team can do its duty. Shall we go for a ride?"

As Cavanaugh pulled the Chevrolet onto Montreal Road and turned toward center city, exactly four miles away, on the third underground level of the Ottawa General Hospital's parking garage, Harris touched Erin Dupres's shoulder, shaking her gently awake.

Erin opened her eyes. She'd dozed for what seemed like minutes, but she knew it had been longer than that. The parking garage, nearly full when they arrived, was half empty. Three hours before, after a few quick turns off Rideau Street and a short drive, skirting Major Hills Park, she'd slowed in front of Ottawa General and pulled below ground. Kirby had been waiting, as he said he would be, on the third level.

Erin stretched and yawned. She was tired. More than that, fatigued. But not Kirby. He looked surprisingly rested for his cross-country journey, she thought. Harris had sat silent as she'd described what had happened at the apartment, waiting until he'd heard her out before telling her about Sassanir. She'd watched him, observing almost clinically as well as listening, although after two days without sleep she hadn't put it all together, at least not right away. She had now, or so it seemed.

The mind was strange, Erin thought. It worked on solutions in its recesses, where without conscious effort, reason and impression, logic and intuition married to produce understanding. Sometimes, it was less than that, a new insight, or maybe just an old one, revived. In this case, awakening, she understood what had struck her. It was the way Harris told the story that explained things. He was back in his element, alive, playing his own game by his own rules, in his own fast lane. It was his animation, an energy that came from the inside out. That was why he looked so good.

"What time is it?" Erin asked.

Harris glanced at his watch, "After 6:00 p.m. It's time to go. Sorry we couldn't have relaxed a bit at the motel. I just didn't want to take a chance."

"Take the chance with what?" she asked.

Harris shrugged, "Frank. He's not all that bad at what he does. Who knows? Maybe he found the Porter. Maybe he knows I got to Sudbury by train, rented a car, drove to North Bay, and flew here. Maybe he's in town looking for me right now."

Erin took a deep breath, "And maybe I told him I was meeting you here."

Harris was in the driver's seat. He turned toward her slowly, as if choreographed, projecting an image of complete control. Harris examined her with an air of detachment, "No, you didn't do that."

The certainty irritated her, "Oh? How do you know?"

"You did your civic duty when you told Frank I'd be at Sixteen."

Harris studied Erin's expression, his intensity evidenced only by his unwavering gaze. She stared back as he continued, "Frank DiGenero and the forces of truth, justice, and the American way had you worried from the beginning, didn't they?"

Erin leaned away from him, propping herself against the passenger door. Her lips parted, but she controlled the impulse to answer back.

"If DiGenero hadn't tried to stop me at Sixteen," Harris said, "maybe

I'd have wondered about you. If you'd wanted to end the game, it would have been much easier to tell Frank where I was meeting you in Ottawa. He could have saved the dramatics by arranging to have me picked up at the motel. But you couldn't do that, could you?"

"You had me all figured out, didn't you, Kirby?" Erin heard her own voice. It sounded cold as well as faraway, "You've got everything figured out."

Harris shook his head, "I'm just willing to take a chance, sweetheart. That's what makes life interesting. Don't take it so hard...," he stopped in midsentence, his eyes on the rearview mirror. Behind them, a police cruiser turned off the inclined ramp that led down from the second parking level. Harris could see that the officer was staring left as the blue-and-white Dodge rolled slowly along the row of parked cars directly behind them.

"Shit," Harris hissed.

"What?" Erin asked. She started to turn, but Harris gripped her shoulder, holding her in place, facing forward.

"A cop. Checking stolen cars, parking violations, overdue license plates."

Erin watched him follow the police car in the mirror. Engrossed, he failed to hear the soft mockery in her voice, "Why don't you just sit tight. After all, Kirby, what's the risk?"

Harris, only half-listening, shook his head, "No. If they're looking for the car you've rented, they've got us. If they're not looking for the car, my pulling out and driving away won't make any difference."

For the first time, Erin felt her own fear rising, "Kirby, it's not worth it. I don't care how much money you think they'll pay for what you know. For Christ's sake, Frank doesn't want to hurt you. The Iranians, Von Biemann, they do. Frank's trying to help you. I want to help you. Don't you understand?" From the passenger seat, she reached for his hand, but Harris pushed her arm away and twisted the ignition key.

The Thunderbird's turbocharged four-cylinder whirled and caught. Harris pressed the automatic adjustment button on the driver's door, canting his outside mirror to follow the patrol car. At the far end of the parking garage, the cruiser turned, proceeding slowly down their row. Harris shifted the automatic transmission into reverse and backed out, taking the care of any new-car owner concerned about scratches and nicks in the narrow confines of an underground garage.

Ten yards behind the Thunderbird, Officer Ronnie Aldridge, Ottawa City Police, glanced up from his routine scan of provincial license plates. He'd been looking for out-of-date registrations and delinquent safety inspection stickers, filling in the dead time on Ottawa midtown precinct's typically slow Saturday swing shift. Clipped with his other evening watch notes, the small slip of paper with the RCMP All Points Bulletin hung in the center of his dash. Under the map light, Aldridge matched the rent-a-car license plate number and the car's description on the scrap of paper with the tags, make, and model of the Thunderbird that had just pulled in front of him.

The rest was automatic. He snapped the lightbar's toggle switch into the quick-flash mode, and punched the siren button. The single warning "woop" reverberated off the low ceiling and concrete walls of the parking garage. At 26 years old, with three years of traffic duty on the city force, Aldridge had issued his share of citations to speeders and drunks, but he had never—"unfortunately," he used to say to his wife and friends—found himself in the kind of chase that seemed a daily occurrence on his favorite American police TV shows. At the instant the Thunderbird tore away from him, tires smoking and engine screaming, and the Ottawa policeman slammed his foot down on his accelerator, he knew for a fact he was in for one now.

In less than twenty yards, the Thunderbird reached thirty miles an hour. The undercarriage hit the incline of the "up" ramp, shooting steel-on-concrete sparks to match the rasping scrape as the car bottomed hard. Behind him, Harris heard the Dodge police cruiser accelerate. Aiming upward, he spun the wheel, twisting the Thunderbird around the wall that divided the ramp into a hairpin turn, and shot toward the second level. The turbocharger's needle pegged in the red zone. Under the hood, the turbine impeller howled, its blades packing air and fuel into the Thunderbird's cylinders.

Climbing at fifty miles an hour, Harris was two floors below the street and the side-by-side open entrance and gated exit for the hospital's garage. He spun the wheel, sliding into his second hairpin turn, and rocketed toward the first level. He could hear the patrol car's heavier, throaty V-8 slowing for the 180-degree pivot and then roaring to gain ground. The chase, he realized, didn't matter but the policeman's radio did. If the cruiser reached the street and saw where he turned, the cop's radio calls would position cars all over the map to cover his route.

A split second ahead, around the next turn, Harris knew the plateau at level one and the "up" ramp to the street loomed. He lifted his foot, slowing the Thunderbird. In the rearview mirror, the Dodge grew larger, gaining yards. Satisfied, he twisted the wheel, fishtailing around the corner. Ninety degrees through the turn, on level one's flat apron, he straightened the steering wheel, stomping the accelerator. The Thunderbird shot to the right, up the "down" ramp that led from the street. The surprise wrote itself across Aldridge's face as he turned hard behind the Thunderbird. He frantically reversed his grip, spinning the steering wheel right. In less than a second, Harris heard behind him the squeal of the police cruiser's brakes and then the crash.

At street level, Harris wheeled left, then right, circumventing the lowered barrier for the parking garage's exit, barely missing the half-glass booth, and terrifying its attendant. He snapped on the headlights, turning right on Sussex. The rain had stopped and the traffic along the river was light. He glanced at Erin. She was pale, staring at him with an expression he'd never seen before.

"We're on our way," Harris said. He reached for her hand. It was cold. She didn't reply.

Cavanaugh had turned on the flashers concealed in the Chevrolet's grill and accelerated down Rideau Street when he'd heard the first radio call from the hospital garage, but it was the second, two minutes later from another patrol car, describing a Thunderbird traveling northeast on Sussex toward Princess, that made him pour on the coal.

"Where's Sussex?" DiGenero said, snapping on his seatbelt as Cavanaugh veered around a slow bakery truck.

"It's a drive running along the river toward Rockcliff Park."

"What's there?"

"The park? Oh," Cavanaugh paused, concentrating as he turned right on King Edward Street, "the prime minister's place, and Government House, the governor general's official residence."

"The governor who?" DiGenero furrowed his brow.

Cavanaugh snorted. Like most Americans, DiGenero didn't have the faintest idea what Canada and the Commonwealth were all about despite the fact it had been next door for 350 years. "He speaks for the queen. I'll explain later."

"Don't bother," DiGenero said, "I don't think she's Harris's type. So where's he going?"

Cavanaugh glanced down. The speedometer was moving past the 100-kilometer-an-hour mark, passing sixty miles an hour. "If he stays in that neighborhood, we'll know in about three minutes. At this rate, we're almost there."

The Canadian reached for the microphone, driving one-handed.

"Central, this is Delta Echo One. Contact embassy security and have them fan their cars out in the Rockcliff vicinity to look for the subject Thunderbird."

"Delta Echo One, Central. Already done."

"Good," Cavanaugh dropped the mike on the seat. He pressed the concealed siren's control button, filling the vicinity with its rapid wavering. DiGenero watched the startled pedestrians on either side of the street flinch as the warning blare reverberated, scattering the sparse traffic in front of the Chevrolet. Cavanaugh skidded right without lifting his foot from the pedal, racing up Sussex.

DiGenero grasped the door handle, straightening himself on the seat, "What's embassy security got to do with it?" He glanced at Cavanaugh, who was weaving an ess-curve around a station wagon and two sedans that were dawdling in the northbound lanes. The Canadian cop was in his element, eyes darting from the road ahead to the rearview mirror, obviously enjoying the chase and concentrating on where their route should take them to save time. It was a stroke of blind luck, and Cavanaugh's goodwill, that he had gotten this close, DiGenero thought.

Suddenly, the hum of the tires changed. They were racing over a bridge. On the right and left, beneath them, Rideau Falls and the river, dark and cold, shot by.

"Embassy security?" Cavanaugh repeated, finally answering his question. "Well, aside from being home to the 'Mandarins,' our overpaid federal bureaucrats, Ottawa's literati, and some upscale Canadian yuppies, Rockcliff Park is also the embassy quarter. The RCMP provides security. Actually, the old guard, the natives in the neighborhood, don't care for the international riffraff or for us, for that matter. They think the embassies attract terrorists."

"How can you argue with that?" DiGenero smiled.

The radio dispatcher broke in, "Delta Echo One, Central. Subject Thunderbird just turned left on Springfield from Mariposa. There's an unmarked cruiser following."

Cavanaugh hit the brakes, swerving hard into a narrow residential street. Ahead, DiGenero saw the sign for Dufferin Road. He read the English and French before they shot past. "We're only a minute from where they spotted him," Cavanaugh said, picking up the mike. "Central, Delta Echo One. Advise the cruiser to follow but not pursue or apprehend. We don't want him to jackrabbit."

"Delta Echo One, Central. Subject Thunderbird approaching Mile Circle and slowing." Cavanaugh whipped the Chevrolet through two sharp jags, angling into an odd, three-street intersection, and then sped down Minto Place. "We're almost there," he said.

"What's at Mile Circle?" DiGenero asked. Outside, the oaks lining the quiet residential street appeared a blur of trunks and limbs. They were going too fast to make out many details, but beyond the trees DiGenero could see large yards and a mixture of new and old homes, some stone, others brick and shingle. They were substantial, dating from the 1930s, and eclectic in design.

Cavanaugh raised his voice over the roar of the Chevrolet, accelerating again in passing gear, "More of the high-rent district. Bit of a political stink there these days. Government's allowed three embassies to move to the Circle, and the residents don't like it," Cavanaugh said. "They say it's ruining the neighborhood."

The radio call interrupted, "Delta Echo One, Central. Subject Thunderbird has reached Mile Circle. It's going around the block."

Cavanaugh slowed briefly to forty miles an hour at a stop sign and then mashed the accelerator, glancing over at DiGenero, "Maybe that's it for him. Home free."

DiGenero looked up, "What embassies are there?"

"The Americans, the Germans, and the Saudis. That's all."

"Where are they?"

"I'll show you in less than sixty seconds." Cavanaugh looked both ways at the next intersection out of habit but didn't slow down, "The Germans and the Americans are on the west side. The Saudis just built their embassy on the east."

The radio crackled, "Delta Echo One, Central. Subject Thunderbird just passed the German and the American chanceries and is turning toward the Saudi compound. The car on the scene says it's slowing."

Von Biemann's file, DiGenero thought. In the recesses of his memory, he could see it, the pieces of paper he'd spread so many times on his desk. He'd learned a long time ago never to throw anything away. In this case, he remembered putting the odd surveillance report to the side, the one on Musaani that had been inadvertently included because of the automatic cross-referencing, spit out by the Counterterrorism Center's computerized data bank when Stockman sent him the German's 201. The Arabian prince in San Francisco. Musaani's friend. And now the Arabian embassy.

It was there in front of him, in his mind's eye. Not altogether in place, neatly tied up with a bow, but that wasn't necessary. What he had was enough for an answer. Von Biemann, the radical, Musaani, the terrorist, and finally, the Arab, previously incidental, with no apparent connection. Odd. Out of place. Until now.

The Saudis. They were the target for Musaani and Von Biemann. Naturals. But what or who? Someone or something here, or in the States, or in the Middle East, or in Europe? He didn't know. But whoever or whatever the operation was, Harris had to know. There was no other reason, no other explanation why the Iranians wanted to kill him, or Erin, except to keep them quiet. Harris had to be in the middle. And, he was going for the gold. He had something the Saudis wanted, something the Iranians didn't want him to tell.

DiGenero looked out. Cavanaugh had switched off the flashers and was slowing. The embassies were on the inner rather than the outer rim of the circle, using property that obviously had once been vacant parkland and woods. Even with the new buildings, the center of the rotary was still heavily treed and shrubbed, as was the outer edge of the circular road.

DiGenero knew he was right. He pivoted on the seat, facing Cavanaugh, "Mike, the Arabian embassy. That's why Ottawa. That's why here. That's where he's going. Now!"

"OK. Once he's inside, he's on their turf, not ours. Diplomatic immunity and all that. If you want to stop him, we've got to get there first. It's closer if we take a left turn rather than a right. Wrong way around the circle does it."

A half mile away, Shapur Bazargan watched the headlights make their way slowly along the circumference of the road. Inside his raincoat pocket, his hand curled around the grip of the .357 magnum. Bazargan had studied the site most of the afternoon, following the circle twice on foot and twice driving. The security was less than he expected and concentrated mostly on the Americans' side. The plan was simple. When he was finished, he would turn, walk back to the car that was parked under the trees, and have the chauffeur drive him slowly away. Bazargan stepped from the woods on the outer edge of the circle momentarily to check on his escape route. Fifty yards away, the car was waiting for him, engine running, lights out.

The approaching headlights reflected dully on the wet pavement. Bazargan slipped behind the tree, letting the Thunderbird pass before again stepping out of the shadows. He strode quickly across the road, angling toward the car. It slowed, nosing toward the embassy's gate.

Bazargan slowed his own pace momentarily, surprised that there were two in the front seat. The man was his quarry. He hadn't expected the woman on the passenger side, his side. He walked toward her, keeping in the driver's blind spot, away from the rearview mirrors. The Thunderbird stopped, motor running. He would need to eliminate both. The man was first. He would crouch, shooting across her through the window. It was better to make the kill before the man had a chance to open the door and step outside where he could duck, dodge, or run. She would be an easier target, trapped, shocked, and unmoving. He pulled the heavy pistol from his pocket. It was good. The woman was turned toward the driver, listening or talking. Bazargan raised the .357. Concentrating, he didn't hear the sound of the engine as a car rounded the circle coming toward him the wrong way.

"Jesus H. Christ," DiGenero yelled as he understood instantly what was unfolding before them in the headlights. "Go!"

Cavanaugh slammed the accelerator pedal to the floor. The engine roared, winding up in low gear. DiGenero planted his hands on the dashboard, transfixed. The crouched figure whirled, leveling the gun at the Chevrolet. The man's expression was at the same time cruel and surprised, wide-eyed and openmouthed rather than fearful even as they hit him, dead center on the grill, at thirty miles an hour.

The pistol shot, a death reflex, smashed through the windshield between them, showering both men with fine crystalline glass. Neither noticed. The body bounced up, rebounding ahead of the Chevrolet, before falling to the pavement and tumbling backward at nearly their speed. Cavanaugh braked hard, but not in time. The unmarked car slewed right, sliding sideways with a dull thump as the front wheels rolled up and over the crumpled form.

DiGenero leapt from the car and sprinted toward the Thunderbird. He heard Cavanaugh running behind him. Even from a distance, he could see Erin in the passenger seat, her face turned toward him. The driver's door was open. So was the gate to the embassy. DiGenero ran past the Thunderbird, instinctively drawing his gun, and turned into the embassy grounds. Harris was twenty yards ahead of him, walking fast across the curving, U-shaped drive. To the left of the white stone chancery's formal, canopied main entrance, a side door, marked "Service," had opened. Two men in dark suits, both Arabs, emerged, guns in hand.

"Kirby!"

Harris glanced back, walking faster, almost running now.

Behind DiGenero, Cavanaugh shouted, "Frank, put the gun away! You're in the embassy!" The Canadian caught his breath, "You can't take him. It's their sovereign territory."

DiGenero slowed to a walk. The two Arabs stepped farther away from the open door, spacing themselves several feet apart and leveling short stubby automatics that looked like Uzis. Harris reached them. He stopped between the two men and turned. They closed ranks and moved forward, shielding Harris with their bodies, eyeing DiGenero warily. DiGenero lowered his .38 and stopped, breathing hard.

Cavanaugh's voice rose behind DiGenero, "Hold it! Royal Canadian Mounted Police." DiGenero looked over his shoulder. Cavanaugh was holding up his badge, "Lower your weapons. The officer in front of you is United States Federal Bureau of Investigation." Cavanaugh gestured toward the Thunderbird, "There's been an attempted murder. We want to talk to the man between you."

The Arabs and the two Uzis remained motionless, their stares fixed on DiGenero. Cavanaugh waited. There was no reply. From the opposite side of the circle, DiGenero could hear the sirens' approach.

"You don't give a shit whose life you risk, do you, Kirby?" DiGenero spit out the words.

Harris didn't reply at once. Then, he spoke quietly, "Is Erin all right?"

DiGenero wondered for a moment whether to answer and then nodded.

"Good," Harris seemed relieved.

DiGenero took a step forward. He was still ten paces from Harris, but the two Arabs raised the muzzles of their weapons slightly. It was an un-ambiguous signal to go no further.

DiGenero shook his head, his face suddenly fatigued and sad rather than angry, "I've got one dead and one wounded because of you in Missoula. That's on my head. You know why? Because I wanted to help you."

Harris cocked his head, adding mock puzzlement to his expression, "Who asked, Frank?" He turned as if someone had motioned him from inside the door.

"Kirby," DiGenero called.

Harris paused, "Forget it, Frank. I've got to see a man about some business. You gave me a good run for the money. It just wasn't your day."

"Kirby!"

Harris disappeared into the open doorway.

"Kirby, you son of a bitch," DiGenero called again, but the door to the embassy had already closed.

One hundred yards away, under the low-hanging maple branches that fringed the outer curb of Mile Circle, the black Buick with diplomatic plates idled quietly. Behind the wheel, the driver, a small, dark-com-plexioned man, released the parking brake and paused, still petrified. He ran his fingers through his greasy hair and bit his lip, torn by the fear of leaving as much as by the terror of staying. Even around the bend of the circle, too far away to see Bazargan, he had heard the sound of the body being struck as well as the shot. The sirens confirmed the worst.

He had to return to the embassy to report. He slipped the Buick into low gear and pulled away, his lips repeating a silent prayer. Slow, drive slow. They will not notice. A diplomatic license in the embassy area is protection. Suddenly, from behind and in front of him, the sirens screamed. Run! He had to run. He started to hit the gas pedal hard, but the squeal of locked brakes and the flashing lights surrounded him. The police cars skidded to a halt, boxing in the Buick, front and rear. He saw the drawn guns. Then, his door flew open. Too frightened to scream, he felt the hands close on his arms and legs, dragging him, trembling in fear, into the street.

Six hours later, as the grandfather clock in the great room of Über-spitzensee began tolling the 6:00 a.m. hour, Sunday, September 30, Musaani stood at the window, peering into the morning darkness. Outside, the loading was almost complete. In the headlights, he could see Kahlil and the Shakir brothers, the two Kurds who would accompany the prince, standing beside the Mercedes station wagon. Kahlil was talking rapidly, using his hands, obviously excited. It was his time in the sun. Musaani had stressed that. Kahlil was a risk, as always, but Musaani was confident he would perform as required. He was critical, at least for forty-eight hours more, at least until the operation was over.

The Shakirs motioned away the driver, who had turned for the last item of luggage. They lifted the crate themselves, sliding it gently onto the Mercedes' rear deck. It was the falcon's cage. She had been superb, a better peregrine, his father had said, than he'd ever seen.

Musaani turned at the sound of the footfall. Von Biemann entered the room. The German stepped to the bar, poured a cup of coffee, then spoke, "I think you deserve to congratulate yourself."

The Iranian peered at Von Biemann coldly, "Do I?"

Musaani walked to the desk. The special courier had delivered the messages that lay on its burled wood surface only an hour before. They had arrived at the Iranian embassy in Bonn from the Committee in Tehran with the highest precedence and the instructions to bring them to him immediately.

Musaani picked up the first piece of paper. It was a retransmission of a message from Denver. "One account at least is straightforward," he said. "Sabah did not return and the newspapers have the story about an unidentified foreigner who was shot in a gun battle in Missoula by an FBI stakeout team. The local police have said very little about it except that federal authorities are investigating."

The second cable was longer. It had been sent from Ottawa to Tehran and then, like the first, forwarded to Bonn. Musaani studied the paper before continuing, "The other," he paused, "makes me wonder. It says there is a news story from Ottawa that a man was killed last night outside the embassy of Arabia."

"Your man from New York did well then," Von Biemann said.

"Did he?" Musaani asked. "The message also reports that Bazargan and his driver did not return to our embassy."

"Oh?" Von Biemann interjected. "Were they planning to do so right away, after he completed the assignment?"

"No," Musaani said, "Bazargan did not say."

The German shrugged, "Perhaps, then, he went into hiding or made his way directly back to the United States."

Musaani nodded, "Yes, that is possible. But," he paused again, obviously troubled, "I don't know."

"Well, did the embassy say there was a chance he was arrested, picked up, or that he failed to eliminate Harris? Is there anything else?"

Musaani shook his head, "No."

"So, what are you worried about?"

Musaani fixed the German with a look of cold contempt, the tension obvious in his voice, "Don't be stupid. If Bazargan failed, and Harris is alive and in the hands of the Arabian embassy, and I do not stop this, all we have worked for will be destroyed."

Musaani walked to the window and then spoke, "Everything is ready. Everything. We are on the threshold of an operation that will change the face of the Middle East." He paused, then spoke again, "Bazargan has never failed before. Never. What do we know? A man is reported dead, one man, where it was planned Harris would die, at the time his death was supposed to occur. That is a fact. The rest—the whereabouts of Bazargan and the driver—are uncertainties. I wish they were otherwise but I cannot change that." Musaani rattled the papers in his hand. "I can only act on what I know. If Bazargan was successful, if Harris is dead, and I stop the mission now simply because of uncertainty, our opportunity will be lost, perhaps forever."

Von Biemann smiled, "Good."

Musaani walked back to the desk, putting down the cables. He rapped them with his knuckles, "Tell me, what is the other most important fact in these messages besides the report of Harris's death?"

Von Biemann shrugged, "I don't know. What?"

"The FBI," Musaani said.

"Ah, yes," Von Biemann nodded, "the story of Sabah's gun battle."

"That was my mistake," Musaani said.

"How so?"

"Harris and the woman. From the beginning, both killings were really quite simple. At least, they would have been, I think, if I had made the right choice a few weeks ago."

"What was that?"

"To have DiGenero killed first."

The German furrowed his brow, "Do you think Harris told DiGenero about the mission?"

"No," Musaani replied. "Harris would not have fled halfway across North America to the Arabian embassy in Ottawa if that were the case. If he had told the FBI, then Riyadh could have learned what he knew directly from its American allies.

"No," Musaani repeated, "DiGenero is a policeman, one who understands us and is following a trail. That is all he is at this point, although he is dangerous nonetheless." He smiled, "Fortunately, I did not apprise Tehran of his possible involvement in our operation. Some complications are better left unreported. In this case, I will be able to correct my error without facing the criticism of my superiors."

"He can still die," Von Biemann said.

Musaani's voice was cold, "And so can we all."

Outside, the doors of the Mercedes slammed closed. Musaani walked to the window. The engine turned over once and started. Heavily laden, the car moved slowly down the crushed-stone drive and into the woods. In only moments, the taillights disappeared, following the downward slope out of sight.

Musaani stared at the empty drive. In three hours, they would be in Frankfurt. Then, later, they would board the flight for Riyadh. In thirty minutes, he too would leave for Munich, Frankfurt, and Jidda to play his next part. Tomorrow, inside Arabia and Iran, the gears would begin to mesh. Now, it was too late for changes, for second thoughts, or second-guessing. There was no turning back. The final stage had begun.

Part
Four

The Gift

23

Monday, October 1, 1984

King Khalid International Airport, Riyadh, Saudi Arabia

Kahlil bin Zahel stood behind the dark-tinted plate-glass windows of the VIP lounge, watching the tarmac begin to shimmer. At 9:00 a.m., the sun's baking rays already were transforming the concrete expanse of taxiways and parking ramps from cold to hot white. The flurry of nighttime arrivals and departures had ended several hours before, leaving a few scattered planes and the baggage vans and maintenance trucks that were moving among the warehouses, terminal gates, and loading docks. Kahlil squinted in the morning light at the outlying colony of houses, apartments, and hotels that created a low, colorless backdrop for the new airport complex. Last night, he thought, it had gone perfectly.

They'd arrived in Dhahran from Frankfurt on time. As expected, the immigration officials had bowed and scraped at the sight of the royal family passport, adopting an usher's demeanor and foregoing their usual questions and baggage search, the interrogation and inspection meant to discover the contraband contamination of liquor, videos, and pornography, the corruptions that were embargoed from the Kingdom of Islam. The first-class seats on the Saudia Airlines 727 to Riyadh, always overbooked for anyone but a member of the Zahel clan, had been waiting. They'd arrived after midnight. He had slept a few hours in the airport hotel. In minutes, they would board the Dash Eight, the chartered Dehavilland turboprop for the 200-mile flight from Riyadh to Jabrin.

Kahlil looked across the taxiway. The new royal terminal stood alone, white in the sun. It was big enough to serve a medium-sized city, but the building was exclusively for the king. In front, the rotund, bulbous-nosed shapes of the high-winged C-130 Hercules transports, their rear cargo ramps lowered, seemed conspicuously utilitarian, out of place against the columns and alabaster walls. It was a prophetic coincidence, he thought. At the same hour, on the same day, the king too was leaving for Jabrin.

The three desert-tan Hercules, marked with the Arabian Royal Air Force seal, were parked precisely, angled in military formation at forty-five degrees. The king's was first. It was his alone, with no other use, always ready whenever he wished to return to the desert. Like the bedouin's dress, its drab exterior was unadorned and functional, stripped, or so it would appear, to the bare minimum, the essentials. The Hercules could go anywhere, landing on unimproved strips and navigating with its state-of-the-art inertial system to find the smallest spot in the desert, night or day.

On the rear ramp of the second Hercules, a small cluster of technicians milled idly, half in light, half in the darkness of the cavernous interior. It was the communications plane, identical to the first except for the oddly shaped antennae arrayed like spines along its back and belly. The only other passengers for the two aircraft sat on their haunches beneath the wing, waiting. They were the king's personal bodyguards. Three would travel with Zahel. Three would follow on the second plane.

Kahlil knew them well. For as long as he could remember, they seemed interchangeable, impassive, unobtrusive but always there, the same dark, wiry men from the Quraysh, the nomadic tribe that had roamed the high desert east of Mecca for twenty generations. As guardian of the holy city of Islam, Muhammed abu Zahel had their unfailing loyalty. As his protectors, the Quraysh would die for him in the same way they had pledged their lives to the three kings before him who had solemnly sworn to lead the tribes and to keep Mecca, the holy shrine, pure.

A small convoy of trucks turned onto the taxiway. Kahlil counted four. Two, he knew, would be loaded into the third C-130. Two would stay to be dispatched later, if needed. The first truck, a paneled van with oversized tires for the sands, backed and turned, then drove slowly up the lowered cargo ramp. It carried the falcons, the king's hunting stable, and was provisioned with their food and furnishings as well as the falconer's tools and medications to repair jesses, splice feathers, or heal a bird. The second, a Land Rover with a removable steel top, was the king's car, armored and protected as well as comfortably appointed with a custom-fitted overstuffed couch in the rear, and a built-in cadge for the birds. As the falcons hunted, Zahel would ride, following them to the kill.

The C-130's ramp closed, creating the upswept line of the fuselage. The rest, Kahlil knew, had been loaded earlier. The tents, the food, the water, the electric generators, the air conditioning, the showers, the emergency medical supplies, the portable toilets. At Jabrin, his family would have much of the same, of course. For them, as for all the tribes, the king's visit would signal the twentieth-century revival of an age-old Arab tradition. Whatever they had belonged to their guest. That was how it had been, and how it always would be, never to be foregone or forgotten as a measure of their hospitality.

Kahlil turned, distracted by the banglelike tinkling of porcelain on silver. To the left of the polished mahogany doors that led from the VIP lounge to the lobby, seated on one of the soft couches that were lined up, arm to arm, along the marble walls, the Shakirs also watched the progress of the white-garbed coffee server who was carefully guiding the small wheels of his cart off the intricate oriental details of the forty-by-forty-foot Tabrīz carpet. The wizened old Yemenite moved slowly, pushing the service before him across the terrazzo floor.

Musaani had picked well, Kahlil thought. The Shakirs were dressed alike in linen business suits and white, open-necked shirts. They seemed the perfect picture, two young scions of the Arab elite returning from their watering holes in London, Paris, or Rome. The servant stopped beside them, pouring ceremoniously from the silver urn and then bending low in deference to extend the small cups. Kahlil could smell the coffee's rich aroma. It was better than the taste, he thought. After years in the States drinking the American brew, Kahlil had lost his liking for the thick, bitter liquid that was the Arabs' standard fare.

"Prince Kahlil?" The short, pockmarked Pakistani in the dark-blue business suit had stopped a respectful distance away.

"Yes?" Kahlil turned, recognizing the local station manager of Gulf Flight Services, the air charter firm.

"Sir," the Pakistani half-bowed, "I'm pleased to tell you your plane has landed. Perhaps you and your traveling companions would like to prepare to depart. The aircraft should be at this gate in less than three minutes. You will be on your way immediately for Jabrin."

Kahlil nodded and glanced at their bags. They were stacked on a small cart beside the exit, ready to roll outside to the aircraft ramp. The falcon's crate was also there, but set apart and covered. The bird had trav-

THE GIFT OF A FALCON

eled well, he thought. Normally, it took days, sometimes weeks, for a falcon to acclimate to the desert's conditions. But in the peregrine's case, the time wouldn't be necessary. She would fly only once, early tomorrow at dawn when the air was still cool. It would all be over before the sun rose high enough to sear away the overnight chill.

Outside, the glint of sun on glass caught his eye. Across the tarmac, the king's motorcade was proceeding at a stately pace toward the waiting aircraft.

The station manager followed Kahlil's gaze, smiling deferentially as he spoke, "Ah, yes, the king is departing."

Kahlil stared, ignoring the comment. From the first and the last of the six black limousines, four security men emerged, fanning out as they jogged ahead to cover the last few yards of the route on foot before the long stretch Lincoln pulled to a stop. The Shakirs had stood and were walking toward the collection of luggage.

The blades on the first C-130's left inboard turboprop began to rotate slowly. Closer by, the whine of the Dash Eight, approaching as it taxied fast, penetrated the walls of the VIP lounge.

The Pakistani smiled obsequiously, "Your aircraft, sir." He reached for the attaché case beside Kahlil, but the Saudi grabbed his arm, jerking it away.

"I'll take it."

Flustered, the Pakistani stepped back, "Of course, sir."

Kahlil lifted the case. The package from Tehran was inside, fitted carefully into molded styrofoam and heat-sealed in three layers of heavy-gauge plastic. So were the electronic components. They were fashioned into a bogus portable radio and miniature tape recorder. The radio had the parts for the receiver and the primary transmitter arranged to resemble its own circuitry. The tape recorder was similarly wired, carrying the second transmitter, the backup. The Shakirs would assemble the units tonight.

The Pakistani motioned politely, "This way, please."

Kahlil's mouth was dry. The Shakirs had pushed the door open and stepped outside. The heat of the morning struck Kahlil, a few paces behind, like an oven blast. Leaving the unnatural coolness of the VIP lounge, he felt suddenly sick, weak-kneed. Kahlil swallowed hard, trembling, and walked forward. It was more than fear. It was a terminal sensation, like the absolute helplessness of someone who had stepped off a curb without looking and realized there was no bottom to be found, only falling. The heavy odor of kerosene exhaust and the whine from the Dash Eight's engines surrounded him. With two propellers feathered, the plane had swung into position, opening its passenger door.

Kahlil looked across the field toward the four-engined roar. The first C-130 was angling its nose away from the royal terminal toward the taxiway. His stomach turned over as the image flashed across his conscious mind. He had seen the Quraysh kill once when he was 16 years old and visiting the palace during Ramadan, the month of daily fasting to celebrate Allah's gift of the Koran. At dusk, as was the custom, a man had come through the king's open door, one of many who dined with Zahel and then joined him in the majlis, the sitting room, where commoners as well as princes could talk, petition, and air grievances. Later, it was clear he was a victim of his own religious zeal, deranged because he had taken no water or food during his long desert journey to Riyadh. He had argued, raising his voice, and stood, moving forward toward the king too quickly. The blade of the closest Quraysh had struck before he took a second step, opening him from the navel to the neck in one upward motion.

Kahlil put his foot on the aircraft's stairway and paused. Deep in the recesses of his mind, a wordless prayer for his own salvation welled up. He tried to push it aside, instead beseeching Allah to strike with him as he cleansed the world of old men with old beliefs who prostituted rather than protected the power of the people and the one true religion. Finally, after all these years, it was time. His time. The revolution. There was only success or failure. Nothing in between.

"Thank you, sir. Allah be with you," the Pakistani's voice rose over the whine of the turboprops.

Kahlil didn't reply. He shaded his eyes with a trembling hand, and climbed the short set of steps. God willing, Allah would be with him. When it was over tomorrow, there would be no one between Kahlil bin Zahel and his place as leader of the new Islamic Revolutionary Republic of Arabia.

Eight hours later in Jidda, at exactly 5:00 p.m., Musaani opened the door of his hotel room, beckoning in the three men who had just knocked.

He closed the door behind them quickly and then turned, grasping shoulders and embracing each.

"God be with you," Musaani said in Arabic. Each man murmured, repeating the phrase as he returned the Iranian's greeting.

He motioned the trio to the couch and chairs. They sat silently, eyes drawn to the view of the Red Sea, west, beyond the harbor reef, a mile distant and twenty-five floors below. Through the Meridien Hotel's dark, reflecting glass, the water glinted in the late-afternoon sun, constantly changing texture and complexion.

Musaani examined the three men as he sat, taking his place in the center of the group. As he had instructed them, the Egyptian and the two Palestinians had dressed well in new robes and headdresses. They appeared suitably prosperous, indistinguishable from the Saudis, and therefore inconspicuous coming and going in the five-star hotel. It was like Musaani's own garb, consistent with what would be expected by anyone who inspected the Saudi Arabian passport he carried identifying him as Alireza Ali Zanal, banker, resident in London, late of Riyadh.

Musaani opened his briefcase on his lap, extracting three pieces of paper. He spoke tersely, "These are your instructions. The hour is here."

He paused, examining their faces. It had taken five years to establish the revolutionary network among the Shia faithful and the Sunni expatriates—the Egyptians, the Palestinians, the Pakistanis, the Yemenites, and the others. The Arabian internal security service had stumbled on a few of the cells, bribing, torturing, and in one or two cases, infiltrating, but the losses had been acceptable. The organization was compartmentalized, subdivided into groups within groups, making it impossible for one component to give up more than two others. Now they were all in place, reliable and ready to rise in the name of the true Islam to purge the corrupt, to destroy the western impurity, to scour out the stain of the infidel.

Musaani extended his hand. Each man nodded, accepting his small slip of paper. These three, trained in Tehran, were the top of the pyramid and loyal to the death. Musaani had recruited each one. From them, tonight and tomorrow, the word would go to three more, and from those to yet other triads, spreading by morning to sixty cells in five cities.

"Tomorrow," Musaani spoke softly, "at the hour, 7:00 a.m., when Zahel is dead, the uprising will begin." Each looked down at the folded paper in his hand.

Musaani continued, "You may open your assignment and read." This, he thought, was the final step. He had kept their targets secret to protect their security until the very end. Each slip of paper had instructions for the primary cells. Depending on where their mobs attacked, the subordinate units would have one or another predesignated target. They would strike, creating an incendiary chain, and then, in a few hours, across the country, a conflagration. Tomorrow, in the souqs, or markets, the telephone exchange buildings, the police garrisons, the ports, the western offices, the government ministries, the burning and the rioting would begin. By nightfall, it would be over. Arabia would be theirs.

"This will appear to be grass roots, a revolution from the bottom, occurring everywhere at once. By the time you are on the streets, the military will be neutralized," Musaani said. "If any units are not, they will have only one choice. To fight against you and die, overwhelmed by the masses, or to join with the faithful, the strugglers." He paused, "I do not think they will turn on the people."

The three men looked up, silent, obviously holding Musaani in awe. They sat ramrod straight, bodies taut, the zeal burning in their eyes. The hour was approaching. This man had delivered them to the highest calling, revolution for the people and defense of the faith. Now, following him, they would deliver Arabia.

"Do you have any questions?" Musaani asked. There were none. He rose, signaling the three other white-garbed figures that it was time for them to leave. They stood.

"Remember," Musaani said. "Tomorrow, not one moment before 7:00 a.m." He paused, holding each of their eyes, "And, as Allah is your witness, not one second after."

Six and a half hours later, at 11:55 p.m., Mansour Gobsadeh, third secretary and vice consul, Iranian Embassy Liaison Staff Office/Riyadh, pulled his rented Toyota Carina into the vacant Obeid Hospital parking lot and switched off the lights. He patted his jacket pocket. The prescription vial was there. Overweight, his shirttail lapping over his belt and belly, Gobsadeh stepped from the car, casually scanning the surroundings. The white Chevrolet had stopped across Farazdak Street, parking lights on and motor running. He slammed the Toyota's door. His surveillance by the Saudi interior ministry's secret police, he thought, was as obtrusive as ever.

Gobsadeh walked toward the emergency room entrance, assuming a pained expression and holding his head. His monthly trip from the Iranian embassy in Jidda to handle consular affairs in Riyadh was a simple chore. In fact, there were no consular affairs, although as the chief of the embassy's clandestine intelligence section, Major Mansour Gobsadeh, Revolutionary Guards, used the time to good advantage. It was his opportunity to provide requirements, questions for which Tehran needed answers, to Saval/1, his most valued agent, Gobsadeh's one penetration of the senior Saudi police ranks. He'd completed the task that afternoon, loading the dead drop, the predesignated pickup point on the ledge outside the jewelry shop in the Deera Souq, by dropping the crumpled envelope with premeditated casualness into the small chipped urn.

The Iranian reached for the steel-and-glass swinging door. Saval/1's answers always came a few days later to the post office box in Doha, unfailingly complete, accurate, and on time. They never talked. It was too dangerous and there was no need. Gobsadeh paused, wiping his brow. That was why the telephone call an hour ago had surprised him. That was why Gobsadeh was worried.

The emergency waiting room was empty, as was the telephone booth in the corner. Its number was their emergency contact point. The Iranian had chosen the location with care, a place that was always open in a city that shuttered itself tightly at night, retreating between high concrete walls. Gobsadeh glanced at his watch. He had three minutes to establish his cover with the emergency room staff before he would need to be in the booth to answer the phone when it rang.

At the high reception desk, the nurse on duty, a blond, a Scandinavian or German expatriate, looked up from her reading. A second, a Philippina, seated in the corner, dozed.

"May I help you, sir?"

Gobsadeh shuffled forward, feet splayed outward in a fat man's walk, grimacing, "My migraines are back. They're killing me. Can you give me some medication? My prescription is empty."

The blond examined the empty vial, "I'm afraid this is out of date. Could you wait for a moment, please? I'll try to reach one of the doctors."

"Wait? I can't stand this anymore. How long?"

The nurse started to speak but Gobsadeh interrupted. His voice was loud, irritated, and obviously impatient, "My head is splitting. Can't you fill this now?"

The blond wrinkled her brow, her tone calming, "Sir, I must call one of the physicians. I'm sure he'll be able to see you in just a few minutes. If you'll have a seat..."

The Iranian sputtered, "Where's the telephone? I'm in pain, can't you see? Why do you make me wait for a doctor? You must have a druggist here. If you won't help me, I'll go somewhere else."

Gobsadeh turned his back on the nurse and walked, his gait rocky, to the phone booth. He squeezed inside and sat down, closing the door, and appeared to dig for his address book as he lifted the receiver, his thumb firmly on the hook. Gobsadeh glanced at his watch. As the hands touched midnight, the phone rang.

The Iranian intelligence officer released his thumb immediately, "I'm here."

Saval/1 spoke rapidly in English, "I don't know the significance, but we have the highest-precedence security alert in effect from tonight. This has not happened in years."

The voice of Saval/1, Colonel Husaini Halal, vice commander, Internal Security Division, Ar Riyād Province, Saudi National Police, Ministry of the Interior, was clipped and drawn, obviously strained. Gobsadeh knew Halal was a professional, and on the face of it an unlikely traitor. But he was also from the tribe of the Shammar, who had lived on their traditional land near Arabia's northern frontier as blood enemies of the Iraqis ever since British surveyors had created the invisible line through the sands and along with it, a half century of border wars. Halal had come to Gobsadeh's predecessor as a walk-in, a volunteer, five years before when Tehran's holy struggle with Baghdad had begun and Arabia had allied with Iraq. The enemy of my enemy, Gobsadeh thought. As a source in the top ranks of Arabian internal security, Halal had been worth his weight in gold.

"What does 'highest precedence' mean?" Gobsadeh asked.

"We are watching all internal security threats with twenty-four-hour surveillance. We are also rounding up known suspects. And our military forces are on alert."

Gobsadeh frowned, scratching his head. He knew of nothing that would warrant an Arabian alert, certainly nothing having to do with Iran. His mind raced over the recollections of the cable traffic from Tehran and the latest rumors that had accompanied the visiting bureaucrats who came and went at the embassy with tiresome regularity. A week ago, his intelligence section had been put on a seven-day workweek, a "level-two watch." Rumor had it, the order had come from outside the Revolutionary Guards' chain of command, directly from the top, the Committee. The section was still on "level two." But what of it? Wars were always confusing, with contradictory orders given and rescinded whenever there was major action at the front. He had changed the work schedules but not bothered to speculate or ask. Readiness had gone up and down before.

"Another thing," Halal said. "There is a nationwide search to apprehend a man, an Iranian. It's under way now."

"Who?" Gobsadeh sat up straight.

"I only know the name. The description is being cabled from our embassy in Ottawa."

The sound of voices made Gobsadeh turn, glancing out. Two men had entered the emergency room. He recognized one as the driver of the white Chevrolet that had been following him.

The Iranian spoke quickly, "The name. Who?"

"Musaani. Rajid Musaani. He's to be captured," the Saudi police official paused, "or killed."

Gobsadeh's mouth fell open in shock. Musaani. He wasn't a friend, or an acquaintance. They'd never met. But he knew the name. Only the name. The name was a story. No, a legend. There was only one Musaani. The Committee's Musaani. He had to report.

The Iranian started to turn his bulk again at the sound of the footstep, but the door to the booth slammed open before he could swivel in the seat to look out. He gagged as the open hand, fingers rigid, rammed into his larynx and then closed around his throat. The force of the blow jammed his windpipe closed, slamming his head against the wall. Choking, arms pinned in the confines of the booth, Gobsadeh barely resisted as another hand reached across him to wrench away the phone.

He felt someone going through his pockets, but he was losing all sensation as well as consciousness as his brain pounded, starved for oxygen. Gobsadeh wiggled pathetically, reflexively trying to crane his head to see the threat. Eyes bulging, he could only make out the form of the man who held the phone, as his sight, a casualty of his strangulation, telescoped to tunnel vision.

Next to the booth, the man with the phone signaled with a nod to release the grip on the Iranian. Gobsadeh, unconscious, slumped forward. The instructions had come over the radio only moments before for all surveillance teams to pick up their Iranian subjects "code black." That meant no warning, and detention incommunicado pending further instructions. It was curious, but an order was an order. The Arabian counterintelligence officer put the telephone receiver to his ear. For only a moment, he could tell the connection was open. Then, he heard the click and the line went dead.

24

Tuesday, October 2, 1984

Büshehr Air Force Base, Iran

At the very moment Gobsadeh came to, finding himself sprawled across the rear seat of a car racing out of Riyadh, and realized with a horrifying fear that he was probably living the last hours of his life, 400 miles away on the shore of the Persian Gulf, Captain Nassir Ghazali coincidentally sat frozen in place by the same numbing thought. He'd repressed it for hours, but the image was too real, too much like a premonition to be forgotten. The Iranian Air Force squadron commander pushed himself back from his desk, shaking his head like a fighter who had taken a blow and was trying to clear his senses. He wouldn't let it happen. He wouldn't give in. He wouldn't surrender to the fear.

Ghazali glanced at his watch. At the briefing five hours before, he had moved the hands back, changing the setting from Iran's odd time zone, with its extra half hour. It was 12:05 a.m., Arabian, not Tehran time. The signal would come in seven hours and fifty-five minutes. In the fourth year of the war, the battered Iranian Air Force was anything but a precise military machine, but the mullah who had given them their mission had been emphatic. No, categorical. Ghazali was to have his helicopter squadron fueled, loaded with troops, engines running, and ready to lift off by 7:45 a.m., no later. At 8:00 a.m. they would go.

The tall, spare man stood, staring down at the blank page centered in the circle of light on the table. He had written a farewell letter to his wife and two sons in Tabrīz before, too many times before, but tonight the words wouldn't come. Ghazali snapped off the small lamp and opened the desk drawer, slipping the single sheet of cheap stationery inside. It was a bad omen, he thought. He had nothing to say. No final remembrance. No claim of divine purpose. No brave words that it was all worthwhile. No comfort to offer. No good-bye. He had used them all. He glanced at the unmade cot in the corner of the small room that doubled as the squadron commander's office. He should sleep, rather than just wait for morning, but he'd found that impossible. Ghazali pushed aside the blackout curtain and stepped through the door.

The night wind had shifted, blowing salty and cool from the gulf. Ghazali turned up his collar, walking slowly across the stubble, gravel, and sand. He had survived the front for four years and four times that many "final" offensives, flying back and forth across the Shatt-al-Arab, bringing the faithful to battle in Iraq's marshes, and returning with the same, many of them dead and dying, to be buried in Iran.

Four years. The helicopter squadron was nearly decimated. Machmed and Baldarzi were the only two left from the old corps, from the imperial days. The remainder, the new ones, came from the Revolutionary Guards flying school. Ghazali divided them into two categories: those few who could barely fly and the rest who never should.

He stepped onto the macadam pavement of the helicopter parking ramp. It was cracked and potholed, badly in need of repair, a far cry from the spit-and-polish base he remembered from when he'd arrived for his first assignment as a junior officer, a copilot, ten years ago. Ahead, the six CH-47 Chinooks, fueled and preflighted, were aligned in two rows, spaced to allow room for the platoons to assemble with their weapons before boarding. In the darkness, the heavy-lift helicopters, long rotor blades drooping, seemed to slouch on the ground. Six, Ghazali thought, shaking his head in disgust. They were battered, sand-scoured, missing instruments, and long overdue even the most minimal scheduled repairs. Once there had been twenty-six, in perfect shape. They had shone. Now, there were barely enough parts or crews to keep these, the survivors, in the air.

Ghazali's mind returned to the briefing. Compared to flying over the Shatt, where the ground fire and the SA-7s, the handheld antiaircraft missiles, were everywhere, tomorrow would be easy, at least for the first 170 miles. He would be in the lead. They would fly straight, crossing the gulf at fifty feet, below radar, dispersing to avoid drawing attention when they reached the shipping track where the tankers were thickest, and then reassembling off Al Jubayl for the last-minute run to the shore.

A few things were in their favor. There were no American carriers in the area to find and dog them with their air patrols. The risk that a picket ship off the coast might sound the alarm also was slim. And, they were told, there would be scores of other attacks and unrest in the interior, complicating the Saudis' problems and with any luck, confusing them as well.

He turned back toward the Quonset hut, feeling the fatigue that came from tension and fear. Even if he couldn't sleep, it would be better to lie down, to try. In the morning he would need all his strength and stamina. His six helicopters would each bring forty commandos into the heart of Ras Tanura. Later today, when it was over, he could rest. Of course, if they failed to take the naval base as they'd been ordered by the mullah, sleep wouldn't matter because, Ghazali thought, by this time tomorrow, the odds were overwhelming that he would be dead.

As Captain Ghazali closed the door of his Quonset hut, 130 miles southeast of Büshehr in the small Iranian fishing town of Asalūyeh, Ensign Akhbar Radi laid the parallel ruler on the navigation chart of the Persian Gulf, computing the distance and heading to Manama port in Bahrain for the third and final time. It was 170 miles as a bird flew, but birds didn't need to concern themselves with currents, heavily traveled shipping lanes, hostile patrols, or with the problems involved when wind and water combined to push a hovercraft flying across the surface of the sea at a mile a minute even a few degrees off course.

Radi snapped off the chart light over the navigation table and looked up, letting his eyes adjust to the dark. Seated high above the rounded deck in the compact command and navigation station, the small bridge, he could sense the slight roll of the Winchester hovercraft. Its sixty-three feet rose and fell, nagged into motion by the choppy water that lapped and rebounded off the shore. The same southwest breeze that troubled the harbor made the 33,000 pounds of air-cushioned, British-built fast-attack craft tug at its moorings. The dock was well protected from southerly or easterly winds, but the rocky spit that hooked into the gulf to create the natural refuge offered little help when storms came out of the west.

Radi turned back to the chart and again snapped on the light. If he ran the Winchester's 1400-horsepower Rolls-Royce gas turbine at cruising speed, his calculations showed he could cover the 170 miles in six hours, just short of the hovercraft's maximum endurance time. That meant they should leave in three hours, arriving at 9:00 a.m. He would wake the crew at 2:30 a.m. After departure checks, at 3:00 a.m., they would cast off.

Radi shook his head and lit a cigarette. Their mission was madness, on the face of it, a death sentence with no chance that he and the crew would survive. No chance, that is, unless you were smart enough to figure a way and thereby transform a suicide trip into salvation. In this case, Radi smiled, he was.

He stared at the chart. Dhahran and Manama were almost sister cities—for a ship entering the ten-mile-wide strait between the island of Bahrain and the Arabian coast from the north, a right or a left turn, respectively. With 8000 pounds of small arms and ammunition on board, his orders were to turn right, appropriately he thought, and make for the Arabian reef, where the Shia resistance fighters would be waiting.

The words of the political officer from Qom who had delivered their orders that day had been grand and glorious. The revolution was spreading to Arabia and they would be the vanguard, delivering weapons to the strugglers on the first dawn of the first day, the beginning of a new era for Iran and the world.

That was all well and good, Radi thought, if you wanted to be a struggler yourself, or intended to sit on the Arabian reef, out of fuel, with nowhere to go, waiting for the Saudis to discover your craft, so you could die. The young ensign stubbed out his cigarette, sliding open the window panel and flicking the butt into the sea. Radi shivered. The night air felt cold. He pushed the window shut and walked to the bench at the back of the command station, lying down and stretching out.

"Glorious dawns" were not his concern, he thought. After spending four years avoiding the army and the front, and then the better part of his family's savings to buy a place at the naval officer's school when he finally had to go, Radi had no intention of sailing to certain death at 26 years old, on his first real mission of war. Tomorrow at 9:00 a.m., when he reached the channel opposite Bahrain, a sharp turn east and full throttle would take them straight into Manama harbor at fifty miles an hour, and onto the beach. So much for the rebels awaiting them outside Dhahran on the reef. Ensign Radi closed his eyes, trying to doze. Shia strugglers or not, he thought, the revolution in Arabia would have to wait.

At that moment in Riyadh, 450 miles southwest of the Iranian coast, Senior Communications Officer Major Ahmed Sudairi, Arabian Air Force, sat bolt upright and stared at the red light flashing before him. The bright pulse indicated an incoming call. It was not a phone he would lift from its cradle lightly. Sudairi ran down his mental checklist, reviewing his responsibilities as the midnight-to-8:00 a.m. watch commander for the defense ministry's National Command Center.

The Harris communications network linking the ministry to the ground, naval, and air operations centers was quiet. So were the links to the royal family. The system was new, recently installed by the team of American technicians who had wired and checked the circuitry with meticulous care. Supported by twin IBM mainframes and a cryptographic VAX minicomputer, the network used triply redundant connections—hardened land lines impervious to bugging, microwave relays that spanned the deserts, and fiber-optic technology to handle the thousands of messages a minute that would pour into the ministry during a war. It was fail-safe, and state-of-the-art. Sudairi glanced at the "trouble" board. The software constantly monitored the system, as well as received, decoded, routed, and filed all its traffic. The board was clear, its lights green. There were no systems failures.

Sudairi nervously scanned the giant map of Arabia that hung like a theater screen ten feet away. His eyes raced over its lights and symbols. He prepared from habit to answer questions as he reached for the phone. Only the king was traveling. He was now in Jabrin. In the upper right-hand corner of the map, the bright blue glow beside King Zahel's call sign and code name displayed the fact that his AN/APQ 25/26 was on-line, in electronic contact with its coding control unit beside Sudairi's console, and ready to transmit any command. The lights were out beside the names of the other family members, confirming they were on the main communications system, rather than using portable telephones.

Sudairi swallowed hard and grasped the receiver. The lines that ran to the ministers of defense and interior, the commanders of the national guard and the military services, and the intelligence chief were direct, ringing instantly whenever the instruments were lifted at either end. That was what made him pause. The red light was winking above the phone from the residence of Kahled bin Muhammed abu Zahel, the son of King Zahel and minister of defense. Kahled bin Muhammed had a frightening temper coupled with a vindictive personality, and at this hour, Sudairi knew that a call from him could only mean trouble.

"Sudairi here, your Highness."

Kahled spoke in a monotone, "What is the defense status?"

Projected on the backlit map, the scattered military symbols for ships and planes reflected the fact there were no threats to the kingdom's territorial security other than the usual Iranian and Iraqi patrols. Two Iranian F-4s from Shīrāz and five Iraqi Mirages, F-1s, were cruising, looking for each other's tankers or transports in the gulf. As always, the Saudi Air Force had six F-15s on alert, and the American AWACS was flying.

"The situation is normal, your Highness," Sudairi answered. "There are two Iranian and five Iraqi patrols in the air, all flying within forty miles of the Iranian coast. Our alert aircraft are operationally ready and the AWACS is airborne."

"There is nothing unusual?" the defense minister asked.

"Nothing, your Highness."

"You are certain?"

Sudairi swallowed hard, praying silently that he was right as he studied the map and its symbols a final time before answering, "Yes, your Highness."

"Good. Listen carefully," Kahled bin Muhammed paused. "First, you are to deactivate the king's AN/APQ 25/26."

"But, that is against our standing order, your Excellency," Sudairi interjected, surprised and puzzled. The king's personal command-and-control communications unit always had their highest readiness priority, to be maintained in perfect condition, on-line, twenty-four hours a day.

"Silence!" The defense minister's fury was instantaneous. Sudairi cringed as Kahled bin Muhammed continued, "Then, you are to go to Defense Condition One, and contact each of our senior service commanders to transmit the following instructions. Word for word."

"Yes, your Excellency," Sudairi groped for a pen and prepared to write.

Defense Condition One. The major wrinkled his brow. There was nothing on the map to explain why the armed forces were about to go to immediate war alert.

Kahled bin Muhammed spoke rapidly, dictating his orders, "Initiate Operational Plan Musmak." Sudairi's eyes widened. He scribbled furiously, simultaneously awestruck and praying that he would not miss any details. Musmak. It was the legendary name of the small mud-plastered fort, once a village, now preserved as a near holy place in the heart of modern Riyadh. There, eighty years ago, Abdul Azziz—later known to all the world as Ibn Sa'ūd, the founder of the kingdom of Saudi Arabia— had destroyed his enemies and the enemies of the al'Sa'ūd clan in a lightning early-morning attack. Sudairi felt the hair stand on the back of his neck. Listening to the defense minister as he wrote, scrawling the words hurriedly across the page, he began to tremble at the thought of what the new day would bring.

Two hours later and 550 miles away, security police Lieutenant Ibram Hamdi's footsteps echoed loudly in the deserted lobby of the Jidda Kaki Hotel. Even in the middle of the night, the humidity from the Red Sea hung heavily in the cool air conditioning. The desk clerk, obviously sleepy, looked up, puzzled, watching Hamdi and his three plainclothes officers stride toward him. It was 3:00 a.m., and he was certain the four men were not arriving guests.

"Are you the manager?" Hamdi asked. The voice had the authority of the interior ministry's security police, obviating the need in the desk clerk's mind to request identification. The small man in the dark suit shook his head, "No."

"Get him." The clerk nodded, stepping at once into the anteroom behind the reception counter. Hamdi looked at his watch. He had four more hotels to cover after this, the Jidda Airport, the Sheraton, the Kandara Palace, and last, the Meridien. There was far too little time to do it. The Kaki and the Jidda Airport hotels were small, but not the others. They were massive, modern, and always full.

Hamdi glanced over the vacant lobby with a policeman's eye, displaying his habitual curiosity about the mundane. The hotel was relatively new. The magazine racks at the small newsstand in the corner displayed French and

German covers, testifying to the fact it catered to Europeans. Hamdi flipped open the notebook in his hand. The picture and description had come to them from the interior ministry headquarters in Riyadh only an hour before. It was grainy but recognizable. The man also had some aliases. Normally, it was plenty when they were looking for someone, even if they had to canvass five hotels with 1300 rooms. But not tonight. Not when the order was the highest priority. And not when it specified that if the subject resisted, Hamdi should do his best to kill him.

Hamdi fidgeted, impatiently drumming his fingers on the counter. Night managers were paid to work, not sleep, and yet he had never known one he didn't have to awaken. He had three or four hours at most, and time was already against them.

The night manager emerged, straightening his tie and smoothing his hair, with the clerk in tow. Hamdi produced an identification card, prompting a bow from the hotelier, who was more familiar than most by virtue of his trade with the interests of the internal security officers when they made their late-night calls.

"How may I help you, sir?" The manager glanced past Hamdi, spotting the unmarked van. It was parked under the hotel's covered entryway behind the police sedan. The six men in uniform standing beside it were dressed in combat fatigues, flak jackets, and helmets. Each carried a stubby machine gun.

The policeman pointed to the loose-leaf binder he had placed on the counter. "We are looking for this foreigner," he said, opening the cover to reveal a nine-by-twelve-inch Wirephoto. The picture had been taken from above, showing someone in his thirties, well dressed in a casual western style. He appeared to be standing at an immigration or customs booth, waiting.

"I'm sorry, but I don't recognize him," the night manager motioned to the clerk, pointing at the photo. Nervous, the man shook his head, adding his own wordless "no."

Hamdi nodded, "Get me your registration cards for the last forty-eight hours." The clerk scurried away even before the manager snapped his fingers.

Hamdi tapped the photo, "Are you absolutely certain?"

The night manager bent down, squinting this time in concentration. In the picture, a shoulder was visible, probably belonging to the inspector or customs official who was facing the subject from inside the booth.

The corner of an epaulet, a shoulder board that was part of a uniform, stood out, embossed with a designation of rank, and a symbol of paired lions with a crown. The night manager recognized the British insignia. His eye caught the small type in the photo's left-hand corner. It was blurred, but he could make out the date, "September 3, 1984," and one word, "Heathrow."

On the margin of Arabia's vast and arid sands, the solitary form of a man, stooped low, moved away from the desert camp. He walked with an oddly hurried pace for the hour and the place, following the shadow that defined the contour of the land and angling his path to pick dark over light as he made for the first line of dunes. Between the peaks, the high sand mounds met in a small valley. There, in less than a minute, the darkness swallowed him. Except for tracks that the night wind would soon obliterate, he was gone.

Moments later, a second man moved into the darkness, walking less quickly but with a steadier gait. Although he was short-legged and smaller than the first, he took the more arduous course near the crest of the dunes, stepping surefootedly on the soft-blowing edge. After a quarter mile, without looking left or right, he paused, his bare, callused feet splayed for balance on the slope, listening. For all but those who knew how to hear, there was only the sound of the wind. He cocked his head slightly, closing his eyes, listening. Then he shifted the long, leather-sheathed bundle in his arms, and stepped forward, his feet burrowing soundlessly into the cold sand, to resume his walk into the desert night.

25

Tuesday, October 2, 1984

The Jabrin Oasis, Saudi Arabia

The lingering cold night air belied the promised warmth of the new dawn sky and the false rose hue of the sand. The man breathed deeply, refreshed by the chill. It would soon become oppressive heat, although he knew that the particular transition from the extremes of night to day was not what distinguished this land. Rather, it was where he stood. On the edge. Jabrin. The oasis on the undefined border that marked the end of an unforgiving desert and the beginning of a killing one.

King Muhammed Kahlil abu Zahel glanced toward the top of the nearest dunes. The three Quraysh who had spent the night at their posts rose from their haunches to greet him, bowing low in the direction of their royal charge. They were the sentinels who had guarded the perimeter. The ten massive tents, the supply trailers, the generator units, and the collection of jeeps, cars, and trucks made the scene seem less like a nomadic encampment than a small town, somehow transplanted whole into the desert. Zahel looked east, watching the brightness of dawn define the crest of the far dunes. At 6:00 a.m., the first light came just as the wind died.

He had already prayed, and felt rested despite the late night. The feast had begun soon after dark. A whole roasted lamb, juices dripping and steaming on a mountain of rice, followed by dates, fruit, sweets, and coffee. Then they had talked, continuing into the small hours, with tea, gifts, and compliments to the hosts for their hospitality before he retired. Like his visit to the tribes, the meal was a tradition, a ritual practiced without fail each year, as had been done by the scores of tribal chieftains who had come to Jabrin even before Arabia had its king. To maintain the tradition was his obligation, what he owed to the past, to those who came before him, as well as to those living now. But it also was his greatest pleasure, and each year he would not miss the pilgrimage for the world.

He turned, ready for the day. For Zahel, the falconer and the bedouin, to start his journey each fall at Jabrin also was no chore. On the flyway across Arabia, the oasis offered the finest hunting as the summering birds from the east European plain, the Caspian, and the Caucasus winged south to winter in Africa. And there was more. Jabrin was a haven and an outpost for the earthbound traveler. It symbolized the beginning, the demarcation of something truly special, unique in this world. Isolated and alone, it was the last water for anyone moving north, south, or east into the desert. Not any desert. The desert. The sands. The only true sands.

The Rub' Al-Khali. The Empty Quarter. No more need be said. For 400 miles it stretched arid and killing, with line after line of dunes, to

Oman, and then another 300 miles over the bare rock and gravel of the coastal range to the warm, salty waters of the Arabian Sea. To anyone but a bedouin, it was a mystery why people chose to live there. But to Zahel and the shrinking numbers of those who remembered what it had been like, before the oil changed the land, it was a mystery how any true Arab could stay away. To come back was to return to the unchanging, the perfect, the eternal, the sands, the world that would always be there when all other worlds had passed away.

Even in his seventy-fifth year, after countless trips across the kingdom, innumerable nights in the desert, and a lifetime of roaming the land, like his father and grandfather before him, Zahel found the oasis and the hunt to be the wellspring of life. In the midst of what others might see as cruel nothingness, where an error of judgment, or even a slight miscalculation meant suffering and death, Zahel knew his return to the desert was a coming to the source, to his origins. It was coming home.

The king felt the touch on his sleeve.

"We are ready, sir," Colonel Ali Hassan Kahlafi, the king's aide-de-camp, gestured toward the Land Rovers.

Zahel nodded, "And our luck today on the hunt, Kahlafi?"

"It will be fine, sir. We have located a place where the curlew are feeding. There are three falcons for you this morning." The colonel looked toward the king's Land Rover, "As you requested, the American peregrine, the gift to you last night, is the one we have prepared for you to fly first."

"Ah, yes," Zahel turned, gathering his flowing white thobe, his robe, around him as he stepped toward the Rover, "it appears to be an exceptional falcon, does it not?"

"Indeed," Colonel Kahlafi fell in the appropriate pace behind the king, "an exceptional bird." Kahlafi gestured to the south. "We have found a place a half mile away where you may choose to fly her."

Zahel grunted, satisfied. He loved the hunt for its own sake, but it also had the added attraction of allowing him for even a few hours to be alone, or at least what passed for being alone when one was a king. Except for the Quraysh, he refused to bring the normal entourage of bodyguards and security men when he called on the tribes. To do otherwise, Zahel thought, would be an insult. He visited as their guest, under their

protection, not, as seemed increasingly the case when he traveled elsewhere, as a prisoner who arrived with his keepers, paroled temporarily
from the splendid incarceration in Riyadh where he passed most of his
year. His brothers had argued against his wish for years before finally giving up. It was no use and they knew it. The hunt was tradition, sport,
and liberation. He cherished it as his one, albeit too brief, escape.

Zahel's driver bowed low as the king stepped into the rear of the Land
Rover, settling comfortably on the overstuffed seat. Before him on the
perch, the peregrine was hooded and ready. Colonel Kahlafi, Zahel's only
concession to the demands of national leadership during his desert so-
journs, took the passenger's front seat, placing the briefcase containing
the AN/APQ 25/26 on the floor beside him.

In their Land Rover, Kahlil bin Zahel and Rashad Shakir watched
the king's vehicle lurch slightly, its four oversized wheels in gear and digging into the sand. The falconer's van followed, a car length behind.

Kahlil exhaled a long, nervous sigh. He had wondered until the last
minute whether this time King Zahel might break the pattern, bringing
others with him. Praise to Allah, he had not. He glanced around, puzzled. Other than the small party, the camp was quiet. Only one thing
was odd. There were no signs of the Quraysh.

Kahlil tapped the driver on the shoulder, "Go." He glanced at Rashad,
who sat beside him, "Now, it is time."

The Kurd nodded, staring ahead. He knew his brother, Amin, already out on the desert, was ready. Kahlil and Rashad braced themselves
as their Rover started up the incline, moving south into the desert in
third and last place in the hunting procession.

Fifteen minutes later and three quarters of a mile away in a small
wadi, Amin Shakir heard the man's cry faintly but clearly. It was one of
the spotters signaling to launch. The falconer's assistant had found the
game. Amin's heart pounded. He shivered in the deep shadow as he shifted
his position, crouching on one knee. Five hours before, he had slipped
from the camp, following Kahlil's map to find the dry wash, a half mile
from the first hunting site. The small collection of boulders, the natural
refuse of an ancient downpour and flood, had been some protection from
the desert wind as well as his cover.

Amin stood up and moved into the open. He uncoiled the line with
the feathered lure and removed the small, teardrop-shaped parcel from

his deep fatigue-jacket pocket. It was less than a pound, light enough for the peregrine to carry for some distance. She would be airborne any moment now. He lifted the lure and measured a short length of line. Then, he began to swing the feathered bundle in an arc, letting the line slip through his fingers, widening its invisible circle, as he watched the horizon for the peregrine.

At that moment, Talal Hadi, the king's falconer, looked down from the crest of the dune. His assistant was bringing the new peregrine to the king. It was, Hadi thought, an extraordinary bird. Thirty yards away, King Zahel raised his arm to receive the falcon, smiling, "I have been most anxious to try her."

The assistant falconer nodded as Zahel nudged at the peregrine's claws with his heavy glove, prompting her to step onto his arm. The king paused, examining her, "Ah, you have come so far to hunt, my beauty."

Inside the hood, the falcon moved her head, listening to the resonant low tones of Zahel's voice. The king ran his finger gently down her breast, smoothing the feathers, "Perfection in form, and I trust, perfection in flight. This of all birds is the only one I have never flown. Never a North American peregrine." Zahel smiled, "They are reputed to be the best and also the fewest in numbers." He glanced at the assistant falconer, "When this season is over, remember, the peregrine must go free."

The king turned, facing the wind, watching the falcon tense. "Ah, you sense it is time to fly. The curlew are a prey you have never seen before, but I think you will find them a challenge." The peregrine shifted nervously, sensing freedom in the cold morning air. She knew instinctively the king was ready. Zahel spoke softly to her, "In the next moment, when you see the desert for the first time, it will be very different from what you have known before. Do not be alarmed, my beautiful one. The sky is the same and it is yours." He smiled, "Every sky belongs to you."

Zahel looked up at Hadi atop the dune. The falconer waved and pointed the direction of the quarry, "Launch!"

The king raised his arm to shoulder height, removed the peregrine's hood, and released her jesses. Suddenly emancipated, the falcon lifted from the glove, her powerful wing beats driving her forward.

Zahel's voice betrayed his excitement, "She's climbing." Clearing the backdrop of the dunes, the peregrine became at once a silhouette and a translucent form, the morning sun illuminating her outline as well as shining through her wings.

The falconer pointed, jabbing the air, "Curlew!" In the distance, Hadi could see his two spotters gesturing toward the four stone curlew. Flushed from cover, the birds were flying low over the top of the dunes, gaining speed.

The falcon had just finished one circle and was beginning another, seeking altitude, when she veered hard right. Hadi's voice rang out, "She's found the prey!"

Kahlil stepped back, eyeing the scene. The Rovers and the van were parked twenty yards away. Rashad had positioned himself behind the military aide, who was standing only a few steps from Zahel, just outside the killing zone. There were only four others, the drivers and the falconers, but they were too distant to matter. Kahlil's knees felt weak. He fingered the small transmitter in his jacket pocket. The odds were slim that the explosion would fail to kill both men, but should that happen the Kurd's shots would not be expected in the confusion.

It was Rashad's mission, even if it cost him his life, to get to the AN/APQ 25/26 and to transmit the preprogrammed order that would compel the kingdom's military forces to "stand down," to remain on the ground, in port, and in their barracks until further notice. They needed only a few hours. By then, the demonstrators, the revolutionary cells, and the supporting units that were preparing to cross the gulf at the "request" of Arabia's new revolutionary leadership would be in control of the country.

A half mile away, Amin Shakir saw the peregrine at the instant she spotted his lure. The falcon leveled her wings and hesitated for a split second, the genetic circuitry of instinct charged and clashing with the conditioned response imprinted on her nerve fibers by a month of careful training. The curlew, accelerating, were skirting the low line of dunes to the south, getting away. Below, the signal, the familiar amid a wasteland of the unfamiliar, beckoned. She banked once and banked again, torn. Then, as it had been choreographed a hundred times above the Bavarian woods, the peregrine pivoted on one wing and dove.

Amin shortened the line, tightening the arc to draw the feathered bundle closer. The sequence would take only seconds. When the peregrine landed on his glove, he would kneel, securing the small parcel to her jesses with a single slipknot before allowing her to grasp it in her claw. Then, she would launch. The falcon's flight would be thirty seconds, no more. Shakir knew it would be straight, with no deviations, to her master, the king.

At fifty feet above the wadi, the peregrine flared her wings, braking for a landing, legs and talons thrust forward. Shakir dropped the lure and raised his arm expectantly. Then, without warning, he lurched forward sharply.

The noise and unexpected motion, sudden and violent, alarmed the falcon. The peregrine turned sharply, rocking as her wings lost lift, then veered away. Shakir spun and crumpled to his knees before he caught himself, as if finding his balance after a mischosen step. The 7.62-mm bullet had struck him in the soft flesh of the neck above the collar bone, passing cleanly through muscle, larynx, trachea, and arteries, and releasing the deluge of blood that was rapidly filling his lungs. Dying but not yet dead, from a distance he seemed to sway like a man communing in a morning devotion.

Two hundred yards away, Ali Abar Jabal, the finest rifleman of all the Quraysh, chambered another round, muttering a brief prayer of thanks for Allah's guidance and the clean shot. As instructed, he had followed the man from the camp, watching and waiting through the night. The man was not one of the desert, but he had been careful, following the dark side of the moonlit dunes, crossing the open spaces bent low, and passing the night protected among the shadows, unmoving. It was evidence enough for the Quraysh to recognize the trained habits of the spy or assassin, but the orders had been clear: be certain.

Ali lowered the long, matte black barrel of the U.S. M-21 sniping rifle an imperceptible amount, placing the cross hairs of its nine-power telescopic sight on the small of Shakir's back. The adjustment, framing the body from shoulders to knees in the small crosshatching, compensated for Ali's own elevation above the target and for the arching trajectory of the bullet. The dark, wiry marksman exhaled slowly, relaxing himself from head to toe, and nestled his cheek against the walnut stock. Then, with a steady motion, he hooked his right forefinger around the trigger and squeezed.

At the instant Amin Shakir snapped to attention, throwing his shoulders and arms back as the slug smashed through his spine and ended his

life, the rear doors of the falconer's van slammed open and a horrified
Kahlil bin Zahel watched the four Quraysh spill out. The distant sound
of the two rifle shots had frozen him in shock, although not Rashad Shakir. Stepping toward the king, Shakir was clawing for the Astra .357 magnum inside his jacket. At less than twenty yards from him, the first
Quraysh loosed a full automatic burst from his FLN assault rifle. The
bullets stitched a series of vicious red wounds across Shakir's buttocks and
legs, knocking him sprawling to the ground. The fusillade from the three
other Quraysh poured into Rashad before he could move further. Kahlil
wobbled fearfully as he watched Rashad roll sideways, half-twisting, legs
askew, tumbled by the simultaneous high-velocity impact of eighty rounds
burying themselves in his body.

Kahlil sunk to his knees, feeling and yet not feeling the hands that
grasped his arms, yanking and binding them behind him. He tried to
rise, a reflex action, but the boot of the Quraysh that jammed into his
neck bent him like a supplicant, forcing his face into the sand. The recognition that he was dead, even while he was living, permeated every
fiber of his being, evoking a long, pathetic moan.

"Why did you betray me, Kahlil, son of my brother?" King Zahel's
voice came from above him, its sound sad, rather than angry.

Kahlil sobbed, "No, Zahel, please." He tried to raise his head, but
the weight pressed down, doubling him into a fetal position. Kahlil felt
the warm wetness spread over him as he lost control of his body, waiting
in paralyzing fear for the destructive force of the bullet that would blow
out his brains.

"Do not worry, Kahlil, you are not about to die. The Quraysh will
not kill you, not one of the Zahel clan whom they are sworn to defend."
Zahel paused, watching the shudder wrack the bent human form before
him. Kahlil wept. "Your friends, the Kurds, did not matter to us," Zahel
said, "but you do."

Kahlil choked, breaking his silence, "Oh, thank you, please, thank
you."

Zahel bent low, his robes brushing his nephew, to stroke Kahlil's head,
"You are part of my flesh and blood. We must talk. We must have a
long talk. You must help me understand."

"Oh, please, thank you," Kahlil whimpered in gratitude.

Zahel straightened, shaking his head slowly. Kahlil could not see the pained expression on the king's face, "Do not thank me, Kahlil. I still must do what I must. You will explain everything. Every detail. To my satisfaction. Then, and only then, my brother's son," the old man said, his voice touched with pity, "when we have learned what we need to know, you will die."

Kahled bin Muhammed was a man of the evening who enjoyed the cool that came after the desert's scorching heat and before its nighttime cold, a preference that required the minister of defense's office in Riyadh to be perpetually in twilight, lights low and curtains drawn. A tall man, he sat with the same imperious bearing that distinguished him when he stood, causing even his aides to pause, waiting to be summoned, before they approached his desk.

Lieutenant General Haya bin Suleiem, the vice commander of the Royal Arabian Air Force, was no exception. As always, he had stopped on the edge of the circle of light, the only brightness in the expansive office, that illuminated the minister's giant glass-and-gilt desk. Suleiem watched Kahled as he held the secure telephone, listening to his caller without speaking. Aside from his temper, Suleiem thought, the defense minister was unusual in one other respect, the lack of the usual Gilbert and Sullivan comic-opera adornments favored by the royal family on their military dress when they chose to wear a uniform rather than a thobe, their traditional flowing robes. Kahled was dressed in the simple khaki of a desert soldier, the only distinguishing brass the four stars on his collar and the command pilot's wings above the left pocket on his chest.

Suleiem automatically pulled himself to a stiffer attention as Kahled bin Muhammed put down the phone. They had been waiting for the call. "That was Jabrin," the defense minister's voice was a monotone. "The two are dead and we have Kahlil."

Suleiem nodded as Kahled continued, "You are ready?"

"We are. Three flights and two squadrons." The Air Force vice commander looked at his watch, "It is 7:15 a.m. Their engines are running and they are ready for launch."

"Then," Kahled bin Muhammed said, "send them."

The defense minister watched Suleiem turn and stride to the door. The F-16 Falcons would be airborne, flying their low-level evasive triangle course across the Persian Gulf within three minutes. The F-15 Eagles, the protection for the strike fighters, also would take off to climb and hold at 25,000 feet, just inside the ADIZ, the Air Defense Identification Zone, that left them within Arabian airspace but still poised to provide air cover for the F-16s on their homebound dash over the gulf.

Kahled bin Muhammed glanced down at the red-striped folder before him. The bold lettering spelled "Top Secret/The Minister of Defense Only" in Arabic and English. Kahled lifted the cover. The long fifteen-part cable was the only paper inside. On the first page, the "From" line was printed in boldface just below the "Top Secret Sensitive" security classification. He read the words aloud, "Embassy of Saudi Arabia/ Ottawa."

He stared for a moment, lost in thought, and then snapped his fingers. Misha'al Salman, Kahled's private secretary, stepped from the shadows, pausing beside him.

"God works in strange ways, Misha'al."

Kahled closed the folder, extending it without looking to his aide, "But his will is always done, whether it is written plainly, generations in advance, for all to heed, or revealed by the Almighty to only one among the millions, a half a world away, just in time."

"In truth, minister," Misha'al Salman took the folder with both hands in the traditional pose of a retainer accepting a gift, "Allah be praised."

At that moment, 550 miles away, on the twenty-fifth floor of Jidda's Meridien Hotel, Lieutenant Ibram Hamdi fingered the key to suite 2512 and straightened from his crouch. Even with his ear pressed to the door, he could hear no sound inside. Hamdi looked at his watch. It was 7:20 a.m. Ten minutes ago, downstairs, the day manager had recognized Musaani at once. Hamdi motioned to the two men on either side of the hotel suite's door. They stepped in front of him, leveling their Heckler & Koch machine pistols. Behind them, two others moved forward to take their place as the second pair who would crash through the door.

Hamdi reached between the two special-action-team officers, inserting and turning the key. The door opened without a click. He pushed it gently, waiting for the restraining tug of the security chain. There was none. Puzzled, he paused, but there was no other choice, "Now!"

The two boots crashed into the door. The five men surged down the narrow hall. Hamdi and the first two officers ran straight, dropping to their knees as they crossed the threshold of the sitting room. The drapes were drawn back, revealing the Red Sea sparkling in the new day. The room was empty. Behind him, Hamdi heard the crash as the bedroom and bathroom doors slammed open. The cries were simultaneous and identical, "Nothing!"

Hamdi stood, rubbing his eyes, feeling suddenly very tired.

The voice came from the bedroom, "Lieutenant."

Hamdi holstered his pistol, and walked slowly down the hall. Inside the bedroom, the suitcase was open on the queen-sized bed.

The officer stood back, "These are his only belongings."

Hamdi stared at the clothes. The robes, a silklike Egyptian cotton, were finely made and new, as were the linen slacks, French knit sport shirt, and Italian slip-on shoes, clothes that would be owned by any well-to-do Arab. The passport was lying on the bed. Hamdi picked it up, examining the document. It was stiff, unsoiled, obviously new. He opened the cover. In the photograph, Musaani's face looked familiar, although this time from a different, full-front angle, a bit younger.

He turned the page. Name, Alireza Ali Zanal. Born, Riyadh, August 28, 1944. Now resident, London. Occupation, banker. Hamdi dug through the suitcase. There were no other clothes or personal effects, no socks, underwear, or toiletries. He stepped to the closet, peering inside, and glanced in the bathroom. Both were empty. Someone had already pulled open the dresser drawers. They were the same.

Hamdi looked at the passport photo again. He remembered the Pakistani he had overheard in the coffeehouse a few weeks ago, railing against the Indian Hindu infidels who believed man died and was reborn. Hamdi shook his head. In this case, the odd belief seemed appropriate. With the only mortal remains of Alireza Ali Zanal before him—a passport, two new robes, a shirt, a pair of slacks, and shoes—the Saudi banker had indeed found rebirth.

Hamdi frowned, tossing the passport into the open suitcase, and stepped into the hall. He walked to the windows in the sitting room. Even through the tightly sealed smoked glass, the morning sun already felt and looked hot. In the distance, Hamdi saw smoke rising along the waterfront.

Odd. It was the district where they had just completed the telephone exchange and government center. All the buildings were new, with concrete and steel construction, sprinkler systems, and alarms, not like the wood-and-stucco godowns on the old wharves where most of the blazes took place. The sirens sounded faraway, muted. Hamdi stared and listened for a moment, wondering again about the fire, before turning away. Reborn or not, he thought, the Iranian wasn't here. The fact was, Hamdi had started checking hotels at the wrong end of the list. After a night's work, he had nothing. Rajid Musaani had disappeared.

Twenty-five minutes later and 950 miles northwest of Jidda, at exactly 7:55 a.m., Captain Hassan Walid Raman stared through the HUD, the Heads-Up Display that projected his F-16's speed, altitude, bearing, and bomb-target computer data before him. The small glass plate mounted above the aircraft's instrument panel glare shield allowed him to monitor his instruments as well as watch the Iranian coast streak beneath him. At 150 feet and 500 miles an hour, the digital counter that measured his distance-to-target was rolling to zero. His flight had traveled east over the gulf and then swung northwest, paralleling the Iranian shoreline to disguise its approach. Strung out behind Raman's lightweight fighter-bomber at ten-second intervals, four other F-16s were also preparing to pop up, to shoot skyward toward 2000 feet in a split second, in order to identify their target.

Raman eyed the miles-to-target counter. Five, three, one, zero.

He touched the mike button, "Popping up."

Raman pulled back on the small control stick in his right hand. The minicomputer mounted forward of the cockpit responded to the electronic message instantaneously, signaling the hydraulic servo units to activate the horizontal stabilizers. The F-16 stood on its tail, compressing Raman's body with six Gs, six times the pull of gravity, as he angled into the sky. At 1900 feet, Raman pushed the stick and rudder pedals right, looking down at the world through the top of the bubble-glass-dome canopy as the F-16 arched. The two parallel runways lay ahead of and beneath him.

He touched the mike button for a final time, "Rolling in."

For him, there was only one more act. To release the two 500-pound cluster bombs under his wings on target. Then, he would push the throttle to the wall, lighting the afterburner to energize the 24,000 pounds of turbofan thrust, point the nose south over the gulf, and climb at twice the speed of sound toward home and the protection of the F-15s that were heading north to meet them.

One mile distant and 2000 feet below the Saudi Air Force F-16, on Büshehr Air Base, Radar Officer Sadeq Hedayat only had time to yell. In the darkened aircraft-warning-and-control center, the morning had been quiet because of the special flying stand-down, making him sleepier than normal for the first day shift. The blip that suddenly shot across his empty ground-control-approach radar screen at first made him blink. It was in the middle of the flight path and climbing above the base. There had been no warning of impending attack—only the advice that there were Saudi fighters at 25,000 feet circling in their own airspace across the gulf —and no air traffic authorized at Büshehr because of the secret mission. Hedayat's eyes widened. Another blip was climbing at almost 600 miles an hour behind the first, which had arched and started to descend.

Hedayat reached for the command center phone, "Unidentified bogies, unidentified bogies, zero miles out, 1000 feet." A third green dot appeared behind the first two, then a fourth.

"Two more bogies, two more bogies," Hedayat screamed into the phone. He punched the red alarm button. Outside he could hear the wail of the air-raid siren he had just activated followed by ragged fire of a heavy machine gun. Then, the room vibrated, shaken by the first heavy crump of an exploding bomb.

A half mile from the windowless, darkened radar control center, Captain Nassir Ghazali felt, rather than heard the explosion. At idle, the vibration and noise from the twin turbines and rotors of the giant CH-47 helicopter more than dominated his senses, blocking out any other sound on the flight deck. Puzzled, Ghazali glanced at his copilot, about to key his microphone button, when he saw the horror in the man's eyes. He was looking past him, skyward. Ghazali turned, following the copilot's line of sight. Above them the sleek jet was glinting in the sun as it grew in size, falling in a graceful earthbound arc.

"Attack! Attack! Take off! Take off!" In Ghazali's earphone, the tower controller's frantic voice seemed somehow jarringly discordant as he watched, mesmerized. The fighter was beautiful, a perfect symmetry of form and motion, an exquisitely designed shape in a strikingly dramatic diving flight.

Ghazali felt the familiar vibration as the copilot advanced the throttle to takeoff power. The two specks were falling from the wings of the silver plane in slow motion, tumbling in unison as well as in tandem. Fascinated and unable to turn away, Ghazali ignored the screaming voice beside him. The copilot pulled up on his own collective and control sticks, wrenching Ghazali's out of his hands. He felt the Chinook's tail lift. The helicopter pitched forward, struggling to rise, just as the two oblong shapes struck the runway.

It was a wonderful bloom, orange at the center, with fragile soft edges, like the rare hibiscus he remembered seeing with his father and mother at the arboretum in Tehran as a young boy. Like the flower's, the petals spread, folding and closing over themselves. Then, coming toward him, he saw the specks. They were black flecks imposed on the brightness behind them. They seemed to create a cloud, like seeds from a broken pod spread by the wind.

The shower of two-pound cluster bomblets ripped into the helicopter at 400 miles an hour, exploding and tearing it to pieces. Behind the cockpit, there was barely time for those of the forty heavily-laden commandos strapped into the canvas sling seats who survived the blasts to scream. The spray of fuel from the ruptured tanks vaporized, filling the inner space and hitting the hot turbine blades exposed as the bomblets tore open the twin engines above them. The fuselage flared, a single inferno, and then exploded as the ammunition, hand grenades, and mortar shells incinerated.

The bulkhead between the flight deck and the cargo bay held the flames for less than a second before the 1000-degree heat melted the aluminum. In the pilot's seat, Ghazali saw the arboretum. It was more beautiful than he ever remembered, and his mother and father were standing beside the flowers. For only an instant, he felt more heat than he had ever known in his life. Then, the second bloom, redder this time, more like a rose than a hibiscus, opened and closed around him.

Forty-five minutes later and 200 miles to the south, Ensign Akhbar Radi saw the white bow wake roll upward against the gray sides of the Saudi corvette as the missile boat veered toward them. The voice of the lookout standing beside him went up the scale several octaves, "Enemy ship, enemy ship! Starboard quarter. Two thousand yards."

Radi glanced at the channel traffic. Their nighttime crossing of the gulf had been uneventful, but he had started to worry at dawn when he saw the patrol planes. He had changed course toward the west, aiming for Doha, and then, close to land, turned east before heading south again for the run into the Bahrain channel. There were only a few other ships nearby, two oil lighters and a cargo ship in front of them and a container ship and two tugs to the port side. Faster now, with most of its fuel gone, the hovercraft was skimming the water at forty-five miles an hour.

The frantic beeping made Radi start. Behind him, at the radio-and-radar workstation, the communicator had turned a ghastly white.

"Radi, they are painting us," the man's voice shook. The hovercraft's electronic warfare sensors had picked up hostile radar, identifying the signal from the corvette's fire-control system. It was "painting" the hovercraft with the radar's electronic pulses, identifying their distance, course, and speed, before feeding the data into the computer that would aim the ship's weapons.

Radi turned to the lookout, "Musaavi, what is it?"

"The number is 612," the lookout squinted through his binoculars, reading the serial number on the ship's bow. Radi flipped quickly through the laminated plastic pages of the Saudi Arabian naval order of battle that was clipped to his chart stand. Missile Corvette 612, the "Badr," 245 feet long. Carries eight Harpoon ship-to-ship missiles in four quad mounts. Also one 76-mm gun, one 20-mm Phalanx rapid-fire gun, and six anti-shipping torpedoes.

Radi felt the perspiration drip from his chin. They were too elusive for the 76-mm gun, too far away for the Phalanx, and an impossible shot, cruising on a cushion of air six feet above the water, for torpedoes. The Mark 92 fire-control radar on the corvette was painting them to fix the target for the Harpoons.

Behind him, Radi heard the fast beep of the radar warning signal shift to a wavering squeal. The corvette's acquisition-and-targeting radar was preparing to lock on, to hold them in a permanent grip, feeding the data into the weapon system and readying it to fire.

"Hard to port, full speed!" The hovercraft banked left, pounding over its own wake, and accelerated. "Make for the container ship and the tugs!" The radar warning tone was now a steady whine.

"Lock on!" The communicator cried out.

A half mile ahead, Radi could see the deck crew of the tugs staring up from their work at the hovercraft. He looked back. The slower Saudi corvette, bow wake boiling white, was dropping behind but following dead on their trail. Their only prayer was to make the captain of the corvette pause. They were dead men if the Harpoon fired, but a miss close by the tugs and the container ship could destroy the innocent. They might be safe if they were close enough. If. The steady warning whine filled the bridge. Radi felt his lips moving silently in prayer. The hovercraft shot past the first tug.

Radi pointed at the container ship, its ungainly square shape, seemingly overloaded and unseaworthy for all but the calmest water, looming before them. The Japanese flag hung languidly from the stern. Off its bow, Radi could see the blue and white Manama harbormaster's launch approaching with the Bahraini customs and immigration officials. They would pull alongside and board, preparing the cargo ship for entry into port.

"Twenty degrees to port. Head directly for her."

The helmsman swung the small wheel, aiming for the container ship's massive, high square stern. The hovercraft was a quarter mile and closing. Suddenly, Radi froze as the silence overwhelmed them. The radar warning whine had stopped. The Saudis had broken off, or fired. He spun, fixing his binoculars on the corvette. Radi felt the relief wash over him. There was no smoking trail, no exhaust from a Harpoon shooting toward them. The "Badr" was heeling hard to starboard, turning away. Around him, the laughter was hysterical.

The towering side of the container ship sped past. The helmsman spun the wheel, putting the container ship's bulk between the hovercraft and the corvette. Twenty yards away, the Manama harbormaster's launch veered, dodging the gray shape that roared by at sixty miles an hour. Radi watched the white-clad officials standing in the stern grab for the rails and tumble as the hovercraft's wake rolled the boat beam to beam.

He clapped the helmsman on the shoulder, "Good work. To the harbor, full speed." Ahead, at the harbor's mouth beyond the entry buoy, he saw the Rapier coastal patrol boat turn sharply. The harbormaster's launch was already on the radio, reporting. The Bahraini coast guard would be waiting. Radi broke into a broad grin. Whatever they had in store for him, it would be better than the revolution and most certainly, much better than a flaming death at sea. But best of all, Radi thought, Manama was their port of call, and for him, the war was over.

At that moment, in Jidda, 820 miles away, Rajid Musaani slammed against the front seat of the taxicab, thrown off balance as the driver suddenly braked. The mob was eddying before them, blocking the way. Across the street, the smoke from the shopping arcade billowed from the first story, forcing the crowd to change course. A brick caromed off the hood, barely missing the windshield.

"Left! Turn left here," Musaani regained his composure, pointing down the narrow alley. The driver nodded vigorously, frightened and thankful for any advice, and wheeled the old Buick four-door sedan down the side street. It was deserted. The taxi accelerated, leaving the noise and the smoke momentarily behind.

Musaani sat back. It was over, over before it began. There had been no signal from Jabrin. Nothing. No word from Kahlil or the Shakirs. The riots and destruction had started on schedule but that was all. The army was on the streets in Jidda, out of its garrisons. The police were everywhere. There had been no stand-down order. It had gone wrong, badly wrong.

"The road ends," the taxi driver slowed, pointing to the heap of rubble, a demolished apartment, and the new construction that marked the terminus of the alley at a building site.

"Turn right," Musaani instructed, "and then, left again on Ruwais Road. Take me to the port." The cabbie swung into the alley, hitting the brakes again. Forty yards ahead, the roadblock, two police cars and a portable sawhorse barricade, sealed the intersection with Ruwais Road. There were four policemen, armed with automatic weapons. Two had turned to stare down the alley, waiting for them to proceed.

"Go ahead," Musaani dug for his identification, his stomach knotted. The ID was in the inside pocket of his jacket. He opened the high-buttoned neck, pulling out the Pakistani passport, and straightened his soft white cap. It matched the Karachi cut and labels of his gray-white cotton coat and slacks.

Musaani began bowing from the backseat even before the officer reached the car and nuzzled his rifle barrel against the window, signaling for it to be lowered.

"Yes, officer, terrible, terrible, isn't it?" Musaani slipped into the clipped hybrid English and rolling r's of a South Asian public school accent, ignoring the peremptory request in Arabic for his papers, "I'm sorry, so sorry. I only speak English."

Nervous and obviously short-tempered, the policeman asked again. Musaani watched his officer-in-charge walk toward the car. He was a sergeant. The senior policeman's hand thrust through the window, "Identification." Musaani handed him the passport.

"Muhammed Ali Singh?"

Musaani nodded vigorously, "Yes, officer, one of the faithful, Allah be praised, and a dealer in fine textiles from Karachi."

The pencil-thin artificial moustache and the makeup had darkened Musaani's complexion and visage considerably, matching the photograph as well as aging him to look fully the 51 years of age of the bearer described in the travel document.

"Where are you going?"

"Going? Oh, yes, going. Of course. To the hotel. This looks very dangerous, very dangerous, indeed."

The policeman returned the passport, "Get off the street. If we find you again, you will be arrested. Jidda is under curfew." The officer turned, motioning the two men to remove the barricade.

"Yes sir, yes sir." Musaani tapped the driver's shoulder, "Go, go." The Buick lurched forward and turned at the intersection.

Musaani sat back, breathing deeply. He spoke rapidly in Arabic, "To the port, quay 26, the Transcon shipping pier." The Iranian freighter was waiting for him. He looked at his watch. The arms and ammunition on board were useless now. He was to have directed the unloading. Instead of the beginning, it was the end. When he arrived, they would sail.

Musaani glanced up. The traffic was slowing, funneling into the right lane before it reached the high white wall that fronted the east side of street, on the left. Musaani reached for his passport, expecting another roadblock, before he saw the sandbagged bunker and above the wall, the flag. The taxi, moving in line, single file, rolled slowly past the two United States Marines in green battle dress, flak jackets, and helmets, who eyed them warily from behind the leveled M-60 machine gun. They were the first outpost, the first line of defense and security at the corner of the

American embassy compound. Fifty yards ahead, Musaani could see the larger emplacement, a hastily constructed, sandbagged pillbox with firing slits, reinforced with a cordon of trucks, blocking the entrance.

It was so like the Americans to have an army at their embassy, as if the world was theirs and they could not protect themselves without making Jidda's troubles their war. Musaani thought of DiGenero. In a way, what the FBI agent had done was the same. Musaani had used one American, and only one, Harris, to achieve the mission. Harris was important, but only a cog in the wheel, only an instrumental actor in the drama, not a central character. But because of him, DiGenero had doggedly pursued. He was only one FBI agent who had nothing to do with them, no duty to stop Iran, no personal connection to their cause, but it hadn't mattered. He had not stopped. Musaani couldn't prove it. But he knew, deep inside him, that DiGenero was the reason for all this. He had been enough. No, more than that. He had been too much. He had destroyed them.

Ahead, the traffic on Ruwais Road spread out, moving back into three lanes. Musaani glanced through the cab's rear window. Behind, beyond the American embassy, the smoke rose in columns straight up, hanging black against the sky. He sat back, exhausted and depressed, and closed his eyes. He could picture DiGenero's face in the eight-by-ten-inch print of the photograph they had taken in Montana. Unexceptional. Anyone's face. Anyone's at all. The fires would spread for a while longer and so would the mobs, roaming and burning, but neither mattered. It was already over.

Musaani looked out, staring as the old-and-new jumble of Jidda's bleached white buildings slid by and wondering whether Frank DiGenero ever would know what he had achieved.

26

Tuesday, November 13, 1984

Café Kopenhagen, 204 Kurfürstendam, West Berlin

"The message has come," Musaani twirled the glass desultorily in his hand. The beer was almost gone, leaving a trace of effervescence from the Pilsner

Urquel to coat the sides and the bottom. On the marble between them where the pitcher had been resting and then removed, the small, damp ring mimicked the roundness of the café table. Outside the window, the November rain made the midday light seem prematurely gray, presaging the early darkness that came with a north German fall afternoon.

Von Biemann looked up, surprised. His eyes darted nervously and then fixed on Musaani, trying to discern from his expression what he thought was in store. He waited anxiously for an elaboration. The Iranian was quiet. Finally, the German asked, "When?"

"When what?" Musaani repeated, obviously distracted. His voice sounded distant.

"When are you supposed to go?"

"Whenever," Musaani shrugged, "tomorrow, the next day, the day after. They merely said they were expecting me before the end of the week. I am to arrange my own transportation," he continued, his tone ironic, as he quoted the cable from memory, "'being careful to ensure my security and the secrecy of my travel.'"

Von Biemann bit his lip, fidgeting anxiously on the chair, "What else did they say?"

"Only that I am to report to Tehran." Musaani paused, sitting silently, his gaze holding the German's before he continued, "That's enough, isn't it?"

Von Biemann exhaled a long sigh, trying to compose and reassure himself. "Well," he cleared his throat, running his fingers through his hair, "so they want to talk. What's wrong with that?" He waved his hand, motioning for another beer. The waitress, her back turned, failed to see the signal. The German frowned.

"Talk?" Musaani looked away. "I said I'm to report to Tehran, not Qom."

"So?"

"Tehran is the intelligence headquarters of the Revolutionary Guards. It's not where people find casual conversation." Musaani sat back. "It's where they conduct formal interrogations and discover the causes for failure. And, after that, where they make judgments about who shall pay the price."

"And me," Von Biemann lowered his voice. "Did they say anything about me?"

Musaani stared at his table partner and then spoke flatly, "No." Von Biemann seemed to take no comfort in the negative reply. He looked away, still upset, watching the passersby who crowded beneath the neon, glass, and glitter of Berlin's most famous shopping street. Most were wrapped in raincoats and covered with umbrellas, bent forward as if to make their sizes and shapes conform with their small cones of portable protection.

Musaani noticed Von Biemann's pallor. He hadn't paid any attention until this moment. Klaus was not sporting his usual healthy, perpetual tan, but appeared worn, tired, and older, much older. Their six weeks of hiding in the East Berlin flat had taken its toll in more ways than one, he thought. After the catastrophe, Musaani had taken the Iranian freighter to Djibouti, flown to Addis Ababa, and then on Ethiopian Airlines to East Berlin. Von Biemann had been waiting. They had gone underground at once.

He was tired of being holed up as well, Musaani thought. Today's drive into the western sector of the city was their first outing since October. They had parked around the corner and walked directly to the small pub, one that Von Biemann remembered as a favorite spot from years ago. Von Biemann had wanted to go out sooner, Musaani recalled, but he had refused until today. Until he got the cable. After that, it didn't matter. The message was his death sentence. Under the circumstances, what difference did the risks of an outing make? Now, the question was—did he obey the cable or not? He would see. At least he had a few days to decide. At least it had not ordered him to Tehran immediately.

Von Biemann's voice broke his concentration, "You shouldn't worry." The reassurance sounded hollow, without conviction.

"Oh?"

The German spoke too categorically, trying to convince himself, "We did our best. You have your reasons. Besides, if the intelligence bureau was so interested in answers, they would have called you home earlier. Why would they wait until now? We've been in hiding for almost two months. They know you have friends here who can help you. They could have located you earlier if they had wanted."

Musaani examined Von Biemann's face. His eyes were open wide, searching for an explanation, an excuse, a reason to believe. It was the expression of a small boy who wanted to avoid accounting for a transgression, hoping against hope for an absolution that he knew would not come.

The Iranian sighed, "Anything you say, Klaus."

Von Biemann was agitated, "No, no, I mean, really..."

Musaani broke in, tired of the fear and whining, "Like everything else, this too has its time. Perhaps there were other questions to be answered first. Perhaps there were other people to be asked. Perhaps there were even some decisions to be made about who should bear responsibility. And, of course, there is the matter of technique."

Musaani shook his head as if silently sharing a joke with himself, "If the failure was mine, let us say for the purposes of discussion, they would not make the mistake of calling me home immediately. In that case, I might realize too soon what was in store and choose not to accept their invitation. Not to come. Instead, they would judge it wiser to wait. After a while, what am I to think? Weeks have passed. No one has questioned me. No threats have been made. Not even a hint that someone may have been dispatched to eliminate me. Perhaps this is simply to give me another assignment. Another mission. Perhaps. Hope springs eternal in the human breast, does it not?"

Von Biemann's hands were shaking, his eyes watery, "I don't like it."

"You don't like what?"

"I don't like being the hunted, the prey."

"Indeed? What makes you think you are?"

"Don't be silly," the German snapped, "Erique is dead."

They had found Von Biemann's brother in his hiding place, a house in Hamburg, a week after the operation failed, his throat slit, with wounds on his body that suggested the final knife stroke was a long time in coming. The Saudis, or perhaps the Iraqis, but someone on behalf of King Zahel, was beginning to exact revenge. Von Biemann was agitated, "The last six weeks, never going out, now, looking over my shoulder, waiting, watching. I think that's evidence enough."

"To prove that we're the prey?" Musaani asked, cocking his head.

"That's right."

"Oh, no," the Iranian's tone was matter-of-fact, "we are still the hunter, the predator. We are the same as we have always been. It's just that we've served our purpose. Now our masters as well as our enemies want to kill us. It's time to kill the wolf. Neither we nor they have changed.

Only our usefulness. Now all are joining in the hunt for the predator, rather than letting the predator hunt the prey."

"What's the difference?" Von Biemann looked perturbed. "It's a matter of semantics."

"Semantics?" Musaani rose, tossing a handful of deutsche marks on top of the check. "Not if you survive." Von Biemann stood slowly, preoccupied, his movements seeming unsure, not himself. It was time, Musaani thought, for them to go their separate ways. But for now, he would defer the decision. There were still a few days left, Musaani thought, to consider what to do next.

Outdoors, in the damp cold, the afternoon throng of shoppers, tourists, and office workers parted slightly to allow the two men onto the street. They turned right, joining the flow of pedestrians along the Kurfürstendam. After two blocks, they turned right again, edging sideways to slip past a paneled delivery truck that had stalled, blocking the alleyway, and walked, collars up and heads down, toward the burgundy Peugeot twenty yards ahead.

The East German diplomatic license plates gave them the privileges of the Berlin consular corps, including diplomatic immunity, allowing for the violation of no-parking zones at will. Because of the narrow street, they had pulled the Peugeot over the curb, leaving no room to open the passenger door. Von Biemann stood back, letting Musaani slip across the front seat before he sat behind the wheel. The German shut the driver's door, fumbling, his hands still shaking, with the key and ignition.

Beside him, Musaani waited, staring through the rain-covered windshield at the narrow street. It was then, when he saw the BMW, that he felt the sinking sensation and the chill. Ahead, a half block in front of the Peugeot, a gray four-door sedan, its windows tinted dark, had pulled into the next intersection, blocking the crossroad. Musaani twisted, scanning left and right. Unlike the Kurfürstendam and the alleyway they had passed before turning to walk toward the car, this narrow street was emptied of people. There was no one on the sidewalk. Either sidewalk. He swiveled, looking through the rear window. The stalled truck was coming toward them fast. They were trapped.

"Get moving, now!" Musaani screamed.

"What are you talking about?" Von Biemann had found his keys. He looked up, startled and annoyed, turning toward Musaani just as the truck pulled alongside the driver's door.

The paneled truck's sliding side door opened. The rain on the windows of the Peugeot made the truck's dark interior appear blurred and indistinct, but there was no mistaking the outline of the men who pointed the gun barrels at them. Von Biemann was about to speak again when the bursts from the Kalashnikov automatics, firing simultaneously, caught him, the hail of bullets suddenly lifting his lifeless body up from the seat and then sprawling him sideways in the front foot well across Musaani's legs.

Blinded by the spray of fractured window glass, blood, flesh, and torn upholstery, the Iranian instinctively raised his arms and ducked. But Von Biemann's dead weight on his legs now trapped him upright. The AK-47s' second chorus, more ragged but longer than the first, caught Musaani in the chest, slamming his torso against the passenger door. It was over in less than five seconds. As the truck's door slid closed, two apple-sized objects dropped through the Peugeot's shattered side window, bouncing on Von Biemann's twisted body, then rolling to rest on the blood-soaked seat.

Twenty-five yards away, at the corner of the Kurfürstendam, a few frozen bystanders peered down the street, watching the truck accelerate, following the fleeing BMW. In the awful vacuum of silence, one or two moved tentatively, venturing to overcome their shock, only to recoil again from the concussion, flash, and flying glass as the Soviet RGD-5 hand grenades exploded, tearing Musaani, Von Biemann, and what remained of the Peugeot's interior apart.

Eight hours later, at 10:30 p.m., the Berlin police captain put down the phone and regarded the grisly photographs and the plastic bags with the blood-soaked identification documents and the tattered East German automobile registration on his immaculate desk. Under the fluorescent lights of the municipal office, they appeared like stark specimens from a distant horror. The two homicide inspectors who stood before him waited silently for the captain to speak.

"That was Frankfurt. They've been helpful."

"Oh? What did they learn?"

The captain leaned back, playing with one of the AK-47 shells they'd found in the alleyway. "The man who rented the truck, in fact, took a flight from Tegel to Frankfurt. So, leaving the truck at the airport was not meant to deceive us. He's not in West Berlin or in the East. He's gone."

The first homicide detective, short, pudgy, and tired, rubbed his eyes,

"Wonderful. He's not in Berlin. Frankfurt's efficiency as always astounds me. That's very helpful."

The captain let the comment pass. The two detectives had worked all day before the murders occurred and now, because of them, were just completing their second straight shift. Given the fact they would work through the night on the case, the sarcasm was well within the limits of his tolerance.

He smiled paternally, "There's more. They held his connecting plane for him, and for four others who were on the same flight."

"That's not so unusual."

"That's right."

"So?"

"The five from the Berlin flight made up a group."

"Seating?"

The captain nodded, "The passenger manifest showed that they all requested seats in the same row."

"Where did they go?"

"Belgrade and Athens."

"Where else?" The homicide detective rolled his eyes, "This is even better than we could have hoped for." The Yugoslavs and the Greeks were next to worthless in any political case, preferring to make their own peace with terrorists, and turning a blind eye to their comings and goings.

The captain spoke, "I don't think the Jugs and the Greeks are our problem."

The pudgy detective knitted his brow, "The flight continued?"

"Well, yes and no. It seems on Tuesdays, Thursdays, and Saturdays, Athens is its last stop, but today the pilot said they had maintenance trouble. For some reason, he knew the Greeks couldn't fix it. So, he didn't overnight in Athens."

"And?" the detectives waited.

"And," the captain paused, "at 8:00 p.m., Iraqi Airlines flight 9938 made an unscheduled departure. For Baghdad."

Friday, November 16, dawned gray and overcast in Qom. The daybreak was coming later each morning as the winter approached, adding to the stillness of the hour. At 7:00 a.m., only one light burned in the Qara Su compound, on the top floor. It outlined a single form, a tall man, robed

and dark, who stood at the window of the office of the executive director
of the Committee, looking down.

Ayatollah Reza Hosein watched the small processional cross the central courtyard. The five men were there by his order, four in fatigue jackets who walked with purposeful steps and one in only a shirt who appeared
to be in the grasp of the others, moving with a shuffling gait.

Even from a distance, Reza Hosein could tell that Azhger Navadeh-
Taheni, the former executive director of the Committee, had already left
his mortal being behind. Reza Hosein watched until the group reached
the far wall. Taheni stood where they placed him, his back to the center
post, as they made the bindings fast. If he had looked up toward the suite
he once had occupied before the blindfold was cinched around his eyes,
he would have seen turn away the man who had chosen him to direct
the Committee as well as condemned him to die. The brief tattoo of rifle
shots broke the silence before Reza Hosein reached the desk. He paused,
waiting. The pistol shot, a single crack, followed.

Reza Hosein sat down, staring at the English text of the wire service
news ticker that lay atop the file before him. The Reuters story was two
days old, with a West Berlin dateline. It gave few solid details, but what
it said was enough to convince him the killings had the mark of the Iraqis.
Bloody, public, with no finesse. Whoever had pulled the trigger, however, he knew it was Riyadh's revenge.

Hosein put the news story aside, thinking. The Revolutionary Council had demanded a full accounting. He had wanted to question Musaani
himself, to learn from him where he needed to go in order to take care
of all the loose ends, but in a way it was just as well. The interrogation
would have been more a matter of form than substance. Hosein had already advised the Council that the final report on the case, when it was
concluded, would contain no new details other than those he had already surfaced. One always has enemies who look for weaknesses and
openings, Hosein thought, and he did not want to give them such op-
portunities by contradicting his own statement.

Nonetheless, he reminded himself, there was a task yet undone. He
opened the desk drawer, removing the red-tabbed folder. He thought of
Taheni. Even to the end, with the operation collapsing around him,
Taheni's lawyerly mind, schooled in a punctilious attention to detail, had
been in command. Red tabs were target folders, designating those people
who could threaten the Committee's mission. The folder was the only

remaining one that required Reza Hosein's attention and, given what he had told the Revolutionary Council, his attention only. The name, in English, was stenciled, black on red, across the protruding tab. With Musaani, Von Biemann, and now, Taheni gone, the postmortem on the operation was almost complete. Almost.

Hosein slipped the file into his briefcase. He would dispatch someone personally to accomplish the task in a few months, when the time was right, after attention to the mission and its failure had waned. After there no longer appeared to be a requirement for vigilance and watchfulness. Then and only then would it be done, when the odds favored success and their target's guard was down.

Hosein rose. A single folder remained on the desk. He opened it to see Rajid Musaani smiling at him in a full-front photograph taken by the counterfeit-passport technicians. Hosein removed a manila envelope that had been inserted loosely behind the photograph. Yellowed with age, it was covered with initialed and dated routing stamps, cachets that had once moved it from one bureaucrat's in-box and file drawer to another. The largest stamp was fading, a circle enclosing the letters "IIA" imposed over a winged eagle background. Beneath it, the fine print was still legible, "Iranian Imperial Army, Retired Personnel File, Major Machmed Musaani." Reza Hosein stood, putting the manila envelope under his arm. It too was another detail. Then, he picked up his briefcase and walked out.

Eighteen hours later, on the outskirts of Tehran, the sense of an early winter permeated the night air, causing the old man to draw the thin blanket more tightly around him. Despite the tiny high window, the thick walls, and the narrow confines that trapped the heat and smell of even a single body in the cramped cell, the small cubicle was always too cold or too hot, never varying more than a few degrees in temperature from the outside, scorching in summer and, as he knew, chilling like ice on flesh when the winter started to come.

Machmed Musaani felt himself beginning to doze until he heard the sound. In the distance, the approaching footsteps echoed hollowly. It was the guard's tread, unremarkable but nonetheless a subject of interest for anyone in solitary confinement. Such mundane things created the events that were the only distinctions in the empty hours, day and night, he spent alone in the cell. The rough metal-on-metal insertion of a key grated on the silence. The cell door clanged open.

"Get up! Follow me!"

The old man struggled stiffly to his feet, blinking in the shaft of harsh light that bisected his darkness. He pulled on his laceless shoes and straightened, automatically assuming a military bearing. Oddly, instead of waiting for him to emerge from the cell, the guard turned his back and disappeared after signaling him to follow.

Thirty yards down the corridor, the guard stopped, motioning Musaani into an open doorway. He recognized the interrogation chamber. He had passed it many times on his way to the exercise yard, but this was his first visit during his two months in the small prison. In a way, the fact that he could not even expect interrogation after a time had made it all the worse. Two months. Eight weeks. No reason to be there. No one to talk with. Nothing, day after day. Only waiting, alone. He walked in slowly.

"Sit!" The guard pointed at the wooden stool that was positioned before the scribe's small desk and chair. Bewildered, curious, and frightened, Musaani stepped obediently forward and sat. The door closed with a solid, final sound.

Five minutes later the man appeared. Musaani rose, as he had been trained to do. He recognized him as one of the senior prison officials, or so Musaani thought because of the deference he once saw the guards pay him. The man sat. He wore no uniform, but dark pants, white shirt, and mismatched suit jacket. He placed a single file before him, letting several moments pass before motioning the old man to resume his place.

Musaani watched him read silently. Then, he spoke, "Machmed Musaani, Major, Imperial Army of Iran. Assigned last to the Niavaran Palace. Position, falconer to the Shah." The man looked up, his face contorted into a sneer of contempt, "Excuse me. The ShahanShah. The Shah of Shahs. His Imperial Highness." He turned slightly and spat, barely missing the edge of Musaani's stool.

Musaani felt himself looking down from above, as if he was watching a scene that had already been recorded, played, and chronicled for posterity. He had heard the gunshots before. Sometimes during the day, sometimes late at night, and waited, wondering when it would be his turn.

He had to concentrate, listening hard to the next words. The man appeared to be perusing the paper for the first time before he read from the file, "Machmed Musaani, you are released as of this hour. You are to return to your home." The old man stared, obviously confused, as if hearing a foreign tongue. "You are to adhere to two requirements if you wish to keep your freedom. First, you will not tell anyone of your work in Germany." The man looked at Musaani, this time speaking more slowly, "And, you will never mention or seek after your son."

Suddenly, Musaani understood. He felt no pain, only a dull emptiness. The anger, grieving, denial, and regret were behind him. It was as if after a long and tiresome search, he had finally concluded that a once-prized object was irretrievably gone. He voiced his thought, "He's dead."

The man stared back at him for several moments, then rose, closed the folder, and walked to the door. There, he paused and turned, "I know nothing of this. I have only one piece of advice. Treasure your good fortune, old man. You have been given your life, or whatever is left of it. That is all. You have no right to ask for anything else, and there are no obligations to give you any answers." Musaani stared after him, hearing his steps fade. There was no clang of locks or keys. The door was open, unguarded, and the man was gone.

For the three street sweepers who stood, taking their first break of the day in their usual place across from the entrance to the Riyadh Zoo at 7:00 a.m., on Thursday, November 29, the bleak desert dawn was unexceptional save for the procession that sped past them and turned sharply left, tires squealing on Jareer Street, disappearing west. The prison was only a half mile away and the white, unmarked Volvo van was a familiar sight. It regularly transported the unfortunate from the Directorate of Public Security in the North Murabba district of Riyadh to the prison's high white walls. But the limousine and the dark sedan accompanying the van were unusual. One of the men, the oldest, bent and toothless, cried out, pointing at the rear of the long black Cadillac, claiming that he had seen a palace license plate. The other two, younger with better eyes, laughed, chiding him good-naturedly about his confusion. The trio then returned to their sweeping, the younger two not knowing that their friendly derision was unfounded. The old man had been right.

The small procession had left the prison minutes before. A half mile further west, the two cars and van decelerated slightly, turning at the sign for the Riyadh Stables. The road to the stables was deserted, as were the clustered stalls and corrals. The van and cars veered onto a service road that led away from the long low buildings housing the purebred Arabians and the riding stock, and toward feed storage sheds. Ahead, the van's driver saw that the police lorry and the ambulance, having arrived earlier, were waiting, parked in a semicircle in front of the storage sheds.

As the van, the car, and the limousine slowed to a stop, the figures appeared from the waiting vehicles simultaneously, moving purposefully and without ceremony. The doors of the white van opened, allowing the two police officers who had climbed out of the sedan to step up on the bumper and reach inside. Each grasped the arm of the dazed and blinking man who emerged unsteadily. His white robe, uncinched at the waist, seemed to catch on his heels, but the policemen caught him before he fell, easing his weight to the ground. They bound his wrists swiftly behind him, pausing when they were through to yank once on their handiwork, checking the knots. Then they began to walk, keeping their grip tight as they led Kahlil bin Zahel into the center of a small parking area that fronted the storage sheds.

Defense Minister Kahled bin Muhammed lowered the rear window of the stretch limousine, watching, his breath frosting in the morning air. Beside him, the prison superintendent, an obviously nervous if not frightened man, studied the defense minister with trepidation, leaning forward in attentive deference on the small jump seat.

Kahled's voice was low and final, "There will be no records."

The superintendent bobbed his head vigorously, "Yessir. You have every scrap of paper in the folder beside you. There is no other document that would even suggest that the prince has been in our charge."

"And these men?"

"They know nothing. Simply that it is a summary execution ordered by the defense ministry. That is all."

The defense minister's face was a portrait of disgust, "At least Musaid, Faisal's assassin, could pay his price publicly." Nine years before, in 1975, Faisal bin Musaid, a nephew of King Faisal, had shot his uncle in his chambers. Kahled continued, "Musaid was deranged but he acted alone. Not like Kahlil. Not like a dog on the Iranians' leash. In the House of Zahel, we have never had a traitor in our midst. Those who would kill for revenge or retribution, yes. But never one who would sacrifice the kingdom to its enemies. Until now."

The superintendent shifted uneasily on his seat as the defense minister continued, "Kahlil does not deserve the honor of a public death. His life deserves only to be ended and forgotten. Do you know what that means?"

The superintendent swallowed hard as the defense minister, eyes cold as ice, continued, "Bury him in the sands, with no marker or map. Nothing to show the spot. Do you understand?"

"Yes, sir."

Defense Minister Kahled bin Muhammed now turned his gaze to the group outside. Kahlil and his two police attendants had stopped before a man who stood waiting by two hay bales, his arms locked behind him at a stiff parade rest. He was short, dressed in a dark winter thobe. Seeming to ignore the trio who had just joined him, his gaze remained riveted on the limousine. Then, the defense minister nodded. Unaware of the signal, Kahlil bin Zahel stepped forward as he felt the two policemen's restraining arms fall away, leaving him suddenly free.

The illusion of liberation was momentary. The hands that had held him now pushed hard, shoving him to his knees. Arms bound behind him, Kahlil hit the ground off balance, his body rocking forward until stopped by the hay bale. Then, the sharp prick of the executioner's sword jabbed his right side. He stiffened, jerking in a reflex, and pulled erect, surprised more than pained. The long thin blade came from above with a rush of breeze, severing his head cleanly two inches above the shoulder at almost the exact instant the sound of its wind, the last he would ever hear, struck his ears. His headless body sprawled spastically in final meaningless motion, then was still.

Almost at once, the long black Cadillac slipped into gear and turned. The two jailers bent over the body as the executioner slowly wiped his blade. None of the three looked back as the sound of tires and engine recorded the limousine's acceleration down the empty road.

27

Thursday, January 24, 1985

Federal District Court, Alexandria, Virginia

Under the ugly, suspended fluorescent fixtures, the courtroom already seemed to hold its full share of light, unneedful of the contribution from the long, church-style windows that arched toward the ceiling. Its heavy

oak benches and rails were polished to a dark sheen by age, the soft cloths
of a hundred years of courthouse custodians, and an uncountable number of hands. The chamber was sparsely filled and, on this winter's day,
too warm.

In the second-to-last row, DiGenero leaned back, the radiator beside
him banging its sharps and flats in no particular rhythm. Outside, the
overcast spat out a gritty snow. A few blocks east along Old Towne
Alexandria's dock, where he had paused before walking uphill to the court,
the raw northwest wind roiled the expanse of the Potomac River, hurrying the cold gray water downstream beneath the long, shallow arc of the
Wilson Bridge.

DiGenero studied the three men who were center stage in the courtroom. The prosecutor, a young assistant federal attorney, and the defense lawyer, older and taller, stood side by side at the bench, talking
quietly with the judge. In front of the robed, white-haired figure, the two
made a before-and-after picture, one on his way up the ladder, serving
his trade's internship for the state, and the other, silver-haired in a $1000
suit, on the top rung looking down, remembering when he'd done the
same, while anticipating the younger man's every move.

In the quiet, their low buzz of conversation died away. The prosecutor and the defense attorney returned to their places, two long tables
positioned an aisle's width apart, each an equal distance from the bench.
Harris was seated, his back to the spectators' gallery, beside his silver-
haired lawyer. He'd nodded at DiGenero ten minutes before when he'd
entered from a side door, then paid no more heed to him. Tanned, dressed
in an expensive blazer, conservative tie, and slacks, he looked casual and
at ease, although to DiGenero, a Harris not wearing blue jeans and
workshirt somehow seemed out of place.

The judge's voice, a deep southern accent modestly amplified by his
microphone, filled the courtroom, "The defendant will rise."

Harris stood. The Bureau liked to have the Justice Department do
business in Alexandria. The venue, the Federal District Court for the
Eastern District of the Commonwealth of Virginia, had its advantages. It
was convenient for arraigning fugitives extradited from abroad, a mere
thirty-minute ride from Dulles airport where they would first touch
American soil. And, thanks to Virginia politics with its Old South, old-
school ties, the Department could count on a stable of now fashionably

conservative judges who had been raised to the bench by presidents heed-ing the advice and consent of the old boys in the Senate, the pickers and choosers from among the right thinking. Most did their best to make cer-tain that spies, subversives, and other politically dicey cases that were even less clear-cut matters of law to the judicially faint of heart didn't get away.

Across the courtroom, to the rear, the motion of the swinging door caught DiGenero's eye. He started involuntarily as Erin entered and sat down at the end of the last bench, the first available place. He hadn't seen her since Ottawa. She looked wonderful. He found that he couldn't look away from her, any more than he had been able to stop missing her. The feeling of emptiness was physical, like a hollow in the pit of his stomach.

He watched her smooth down her upturned raincoat collar. Her wind-blown hair and reddened cheeks testified to the fact that she had just come indoors, probably hurrying after a late arrival and a rushed cab ride from National airport two miles away. For a moment she seemed distracted, as if nervous that she was an unauthorized intruder, off-limits in an of-ficially proscribed place. Then DiGenero saw her relax, collect herself. He turned away and then looked back. She didn't notice him, but in-stead stared straight ahead at the proceedings.

"In the case of the United States versus Kirby Harris, a plea of guilty having been entered by the defendant to the charges specified in the In-dictment 84-4325 handed down in the Federal District Court, Eastern District of Virginia on December 2, 1984, I hereby render my judgment."

The judge glanced up, examining Harris, who stood impassively, be-fore he continued. He spoke succinctly, "Kirby Harris, as specified and pled, I sentence you to serve a term of incarceration in a federal correc-tional facility for a period not to exceed five years. In addition, under the penalty provisions set forth in the federal Endangered Species Act, you are ordered to pay a fine in the amount of $100,000 to this Court in cash or certified check not later than February 1, 1985."

The judge paused, harshly clearing his throat, "In light of the exten-uating circumstances presented by your counsel and attested to by the United States attorney, it is my judgment that your sentence of incarcer-ation, but not your fine, should be suspended. I am therefore placing you on a supervised probation for the aforementioned five-year period."

The yawn from the front left of the gallery was inappropriately loud.

The microphone caught the sound of rustling paper as the judge tabled the documents, perturbed as he scanned the spectators for the culprit. DiGenero followed his gaze. Four rows away, he spotted the new press card clipped to the sport coat pocket of an obviously bored junior reporter, who was scrawling his notes, listening halfheartedly and oblivious to the judge's scowl.

The newspapers. DiGenero shook his head. What they found out, they usually got wrong, he thought, and what they didn't know would fill a book. The fuzzy-cheeked novice probably wrote for the suburban section. If his copy on Harris's case got more than a paragraph above the garden store ads, he'd be lucky. It was too bad. The real story would give him the front page.

The deputy assistant United States attorney at the prosecutor's table had spelled out the bargain the week before, when he informed DiGenero there would be no need for his testimony in court. DiGenero remembered his office. It was small, with just enough room for a desk and two chairs. Next door, the much larger corner suite for the assistant United States attorney was vacant. The deputy assistant's name was in the hat for the job, a candidate to move up, but for the time being he was "acting," filling the position held by his former boss, who had just left Justice for six figures in a well-known private firm. In retrospect, DiGenero thought, it explained a great deal.

The deputy, he remembered, had feigned a suitable degree of outrage, albeit well short of any hint he was about to fall on his sword to protest the deal. The telephone call, he said, had come from the legal counsel in the White House. What was he supposed to do? He had opened the safe behind his desk and shown DiGenero the cables. There were two "back channels," private communications that were distributed to only the addressees, both stamped "Secret, Eyes Only." One was from the American ambassador in Saudi Arabia to the secretary of state, and the other from the secretary of state to Riyadh.

The messages were informal, almost chatty. It seemed the Saudi defense minister had raised the matter with the ambassador at a small, private dinner two weeks ago, strictly as a "question" on behalf of the king. There was no request, really. Only the suggestion that the king had a personal interest, much as he did in the negotiations on emergency military base rights for American forces and, of course, the timing of the president's postelection visit to Arabia to announce his new Middle East peace plan. The outgoing cable from the Secretary a week later was short and to the point, instructing the ambassador to pass on the president's greetings to the king and to assure him his personal interests were well understood.

At the front of the courtroom, the judge slowly removed his glasses, folding them carefully before he spoke, "Mr. Harris, $100,000 is a small price to pay for your long and lucrative career in an illegal and dangerous business. You should count yourself lucky. And," the judge paused, "for reasons you know better than I, you should take a great deal of care." The gavel sounded once as the black-robed figure rose, stepping down from the high bench.

"Well, not much to that." Seated a few feet from DiGenero, the old man, one of the permanent spectators who made the courtroom theater a regular feature of his daily entertainment fare, muttered as he stood. DiGenero nodded, "Not much." Satisfied that his disappointment had been confirmed, the elderly retiree shuffled from his favorite place in the gallery.

Alone now on the long wooden bench, DiGenero sat, watching. Harris had half-turned, waiting for Erin who was walking toward him in the far aisle. Without looking back, the two stepped through the side door, following the attorney. From the rear of the courtroom, there was no way DiGenero could see Harris's face, but he didn't doubt that it was marked by a broad smile.

In moments, the room was empty. Behind DiGenero, the sound of voices faded, even outside in the hall. He didn't know why but he kept his place, his thoughts accompanied only by the ticking of the old clock high and to the right of the judge's bench. With each long stroke of the pendulum, the hollow inside him seemed to grow until he felt empty of everything except a dull ache.

The late-afternoon light was almost gone when the hand on DiGenero's shoulder made him start. He didn't know how long he'd been sitting since the courtroom had emptied. Nearby, southbound on Washington Street, the rush-hour traffic from the capital, the Pentagon, and Crystal City droned steadily. Along with the effects of the half darkness, the sound had buffered his senses, blocking the echo of footsteps behind him.

"I was outside, waiting. I wondered if you'd left by another door and I'd missed you."

DiGenero turned his head. Erin stood there, her coat buttoned, seeming uncertain at first like someone who had either just arrived or decided to go. Then, tentatively, she sat on the edge of the bench, one row behind him.

He had concentrated on the fact it was her, rather than on her words, "Waiting? For whom?" He winced at the stupidity of the question almost as soon as he said it.

"For you."

"Why?"

"To talk. It's been a long time." She smiled slightly and looked down, as if momentarily embarrassed. "Missoula seems another world, a lifetime away."

DiGenero noticed that the color of the cold was still on her cheeks, although Erin had paused to brush the wind's braiding and the dampness of the snow from her hair. The dark, full curls fell luxuriantly, bunched by her collar in a naturally soft adornment. She had caught him off guard. In the sudden presence of her beauty, his attraction to her made him feel oddly uneasy, like an adolescent who wanted to make a pass but feared the rejection that such a risky move might bring.

"Kirby skates again, doesn't he?" DiGenero said. The remark was a temporary refuge as he assembled his thoughts. "Why aren't you celebrating? One-hundred-thousand-dollar fine or not, I imagine he's still got enough loose change to buy you a drink and dinner."

"You don't understand, do you?"

He didn't reply.

"It's over, Frank."

DiGenero snorted, unable to repress his sarcasm, "You've got that right. Kirby pays his bill with Uncle Sam, the Saudis go away happy, the Iranians live to skulk another day, and I fly back to Salt Lake City toting the minor memory of two FBI agents, one dead and one shot-up, in my cerebral carry-on baggage."

Erin kept her hands thrust deeply in her pockets as she reclined against the bench, gracefully crossing her legs. It was the posture of someone who was settling back with something particular to say, "Don't blame yourself, Frank." She paused, "And don't blame me. If you do, you're wrong. We both did what we did because we loved him, each in our own way. That fact only affects us. It hasn't affected him."

DiGenero felt the muscles in his jaw harden, embarrassed and then angered that his verbal diversion had provoked this unsolicited sympathy, but he held himself back, keeping still. There was no pity in her voice, but a distinctive meter, a pace and pattern that gave away the fact she had thought long and hard about what she had said and was about to say, "Kirby is Kirby."

Erin captured his eyes with the singular warmth of her own, as she had the first time he'd seen her, "You know what Kirby likes to say? 'You pays your nickel and you takes your choice.'"

She looked toward the front of the courtroom, dark now in the evening shadows, as if searching for someone, "How did the judge describe it? A dangerous business? He was talking about the falcons, but it's more than that, isn't it? Laos, Cambodia, Vietnam. Kirby isn't satisfied with just remembering. It's over but he can't let it go."

Erin studied DiGenero as he listened to her speak. The hard outline of muscle along his jaw had softened. Her voice continued steady but low, just above a whisper, "He brought you into his world when he saved you. Then you discovered how different he was." She smiled, "And Kirby? He knew that you were different, too. Kirby knew that you understood what it was like. You do, undercover. You know because you were there, too."

She reached out, putting her hand on DiGenero's sleeve, "You know why you couldn't persuade him to stop? It didn't make any difference what you did. You couldn't warn him away. Everything you suggested— quitting, leaving the business, dropping Von Biemann—for Kirby, to drop the deal would have been the finish, the end, dying, suicide.

"You see, he wanted you to know. It mattered to him," Erin shook her head slowly, as if to emphasize the point. "He wasn't toying with you. You did him a favor. He knew that ultimately you'd have to come after him, but that was all right. That made it even better. That made you part of him, part of what kept him alive. That's why he couldn't give it up. And, you understood. That's why you mean so much to him."

Erin's eyes glistened softly with the sheen of dark water reflecting low light, "Besides, I wasn't talking about Kirby or the trial."

"What do you mean?"

"When I said it was over."

"Oh?" DiGenero raised his eyebrows.

"It's over between Kirby and me."

"Why?"

The tremor in her voice was barely perceptible, "I can't keep going up to the edge and looking over. I can't do it anymore." Erin smiled faintly, remembering, "I could once. He never fell off and he made it look so easy. I suppose it was the excitement that kept me going. It was as if I could do the same thing too. It was more than the fact he was different. It was as if his magic extended to me. I thought he was protecting me. I knew inside that he wasn't, of course. I cared and I was frightened that he would be caught, but it didn't happen. He never lost. Not until now."

"Lose?" DiGenero asked. "Look again. Kirby's walking. He didn't lose."

"Yes he did."

"What did he lose?"

Erin wrinkled her brow, momentarily puzzled, before she understood he had missed her point, "Me."

She bit her lip and then spoke, "I can't watch anymore, Frank. I can't. One day it will end and I don't want to be there. I loved Kirby for something I can't love him for anymore and Kirby won't stop."

"Even if you go?"

Erin paused momentarily as if mentally reviewing a complex chain of calculations, checking the subtotals, the additions and the subtractions, before arriving once again at the remainder. "Even if I go," she said.

"Does he know?"

"Does he know?" Erin repeated the question, surprised, as if its answer should have been understood. "Yes and no, I suppose. The same way he knows other things. I told him. He heard me say the words." Erin glanced away and then back. DiGenero saw her chin tremble as she continued, "It'll sink in after a while. After I stop coming to the ranch. After I leave Missoula." The tears that began streaming down her cheeks seemed incidental to the sadness of her words, "I don't hate him, or blame him, or want to have him out of my life. It's simply over. I can't love him anymore.

"Yes and no," Erin took a deep breath and wiped her eyes. "That's the right answer." She studied DiGenero's face in the shadows, trying to discern his expression, "Over isn't through, you know. You can be through with things, a book, a job, a place, but none of us are ever really through with each other."

DiGenero nodded. The words came automatically, simply, more easily than if he had planned to say them at that moment, "I love you."

Erin's eyes widened. Oh, she had heard him, but she wouldn't reply. At least not yet. Instead, she continued speaking of Harris, needing to finish one subject before beginning another, "And even if we could leave some people behind, no one can ever be through with Kirby." Her voice had sunk to a whisper, then stopped.

They sat without speaking for several moments. It was darker now, but through the long windows of the courtroom, the evening glow from the streetlamps had substituted a subtler, warmer light for the colorless, fading flatness of the winter afternoon. Finally, DiGenero stood, gazing down at her. His expression seemed neither happy nor sad, but familiar, with a clear look of understanding. She rose. They walked out of the building not touching but as close to each other as if they were.

Outside, they turned under the high lamps and the tree branches that were bent lower over the street. The snow had begun again, more than flurries, falling harder. The brick sidewalk, covered now with the heavy flakes, extended untracked before them. The street, quiet and empty, seemed cleansed, renewed by the whiteness. Neither spoke. DiGenero felt the pressure of Erin's hand tighten as she held his arm. He glanced down. Side by side, they paced in steps that were almost perfectly matched. Erin looked up at him and smiled. DiGenero noticed that the hollowness and the ache inside him were gone.

As they turned on the narrow sidewalk where St. Asaph met King Street, a Chrysler sedan pulled close to their side of the curb and honked. The frost and sticking snow obscured the face of the man who was leaning across the passenger seat.

"Hey, Frank!" Above the top of the fogged, half-open car window, Harris's voice was unmistakable as was his smile. "Can I give you a lift?"

DiGenero glanced at Erin, who had stopped abruptly, neither stepping toward the car nor continuing.

"Thanks, I think we'll walk."

"Oh, come on," Harris feigned a hurt expression, "here I am with this big, rented pimpmobile and nobody to put in it. Hey, no hard feelings, right? After all, just consider it the first game in the series. Lions one, Christians nothing." Harris laughed out loud, "Why don't you two let me buy you a drink?"

DiGenero looked at Erin who shook her head, before he spoke, "Some other time."

Harris snorted in mock anger, "Well, goddamn, a sore loser. OK,

J. Edgar, I'll just forget about your unsportsmanlike conduct this time, but when you're back in god's country, I'm going to be mad as hell if you don't stop by the ranch. I've got a couple first-class birds I'm saving just for you."

DiGenero couldn't repress his smile, "Kirby, you're a prizewinning, no-good bastard."

The laugh, this time louder, hung in the cold air. The Chrysler's rear tires sung on the pavement, spinning and fishtailing the car as Harris sped away.

Five miles away, on the corner of 20th Street N.W., the glass-walled top floor of 1995 K Street, the windows of the law offices of McNally, Hardesty and Markham, glowed brightly as it did late into every night. Most of the partners had already gone about the evening's business—dinner appointments, embassy and Capitol Hill receptions and cocktail hours, or for a few, home. Only the firm's junior attorneys were still hunched over their desks. Among them, the truly ambitious were getting their second wind. They would work until midnight or later, researching and recording the fine points of law. Their mind-numbing tasks provided the minutiae, proving their professional betters' instincts were right and allowing them to hope their endurance ultimately would earn the accolade "partner," rather than consigning them to remain, until asked to leave, an "associate" of the firm.

Shortly after 6:30 p.m., the few who bothered to look out of their offices noticed the uncharacteristic pattern at once. "The Gray Ghost," their nickname for the most imperious as well as silver-haired partner responsible for the firm's lucrative international business, was walking the tall dark man, obviously a foreign client, along the inner corridor, seeing him to the door. It was unusual, to say the least. The attorney had just returned from concluding a case in Alexandria. He almost always delegated such social obligations to his secretary, and the courtesy, when extended, marked those who received it as his most privileged and powerful clients.

When the attorney again entered his office, his secretary was waiting, stenographic pad in hand. The heavy manila envelope was resting where his visitor had left it on the edge of his long, polished teak desk. He lifted the bronze letter opener and slit the fold of the heavy paper gently, removing the oversized certified check.

"We'll need two transmittal documents, Harriet."

"Yes sir," his secretary watched as he placed the check on the table and turned, eyeing the driving snow illuminated by the headlights of the snarled traffic on K Street.

"First, the $200,000 deduction to our account to cover our fee and the fine. In the case of the latter, the $100,000 should be sent via our certified check to the Clerk of the Federal Court, Eastern District, etcetera, etcetera. You know the transmittal format."

"Yes sir."

"And, the balance," he glanced over his shoulder, needlessly but habitually checking his calculations, "$800,000. That should be transmitted to the account of Mr. Kirby Harris."

"Yes sir."

The attorney turned away from the window and lifted the check from the desk. The paper was heavy, almost clothlike in texture. The round seal with its Arabic script and sword, surrounded in light green, was embossed in the center. Beneath, the words, "Embassy of the Kingdom of Saudi Arabia," were printed plainly in English.

"Eight hundred thousand dollars. A tidy sum for Mr. Harris," the attorney handed the check across the desk. "In Arab culture, gratitude can run deep indeed."

The secretary nodded.

"Oh, yes," he continued, "have the check delivered to our New York office first thing tomorrow to be handled by Credit Suisse and deposited in our Zurich account." He smiled, "I think it would be in the interests of all concerned if this particular transaction didn't clear the books here."

28

Sunday, March 10, 1985

The Harris Ranch, Broadwater County, Montana

Despite the distance across the yard, the unoiled squeak of the spring on the kitchen door of the ranch house sounded close, only an arm's length away. In the rear of the shed, the assassin shifted to a crouch, readying and tensing. The motion suspended the Beretta like a free-hanging weight in his jacket pocket. He grasped the automatic. As ordered, it had been stolen for him two weeks before from the gun shop in Denver. He would leave it here, wiped clean, when he was finished. It was a disposable, safer discarded than kept, but he also had acquired the habit of leaving the pistol at the scene as his personal trademark. In his faceless, nameless world, it was a statement testifying that he was neither concerned with those who would find the gun nor in need of its protection.

The light through the old window glass in the shed produced a gray hue that fell short of penetrating the dark corner behind the trunks and boxes where he had settled to wait. Harris's routine had been the same for weeks, a feeding shortly after 9:00 a.m. Ten feet away, the peregrine moved on her perch, calling softly in anticipation. She too sensed it was time. He had ordered a thorough surveillance, waiting until it was certain Harris had relaxed his guard. It was inevitable, of course. Harris was more careful than most, but finally the rifle was gone, no longer constantly by his side. So were the tension, the quicker step, and the roaming eye, all signs of someone who expected the unexpected.

Then there had been the final preparations. He shivered. It was colder in the old shed than outside. He'd driven from Bozeman last night, late, leaving the rented car two miles away. Dawn had come a few hours ago. The hills were still white but the south winds had already melted the snow in the valley. He had crossed the dark, rutted fields, still frozen hard by the deep frost, leaving no tracks. Closer to the ranch, he had hugged the edge of the irrigation canal. In the house, the lights were out, but he had stayed low as a precaution and approached from the rear of the shed before slipping inside.

Fifty yards away, the footfalls struck the back porch of the ranch house and then paused as the door banged, rebounded, and banged again, more weakly the second time. He snapped the Beretta's action, chambering a bullet and cocking the automatic. The sound distracted the peregrine. Hooded, she turned her head, listening in the silence but not seeing. Then, like him, the falcon stilled, watching in darkness as she waited for the door.

At that moment two miles distant, DiGenero lifted his foot from the accelerator, slowing as he eyed the car parked by the side of the highway, before resuming speed, "Wonder why he's pulled over."

Distracted, Erin looked up, "Hmm?"

DiGenero nodded toward the sedan they'd just passed, "The car. Strange place to park. In the middle of nowhere."

Erin spoke, "What do you suppose it is?" In blue jeans, boots, and sweater, she still wore the warm, dark colors of winter.

"What?"

"Kirby's surprise."

"I don't know."

Harris had called Salt Lake City the week before, inviting them to the ranch. DiGenero had demurred. It wasn't their first conversation since the trial. They had talked on several occasions, mostly about the old days, ritually repeating words about getting together. Neither had pushed it. But this time Kirby had insisted, saying there was something he wanted to show them. DiGenero had to be in Bozeman tomorrow, Monday, on business. Erin had listened to his rendition of what Harris had said. Finally, she'd agreed reluctantly to go along.

He reached across the seat, touching her hand, "It's been a while, hasn't it?"

"Since last summer."

"Is it hard?"

"What?"

"Going back."

Erin shook her head.

"How about seeing him again?"

She smiled, recognizing that he had been searching for a different answer, "Not with you."

"Jesus, you're brilliant."

She laughed out loud at DiGenero's mock amazement, watching the familiar highway unroll.

It had happened to them at once and slowly, she thought. All of a sudden and over a long time. A funny contradiction. That January night in Washington, after the courtroom, they made love as if it wasn't the first time. In a way, their beginning was so natural she almost hadn't noticed it. When she got home, the change in her and what Frank meant were plainer, obvious because of the surroundings. With Kirby behind her, Missoula was the past. Somehow, she remembered, moving to Salt Lake didn't even seem like a decision.

The car leaned into the curve. Erin recognized the sensation, the highway's familiar long bend leading to the turnoff for the ranch.

The rest, what the future would be like with Frank, was taking longer to unfold, emerging more slowly. There was no question it would happen eventually. She could even picture what it would be like after they had lived together for a year or two. But until then, it was taking time. That was all right, she thought. They knew each other already. The rest, the understanding, not the knowing, would come little by little, building the whole from the parts. It was like putting together a jigsaw puzzle with 1000 pieces. You could only see the picture if you worked on it day by day. That was one of the reasons she loved DiGenero. He was willing to be patient, to take care, to give her the time, to give himself time, too.

The road leveled, resuming its straight-line course. To the west, the square corners and peaks of the ranch buildings, small in the distance, angled against the soft curving backdrop of hills. The low roof of the original barn, the falcon house, stood out. Erin glanced at DiGenero. Under his sweater, just above his hip, the bulge outlined the butt of his .38 Smith & Wesson. She wished it was otherwise, but she understood. He seemed tense. But that figured. It was the first time since January he'd seen Kirby too.

"Do you suppose he's in the business again, Frank?"

DiGenero's expression was noncommittal. He touched the brakes. The oversized country mailbox and the weathered sign for the Harris ranch marked the left turn onto the dirt-and-gravel track. Despite Erin's silence, he could see the question was still in her eyes.

"I don't know," DiGenero furrowed his brow, turning the steering wheel one-handed. "For his sake, I hope not. Someday even a cat uses up all its nine lives."

Harris stepped off the porch and looked south. Across the bare brown fields, the highway was empty except for the single car that had begun to turn. He paused, picturing Erin in the small office behind the courtroom, the last time they'd talked. He hadn't tried to change her mind. Even in Ottawa it had been plain there was no point. There were long shots and lost causes, he thought, and the winners knew which were which. Just like the old movies, Harris thought. The cowboy shakes hands with the girl, kisses his horse, and rides off into the sunset.

He slipped the heavy leather falconer's glove on his hand and walked toward the shed. Who would have believed the call from his attorney, telling him to pick up the air-freight package in Bozeman? The private Learjet was waiting for him with the crate and a message, a gold-plated special delivery. They had sent her back. The peregrine was a token of their gratitude. There was no other explanation. Just the falcon and an envelope enclosing the heavy bond paper with the royal Arabian seal and the single handwritten name, in Arabic and English. Muhammed Kahlil abu Zahel. Harris shook his head, smiling. He could picture DiGenero's face. It would lay him out. Poor Frank. He took life too seriously. Ain't that a fact?

Thirty yards away, inside the shed, the Iranian knew there was something badly wrong. The sound of the car doors had surprised him, making his blood run cold. Harris had called out a greeting, but his footsteps had continued to approach, scuffling on the hard ground. He listened. The voices that replied were muffled, indistinct. His mind raced, sorting his options. The orders for retribution were clear. There was no room for failure. Harris must die. As for the newcomers, it was their fate to be present at this moment. He cradled the Beretta, watching the door through the narrow crack between the stacked boxes that hid him from view. He had only one choice. Whoever they were, they would die too.

Erin and DiGenero saw Harris wave and heard his call as they rounded the corner of the ranch house. He was walking away and motioning them to follow him toward the shed, "Come on, I've got something to show you."

"Hey, Kirby, don't bring a bird outta there that's going to make me throw you in the slammer," DiGenero yelled.

Harris looked over his shoulder, laughing, "You had your chance. Besides, you know I've gone straight. I'm an honest man."

"Bullshit," DiGenero smiled.

Harris had almost reached the falcon house door. Twenty yards behind, DiGenero glanced down at Erin who was walking in silence beside him, "Notice any differences?"

"In Kirby?"

DiGenero nodded.

She tightened her hand on his arm, "Only that he's still better looking than you."

DiGenero grabbed his heart, "Jesus, that hurts."

Harris swung open the door, letting the morning light spill inside. The brightness of the day surrounded the peregrine who was waiting, alert, on the perch. Fully mature now, she was bigger than when he first took her from Sixteen, her feathers the color of dark, weathered steel.

The falcon held herself still at the sound of his familiar voice, "Hey sweetheart, this is it. Hope you're ready. It's time to say good-bye." He ran his fingers gently down her breast, feeling the strength in the band of muscles that drove her wings. He had flown her three times in the past week. She had been well trained, but he knew she'd come back to him for one reason, and one only. She knew it too. Each time, in the air, she'd delayed sufficiently when he had raised his arm, calling her home. If only a single climbing loop before turning toward the glove, the act was the mark of the wild-caught who knew freedom, a testimony for those who knew to see it that she was her own, not the falconer's, and always would be.

Ten feet away in the darkness, the Iranian leveled the Beretta, holding his breath as he watched Harris unfasten the falcon's jesses from the metal ring on the stanchion of the perch and remove her hood. Beyond him, he could see the two figures through the open door. Harris would be first. Then the man and the woman. As Harris turned his back, he rose quietly, slipping forward in the shadows that still clung under the low eaves of the shed.

Erin and DiGenero watched Harris step from the falcon house. The peregrine, unhooded, was perched stately and straight on his arm.

Harris grinned, "Who do you suppose I've brought to say hello?"

DiGenero stopped, about to speak, when he saw the motion in the darkness. The surprise was less in the fact that it was the form of a man than in his unmistakable movement as he centered himself in the doorway, arms sweeping upward in the classic two-handed shooter's grip.

"Kirby!" DiGenero felt the horror well up inside him as he saw the confusion on Harris's face. In an instant, he knew it was too late to stop it, too late for Kirby to understand.

The sound of the first shot echoed, amplified by the emptiness of the falcon house. DiGenero spun, shoving Erin with all his strength. She sprawled, hitting hard on her side as he threw himself prone, grappling for the Smith & Wesson in his belt. In front of him, Harris seemed to flinch when the second and third shots struck. He groaned, crumpling slowly, like someone who was simply losing his strength. Startled, as Harris's hand released her jesses, the falcon rose from his arm, wings beating hard, veering away and upward.

DiGenero stretched his arms full-length, jamming the butt of the .38 into his left palm to stabilize the stubby pistol against the cold, rock-hard earth. The man was still stepping forward, half in the dark and half in the light, following the slumping Harris with a downward motion of his gun. DiGenero leveled the snub-nosed muzzle at the belt line. It was the optimum aiming point, centering on the body's bulk. Firing prone, with a rising trajectory, a bad shot would still have a chance, hitting the chest rather than passing harmlessly over the shoulders.

DiGenero squeezed, squeezed, and squeezed again. The three slugs climbed the Iranian's torso, whipping him up from his crouch in a series of spastic jerks. Erect, he leaned against the doorjamb, the automatic dangling, seemingly puzzled that the prone figure rising from the ground could have shot him at all, much less done so well. He opened his mouth, as if to speak. Then, a fourth shot tumbled him backward into the dark.

DiGenero scrambled to his feet and ran toward Harris. A few feet away, Erin rose unsteadily and then did the same. Chest down, Kirby seemed to be resting, motionless, his face turned comfortably to one side. DiGenero knelt beside him, steadying Erin momentarily as she plunged to her knees next to Harris. She reached toward Kirby, at first touching and then brushing back his hair. DiGenero's words were as meaningless as they were automatic, "Hold on, Kirby, you're going to be OK."

DiGenero started to speak again but stopped. Harris was moving his lips almost imperceptibly. He bent lower, trying to listen, but there was only breath, shallow and slow, and no sounds. Harris was staring skyward, past him. DiGenero turned. Erin, sobbing, also looked up. At 500 feet, free, the falcon was climbing into the morning sun in a tight, rising spiral.

DiGenero turned back, "You were going to let her go, weren't you, Kirby?"

There were no words, although it didn't matter. DiGenero could sense the answer. Harris wasn't trying to talk. He was trying to smile. DiGenero rested his hand gently against Harris's cheek, but the light had already left his eyes.

Above them, the falcon tucked a wing and swooped low, passing once over the three figures. Then, pulling out, she gathered speed, flying hard and climbing northwest toward the Big Belt Mountains, Sixteen, and the high valley from where she had come.